# All Worlds Wayfarer

## A Quarterly Speculative Fiction Literary Magazine

www.allworldswayfarer.com

Current issue available free to read.
Previous issues available through Amazon Kindle

www.allworldswayfarer.com/pastissues

## All Worlds Wayfarer Anthologies:

**Through Other Eyes (December 2020)**
**Prismatic Dreams (June 2022)**
*Each Our Own (Release TBA)*
*Into the Dark (Release TBA)*

# ALL WORLDS WAYFARER:
# PRISMATIC DREAMS

**Edited by:**
**Rowan Rook**
**Geri Meyers**

**All Worlds Wayfarer**

**2022**

**All Worlds Wayfarer**
**Greenbank, WA ; Woodbridge, NJ**
**www.allworldswayfarer.com**

Copyright © 2022 by All Worlds Wayfarer.
All stories copyright © 2022 their authors.
Cover Art © Liu Zishan.
Book Design by Rowan Rook and Geri Meyers
Fonts used include EB Garamond, Merriweather, Georgia, Flamingo Shadow,
Charlemagne Std, and Annabel

Edited by Rowan Rook and Geri Meyers



These stories are works of fiction. Names, characters, places, and incidents are products of the authors' imaginations or are used fictitiously. Any resemblance to actual events or locales or persons, living or dead, is coincidental.

Published by All Worlds Wayfarer, Printed and Distributed by IngramSpark.

Library of Congress Control Number: 2022939349

ISBNs:

9781736150559          (hardcover)
9781736150535          (trade paperback)
9781736150542          (ebook)

FIRST EDITION

# Table of Contents

# Content Warnings

**Tea With Elaine:** Loneliness
**A Shadow of Light:** Violence
**Stormcalled:** Violence, Grief, Homophobia
**Apocalypse Sasquatch:** Hunting, References to: Bullying
**Fluorescent Clouds, Neon Rain:** Violence, Gun Violence, Alcohol
**For Esnan:** Grief, Death, Serious Illness
**Resistance:** Grief, References to: Violence
**The Green Star Bar:** Violence, Gun Violence, Alcohol
**The Trunk:** Violence, Gore
**Change:** Bullying, Transphobia, References to: Mild Violence
**Like the Stars:** Violence, Transphobia, Sexual References
**Sailing Blind:** Mild Violence
**Different Ways:** Alcohol, Sexual/Suggestive Content
**Compilation Error:** Memory Loss, Grief
**Come and See:** Violence, Sexual Abuse, Serious Illness
**The Nature of Stones:** Relationship Breakup, Pregnancy, Childbirth
**The Moon Rabbit:** Gender Dysphoria, Menstruation
**Hunters:** War, Violence, Injury, Sexual/Suggestive Content
**The Sword of Death:** Violence, Abuse, Death, Grief
**The Wolf's Den:** References to: Violence, Abuse
**Of Feathers and Flowers:** Abuse, Captivity, Self Harm, Mild Gore, Sexual/Suggestive Content
**The Bone Merchant:** Death, Mild Gore, References to: Abuse
**LV2RD:** Grief, Car Accidents
**Mishael's Love:** Inappropriate Teacher/Pupil Relationship
**What's Ours is Ours, What's Hers is Everyone's:** Illness, References to: Death
**Let Our Song Be About Love:** n/a
**A Banquet in Turquoise and Indigo:** Violence, Captivity, Mild Torture
**Mirror, Mirror:** Captivity, Possession
**The Only Lesbian in Space:** Homophobia
**Evergreen:** n/a

# Tea With Elaine
## *by K.G. Delmare*

Every day at three o'clock, I had my tea with Elaine. I was sure to never miss it, as it was a tradition carried over from the earliest days of our marriage. Even through the distance and time-zone changes, I never missed a single one. The setup of it all was really quite simple. We started making our pots of tea around the same time, settled down at our computers, and initiated a call at exactly three in the afternoon. There used to be a need for further coordination, but it long ago became unnecessary as the affair entered the realm of the commonplace.

I loved to see my wife. I could never understand the surly men of the sitcom world, always dreading their spouses. And in my case, absence, as always, made my heart grow fonder. Ever since my job took me away from her, I found myself ever more longing for the stroke of her skin upon mine, the sound of her laugh without the crunch of a computer speaker. I felt greedy for her presence, always wanting more than the pittance of time I'd been given every day. There was no mincing words: I missed her constantly.

That day, Elaine was waiting as she always was when I booted up the video call program. It took just a moment for the delay of the internet connection to kick in, but when she saw me, a smile widened across her face. I thought of the smell of her perfume, the way it would soak into our pillows.

"Good afternoon," I said.

"It's night there," she said, "isn't it?"

I smiled back at her. "Isn't it always?"

She held up her mug, taking one of her usual delicate sips. She was always careful when she first started her cup, always vigilant to avoid a burn. She had a tendency to tease me for my more rushed approach, which often led to a scalded tongue that she would have to comfort me over.

"What kind of blend do you have today?" I asked. I thought back to the packed tea shelf in our home, our matching Hers and Hers mugs where she would lovingly pour over our numerous favorite varieties.

"Oh, just some plain old green tea," she said, tapping the cup with her finger. "I added a little honey, that's all. How's work going?"

Something of a glowering look no doubt came to my face then. I didn't really enjoy talking about work during our tea time, even if she had every reason to ask upon how things were progressing. I delayed my response with a sip of my own drink.

"Same as ever," I said finally. "I had a call with the command center this morning. They want me to try recalibrating the main computer so it's back to an older operating system. Their theory is that it might kickstart the directional mainframe to remember how it was meant to function."

She was silent for a brief juncture, steam floating up from the mug to frame her face. Her tea didn't need artificial gravity to stay in its cup.

"Do you think it'll work?"

I found myself equally quiet in the face of this question. The truth was, I didn't know the answer. That reality was arduous to grasp, of course, and I didn't want to press it upon my beloved wife. The alternative, however, would be to lie to her, and that was unthinkable.

I settled on, "I'm not sure."

She looked at me, and through the pixels of the screen, I could see her jaw working. Finally, she nodded. "Well," she said, "if they're recommending it, you might as well try."

She was right. I didn't have much in the way of other options. If I couldn't figure out some way to get the ship working right again, I'd likely never come back to the home I was looking at through the screen. Lately, I could sense the command center giving up on me, and it was like feeling someone's grip loosen as they held you from the edge of a cliff. When I was first stranded, they did everything they could to look for solutions and occupy my time. Now, it seemed like all I got was the occasional call with some halfhearted troubleshooting.

But no matter how much they wanted to leave me in the expanse of space, there was Elaine. I knew that with every rotation of the Earth below, with every star that twinkled out beyond the ship's windows, she was somewhere wondering why I wasn't with her. That was enough force to propel me to keep trying, every day.

"So," she said, "is that the plan for the day? To turn back the computer system?"

I nodded. "Other than that, it's just routine maintenance. But that can wait."

"I hope it works," she said.

"Me too."

Somewhere beyond our words hid a chime of surrender. It happened more than scarcely lately. The first few times we had our daily meeting after the ship's system failed and my fate became uncertain, she would often weep for me over our tenuous connection. We had tried to give way to hope after the initial sting, but as the days ran on, the duller but all the same potent pain of capitulation to reality was setting in.

From the corner of my eye, through one of the ship's small, circular windows, I saw Earth. It was difficult to understand that somewhere there, millions of miles from my ship, Elaine was living her life, while I sat floating and hoping for solutions that likely wouldn't work. But it was because of Elaine that I had to hold on to hope. If nothing else, I had to keep trying for her.

"I'm going to come home, Elaine," I said. "I'm going to come back to you."

Her voice cracked when she responded: "I know you will, Aisha."

After that, we left it behind. We drank our tea.

"I love you," I said, because I did.

"I love you too," she said, and I believed every syllable. The Earth turned on below me. The ship creaked with age. And when the call was over, I left the screen to go have a talk with mission control.

The ship had once been state of the art. Now I'd been away from Earth for so long that I wondered if any of the technology was worth anything at all anymore. I'd come to know the interior of the ship in the way that one knows a lover, having to sweep every crevice for a solution that never seemed to arrive. The ship had simultaneously become my greatest enemy and my closest friend, the reason for my current predicament and yet my only company. As I walked through the halls of the old thing, groaning here and there with my weight as I traversed the artificial gravity, I was once again consumed with my one greatest desire: to see my wife again.

I fired up the communications console and waited for someone to pick up. No doubt they would be sour that I was wasting their precious time on a lost cause like myself. Still, the screen blinked to life after a few minutes.

"Good afternoon, Commander Cherian," said one of the many scientists at mission control who was charged with checking in on me as I floated about in an expanse of nothing. He was wearing a suit and tie, and his face didn't look familiar. Maybe he was new. Maybe my memory was starting to go. "You're looking well."

Regardless of how I looked, I certainly wasn't feeling well. "Hello," I said, not remembering the man's name, if I'd ever known it at all. "Are there any updates for me? Any new strategies?"

The man consulted a clipboard he was holding, and I had the strangest feeling that there was nothing related to my mission or its bizarre sort of failure written on it. "No, not that I can think of. Have you tried changing back to the old system like we suggested in our last meeting?"

"I was just about to," I said. "But I wanted to double-check and see if there was any news." A fool's errand. There was never any news for me, it seemed. Just twinkling stars and dark swathes of sky surrounding my ship.

"Well, I would recommend giving it a try before you contact us again." He said it with an air of professionalism, but I could detect the bite of frustration with me behind his words. I had no room left to feel shame for wasting their time. I was the one who was stuck in space; I felt that I had the jurisdiction to pester the people who had sent me up there in the first place.

Still, I wasn't in the mood to pick any fights: "All right. I'll go do that."

The wide array of knobs and buttons on the main console stared me down as I wrapped up the call. In my mind's eye, I saw myself tearing them apart and destroying the ship, making it feel my pain in turn until it decided to send me back to the place from which I came.

As I had fully expected, recalibrating the system didn't work as intended. Instead, the internal computer of the ship was just running slower now that it had been set back to an inferior operating system. This meant that I now had to wait an extra handful of minutes when trying to connect with Elaine for our daily tea, which for me took a rotten situation and made it downright excruciating.

"Hi, honey," she said once the connection went through. She then held up a bear-shaped bottle of gold that she had no doubt just poured into her tea. "Get it? Honey?"

I was glad that one of us could be in a good mood. I made the effort to crack a smile.

"Cute," I said. Every time we spoke like this, there was a tension in the air that my being stranded had left permanent. No matter what pleasantries we exchanged or what sweet nothings I spoke to her over an intergalactic connection, it did nothing to ease the pain of our situation. To be unable to provide comfort to the woman I'd vowed my life to made me feel powerless in a way that being aground could only hope to achieve.

"So," she said, "how did the ship recalibration go?"

She knew the answer. We both knew the answer. If anything about my situation had changed to that extent, it was clear that I would have burst onto the call all but throwing confetti and singing praises to whatever deity had granted me passage home.

"Not what we had hoped for," was all I could offer, because tears threatened to pour out of me if I tried to extrapolate anymore.

She was silent, but only briefly. As I said, we were both aware of what had happened from the moment I entered the call with what had now become a typically solemn look on my face.

"Well," she said, "we'll just have to keep trying." She blew on her tea before taking a dainty sip.

"We'll just have to," I echoed. What else could I do?

There was a long silence then, filled with the soft sounds of slurping as we drank our tea. There were often these periods of quiet, usually because we just wanted to appreciate that we were spending any time together at all. The ship hummed around me, its various machinations churning onward even as we went nowhere. I'd long become used to that dull, droning noise, always surrounding me and reminding me acutely of where I was and how I got there.

Finally, Elaine spoke: "Connie asked me to come to a party with her."

Connie was one of our few unmarried friends who lived a few houses down from us. I remembered the last time I saw her quite vividly. She'd held a grand party at her large, comfortable home to commemorate my journey that everyone was so certain would go according to plan. Now, months into being stranded in space, the memory felt like a bitter pill.

"Really," I said. The idea that Elaine was going out while I stayed up in space was a quandary. Of course I didn't want her life to stop just because mine had ground to a halt in this most peculiar of ways. Still, I couldn't deny the twinge of distaste at knowing what I was missing out on.

"A party," she said, "for single people."

The silence returned, and the idle hum suddenly began to feel stifling, as if it were sounding from deep inside of me and pouring out of every pore. It was one thing to be faced with Elaine going out to dinner or seeing friends without me. It was quite another to face the implication that I was no longer in the picture, that the ring on her finger had lost its meaning.

"What did you say?" I asked, my mouth parched dry. I could feel my hands shaking in anticipation of her response.

"No, of course!" she said, and I could see her flush even over our rough connection. "I would never."

"Oh." I was left even more adrift than usual, unsure of how to handle this unexpected turn in the conversation.

"I thought it was pretty rude of her," said Elaine. "To even suggest that I would... well, I don't think I'll be able to look at her the same way again after that."

I was consumed by a strange feeling then. Relief had poured over me when I heard about Elaine's refusal, but something like guilt soon followed it. I'd reckoned many a time with how lonely I had left Elaine in my time in space, but I'd never considered the idea that she'd start dating again while I was still up there. It seemed utterly incomprehensible. As long as I was breathing, I thought Elaine and I would still have each other. But was that selfish of me? I didn't know the answer. And it terrified me.

The conversation wandered off to somewhere more benign, but I couldn't shake the curious, unwanted sensation I'd been imbued with by this little anecdote about our neighbor. But Elaine smiled at me again, and I found it in me to smile back.

"I love you," I said as the call came to its usual close.

"I love you too," she said, and I knew it was as true as always.

The next time I called the team back on Earth, I got the small man whose name I could not remember again. He stared at me from behind large glass frames, and I was overwhelmed by the idea that I might never do something so mundane as going to the optometrist again. It was those realizations of the little losses that made the daily grind of life left in space so very tortuous, and at the top of the list of all those missing things was waking up and seeing Elaine smile back at me.

"Commander Cherian," said the man in a way that, intentional or not, made my presence feel quite unwelcome. "We didn't expect to hear from you again so soon."

I wanted to cut to the chase: "Resetting the computer didn't work. If anything, the ship is running worse now. What should I try next?"

The man with no name adjusted his spectacles, surveying that same clipboard that I was now certain had very much nothing to do with me.

"Well," he said, "I'm afraid that we don't have anything else for you to try right at this moment. If you could just give us a few more days, I'm sure we can be in touch with something for you to try—"

"I don't have a few more days," I said, my voice threatening to tremble in a way I felt most unbecoming. "This is my only life, you know. Every day that goes by is one less day I get to live with my wife. Do you even know what it's like to live without your wife? Are you married?"

The man's mouth hung slightly agape for just a moment, then he cleared his throat. "I am," he said. "We understand that you're in a deeply stressful situation right now, Commander, but I can assure you that we take this very seriously and we're doing all we can. This process cannot be rushed, or we very well run the risk of you not coming back at all."

"I know!" I said in a tone that sounded more like a sob. "I know that. But you can't just leave me here. I need to go home. I can't be stuck like this anymore."

The man was silent. I don't think either of us had expected me to crack like that. In all of my time stuck in space, I had never quite come close to being this overwhelmed. But the days had worn me down. So many rotations of the Earth below without me on it had left me desperate and tired, and there was nothing that could stem the flow of my anxiety now. Especially not what I was coming to view as a very incompetent and unprepared crew back home.

"We've got one possible solution at the moment," he said in an uneven voice. "But it's completely out of the question right now. We can't sign off on it yet. It's too risky."

"Tell me," I said. "Anything. Come on, out with it."

He pushed his glasses up the bridge of his nose. I don't think he'd expected me to be so short. All the while that I had been stuck up there among the expanse of stars and planets, I'd tried my best to be the idyllic, stalwart commander who they had known they could count on when they chose me for the mission. Now, I could sense myself transforming into a hysterical, desperate woman trying to find purchase while surrounded by nothing. Fine. Let them see what became of me. I'd like to see any of them be subject to what I'd endured and remain just the same as they were when it began.

"Well," he said, in a way that let me know he ought to not be telling me this at all, "you of course have the option to completely override the system and make an emergency return. But I can't stress enough how much we advise against that. The odds are that you'd burn up upon reentry—the ship just isn't prepared."

"So why install the system in the first place?" I asked, practically through gritted teeth. My one big option, and it would likely burn me to a crisp.

"Well, you see, we have to keep those sorts of things in our back pocket," said the man. "You never know what kind of emergency situation may come up."

"What situation could possibly be more of an emergency than this?"

He was quiet, as if he hadn't been prepared for this most obvious of questions. "Things could always be worse," he said. "And we don't want to put you in danger when there's a chance something else could work."

"What else is there?" I asked. "I might as well try."

"You mustn't."

I felt tears pricking my eyes, hot and humiliating. I found my hands clenched into trembling fists, weakening me in the face of a man whose name I couldn't even have been bothered to remember. Even over the strenuous connection, he had to see how much I was crumbling. Even worse, I doubted it would do much to convince him to let me do what needed to be done.

"We're very sorry, Commander Cherian," the man said finally, closing the conversation off with his stiff tone. "But I can assure you, we're already doing all that we can."

"Are you?" I asked. "Really, tell me, are you? Be honest."

More silence. And then, "Yes."

Lies. Stalling. I was tired of it all. I disconnected the call.

I had no idea what time it was back on Earth. I only ever knew when it was three in the afternoon in my wife's time zone. I sat at the computer, anxiously waiting as the computer let me know that my signal was pinging Elaine, letting her know that I was calling. My heart was pounding in a frenzy in my chest. I had to see her. Now, more than ever, I had to see her.

"Aisha?"

She looked out of sorts, as if she had just rolled out of bed, which was very likely what had just happened. Even with every curl out of place, with her eyes ringed dark and tired, she was beautiful. She had only ever been beautiful to me.

"I'm sorry for waking you up," I said in a trembling voice. "I just wanted to talk to you really badly."

She sat down at the computer chair, the one that I used to sit in when I checked my emails in the days leading up to the mission. "What's wrong, baby?" she asked in her most tender of voices.

"I spoke with mission control."

"And what happened?"

"They're totally lost," I spat out. "They have no idea what to do with me. Most days I think that they're happy just to leave me floating around up here. It's easier than coming up with a solution." I felt these thoughts just pouring out of me, haphazard and sloppy. If there was anyone in the world I could bare my tired, tired soul to, it was my wife.

Elaine was quiet then, looking at me in the crackly webcam video, the one that so often stuttered and hiccuped with the burden of intergalactic travel. I wondered if I would ever see her face in the clarity of reality again.

Suddenly, her face contorted into tears. I watched in horror as she began to cry, just like she did that first day when we reckoned with me being stranded. I could hardly handle it then, and I was certainly in no state to do so now. My heart sank into its furthest depths at the sight, and she continued to sob unabated.

"Elaine," I said, and I could hear my voice creak.

"I'm sorry," she wept, "I just miss you so much, Aisha. I can't take it anymore. I just want you home."

"I know," I said, barely scraping the words out from my throat.

As I watched the tears cascade down her face, I couldn't help but think of our last day together, before I set out on my mission. We had a picnic on a sprawling green hill in a nearby park, overlooking a pond filled with fluffy little ducks. We'd spent the afternoon luxuriating in the beauty of it all, then watched the sunset, and I'd noticed how beautiful she looked in the glow. If I had known what would happen, I would have stared at her a little longer.

"Elaine," I said, "I know I've said it a million times, but I mean it: I'm going to come home to you."

She said nothing, just continued to cry. It was all entirely cruel, the way I was miles away and unable to offer her any sort of tangible comfort. It was wrong for her to feel this way without me beside her to make the pain go away. I felt gutted, as if my insides had been laid bare before me in the face of her despair. I was tired. I was destroyed. I was done.

"I love you," I said, firm and solid and with all the meaning I could possibly put into it.

"I love you too," she croaked. I knew if I did anything in this life, it would be to return. I ended the call and headed off into the bowels of the ship.

The clacking of my boots against the floor of the ship rang through my ears as I headed toward the center console that housed its wide variety of tools and pieces, all meant to help keep me in tip-top shape as I rotted in the middle of nothingness. When I reached the console, I stared down at all of the little devices I'd been using for days and days since I had been sent up here with no idea of how long I'd be meant to stay. The buttons and knobs stared back at me, beckoning for me to turn them any which way until I was on my way back home, no matter how dangerous.

My breathing was ragged, though I had only walked a short distance from the correspondence room to the main console. The hum of the ship around me was turning into a drone, drilling into my skull and taunting me with its ever-present stillness. I would be still no more.

As I said, I knew the ship like a lover. I knew it perhaps just as well as I knew every curve of Elaine. I went into something like a trance, frantically pressing the buttons and turning the knobs in the sequence that I'd been shown in training. My memory was as clear as crystal, my hands moving with an automation that rivaled even the ship's most mechanical of systems.

After a particular twist of one knob, an alarm began to blare, and it jolted me out of my state. The screen that the console was hooked up to began to glow red. "Emergency return processes initiated," said a computerized voice in a way that felt all too calm for the situation at hand.

I stared at it, my mouth slightly open in something like awe as the ship started to steel itself for a return trip home, regardless of how successful it might be. There was only one step left in an action as dire as this, and I waited for the computer to ask me the question that I trained for in many simulations back on Earth. Finally, the automated voice spoke to me again: "To confirm this action, please give your Commander's password."

My mouth was dry. I felt closer to home than I had in a long time, so close that I almost forgot my password in the mess.

But of course I couldn't. Not if I tried. I steeled myself for whatever was to come next, good or bad, and no matter how my body made it back to the warm arms of the Earth, I would not let myself be left behind. I would come back to her. The word the computer was after left my lips as easily as it always had: "Elaine."

# A Shadow of Light
## by *Isabel Yacura*

When Davin looks up from putting away the last of the silver coins, a boy is standing in front of his stall. "Hi, how can I help you?" comes out of his mouth automatically, and Davin has never been so thankful for the knee-jerk reaction of working retail.

The boy is—beautiful. Davin's not prone to flights of fancy, or thinking other boys are beautiful, but he's rapidly re-thinking his stance on that.

Because the boy in front of his market stall is incandescent, little smile turning up one corner of his mouth, a dimple tucked into the left, eyes bright. And his hair is like starlight.

"What do you sell?" the boy asks, and Davin blinks, has to look down at his wares to remember what he comes to the night market to sell. He can feel a blush darkening his neck.

"Oh, this and that," Davin says through a dry mouth, and the boy laughs. "Mainly, ah, potions. Amulets. We deal with small curses, if you've got them." He can't imagine that the boy does.

"No curses," the boy confirms, mouth still tipped up. "What sort of amulets?"

"What are you looking for?" Davin counters. He can do this.

The boy taps his chin, mouth pursing. "Maybe something for luck," the boy says. "I'm very bad with directions, you see, and I'm a bit, ah, lost."

Davin frowns. "Do you need help? I know the night market and the surrounding area pretty well, or I could take you to one of the cartographers—if you tell them I sent you they won't rip you off too badly."

The boy's smile slants toward something bittersweet. "Ah, no, it's more a metaphorical lostness, I'm afraid," he says apologetically.

"Luck can help with that," Davin says, kind now even as his cheeks still feel hot with blush.

"Luck it is," the boy says.

Davin reaches for one of the little charms that is supposed to give you a boost—help you make the last train, find an old umbrella when it begins to rain—and pauses. He looks up, makes eye contact with the boy. "What's your name?"

He looks surprised at the question, eyes going wide. "Shain," he says.

"Right," Davin says decisively. He wraps the little charm —it's shaped like a little ladybug, the paint cheerful and startling red against the black of the wrap. "On the house," he says, and holds it out for Shain to take.

"That doesn't seem like a good business practice," Shain says, but he takes it from Davin anyway.

Davin summons up old arrogance, shrugs. "Not everything's about business."

Shain grins at that, wide and delighted, and Davin, to his dismay, goes red to his ears.

Davin doesn't see Shain at the next night market, but he sees him at the one after that.

"You know, I didn't get your name last time," he hears a voice say, and Davin looks up from his newspaper to see Shain standing there, ethereal and grinning.

Davin smiles back, folds his paper. "Have you been feeling lucky?"

"Oh, very," Shain says, and his voice is so unexpectedly dry that Davin barks out a laugh.

"I'm Davin," he says, and holds out a hand for Shain to shake. Shain's hand is very cool and dry, but his grip is firm. Davin pauses at the last shake, tilts his head. "Is your—you look like you're glowing."

Shain raises an eyebrow, though there's a faint pink tint to his pale cheeks. "My goodness, are you so forward with all your customers?"

"I don't think you count as a customer if you haven't bought anything," Davin says.

"I knew there was an ulterior motive," Shain sighs, but he's still grinning.

"Can I help you with anything?" Davin asks.

"I think I'd like to buy something this time," Shain says, so innocently that Davin laughs again. "I'm looking for something to help me find something."

"Specific," Davin comments. "What're you looking for?"

"Does it matter?" Shain raises an eyebrow again.

Davin shrugs. "A little. Person, place, thing?"

"Mineral, vegetable..." Shain mutters. "It's an object."

"Right," Davin says, and turns on his heel. "Be right back." His caravan is backed up to his little stall so that he can use it as extra storage, keep his more expensive—or dangerous—items out of view of the general public. He's back out a few moments later, but Shain's no longer alone.

"Oh no," he groans, coming to a stop just outside his caravan. Shain's laugh floats to the back, and as Davin pushes his way to the front, Kharaman shoots him a sly grin.

"Captain, my captain, who do we have here?" Kharaman asks.

"Captain?" Shain sounds delighted.

Davin rubs a hand through his hair. He really wishes he could stop blushing every time Shain rolls around. "Not anymore," he says, glaring a little at Kharaman. "Where's your keeper?"

As if on cue, a calico cat jumps up on Kharaman's shoulder and perches there as disdainfully as a cat can. Kharaman scratches them under the chin fondly. "Never far behind, cap'n," he says blithely, ignoring Davin's near audible eye roll.

"I'm Shain," Shain says. "What does 'not anymore' mean?"

"Oh, our dear Davin here used to be the best—that is, the best captain on any of the six seas," Kharaman says, leering at Shain. The cat bats at his face. "And now he sells his little trinkets."

Davin levels Kharaman with a real glare for that one, and Kharaman straightens. "We miss you, cap'n," he says, unrepentant. He tips his hat to Shain and saunters off, his long coat flaring out behind him.

Davin sighs, shakes his head. Shain's got his head cocked, looking at Davin with a gaze he can't read. He rolls his shoulders. "This is a divining tool," Davin says, choosing to ignore the entire incident. "It's got instructions in there. You should be able to use it just fine." It's a neat little leather packet, and Davin holds it out to Shain.

When Shain takes it, their fingers brush again, and his hand is just as cool as it was when they were introduced. "How much do I owe you?" Shain asks.

"Come back?" Davin tries for a charming grin. He's not sure if it works, because Shain throws his head back and laughs.

"Captain," Shain says, grinning, and Davin doesn't want to think about how he feels hearing that from Shain's lips, "you couldn't keep me away."

Shain's there the next time Davin's at the night market. And the next, and the time after that.

He doesn't buy anything of note, really, just a couple of pouches for sleep, or a candle for help concentrating. "You look like you need the sleep," Davin says gently the third or fourth time. Shain's got dark circles under those pretty eyes of his.

"I'm just adjusting, still," Shain says, sighing. "I used to be pretty nocturnal." The night market is something of a misnomer—in actuality, the market ends when the day reaches full dark.

"Weird job?" Davin asks, and Shain laughs brightly.

"You have no idea," Shain says, shaking his head.

Every time Davin comes to the market, Shain's there. Eventually, Davin invites him into the stall, behind the counter, and now Davin has the unmistakable pleasure of having Shain perch on the steps of his caravan, laughing and spinning tales.

Shain knows more stories than Davin knew there even were.

"You are very cozy back there," Kharaman says one night, visiting them. Shain waves from the back. The calico cat hops off Kharaman's shoulder, saunters his way to the back, and curls up in Shain's lap.

Shain pulls his long, pale fingers through the calico cat's fur, and the cat purrs. Kharaman and Davin watch for a long moment, then exchange glances. "Should I be jealous?" Kharaman asks, a little bewildered.

Davin shrugs. "I have no idea."

Kharaman shakes his head, still staring back, when his expression changes. It closes in a way that Davin's been in tune with for years, and his eyes narrow. "Davin," he says, too casual, "is your boy glowing?"

Davin doesn't look toward the back. He knows what's there. "Yep," just as casual.

Kharaman sucks his teeth. "All right," he allows. "You think that's a good idea?"

"Nope," Davin says.

"No changing your mind, huh?" Kharaman says.

"Nope."

"Right," Kharaman says. "Guess I'll spread the word, then."

When Davin turns to him with raised brows, Kharaman shrugs. "Got to let the rest of the boys know to keep their ears out, just in case anyone does come looking for your precious one."

Davin closes his eyes for a brief moment. "Thanks, Kharaman."

Kharaman claps a hand on his shoulder. "You got it." He raises his voice then, calls toward the back, "Caelan! Let's hit it!"

The calico cat jumps out of Shain's lap, lands lightly on the packed dirt, and then stretches up—and up—and up—

And Caelan stands there, stretches their skinny arms above their head, rocking on their toes, before settling back down. They're dressed in white and gray, fairly swamped in fabric that Davin knows must be Kharaman's. Their hair has grown out quite a bit.

"Good to see you," Davin says, nodding. Shain's still sitting down on the steps, open-mouthed.

"Davin," Caelan nods at him in their soft, monotone voice. They shoot a look at Shain over their shoulder, and their mouth curves into a slow smirk. "Shain."

Kharaman sighs deeply, but there's something smug and fond tugging at the corner of his mouth. Davin raises a hand and they exist through the fabric side of Davin's stall.

When Davin turns back around, Shain's pink across the cheeks and still staring. "I didn't know—"

Davin shrugs. "Caelan sort of does what they want."

"Could've bought me a drink first," Shain mutters, and Davin laughs.

One day Davin asks where Shain goes, after the night market.

"My home?" Shain asks, raising a pale eyebrow.

"I just meant—ah—I wanted to make sure you're being safe," he finishes, fumbling and a bit too honest.

"Safe from what?" Shain asks, and there's a tightness to the corners of his eyes now.

Davin sighs. "It's a dangerous world out there," he says slowly. "I just want—" He's interrupted by a blur of gold hair that almost slides into and over the counter. As it is, the counter jostles, and a few things fall over or shiver warningly.

Shain stands up from his perch on Davin's caravan steps. "What—"

"Cap'n," Kendall says breathlessly. Her eyes are wide and bright. "Someone's coming."

Davin's shoulders tense, straighten, and his mouth flattens. "For him?" He jerks his head over his shoulder. Shain makes a questioning little squawk.

Davin doesn't turn around, just watches Kendall's head bob up and down frantically. "Thank you," Davin says sincerely, nodding, and then, "Go."

"But, cap'n—" Kendall protests.

"What's going to look worse?" Davin asks sharply. "A bunch of known pirates hanging round my stall or a simple shopkeeper selling his wares in the night market?" Kendall still hesitates, shifting nervously from foot to foot, and Davin's voice hardens. "That's an *order,* Kendall."

Kendall squeaks and takes off again, just as fast as she had come.

Davin runs his hand through his hair, making the short strands stick up wildly, and turns to Shain. Shain, who is staring wide-eyed at Davin, still standing on his caravan steps.

"What's going on?" Shain says. "Wh— Pirates?"

"I'm really sorry, and I promise we can talk about this later, but you need to get in the caravan right now," Davin says, and in a moment he's gently but firmly pushing Shain up the final step and into the caravan.

"Davin—what—" apprehension creeps into his voice.

Davin leaves him for a moment, heads to the massive chest in the back, opens it with a black skeleton key and a hefty bit of magic. "I'm sorry," Davin repeats. "I need you to get in the chest, though."

"*What?*" Shain asks.

"They're coming for *you*, Shain," Davin says urgently, throwing a glance over his shoulder toward the entrance.

Shain stills. "Why would someone be coming for me?" he asks warily.

"I've had my crew keep their ears open for anyone who says they're looking for a dragon," Davin says, and watches the little color Shain has in his face drain away completely. "The fact that they sent Kendall to warn me says that someone is, and that they're coming *here*. Fast. They know, Shain."

"How long have you known?" Shain says, very still and very pale.

"*Please*, Shain," Davin says, "get in the goddamn trunk."

Shain swallows, and then carefully steps inside. It's much bigger than it seems, deep enough for Shain to fully sit up, but in a moment he's laying down, flat on his back, staring up at Davin.

Davin gets a hand on the heavy wooden lid of the trunk, stares right back, down at Shain. Shain's pale hair is spread around his head like a halo, and his hands are laced tightly across his stomach. "I'll be back," Davin says, and the way he says it sounds like a promise.

Shain just nods, jaw clenched, and then Davin's lowering the lid to the trunk. It clicks into place very softly, and Davin's turning the key, and then rushing out of the caravan, closing the doors and locking them behind him with the same skeleton key.

Davin stares at the skeleton key, the heavy black metal bisecting his palm for a moment. Then he flips his hand, makes a fist, and when he opens it a moment later, the key is gone.

When the black clad men come to his booth two minutes and thirty-three seconds later, Davin has his feet up on a box, his pipe in his mouth, paging through yesterday's newspaper.

He looks up at the men as they approach, but doesn't fold the paper. Yet. "Evening," he says around the pipe. Smoke trails out of it and wreaths his head.

"Good evening," the man in the front says. He's got a narrow face, black hair smoothed back, a thin mouth.

After a moment, Davin folds his paper. Sets it to the side. Plants his feet on the floor. "What can I get you, gentleman? We've got potions, amulets, do a little minor curse-breaking—"

"What about rare items?" A blond man says from behind their point. The narrow-faced man shoots a foreboding look behind him, and the blond subsides.

The narrow-faced man sighs. "What about rare items, indeed?" he asks. His tone is forcibly light.

"Aye," Davin says, "I've got one or two for you. A beautiful silver matchbox, charmed with never-ending matches, never be without a fire, a first edition copy of—"

"Not quite what we're looking for," narrow-face says. "We're looking for something a little more... lively."

Davin frowns. "I don't deal in exotic animals or any of that nonsense," he says, tone heavy with disapproval. "Can't be dealing with the feed and the shit and the stink."

"Sir," the narrow-faced man says. "We're looking for a dragon."

"Well, I have some scales I picked up a few years ago—blue, and given willingly—"

"A shifted dragon, sir."

Davin goes quiet for a moment. "A shifted dragon?" he asks, soft.

The narrow-faced man grins. "Heard report that one was hanging round these parts," and the way he looks around Davin's little stall, hung heavy with carpets and thick fabric draperies, makes it known that *these* parts really just means *this* part.

"Funny, that," and Davin stands up. "I haven't heard anything like that."

The man doesn't take a step backward, but his weight shifts onto his back foot. "Fallen stars are very valuable," he says. "Who knows who'll be sniffing around here before long."

Davin folds his arms. "I don't think anyone'll be sniffing around here," he says. It's not a threat. Davin says it like fact.

"Maybe you'll let us have a peek around your cart," the man says, and Davin scowls at the deliberate insult. "Just to assuage our... curiosity."

The men behind narrow-face take a step forward. One puts a hand on the hilt of his sword. Davin sighs. "Fine," he says, steps aside. "Make it quick."

Davin has to come into the back with them to unlock the doors, and watches with a heavy glare as they look around the caravan. They do that, at least. Their search is quick and disturbingly professional. They're on the way out when one of them kicks the chest. "What about this?" It's the blond again.

Davin raises his eyebrows. "My clothes?"

The narrow-faced man has turned back, however, and now he too is looking at the massive chest with interest. "Open it?"

"You trying to get a look at my underwear now?" Davin asks, unimpressed.

Narrow-face glares. "Open it."

Davin grumbles, and flips open the lid.

When the lid comes up, it reveals stacks of neatly folded shirts, trousers, and yes, underwear.

The blond reaches out as though he's going to rummage through it, and the narrow-faced man snaps, "Enough, you idiot. C'mon."

He's obviously unhappy, but he and his men exit the caravan, with Davin carefully locking up behind them. They walk out, single-file, to the front of Davin's little stall, and the narrow-faced man scowls heavily. "We'll be around," he says, and it's a threat. "You let us know if you see anything."

"I'll be sure to tell you if I see a shifted dragon walking around," Davin says, dry as the desert.

They leave, then, the other customers of the night market giving them a wide berth and suspicious looks.

Davin picks up his pipe, re-lights it. He has to light two matches, as the first one goes out when his hand shakes for a brief moment. He picks up his newspaper. He sells two charms, one for sleeping, the other to help keep track of a dog who keeps running away.

In the late hours of the market, when there's only a few slivers of light left in the sky, Davin packs up his stall. Collapses his counter, folds up draperies, and rolls up carpets, tucks it all away in the caravan. Closes the doors and heads to the front, gives the caravan instructions and a healthy dose of magic to get it started. The caravan begins to roll forward.

It's only once they're well away from the night market, ten minutes on the road, that Davin crosses over to the chest. He kneels in front of it, palms the key from its place, and unlocks the chest. This time, there are no clothes. There is just Shain, sitting with his back to one of the walls, knees up in front of his chest.

He's glowing, ever so faintly, in the dark.

The light comes in then, Davin with a candle leaning over him, offering a hand up and out.

"Thank you," Shain says, quiet and a bit hoarse. He moves a little stiffly.

"D'you need some water?" Davin says, frowning at him. He doesn't wait for an answer, just lights candles with a flick of his wrist as he moves around the gently bumping caravan, heading to the pitcher.

"You have more magic than I thought you did," Shain says.

"Oh, this?" Davin says in surprise. "Not really. Just enough to light candles and the like. Most of this stuff has been enchanted—I have just enough to activate and deactivate it, not enough to actually construct or cast. The caravan cost me a pretty penny," he says with a little half-laugh. "I'll be sad to see it go."

"See it go?" Shain says, eyebrows drawing together. "What do you mean?"

"I'm sorry," Davin says mildly. "Did you not see the pack of bounty hunters who were here to kidnap and murder you?"

"Who says they were here for me?" Shain shoots back.

Davin raises his eyebrows.

Shain relents. "All right, fine," he says unhappily. "I'm very sorry for all the trouble I've caused you," he says, and there's a miserable little twist to his mouth that hurts Davin's heart, a little.

"Eh," he shrugs. "You'll have made Kharaman's day, at least."

"...What?" Shain asks, off-balance again. He stumbles when the caravan bounces over a rut.

"Well, we'll be going back to the ship," Davin says, and gestures to one of the chairs that's bolted to the floor.

Shain sinks down into it, stares at Davin. "You—you're going back to your ship?"

"Bout time we got back in the water, I guess," Davin says, leaning against the wall of the caravan. "It's been long enough, and we have to get you home somehow. You're looking for your skin, right?"

"I—yes," Shain says weakly, still staring. "How did you know?" His hair is starting to look different, and the inside of the caravan is becoming less dim.

"You were looking for something to help you find an object," Davin reminds him. "If I'd've known you were looking for a damned dragon skin I would've given you something a hell of a lot hardier than the little silver rod I gave you."

"How'd you know?" Shain asks again.

Davin grins at him, unable to help it. Shain's face is open and sort of—bemused, his hair like a firefly, filaments of light. "Really, you think I get many glowing men who plant themselves in my stall?" he teases. "It's not particularly subtle, Shain."

"And you want to help me find my scales, so I can—"

"Get back to dragon-ing? We can sure as hell try," Davin says. "Or at least take you to someone who can."

Shain looks at Davin like—like he's the one glowing. Like he's something precious. Like he just offered to give a dragon back his scales.

"You foolish man," Shain says, and there's a slow smile breaking over his face. "Who says I *want* to go back to that form?"

"What?" Davin drops his arms to his sides.

Shain laughs, shakes his head. He's very bright now, bright enough in the dimness of the shuttered caravan that Davin can really see that he *glows*. "I don't want to go back," he repeats. "At least, not yet. Why on earth would I go back to just sit on my mountain and watch when I could stay down here and —do things? Be something? Meet people?"

There's something sweet and mischievous in the curl of his smile as he stands. He almost stumbles again when the caravan jolts, but catches himself on the table. "I'll go with you on your ship, Captain," he says, and Davin swallows. "You can even help me look for scales—I really do need those back, after all. But I want to help *you*, too."

"All right," Davin says. "I mean—yeah."

Shain grins. "What was this about pirates?"

Davin goes pink, tries for a charming grin. "Pirate is such an ugly word," he hedges.

"Please tell me you were some pirate captain hiding out as a humble shopkeep to keep the heat off you and your crew after a big heist," Shain says, delighted.

Davin blinks. "That's a shockingly succinct way of putting it," he says.

"I know a lot of stories," Shain says.

"I know," Davin says. Grins. "You'll be popular with the crew."

The next time the caravan jolts, Shain manages to fall directly across the caravan, straight into Davin. Davin catches him around the elbows, hauls him back upright.

"How are you not falling over?" Shain complains. It goes a little breathless at the end.

"Sea legs," Davin says. He drops his hands from Shain's arms, but Shain doesn't step away.

"Y'know, captain," Shain says, his voice low, "there's a few things that one simply can't do as a dragon."

"What's that?" Davin says, blinks against the light that emanates off Shain in waves.

Shain kisses him in response, a little soft and hesitant at first, a far cry from his confident words.

When Davin kisses him back, in the dark of the caravan, the light that shines through his eyelids is almost blinding.

# Stormcalled

## *By R.K. Nickel*

I tensed as fresh flakes of snow struck my cheeks. They were light, soft, quick to dissolve, and above all... ominous.

"Don't go," pleaded Enooya, and I turned to see her stepping up beside me. Behind her, the tundra shone with a haunting beauty, cold and rock and snow dotted with purple sedges that refused to be buried.

"I'm sorry," I said, taking her hand. I wanted to stay. Of course I wanted to stay. But the council had spoken. This was my storm to thaw, and if I failed, the whole village would be in danger. All the villages would be. And more than that, the pulsing heartbeat of the storm called to me in a way I couldn't understand, a summoning drumbeat, unnatural, somewhere out there across the red ravenberry plains.

Enooya held my gaze, and I felt the worry eddying behind her eyes. She had thawed a storm once, but the thawing was a rite of passage each Qimuja needed to walk alone. To speak of your journey was forbidden.

"Whatever you run into out there, just know," she said, "you're strong enough to face it."

I smiled. We kissed.

Then I turned and marched into the white.

The white. No telling how far it stretched or what lurked behind its frosty veil. I marched, and with each passing hour, the storm grew denser, fiercer, until soon I'd lost all sense of home. The thrumming pulse of the storm drove me forward, and—

A shape materialized ahead, stepping from the snow, and even from a distance, I could feel the rhythm of its ill intent.

I siphoned.

A thin stream of mist poured from my lips, snaking out into the universe, shifting the nature of things, attracting cold. Mist turned to frost turned to ice, forming two lenses atop my eyes. Such an intricate weaving had taken me years to perfect. A chill entered my blood, some of my heat lost, but I could see the beast clearly now, even from here.

A feline thing, formed from the purest snow. It barreled toward me, a powerful, rippling-muscle lope. I met its icy eyes, and—

*I laughed as the cat pounced upon my chest. Only two months old, little Kretu brimmed with boundless energy. My first lynx. I couldn't believe my father had gotten her for me.*

*"Now, Auka," began my father. A tall man, and wide, his clothes always smelled of sweat, and his green, thimbleberry-leaf eyes sparkled with delight. "Raising a living thing is a tremendous responsibility. I didn't get my first pet until I was fourteen."*

*"I know."*

*"I know you do, my little snow wolf," he said, ruffling my hair. "Just remember, Kretu is yours and you are hers." His beard tickled me as he kissed my forehead.*

*"And you are mine," I whispered to the lynx, stroking her fur. She leapt—*

—and soared through the air, almost on me. "Kretu..." I muttered, barely coming to my senses in time to siphon a shield of ice in front of me. The feline creature of cold and memory crashed into the shield, shattering it, and I tumbled backward. It paced, its massive, twisted form bent on death.

And yet, somehow, the eyes were the same.

It charged again. I siphoned, forming ice along the ground, and the creature slipped and skidded toward me. With another burst of concentration and breath of mist, I conjured a hunting spear into my left hand, shooting bolts of ice from my right.

We came together, a being of ice against a mage of ice. I stabbed into its frozen hide, spear shattering, beast chipped. *And I was a girl again, Kretu pouncing*, and I was alone in the cold and the white, claws raking the thick hides I wore, *and I siphoned mice of cold for Kretu to chase*, and I siphoned spiked gauntlets to pierce my feline foe, *and my father smiled at me as I taught Kretu to fetch*, and finally, knocked onto my back, panting, weakened, I watched as the beast came for me, jaws wide.

Jaws wide...

As it struck, I siphoned a spike straight into its mouth and rolled. The jaws snapped shut, and the beast's own strength drove the icicle into its skull.

I sank to the snows, shivering so hard my muscles cramped. So much heat had drained away, frozen and cracked and lost to the winds. Some would return over time. Some, but not all. Lose too much, and I would hasten the fate all Qimuja must one day face.

Is this what the storms did? Why no one on the council spoke of them? Did they tap into the heart of the Qimuja sent to thaw them? Did they turn memories to solid snow, unraveling their foes from inside and out?

I'd been prepared for cold. I'd been prepared for pain. I wasn't prepared for this. Kretu, my father... Snows, how I missed him. But Enooya and I had left to start a life in a distant village. It had been years since my father and I had spoken, and moments ago, there he'd been, real. I could've sworn he was real.

I pushed down the memories, the fear, the loss, because the thrumming heartbeat of the storm was growing stronger. Days, at most, before it would overtake my village. I examined my wounds. My ice-shielded furs had withstood most of the attacks, though the cold claws had found blood in half-a-dozen places. I siphoned, surrendered the barest breath of heat, of life, and cauterized the wounds with cold.

I pressed on. No sun pierced the swirling snow. I could not track the passage of hours. My world became nothing but gray and dark gray. Cold, and colder, with spikes of hunger to demarcate the turning of the Earth. When I could walk no further, I slept beneath a dome of ice, siphoned tight around my body.

*"Each being on the tundra has a heartbeat, pumping our blood, keeping us warm. But in truth," my father said, "heat and cold are one. Opposites that revolve around the same center. Just as we must feast on fish and fowl, trading death for life, we must trade away our warmth in order to shape the ice. But give too much of yourself, and there will be nothing left."*

*"The Illuptingi," I said.*

*"The Illuptingi," he replied. Beings of crystal who roamed the land devoid of compassion, mere shells of their*

*former selves.* "You are strong, Auka. I know you would never let the ice into your heart."

"I would never," I told him.

"I love you, my little snow wolf."

I spent the next day limping forward, wind whipping at my furs, the drumbeat of the storm hypnotic. Everywhere I looked, forms swam and danced, dissipating just as I thought they might draw into focus.

And then she was there. Enooya. As beautiful as when I'd first seen her stepping off the ship.

No. I wasn't thinking clearly. The snow, the hunger, the thirst, the cold, that thrumming heartbeat rippling through the ground, crackling through the air. A vision. She must be.

She strode forward, just as Kretu had—

*And fell into my arms, lips pressing against mine. I'd been with others before, boys at first, but with her it was different. I could taste the rightness of it. Her touch filled me with life. Her smile lit a flame inside me that burned pure heat.*

*"What is this?" my father asked, towering in the doorway. The scowl in his eyes robbed them of their thimbleberry shine.*

*I tried to explain. I tried desperately to explain, and he was a kind man, the kindest man, a man who had taught me everything, but perhaps not everything, because I had grown into someone whose mind was ready to confront the unknown. And he tried his best, staying silent when my explanations ran dry, because he knew his words would sting. His silence stung all the same.*

*Enooya reached out to comfort me, and—*

Her hand landed just above my wrist, so cold it burned, my flesh freezing despite the layers that separated our skin. "You must go back."

I had left her behind... how long ago? I tried to process, but my muscles ached, and my throat was ice-burn dry, and my reason was slipping away.

"I came all this way to find you," she continued. "Auka, please, the storm, it's killing you."

"What do you mean?" She had to be a vision.

"You haven't eaten; you're siphoning too much, far too much. Please."

"I left you behind."

"You can never leave me, my love. Not truly. Snows, I'm so glad I found you. You've gotten so turned around."

Seeing her was such sweet relief. I didn't want to go deeper. I wanted to go home, to curl up and drink tii and forget the world, to drift into a pleasant sort of oblivion.

"You needn't fight," she said. "Life is meant to be enjoyed, my love. It shouldn't be so hard."

And it was easy, so easy to let her guide me back the way I'd come. My mind flickered, weakening, drifting.

*As my father turned his back, leaving the home Enooya and I had built together, she looked me in the eye and told me how proud she was. That I was strong, and that the fight was always worth it, that the fight itself was what mattered, rather than the outcome.*

*That there was strength in unity.*

I stopped.

"No," I said.

"Come, Auka."

I tried to pull away, but her frozen fingers dug into my arm.

"You will go no further, stormwalker," she said as her face shifted to pure snow, a projection of the storm, just as Kretu had been.

I let out a bellow of rage and exhaustion and hurt. And I siphoned, reaching deeper into myself than I ever had, ripping heat from my core. Cold exploded outward, and half-a-hundred crystals of ice tore through her, shredding her to nothing. She screamed. It sounded just like her.

I collapsed, no longer warm enough to stand, and in the comfort of the snow, I allowed my eyes to drift into the dark.

*Thu-thud. Thu-thud. Thu-thud.*

I awoke to the heartbeat of the storm reverberating in my soul. I tried to focus, to rise. How many months had I shaved off my life? How much closer had I brought myself to becoming Illuptingi? If I did, would I end up hurting Enooya? Would I be capable of such a thing?

*Thu-thud. Thu-thud. Thu-thud.*

I pushed myself to my feet, not knowing if my own heart pumped the strength into me or if I was being otherworldly pulled by the center of the storm.

*Thu-thud. Thu-thud. Thu-thud.*

The rhythm pulsed through me, obliterating my thoughts. My steps landed on the downbeats. Nothing existed except forward. Forward and forward and forward and white, always white, a blinding, changeless, howling, burning white.

And then I was there.

The eye.

The sun poured straight down into a clearing devoid of wind. Some invisible barrier held back the snow on all sides in perfect symmetry. The heartbeat stopped all at once, though I could see the sound of it all around me, pulses spiking in the whirling snow that battered up against the magical barrier. For the first time in recent memory, I could think, could hear, could breathe.

"Hello, Auka."

My father stood in the very center. How had I not seen him there?

"Father?" I asked, overcome with emotion.

"Yes."

But he was not my father. He was pure ice, through and through. Someone had taken his soft, kind face and carved it into a lattice of interlocking blades. Broken icicles clung to his chin, forming a jagged beard. Barbs ripped through what had been his skin, as if he'd melted and refrozen over and over. Pale, pupil-less orbs of milky-white sat in the holes where his eyes should have been.

Not some storm vision made manifest like Enooya, like Kretu.

An Illuptingi.

"You're not him."

"I am him, a better version of him. Wiser. Everything has crystalized for me, Auka. And it is an ascension. How I long for you to see it."

"You're not him."

"My little snow wolf, you are so young." He took a step toward me and placed his hand upon my cheek. His touch felt empty, like being caressed by a cold night sky. "To have your innocence, your youth. It's a beautiful thing, but you don't understand how the world truly works. You, your whole generation, they share a rosy vision. It's pretty to look at, of course, but it's not real. You would lead our people to their destruction, traveling on a road of smiles and hope straight into the jaws of famine."

He gazed out into the storm, unfocused, as if looking far, far away. He'd had plenty of heat left when I'd moved away. What had drained him? My absence? Had I done this?

"I'm sorry I left," I said, "but this storm—we need to find a way to stop it."

His face swung back to me. He tried to smile, but his teeth melted and reformed as he spoke, dribbling down his chin and freezing at the tips of his beard. "You have to trust me to guide you. You have to trust that I know better. Believe me, once you are grown, you will see things as I do."

"See what?" I scanned the clearing, looking for some way to end the storm. Other Qimuja had stood where I stood. How had they done it?

"When I was your age," he said, "people knew what was right. But you make these choices, Auka, they—" He clenched a fist, holding back.

"Enooya?" A bitter taste rose in my throat.

"Have you not seen how she pours cold into your heart? She divided us. Father and daughter. Please, come home to me, little snow wolf." He held out his icy hand.

I thought back to the heartbeat, the call. The white. The council hadn't chosen me because I was ready. They'd sent me because of him. This storm and I had been linked from the beginning. And suddenly I felt it, felt the thudding truth of it, the memories. This—this was the journey Qimuja were forced to walk. This was the unspoken sorrow that bonded us, that shone in Enooya's eyes. Shattering the ones we loved most, the ones who had grown cold.

"Please, Auka," he said, milky-white eyes begging, "come home to me."

I thought of all the wonderful days I'd spent in my father's arms. Of the laughter as he'd taught me to fish, to siphon. Then I thought of Enooya. And met my father's cold gaze. "I have a home."

He scowled, and his lips cracked, long crevices opening up along his face. "Just know," he said, "I'm doing this for you, though you are too blind to see it."

"Doing what?"

"Laying down a fresh coat."

And with that, he siphoned, and his weaving radiated more powerfully than anything I'd ever felt. He pulled heat from the world itself, chilling the earth, the air. A crystalline blade appeared in his icy hand.

"You've always fought me," he said, swinging the great pana. I scrambled backward, barely dodging a killing strike. "Every step of the way."

"Dad, I—"

Another swing. I siphoned a shield—nearly three fingers thick—but his blade shattered it with ease. My arm screamed in pain, then hung, unmoving. "You act on any desire that pops into your head, not thinking of the consequences." He swung. I stumbled backward. His blade nicked my shoulder and hot blood froze in the cold air. "Not thinking how your actions might affect those around you."

"The village—"

"Will be remade, untainted. Purest white."

I'd lost him. I'd truly lost him. If I wanted to save the people I loved, I had to destroy this Illuptingi, this—thing. I told myself it was just a thing. An empty vessel of ice. That's all.

He raised his sword, and I screamed, a scream of loss and defiance, and siphoned my heat into a sword of my own. With a single hand, I met his blow. The sound of ice striking ice reverberated outward. The echo collided with the unseen barrier holding back the snow.

And punched through.

Snow poured in through the holes, encircling us, drawn to our magic. Every swing of the sword, every thrust and parry, was accompanied by swirling white.

I siphoned hills of ice, footholds to give myself high ground, but he climbed with me. I siphoned missiles of cold, wove icy mirrors to scatter my reflection, but he batted them away. And kept coming.

I had to stop him, to save Enooya. But if I kept siphoning like this, I would lose myself. The bitterness and rage would turn me into a beast of crystal. To fight him was to become him. To cease fighting was to allow his will to shape the world.

The snow raged.

The sun shone.

And I knew what to do.

*There is strength in unity.*

I poured the last of my energy into one last weaving, shooting a sphere of mirrored ice straight into the sky. My beacon rose above the storm, where it met the rays of the sun and cast them in every direction, great glowing beams of pure light.

The light would reach my village, would reach other villages. They would know where the center of the storm lay. I might have been the only one who could feel its call, but with the beacon, they would be able to find him, to stop him. They would come, and when they did, they would come as one.

Spent, I dropped my sword and released my magic. All but the beacon.

"I did not train my daughter to quit so easily." He kicked me, straight in the chest, and the force of his crystalline blow sent me flying backward into a snowbank.

I wobbled to my feet, coughing red spatters of blood that froze and landed on the white.

"You can't stop us all, father."

He screamed, smashing the pommel of his sword into me with a crunch that I heard more than I felt.

I wheezed and clutched my ribs. Something inside of me was broken.

"You can't stop us all," I said again, more weakly.

He lifted his sword. I lay crumpled on the ground, unmoving, snow swirling around me in great bursts, threatening to bury me. But I had made my choice. I would not become Illuptingi. I let my eyes rest. It was a strangely pleasant feeling, to know the end was upon me. I had done my part.

I would have liked to hold Enooya again.

I would have liked to hold my father again.

"So be it," he said, and he sounded... indifferent.

It had been a warm life...

Warm. I was warm.

My eyes flew open, and the world seemed aflame.

"What have you done?" he bellowed.

I wove dark lenses atop my eyes and looked up. Straight above me, the beacon burned with an intensity I could not fathom. From what seemed every corner of the earth, beams of light poured into that sphere, and suddenly, I understood. My friends, my village, my people—all across the land, home to home, family to family, they had seen my light shining above the storm and known it for what it was. And each Qimuja had added their strength to mine, conjuring mirrors of ice to reflect the sun, sending me their light, trading their heat to bring me hope, each one dying just a little, turning the beacon above me into a star that shone with a fury that said we were not alone. I was not alone.

I siphoned, shaping the flare above me so that every ray—no matter how small, how weak, focused into a scorching blaze that burned straight into my father's chest.

The sword tumbled from his fingers, steaming, and he began to melt away. His face twitched into some new expression. Remorse or sorrow or simply disappointment at his failure, I could not tell.

"My little snow wolf," he managed to say as he reached for me, turning to nothing.

The beacon blinked out, consumed, and I looked toward the space where my father, my once-father, the Illuptingi, had stood, but all that remained was a rivulet of water.

He was gone, truly gone.

And with him, the snows died. The winds stopped. I heard the howl of wolves again, the cry of distant birds—once more saw the plants beneath the white, felt the sun's warmth upon my skin, and as I took in a breath, fresh, deep, crisp, light, I thought of Enooya, pictured her holding out a cup of tii, smiling, beckoning, safe, and finally, I was at peace.

# Apocalypse Sasquatch
## *by Joanne Askew*

Birdie rotated his tiny dark fingers through the worn ropes of the traps, setting them again in the sparse woodland grasses, a wanting building each time. He knew he was the only *boy* in the village who could catch rabbits like this. If only they saw him as that—as the boy who caught the rabbits—not a weird little girl. He had known for most of his life that he wasn't, and had never been, a girl. So why did no one see what he saw within? He was Birdie, the bravest boy and the best hunter. He squinted with one brown eye at his work, a feat for an eight-year-old. That would do.

His short fingernails ran through his even shorter hair. It settled in tight curls that threatened to overflow if he forgot to trim it. He looked around, eyes darting to branches and trunks and piles of dried needles. The pine forests seemed to tell him to return home. Their boughs ached and groaned at him. The sun was setting. His father would not like him being back late, not since the apocalypse happened.

Birdie's dad said it was because people had all sinned, but when he was five, he spoke to one of the younger men in their village. The man told him it was climate disaster and pollution that caused the downfall of humankind. What came after were questions on questions met only with strange answers of a now-gone world. Birdie believed this story over his dad's—his version blamed too much of the disaster on the sins of humankind, and he knew, even at five, there was no such thing as a sin.

He admired his rabbit trap once more. He'd gotten better at trapping since his eighth birthday and was darn proud he could bring home *at least* two rabbits a night, but he hated it when the rabbits were still alive. He didn't like to kill them if the snare hadn't done the job, so if they weren't too injured, he set them free and promised to get them next time. No one knew this. Birdie was scared it showed a lapse in the bravery he fought so hard to nurture.

This evening, he caught three. He tied their back paws with old shoelaces and strung them all together like a bunch of deflated balloons. He secured them to himself like one would secure extra rounds of bullets—from the shoulder, across the chest, keeping their preciousness close. He pulled his mask down as he started his journey home, just in case marauders saw he was young, fresh-faced.

He followed the sound of a stream until he reached its edge, and then, quite ungracefully, he jumped into the water to cover his scent; there were wolves here too. He often bounced from tree stump to lonesome rock pretending to fight them. His knees were always scraped, his fingers cut, and his face covered in muck, but he didn't care. He didn't care how wet his scrappy clothes got, or the way the drops of water stuck to his dense black hair and rolled off without touching his scalp. If his nails were clean, he wasn't himself.

He continued north once he had shaken off the excess water, and danced through the well-worn trails of the mountains, entertaining himself. His father had told him to alternate his path home.

"Don't be predictable," he had said. His words dug into Birdie's sense of direction and he began a new path home, one that took him through the older parts of the forest and had natural open trails for him to wind through.

It was the time of evening when the darkening night played tricks with the trees and spooked little kids in the forest, but Birdie was the bravest little kid the village had ever known.

His pace was unsteady as he continued home. Sometimes he ran, and sometimes he found something interesting to poke at and stopped for a few minutes. The forest was his home and his playground—it was the place he could be himself. The trees didn't care that he wasn't a girl, not like the village which seemed to muse over it like it was a predicament. The spongy forest ground didn't care either, and he was pretty sure all those rabbits didn't care. He was a boy to them like he was a boy to himself.

"Quit it," he whispered to the pines as they grumbled and creaked at him.

"Quit what?" they asked back. He froze, gripped his rabbits tight, and swung round to the voice. There was nothing but the trees in the evening light. He puffed out his chest and took the form of the older boys back at home, shaking it off like the impending gloom was toying with him. They were brave too, bigger than him, but he knew he could keep up with them.

Birdie resisted the morsel of fear that quelled gently in his soul. He picked up his speed and continued north through the older part of the forest.

"Where are you going, little boy?" the trees asked Birdie.

His eyes darted around the trees but saw nothing that could have owned the voice. "I ain't listening. It ain't funny. Who's there?"

"I haven't seen any men for some time. What happened to everything?" the trees called to him. He reacted by accelerating into a run. The trees continued to talk, but the voice faded the faster he went.

Soon, the trees thickened as he neared home. He was embarrassed, ashamed he had run from fear. Perhaps he wasn't as brave as he thought. Perhaps he was as soft as the other kids he had known in his short life.

The village appeared in front of Birdie at the special angle it took when he arrived through the older forest. He gripped his rabbits even tighter, pushing them into his chest. Two were stiff. Rigour mortis had set in, but one of the rabbits had only been dead an hour or so. That one felt nice, like a comforting word on a cold day.

The men saw him return first and rushed to him to retrieve their meal. The other children stayed clear—they had bullied Birdie a long time ago and he had cut off one of their fingers in retaliation. His father had been somewhat worried about that, but now they left Birdie alone. He did what he wanted, and often, what he wanted was exactly what the older men did in their village—hunt, build, protect. He was one of them, despite what puberty would eventually bring.

Two of the older boys slapped Birdie on the back with the same force they would each other. He bent slightly at the impact but smiled.

"Birdie? Is Birdie back?" an elderly voice called.

"Dad, I'm back. Got three. Three bigguns."

He showed off his rabbits to the elderly man he called Dad, but who wasn't really his dad. He was Birdie's grandfather.

His real dad left Earth with his mother when they were offered a rescue by the silver things in the sky. They left baby Birdie behind, without falter or hesitation. His grandfather, consumed with guilt, took him in and loved him like the little girl he seemed to be, and not the little boy he really was.

Birdie had already told the older boys he was really a boy. They were nice. They said he could be "whatever the fuck he wanted to be" and smacked him on the back like he was truly their little brother. He loved Noah and Jaxon for that, but the red blush that came every time the other members of their village called him a girl seemed to sizzle and smoulder across his face and make his eyes wet.

The old man, Dad, breathed a rattled breath as he took the rabbits. His generation lived through pollution—their lungs weren't so good. He grumbled as he navigated back to the center of their village. It consisted of huts made of pine, and open fires here and there. It had a warm-brown glow about it and the air was almost constantly filled with smoke. It used to be busier, before marauders found the area and took most of the women. Now there were only three left, and Birdie didn't include himself in that number.

He whistled at Noah and Jaxon and they came to him like obedient dogs. He always got a response from them. Jaxon had dark skin like him, and Noah was as blond as a Viking.

"Lads, I 'eard sometfing in the forest, the old part." They surveyed Birdie with trusting eyes. "It asked me some stuff but I ran."

"You dick," Jaxon said with his crooked smile. "Why you run from that?"

"'Cos it weren't right. Somefing weren't right with it."

"Everyone has problems, Bird," Noah said.

"Na. It weren't human. I fink it was the trees. They ever spoke to yoos two before?"

"It's the tricks, Birdie. We told you 'bout the tricks? The early night plays tricks." Noah's tone suggested it was the end of the conversation. "Tricks, Bird."

Birdie tossed that night. He turned nearly as much, but the guilt of his fear kept him awake for most of the time the others slept. He remembered when the marauders came a few years ago. They took the little girls and the younger women, but they didn't find Birdie because he had hidden deep in the dead hollowed trunk of a spruce. He often wondered if they had been disappointed by the missing finger of one of their young victims. The village mourned for weeks after that. Birdie only blamed himself—he should have fought them off with the men. He could now, he thought. He was strong enough now.

The night felt as lonely as his struggles. The fear that had made him run was not him. It was not the person he wanted to be. How could he defend against the marauders when he was scared of a talking tree? He had asked the fear to go away like the marauders eventually did, but he did not understand why it crept back in sometimes. He did all he could to dispel the fear like he dispelled the gender that was forced on him. If he could dissipate the identity he did not feel one with, he could dissipate any threat.

The next afternoon, Birdie set off early to check his traps. He went through the old wood, straight back to the place where he'd heard the voice.

"'Ello?" he called. His voice echoed off the bark of the trees and tickled the pine needles suspended in the air. "I'm back. I ain't running this time."

There was no response. He found a soft tuffet and sat. His bottom sank into it like it wasn't solid. His hands swung to his sides to steady himself and when he brought them away, they were crawling with ants.

"Bleeding ant 'ill!" he shouted at the ground. He smacked at himself, freeing the hundreds of ants from his dirty clothes. They tumbled down to the forest floor, their world destroyed by a boy searching for bravery.

"Do you need help?" a voice asked. Birdie bolted his neck around, the sensation of crawling on his skin unimportant now.

"Who's there?"

There was no answer.

A bough creaked. Leaves rustled. Birdie called out again. This time, he made his voice deeper and added a growl at the end. There was movement in his peripheries, a few branches swaying like a gentle breeze licked at them. He focused his eyes on the spot. Deep green danced with strings of brown, but his eyes focused beyond the branches, to where a pool of light struck something, something large, menacing.

There, in the forest light, was a creature he had never seen before. It was taller than any human, maybe eight feet tall, and covered in reddish-brown hair from top to toe. Its eyes were ape-like, but Birdie could see a familiar whiteness around the edge of its irises that sang a more humanoid tune. His heart sped, trying to leap from his body, but he inhaled and the air that leaked into his lungs steadied his heart and stopped it from escaping. In his chest, bravery took out fear in a battle that lasted no more than five seconds.

Birdie grasped at the ground for a weapon. He found a stick, not sharp at the end, but pokey—it would still hurt. He raised it at the thing. A gust kicked up the dead pine needles on the ground, creating a spinning circle of brown and green. The breeze shook the monster's fur, made it look like the thing was underwater, its long hair floating around its body like a halo, the pine needles swirling like kelp at its feet.

It moved one foot and let the other follow. Branches gave way to its mass, letting the monster through, and sprung back with more force than the wind could muster. It made Birdie flinch, like the monster was readying its attack. His small fingers gripped his pokey stick. Sweat formed in his palm, saturating and slickening the wood.

"What the 'eck are you?" he burst, spreading his legs wide to make himself look bigger.

The creature laughed. It sounded like a ticking, like something was stuck in its throat.

It eased Birdie, made him feel like the creature could sense just how brave he was, what he could defeat when he tried. "Why you following me? You asked me 'bout men yesterday?"

"Haven't seen any for a while," the beast said to him, its eyes darting away and surveying the afternoon's forest.

"You have. Me. I'm here. You can face me. I'm ready now."

The beast nodded. "Of course, but I would never harm another creature."

"I'm a man. Not a creature."

"We're all creatures." It reached nonchalantly to the tall branches above. It could reach the pinecones without much stretching. It offered Birdie a bite of the cone before it took to eating it like an apple.

Birdie lowered his pokey stick and let it drop to the earth. It barely made a sound as it fell on the moist ground. He tilted his head. Parts of his tight-curled hair tickled the side of his neck. The wind made the trees move and the beast tried to clear his throat. It sounded like the time thunder had come to the forest and taken out the oldest tree. The sound echoed high into the branches and away from them both. Birdie worried that the noise carried all the way back to his village, booming menacingly through their little huts and sparse campfires. Birdie wondered if his village would come running with sharper sticks and rope to bring the monster down to save him from it. But he didn't need them. He could face the creature on his own, identify its needs and wants, just like he had found his own and held them strong inside his heart to become the champion he knew he was.

The creature stared vacantly at him as if expecting some kind of predetermined behavior from a human.

"Are you not afraid, boy?" the creature grumbled.

Birdie puffed out his chest and pulled down the scarf that covered his face. "Na. You don't scare me, not nomore. Not now I can see who you are."

"And who are you?"

"Birdie."

The creature tilted its head much like Birdie. It didn't say anything. It examined Birdie like it was trying to put him into context. Birdie couldn't stand the silence.

"Yous want some rabbit? Better than that pinecone to fill your belly," Birdie asked the thing, hoping to show he was in control of the situation.

The tan creature scoffed at the notion of rabbits, nearly spitting out its pinecone, but its laugh quickly turned into a guttural explosion. The creature wrapped a giant hairy hand around its own throat, gesturing with its other. The sound was a stranger in the forest. The rabbits screamed when caught. The trees swished and whispered. Birdie yipped and hollered. But this creature struggled, agony and despair ascending into the space between them.

Birdie straightened. He reached to the creature thinking he could help by showing he was brave enough to touch it, to comfort it. It coughed more and the sound of its inhales were shaken, strained.

"You need 'elp?" Birdie finally asked.

"Help." Its voice was forced, like words hurt but it needed to say them.

"What you want me to do 'bout that?"

"Help me," it said.

"Kneel down. You're too tall for me. I did this once to Dad. He 'ad a rabbit bone caught in his throat."

The creature did as he said and knelt before him. Birdie circled the creature and approached its back with a mighty running kick. Birdie knew he looked cool doing this. He was disappointed that Noah and Jaxon weren't there to see it. When he made contact, the creature lunged forward. The pinecone caught in its throat flew across the forest like it had just been freed from a snare. Birdie tumbled and fell to the ground. He lifted himself up immediately and smacked the muck from his bottom.

"Thank you, boy," the creature said.

"No problem," Birdie replied. "What are you anyway?"

"Sasquatch."

"Never 'eard of 'em. You a person? Or an animal, like a rabbit?" Birdie narrowed his eyes.

"Bit of both, I expect. You?"

"Person. A male person."

"You live with others?"

"Yes, but you ain't allowed at our village. It ain't for anyone but us."

"That's ok. I'm leaving soon. I am pleased that men are living in these woods again. It is a true example of life and how it adapts to be what it needs to be." It cleared its throat.

"If you shave off your hair, will you look like me?" Birdie asked.

"Perhaps. I need my hair. For camouflage."

"That's weird, ain't it?"

"You're a little weird too."

"What, because I don't look like a normal boy? Well, I am. It doesn't matter that I didn't have it easy like the other boys and couldn't just look between my legs to find out. I had to discover meself by meself. I don't care what you say, Sam-Squaunch."

The old forest boomed with the creature's laugh. It shook and shuddered under the weight of hysterics.

"What's so funny?" Birdie asked.

"Little boy, you sure are brave. Most humans who have seen me run, or threaten me with strange silver squares that flash lights in my eyes. Years ago they hunted me, before the world became quiet again. You are odd for staying in my company."

"I know I'm a brave boy."

"Of course you are. Sometimes bravery is helping those in need, not how many meals you catch. You will grow from here, grow into a strong and wise man. You will protect that village for years to come."

Birdie grinned. "Do you think?"

"I do. I have seen many versions of mankind, over hundreds of years, and its most compassionate form is standing before me. The forest has always been a home for all creatures—perhaps man's cruelness came when they left the trees. Without the woods to guide them, perhaps man forgot their place in the world." The sasquatch turned to the darkening trees and grunted several times. It hollered too, but it didn't sound remotely human. "See you, little boy. Thank you for your kindness and bravery." it said.

There was a secret smile across Birdie's face. He had defeated fear, maybe, but he had something more now—a magic called compassion that he could lead his people with when the time came. He knew he needed bravery, identity, but compassion was new and powerful.

The sasquatch lumbered into the trees and disappeared, its camouflage dissolving it into mirage. Birdie's smile did not ease as he crept into the green and brown forest to empty his traps. He had caught five rabbits today. His people would be happy.

# Fluorescent Clouds, Neon Rain
## *by Daniel Santos Marques*

How long have I been sat here?

I sigh and lean forward, slapping my arm on the tabletop. It's sticky: too many nights and too many drinks. It's barely able to keep itself clean, I bet. Just my luck to get stuck with the only alcoholic table in the place. I lean forward more. The table tilts. Figures—drunks never stand up straight.

I try to lift my hand to grab my drink, but it's stuck. The webbing between my fingers stretches as I peel it off. It looks like a frog's. We were all frogs once...

How long have I been sat here?

I wrench my arm from the tabletop and grab my drink, but it's empty. The table must have had it. "Greedy lowlife," I say, getting up and kicking its wonky leg so it knows. "Now I have to buy another one!"

It wobbles, unfazed, and doesn't even offer an apology.

"Whatever," I scowl and make for the bar.

The place is more packed than usual. Well, I don't know what it is like usually. I've never seen anything like it before, but it feels known. It's an oddly decorated place, somewhere between a quaint country pub and an inner-city bar. Thick, hand-woven carpet stretches across the floor with lavish, vivid designs of flowerbeds filled with fleur-de-lis which small birds flit between as snakes slither among the buds. Framed paintings dangle from the ceiling, depicting a courtroom. I can't make out any of the faces though. The walls are pitch black and bare. They'd be impossible to see if it weren't for the thrumming strobe lights overhead.

I squeeze my way through the densely populated dance floor, banged and knocked by uncoordinated, jiggling bodies. And I always thought I was a bad dancer.

I finally make it through the wall of flesh and to the bar.

"Hey there, hon," one of the bartenders says to me. All of the staff are wearing orange jumpsuits with serial numbers on the chest. "Just one sec," she assures me.

She pours the last couple of glittery, gelatinous cubes into an hourglass and slides it across to a customer.

"Thanks for waiting," she says.

Her jawline is incredible, so smooth and sharp.

"No problem," I say, stroking my coarse, stubbly chin.

"What can I get you?"

"A strawberry da—"

But before I can finish my order, she slaps down a magnifying glass filled with pink sand in front of me and stares at me flatly, with no expression on her face at all.

"Err..." I peer around the bar. People chat away, gulping out of microscopes and pillboxes. "Thanks," I mutter, looking back at her and picking up the magnifying glass carefully.

I take a sip. It tastes exactly like a strawberry daiquiri.

"You're welcome," the bartender says, still frozen to the spot, her lips barely moving, then her face glitches.

I blink to make sure I saw it right, but when I look back at her she's busy talking to a guy next to me. How long have I been here? Maybe this should be my last one.

I take my magnifying glass and brave the arrhythmic abattoir once again. Arms and legs barge into me as I shimmy my way between people, cautious not to spill any of the sand from the shallow recess of the magnifying glass. Everyone else looks like they're having fun. I should have brought someone, but who'd want to come with me? Haven't had a date in almost two years.

I manage to make it through unscathed and take a seat at my table. It wobbles as I prop my arms on it and accidentally spill my entire drink. Strawberry daiquiri drips from my sleeves, bright red like fake blood, onto the greedy tabletop.

"Well isn't that fantastic!" I gripe.

"That's entirely subject to your definition."

I look up, startled. A man is sitting opposite me. I didn't see him when I came over. He must've sat down just as I was giving my shirt a liquor bath.

"I'm sorry," I say, dabbing my sleeves with some loose napkins I found in my pocket, "I didn't see you sit down."

"You think playing stupid will get you out of this, Brian, but it won't?" he chides in his thick New York accent.

I take another look at him and suddenly stop cleaning my shirt. He looks strange. He's dressed like one of those PIs from old film noirs and the pulp novels my dad loved (long brown trench coat; fedora; navy-blue suit underneath). But that's not what's strange. It's his face, his skin: it's entirely grayscale, like an old movie.

"I, err..." I watch him reach inside his jacket and take out a packet of cigarettes. "My name's Jamie," I tell him.

"Ahh," he shrugs, "but what's in a name anyway. Ain't that what you always say, Shakespeare?"

The song ends and the music changes, much to the delight of the dancers who all cheer as it starts up. It sounds warped and backward. I can't make out the lyrics but it sounds like:

*pu ekaw ot stnaw ohw*
*maerd a tub si efil nehw*

"Focus, Danno," he says, snapping his fingers in front of me. "You ain't finished yet."

"I... what are you talking about?"

"We've been sitting here for hours."

"I swear to god, I don't remember."

"Yeah, that's right. Why not appeal to Buddha while you're at it?"

He takes out a cigarette and screws one between his lips.

"Honestly, sir, I have no idea. Who are you? Some sort of detective?"

He sighs, pauses in lighting his cigarette, draws out a business card and hands it to me.

There's not much on it, just a number comprised of nothing but 4s, and above that a name: INSPECTRE LORENTZ.

"Inspectre?" I comment aloud. "I think you've got a typo there," I say, handing him back the card.

"We never make mistakes."

He lights his cigarette. As he does so, I notice the card has disappeared from my fingers.

"Okay. What is this: a Kafka novella?"

"What are you," Inspectre Lorentz quips, "a first semester English major?"

"Well… yeah, I am."

"Mmhhm," he hums proudly as he sucks on his cigarette.

"So what do you want with me?"

"I ask the questions. Okay, Francis?" he snaps, rainbow-colored smoke wisping from between his monochrome lips.

He doesn't wait for me to answer.

"*Hckhh-hmm.*" He clears his throat and takes out a small journalist's notepad. "So, where is she?"

"What?"

"Don't play dumb with me son, we've been through this. The girl—where is she?"

"What girl?" I laugh. This is so ridiculous.

"You expect me to believe that *you* don't know where she is? You two were any closer you'd be an empty sandwich."

I frown at him.

He doesn't explain.

"We're going to find her, y'know."

Over by the edge of the crowd, the entrance door swings open and a woman enters.

She seems familiar.

"We?"

"Yes. We," he affirms. "And when we do, we're not going to stop with her. We'll come after *you* next."

She hovers by the wall of flesh covering the dance floor and glances over at me. Her lips, painted in soft peach lipstick (n.o. 43), stretch across her face. She's beautiful.

"For what?" I ask.

"Milk, cheese, eggs, flour…" He glowers at me.

"That's part of my shopping list."

"You can say whatever you want, Phil, but it won't save you. We've got reams of the stuff."

She's wearing a boho-style, canary-yellow, floral-print sundress that stops just above the knees. The spaghetti straps drape delicately over her broad shoulders, but she doesn't care. She's paired it elegantly with chunky, brass hoop earrings and white strappy heels. She looks amazing, like I always knew she would.

"Wait a sec," I say to Inspectre Lorentz. "You've been spying on me?"

"Spying on you, off you, in you, out you."

The woman by the entrance waves for me to come over. I feel dizzy.

"This is nonsense," I tell him.

"There's more!" He tears through his notepad. "Here!" he announces, stabbing his finger at the page. "'She's with me always. When I look at the moon, I see her face. Luna. That's a good name.'"

"How did you...?"

"WHERE'S LUNA?" Inspectre Lorentz barks, slamming his fist on the table. Lines of static run up his hand.

"She's not here!" I peer over to her anxiously then gaze back at Inspectre Lorentz. "She doesn't exist!"

"'When I look in the mirror I see her face!'" he reads. His eyes cut sharply back to me. "WHERE IS SHE?"

"Why can't you just leave me and her alone?"

"So you *do* know where she is?"

"No!"

The room feels sweaty, heavy. The walls are damp. Dissonant sounds womp out the speakers in time with the pulsating walls.

"DON'T LIE TO ME!" Inspectre Lorentz booms, bolting to his feet.

"I'M NOT!" I shout, rising up and meeting his gaze.

The dancers on the floor seem to have coalesced into an interconnected mass of limbs, flailing in the strobe light. I feel sick, weak.

Inspectre Lorentz snatches hold of my wrist. His skin feels like glass. "Neither of you are getting out of here."

He holds a pair of handcuffs in his other hand.

I can't let them take me. I can't let them take her.

"NO!" I scream, yanking my arm from his grasp.

Inspectre Lorentz glares at me. His eyes glaze over red. Several more inspectres emerge from the surrounding tables. They close in.

I glance across at her. She looks calm. She smiles at me.

This is it.

I flip the table and ram it into Inspectre Lorentz and two of the other inspectres. They drop to the floor. More inspectres appear from across the bar. I cannot stall.

I rush for the exit, skirting round the swelling blob of meat that expands on the dance floor. The inspectres chase after me.

I reach her. She takes hold of my hand without saying a word.

"We have to leave," I tell her.

I snatch hold of the handle and tear open the door. We rush outside, but don't get far. Sludge brown vans marked Inspectre Bureau are parked in a crescent, surrounding the pavement. Inspectres lurk on both sides. Overhead, drones buzz, illuminated under fluorescent clouds.

"You have nowhere to go!" calls one of the inspectres.

Thunder claps ring out. Neon-green rain falls from the sky.

I turn to her, taking both hands in mine. "I'm so glad I got to see you," I say. Tears roll down my cheeks, mixing with the rain. "You…" I choke up. "You look so beautiful."

"Inspectres ready!" calls an inspectre.

"It's okay," she whispers as I throw my arms round her.

"Aim!"

She presses her lip to my ear: "We'll see each other again."

"FIRE!"

I wake up in my bed, alone as usual. It's dark outside. The subtle, breeze-like rush from car engines rustles by on the street below.

I peel back the covers, clamber out of bed, and go to the window. My palms sweat. The night is still young.

I go to my cupboard, take out the duffle bag, and head to the bathroom. It has been too long. I can't keep putting it off.

I set about shaving it all—my legs, my arms, my feet, my hands, my pubes, my chest, my beard. I scrub deep in my pores and moisturize. I open the duffle, take everything out, and get dressed.

I'm almost ready. There's only one thing left. I slide open the drawer beside the sink. The black plastic tube rolls, rattling across the wooden base. I take it out. There's a sticker with the number '43' written on it. I pull the cap off, twist the bottom, and apply the peach matte to my lips. I pinch a tissue from a nearby box and hold it between my lips for a few seconds.

I then toss the tissue away, take a deep breath, and look in the mirror. There she is. In the flesh. Luna. Me. Spaghetti straps drape finely over my broad shoulders. They look thinner than they are, but I don't care.

"You look beautiful."

# For Esnan

## *by Frances Koziar*

Ayari took slow, even breaths as fe applied thick black eyeliner around fer eyes, making points out to either side as was the current fashion in Xyana. Like many fale—the third recognized gender in the world—fe sported a neatly trimmed beard and had already donned the long metal earrings that were citadel dress code for upper servants. Looking at fer own face in the broken shard of mirror that fe had taken from a richer street years ago, fe couldn't tell that fe had been crying all morning except by the extra spark of brightness in fer dark brown eyes.

Fe finished and straightened, picking up the bag fashioned out of old rags that contained fer uniform shoes for work. Fer gaze passed over fer beloved little sister's body, laid out carefully on the floor mattress, but skimmed off like water against oil to stare blankly at the rest of their tiny home: a single room hardly large enough to stand in with a creaky but well-swept wooden floor, a bucket fe had just used to bathe outside with, a mattress, the mirror shard in a groove in the wall, and a small pile of clothing and other possessions. The last thing Ayari wanted right now was to go to work, but this wasn't the sort of job you missed.

Ayari slipped out into the grungy street outside, stones cold against fer tough brown feet, and closed the creaking, battered door behind fer. The sun hadn't yet cleared the horizon, but the sky was already light, a couple of pale clouds moving slowly overhead like grazing animals out to pasture. The street was quiet—a blessing of the mornings in contrast to the endless noise of the night. Xyana was known for its forests, and the capital of Daxar for having so many trees within the city itself, lining neat cobblestone roads and even forming little parks for the rich, but none of that applied to Ayari's neighborhood. Here, buildings were crammed together in a slipshod way with no clear boundaries between them, and the dirty, broken cobbles of the pathways between them might see city maintenance every ten years if they were lucky.

"Morning," one of Ayari's neighbors murmured from where he sat on the ground with his back to the wall, smoking and ready to watch the sunrise. "Royal's maid," he teased, and Ayari managed a small smile as fe walked quickly by. The man would know about Esnan soon enough.

Ayari stopped by the local pyre-maker on fer way to the citadel, a young woman of only fourteen whose face was already lined like she were a decade older from the weight of her job, and handed over a few coins. Fe gave the location of their apartment so that she could pick up Esnan for the evening rites, and walked away quickly, touching a finger horizontally below fer eyes to try to stop any tears from ruining fer makeup.

*Ayari,* Esnan had mumbled last night, the last time she had been able to speak. *I'm sorry.*

*I love you,* fe had promised, hushing her, and tucking a lock of black hair behind her ear. *I'm here.*

*I'm sorry,* she had repeated, her voice strained, *that you have to be here.* And then she had coughed weakly, her head lolling to the side while fe had tucked her in again, hovering so close to her where fe sat on the floor that their legs touched and fer back began to ache from leaning.

As the rising sun changed the sky into a stunning display of fiery pinks and bold oranges, Ayari walked from the poor district to the rich neighborhoods around the citadel, filled with neat square houses covered in flowering vines and tidy potted plants, and then, through the servants' gate itself, nodding to the guards on duty. It had been because of Esnan that Ayari had tried something so daring as getting hired by the citadel, because Esnan had needed potions that no one hawking rich folk's garbage as Ayari had been doing before could have afforded. As soon as Ayari turned fourteen, the age of adulthood and, for rich folks, the age of being able to work if they wanted to, Ayari had begun going to the citadel every day, asking for work until one day they finally gave fer something. Five years later, fe had reached the position of royal's maid only because— as the head cook and one of the household managers had remarked—*fe can keep fer face polite no matter what happens.*

Fe was waiting in the princess' dressing room—now wearing fer soft indoor slippers around fer tough calloused feet, baggy cotton leggings, and a neat tunic in unobtrusive browns and grays—long before the princess woke. Fe waited without moving while the princess' favorite maid, a handsome smiling Dyer named Parvin, stood nearby. Like everyone—or like everyone except people like Ayari who had never figured out what their skill was—Parvin had a single magical skill that manifested in puberty, and his was dyeing: a skill the princess put to use regularly to adjust the colors of her clothing. Like most of the higher servants of the citadel, and most of the *servants* of the citadel at all, for that matter, the man had clearly been born to a far better neighborhood than Ayari's, and didn't see anything remarkable in the silk curtains draping the corners of the room simply for decoration, the broad gilded mirror that sat above a desk where the princess would soon sit in a plush armchair. In a way, Ayari was used to them too, now, but today all the wealth around fer only made fer think how money had always been about Esnan and her wasting illness, had always been about affording the costly potions to ease her pain.

Had always been about love.

*What'll you do, when I'm gone?* Esnan had asked only a week ago, her face drawn with pain and her breathing shallow.

*I'll figure that out when the time comes*, Ayari had deferred, tucking her into bed. *For now I'm taking care of you, and I'll never stop doing that*, fe had promised.

Ayari closed fer eyes and kept fer breathing steady. Fe tried not to think about how, in only two weeks, Esnan would have been turning fifteen. Tried not to think about the present fe had saved up for for months on the side: a dye that would turn her hair permanently red, and that fe knew would have made her smile, as she so rarely had these past few weeks. Fe had thought she was only falling under her depression again; if fe had thought she was about to die, fe would have given her the present, would have given her the world, so that her last days would be as good as someone like fe could make them.

The princess walked out of the bedchamber then, wearing a silk nightgown draped over her healthy, rounded, nut-brown body, her hands and feet soft, her teeth clean, her eyes the same dark brown as most people's, and yet nothing else about her the same. She didn't even look at Ayari but extended her arms to be dressed, and fe and Parvin worked quickly and quietly, their fingers moving easily over the buttons and the fasteners until she looked fit for a rich person's party.

"I would like my hair cut today," she said, sitting down in the chair before the mirror and turning her head to one side to assess her long black hair. "Lady Faya has it this long," she said, holding a hand to the level of her breasts, "but then she curls it. Do that," she ordered idly, and with a quick glance at Parvin, Ayari left the room. When fe returned with the hair shears, the other maid had already brushed out the princess' tangles and draped a silk scarf around her shoulders to protect her from any stray hairs, and had gotten her smiling at something he had said.

Ayari was the best haircutter on a street where the thought never even crossed anyone's mind to pay someone else to do theirs, and so it went without saying that fe was always the one to cut the hair of any citadel dweller who needed it. Fe began to trim the princess' shiny black hair, fer hands deft and sure, but like everything today, it only made fer think of fer sister.

*Keep the hair*, Esnan had said to fer a year ago, when fe had finished cutting hers. She had sat cross-legged in the street outside their door, her black hair like broken dreams on the cobblestones, breathing heavily from the exertion of walking outside, and yet she was smiling in the sunshine. *I can turn it into a doll for the neighbor's boy.*

*They're moving, next week,* Ayari had told her reluctantly, *across town. Navi turned out to be an Illusionist.*

It happened that way, more often than not. If anyone did move out of their neighborhood, it was because their child got a marketable skill during puberty, but even then, it was usually something more ordinary like weaving or clay-working. To become an Illusionist was another thing entirely: a skill that meant the city watch would always be paying closer attention to you, but also one that meant you could do just about anything you wanted, including touring for paying customers.

Esnan, with an irony that hurt Ayari more than it hurt her, was a Compass: someone who could always sense the north magically. Someone who could have made a good living as a guide or navigating a ship at sea, if she only had the health to go.

*It's okay,* Esnan had said, reading fer thoughts that day. *I know you want us to leave like Navi,* she murmured, *but life's not so bad here. We have enough to eat, a roof over our heads. Some don't.*

*I'm sorry,* Ayari had said anyway. Fe couldn't have said more, not without crying.

"Wait, what are you doing?"

The princess' voice jarred Ayari back to the present. Once more fe saw the brightly lit room, the unnecessary silks, the perfect princess in front of fer.

Then, fe saw what fe had done. The cut hair was still in fer hand, the haircut not quite finished, but fe had cut two-thirds of it into tiers. Esnan preferred her hair in tiers: a cut that was bolder than layering, creating clear rows of horizontal lines in the hair.

But the princess hadn't asked for that.

Ayari backed away in alarm, mumbling an apology automatically, feeling Parvin's shocked gaze as the man raced over from where he had stood post in the doorway.

But even then, in that moment when Ayari didn't know what the princess would do, even then fe thought that Esnan would have loved the tiers, that she would have smiled. That fe needed to make her smile, and that fe never would again.

Parvin motioned hastily for Ayari to leave the room, and fe fled ahead of the princess' wrath, her words flung like sling stones after fer, hardly seeing fer surroundings. Fe had lost fer job, that was for sure, but as Ayari raced down the servant's stairwell toward the kitchen and out into the glamorous manicured gardens around the citadel, fer vision blurring like the streets in a morning fog, Fe could only think that it didn't matter anymore, that nothing mattered anymore, because fer job had always been for Esnan.

Fe caught fer breath and slowed to a walk before walking out of the citadel walls, so as not to draw attention. As always, leaving the citadel felt like leaving a lie. Leaving perfect people in perfect clothing in a perfect building where people ate things Ayari didn't even have the names for and had lives fe couldn't even understand. A place where fe had never belonged, and where not hating everyone simply for their ignorance was a good day.

Ayari sold fer palace uniform to a street kid in an alleyway who would undoubtedly sell it to a spy, and walked through Daxar aimlessly, half-dressed and bare-footed again, the cold stone against fer feet the one thing that felt right.

Fe stopped at a berry stall, fer eyes fixed on the giant pink pecha berries Esnan had loved. The berries fe could almost never afford.

*Someday,* fe had murmured when they were children, when Esnan's health was still good, *I'll get you out of here, little sister. We'll go everywhere, anywhere you want.*

*Really?* she had replied hopefully, her eyes wide and bright. *Can we see the ocean?*

"Don't you come over here," the vender warned Ayari, seeing fer poor appearance and how fe watched the berries like a starving person. Ayari turned and left quickly, but then went home by a long route, knowing that there was nothing fe wanted to return to. Nothing but a cramped room full of dreams that would never come true.

Fe was back by early evening, with only half a memory of the mindless wandering and the sitting on rooftops that had filled fer day, to see Esnan laid out on a pire in the neighborhood, alongside a kid who had died in a street fight. Navi was there, to fer surprise, dressed like a noble in a gilded wraparound skirt compared to the other onlookers' rags, his face strong and confident to their haunted eyes and starving faces, hardly recognizable after nearly a year away.

He came over to Ayari. "Do you want me to add anything?" he asked, his pretty face grave.

"Red hair," Ayari found ferself replying, unable to take fer eyes off of Esnan.

As the pire-making poured shining oil over Esnan's wasted body and the sky began to darken with the coming night, Ayari saw Esnan's hair change color. Fe laughed to ferself—bitterly, madly—to see that while fe could see the red, fe could still see the black underneath. Fe had never seen an Illusionist work, but given that they were so highly prized by rich folk, fe thought they'd at least do something worth remembering.

Ayari wiped fer eyes so that fe wouldn't miss a moment for fer tears, fer make-up half wiped away, half streaking down fer face and into fer beard from earlier. Even an Illusionist couldn't show fer what hadn't happened, the life fe hadn't been able to give to Esnan.

The pyres were lit, and the ring of onlookers stood back from the intense heat. Ayari had seen bodies burned before, and so knew that when the muscles burned they spasmed and the body jerked where it was tied, but still fe leaped forward to help Esnan without even thinking when she moved, and let the arm of someone fe didn't look at hold ferself back.

Fer mind raced and stuttered like someone new to the skill of speed learning how to run again. One moment fe could only watch the flames, only sit there without anything inside of fer at all, and the next fe was trying to think of what fe could have done differently, of how fe could have saved her.

*What would you do if you weren't taking care of me?* Esnan had asked once as fe'd held her close. *Tell me*, she had urged.

*I'm going to save you*, Ayari had said instead, though fe didn't know how fe could in a world that didn't care the first thing about the health of a poor person. Fe could feel the hostility and indifference of the world like blows striking fer back, and yet fe shielded Esnan from it, and told her, *You'll see.*

*Maybe I'll save you instead*, she had murmured weakly, *so you don't need to take care of me anymore,* and fe had hushed her.

And yet here fe stood, released from caring for her.

Fer vision swam again, as fe watched blankly as the fire leaped up and formed beautiful images of a world Esnan would never see: dragons and sea creatures and tall ships and blooming flowers. Like the illusion of the hair, Ayari could see which fire was real and which was fake, and fe averted fer eyes from the deception.

"What do you see?" fe asked suddenly of the woman beside fer. Fe knew her face, but not her name. "The illusions," fe added when the woman stared at fer blankly.

"They're so beautiful," she murmured, turning her gaze back to the pire. "They're telling a story."

"But can you see through them?" fe asked quietly. Most were quiet in their circle of watchers, the city noisy in the distance, but a few murmured or sang under their breath.

"No," the woman replied, her voice lilting up in question, and Ayari shook fer head to deflect the question in her eyes.

Fe watched the flames dance and heard the fire crackle as the bodies burned. The sky was dark blue now, the stars just beginning to prick the sky like tiny flecks of hope in the devastation that was life.

This was *an* answer, if not the one fe'd wanted.

Fe could see through illusions. That was fer skill. It was a skill that could get fer employed by nobles wishing to protect themselves from a criminal Illusionist, or the city guard. Fe would be okay financially, going forward.

But Ayari felt nothing but grief and a bone-deep humility that fe hadn't done enough for fer sister. It was ironic, fe thought as the people around fer began to trickle away into the night, and Esnan's ashes and remaining bones were ground up and put into a small box for fer. Ironic that for all the dreams fe had woven around Esnan of hope that fe didn't truly have, that fe was the one who could see the truth.

Fe took the remains and walked home again, the gentle hush of the night wind touching fer beard, fer damp cheeks, fer still-bare chest. Tomorrow, fe could go looking for work, could go begin to build a new life.

But when fe closed their battered wooden door behind fer, Ayari crumpled to the floor, Esnan's box of ashes cradled in fer arms. She was dead and fe was in mourning, but in that moment, all fe could think was that fe needed to protect her.

Because this was the truth: that Esnan—perfect, kind, *good* Esnan—was dead, and fe would never be able to give her the world.

# Resistance

## *by MM Schreier*

Taking my usual shortcut, I ducked into the dingy shadows between buildings and sighed, grateful to escape the heat of the noontide sun. I blinked and the world tilted. It felt like stepping from a black and white film into vivid technicolor, and I paused to orient myself. For a moment, two alleys swam in my vision: the familiar dank, garbage-strewn, and claustrophobic backstreet, superimposed by this new version——a clean, alluring kaleidoscope of light and color. I struggled to maintain a hold on reality, its gritty stench of rot, urine, and desperation wrinkling my nose.

*Damn these pockets of god-induced æther.*

My grubby, war-weary existence faded, memories blurry as if viewed through an oil-smeared lens. Captain, wife, mother. The words lost meaning. Emboldened, the illusion solidified. A string of lights——glass globes filled with fireflies——twinkled against a backdrop of velvet twilight. They cast welcoming pools of liquid gold across the patterned brick walkway. I rubbed my eyes and groaned. Time split, white light through a prism.

The hairs on the back of my neck prickled with the breath of a looming, unseen beast. I spun around, but the alley was empty. Plagued by the sense I wasn't alone, I studied my surroundings.

Movement caught my eye. Tacked onto the wall, a poster featured a handful of dancing warriors. The figures leaped and twirled, stomped tiny, bare feet in rhythm. One dancer, noticing me watching, elbowed his fellows. They waved and beckoned for me to join them in their frenetic capering. I leaned closer. Flat silhouettes bearing angular, inked profiles flashed me wolfish grins. They stretched out their hands. Desire rose in me like a fever. Oh, to whirl and cavort to the heartbeat of beating drums, not just heard but felt deep within the marrow of my bones. I reached toward them. Tiny claws clamped down on my wrist, pinpricks stabbing my skin. I yelped and jerked away.

*Snap out of it. It's not real, only the gods' cursed æther dreams.*

I shook my head and glanced back at the poster. The small men stood frozen on the page, the drums silenced. Hallucinations. Still, my flesh burned with thin lines that oozed crimson. Papercuts or claw marks? Eyes fixed on the motionless dancers, I backed away.

I hesitated, stomach roiling like a nest of eels. Some half-buried, inner voice screamed at me to move. Twenty steps away, a banner snapped in the breeze beyond the mouth of the alley. Or was it two-thousand steps? The red and blue markings on the cloth seemed familiar, tickling the edges of my mind with a spider-web touch––sticky, delicate, unsettling. The banner itself was unimportant, only that it marked the boundary between Here and There.

*Here and where?*

I shook off the strange thought, and bowed to the need to move. My battered combat boots scuffed across the faded brickwork, the smooth rectangles arranged in a basket weave pattern. Occasionally, one stood out, a wan yellow or violet, as if the whole affair was once painted a vibrant rainbow but had been worn down to the russet underlay by countless footsteps. Awash in the feeling of déja vu, I wondered if any of them were mine.

An intoxicating scent, floral and spicy, drew my attention. The urgency to keep moving melted like cotton candy on the tongue as I paused by a dark window. Indistinct shapes moved behind the glass. On either side of the frame, lush creepers climbed up the building, tendrils seeking purchase in the crumbling mortar. Flat, glossy leaves added a shock of green in the rose and amethyst gloaming. Wine-dark, night-blooming flowers dotted the vines. Their heady fragrance filled my nostrils.

*Sybil would love these.*

I hesitated, hand outstretched to pluck the blossom.

*Who's Sybil?*

A moth flapped around my head, powdery white wings brushing against my cheek. I swiped at it, half-heartedly, as I tried to focus on a barely remembered face. Dark skin, warm brown eyes, a halo of wild curls. A secret smile.

*For me?*

The images swirled and teased in a tangle of comfort and unease. Once again, I reached for the flower.

"I wouldn't touch that if I were you, Captain."

Ares' voice snapped the memories in place.

Face flushed, I balled my fists at my sides as I turned to glare at the God of War.

With boneless, wildcat grace, he pulled off his helmet and tucked it under his arm. "Observe." He jerked his square jaw toward the window, steely eyes glittering. Under the weight of his scrutiny I was unable to resist the divine command, and turned back to the vines.

The moth landed on the silky blossom, wings fluttering, and the petals snapped shut. Hidden barbs pierced the soft abdomen, ripped through the delicate membranes. Within moments, the insect's struggles ceased. The flower gulped––once, twice––then unfurled, the moth gone. A waft of sweet perfume filled the air as the flora belched out a cloud of saffron-colored pollen.

A muscle in my jaw twitched. "Is that meant to be a threat?"

Ares laughed, but his blue gaze remained cruel and mirthless. "A warning, perhaps. How's your wife?"

"Don't you dare speak of Sybil." The words hissed between my clenched teeth.

In the window, one of the foggy reflections solidified. My beautiful Sybil, rocking back and forth in her chair, the light gone from her eyes. No one recovered from being æther-addled, their bodies living on as empty shells. The vision faded and I tore my gaze away.

"An unintended casualty of war."

"She was in the æther no for more than ten minutes! Ten fucking minutes and it scrambled her brain."

Ares narrowed his eyes and tapped his nose with a long, scarred finger. "And how long have you been in here?"

*A few minutes? An hour? A lifetime?*

The god winked. "My presence is but a momentary shield." He shot me a savage grin. "How are you feeling? Dizzy? Confused?"

I changed the subject. "Your petty 'Divine War' is tearing apart our reality." The god's face hardened and I tacked on a scathing, "My lord."

"Exactly that. Our war." Ares ground the butt of his spear into the brickwork. "Not yours."

"Except *your* war is destroying *our* world. Zeus' lightning bolts have leveled half the city. There was a chimera loose in the subway last week, for Christ's sake." Ares cocked an eyebrow at the mixed theology, but I barreled on, voice rising. "There are random bubbles of æther popping up everywhere and we can't see them until we've been sucked inside."

"Of course you can't. It's an echo of divine magic." He gestured, taking in the alley with a casual wave. "Gods battle. We leave behind æther." He shrugged. "Who knew exposure to the residue would have..." the god paused, as if measuring his words, "...a surprising impact on the mortal psyche?" I scowled, but he ignored me, nodding toward the end of the alley. Beyond the æther pool, reality shimmered like a mirage. "Ten feet to safety. You'll never make it without me."

I spluttered, but Ares turned and strode away. Where he stepped, cracks grew under his boots. The bricks crumbled to show pockmarked asphalt beneath. A chill rippled up my spine and I hurried after his burly form, sheltered beneath his expansive aura.

At the end of the passageway, Ares stopped.

"If I had my way, I'd leave you here." His voice sounded flat, as if it were no more important than considering whether or not to squash an ant beneath his heel. "Let the æther addle your senses and good riddance."

I shifted my feet, shoulders tense. Beyond the edge of the buildings, I could see a hint of bright afternoon sunshine. The banner drooped as the wind died. Inside the sphere of æther, the fragrant evening breeze tugged at my hair.

"Athena won't let me, though." He gave me a level stare when I sighed. "It's not mercy. She says it would make a martyr out of you." He scowled. "That, we cannot have."

Overhead, one of the lights shattered with a pop, making me jump. The freed lightning bugs blinked then dove, drawn by the scent of the night-blossoms. I watched, both enthralled and horrified, as one by one the flowers devoured them and the tiny lights extinguished.

Ares' voice sounded close to my ear. "This is your only warning, woman. Stop meddling with things beyond your station." I felt, rather than saw, his smile, sharp teeth grazing my skin. "Go. Raise your son. Forget the Resistance or he'll lose both his mothers."

My tongue turned to sawdust. In quick succession, the rest of the bulbs shattered and I flung an arm across my face to ward off a shower of splintered glass. When I lowered it, the God of War was gone.

I sagged against the building, gulped in ragged breaths. I had no doubt he'd make good on his threats. With one step, I could return to the heat and chaos of reality. Still, the temptation to just stay and let the æther steal my memories sang a siren song.

Take the anger; it was welcome to the weariness and pain.

A cloud of dancing lights swirled through the alley. No longer contained, the rest of the fireflies swooped and soared over the broken bricks. From the vision window, phantom laughter rang out in childish delight. My heart constricted in my chest.

*Malcom.*

Too many sacrifices. The gods didn't deserve them.

With effort, I gathered my tattered courage around me like a cloak. Humanity must survive and the people needed me. My son needed me. I squared my shoulders and stepped out of the alley, blinking in the harsh sunlight. I had a Resistance to lead. It was time to drive the gods back to Mount Olympus.

# The Green Star Bar
## *by Julie Cohen*

The bar was backlit in soft neon green. He sat down and touched the smooth surface, watching the counter react to the warmth of his fingers. Circles of color pulsed slowly outward like ripples in a pool.

"Ooh, an Earthian," the bartender said as they swept over, clad in black and silver. Pale purple curls fell around their shoulders as they leaned one of their elbows on the bar top.

He glanced up and then down again—he'd never been great at eye contact, and the Xenelian's gaze was overwhelming, opalescent irises reflecting the neon lights of the bar. He tipped his hat instead, and then took it off in a panicked moment, trying to recall if wearing a hat indoors was rude in Xenelian or in Earthen culture. He'd been in the stars too long to remember, but it was best to be safe.

"Not the talkative type, hm?" the bartender mused. "Going to be hard to tell me what you'd like to drink, starshine..."

"Swirl zzaf," he said, and then remembered to add, "Please."

He glanced up long enough to catch the smile on the bartender's lips before they glided off to mix the drink, humming along as Bowie's "Sweet Thing" drifted out from somewhere nearby.

"How long have you been in the stars?" the bartender asked, and laughed softly at his surprised look. "I can always tell."

"I guess about... three cycles," he replied.

"Business or pleasure?"

"I was relocating a herd of stalaex to an exo off of M83," he said.

"Oh, a *conservationist*," the bartender hummed, delighted.

He nodded, relaxing a little, and took a sip of his drink after the Xenelian set it in front of him. It tasted like trapped fire with a hint of blue.

"Like it?" they asked, their voice pitched a little lower as they leaned close. "I could add a touch of ora-pink to the next one."

Xenelian culture was heavily influenced by color. It was a subtextual language, similar to old Earthen flower language, or Yvenn stone language. Xenelians had more colors than Earthians did, so the auto-translators had to make do with the more limited vocabulary of Earthen general tongue, but most of the color meanings were common enough knowledge now. Blue, he remembered, represented welcome. It was a color for extending friendship or inviting guests, and was imbued with a sense of relaxation, security, and something that felt somehow like nostalgia for future possibilities.

Ora-pink was the Earthen general tongue translation for a color that wavered along the spectrum between orange and pink. It was most often associated with the feeling of hope and romance, the fluttering sensation of romantic and physical attraction. It was the color of flirtation. Ora-pink that was more pink was indicative of physical attraction, and ora-pink that was more orange implied romantic attraction.

He thought he wouldn't mind a touch of orange ora-pink in his next drink. He turned the glass in his hands, smiling faintly.

"I'll take that sweet smile you're wearing as a yes," the Xenelian teased, clearly pleased.

"Sure," he said. He started to add that he preferred orange to pink, but before he could do so he became aware of the doors opening behind him, granting entrance to two men. He took another sip instead as the bartender slipped out around the counter to approach the newcomers—the scent of Ikez roses lingered in the air, candy-sweet; the blue tasted smokier this time.

It was the voice that pinged his alarms. Not that he'd ever heard it in person before, but the sound of it triggered the memory of a grainy recording. It had come through staticky on his phone, out in the middle of nowhere. Just him, a herd of stalaex, a billion stars above, and an unclear video of Vior Ronas, wanted for a laundry list of crimes.

He kept still. Man like that wouldn't show his face unless he was desperate. Or bored.

"Hey, Xenelian," he said roughly. "I need another drink."

The bartender slipped behind the counter, their smile a cautious question in response to the sudden change in his demeanor. He pressed his fingers down on the countertop, making a pattern of color. He watched the bartender's eyes lower to read the message there, felt the tension in the room crystalize.

Silence. And then sound.

He dropped off the barstool, banging his knee on the way down as glass shattered from above. He bit back a swear and then turned, grasping the leg of the stool beside him and using it to propel himself behind the counter. His shoulder bumped the Xenelian and he let out a breath, relieved the other had ducked down in time.

"Friends of yours?" they asked.

"No," he replied, and leaned around the counter, groping for his tranq gun and firing off a quick stun.

"You have a weapon?" the Xenelian asked, sounding surprised.

"They're just tranquilizers," he grunted. "Conservationist, remember?"

"Why are they shooting at us?"

"For the fun of it, I guess. They didn't come here for a drink."

More glass shattered around them as if to emphasize that fact. He leaned around the side of the bar to return fire, and the man that had come in with Vior dropped inelegantly onto a table.

"Zahranvi," Vior spoke into the stillness that followed. He chuckled, boots crunching over broken glass. Ket Zahranvi blinked, trying to process the fact that this man knew him. Came here for him? He felt the Xenelian's opalescent gaze dart toward him. He made himself return it and shook his head.

"Saw your ship docked here, Zahranvi," Vior continued. "Figure you owe me."

Ket frowned. In his periphery, he saw the Xenelian carefully shift and then crawl toward the back storeroom. He took a breath, steeling himself. He didn't know how Vior knew him, but clearly he did and, for whatever reason, he was here to take Ket's ship, and probably kill him in the process.

He glanced down at his tranq gun—four quick stuns left. Well, he was an all right shot. Pretty good, maybe. Of course, stalaex didn't generally shoot back.

"Myn Zahranvi," Vior said, dangerously close.

Myn. Ket bit back a frustrated sound. His goddamn brother, he should've known. What the hell had he—but now wasn't the time. Vior wasn't likely the type to care that he had the wrong brother.

Ket's fingers tightened on the tranq gun, but then he heard a soft, wet sound, followed by a hoarse cry. He jumped up, tranq gun ready, and watched Vior crumple to the floor, twitching. Something bulbous and translucent was stuck to his chest, with long tentacles that left red welts on his face and throat.

He heard a delicate cough, and inhaled the scent of Ikez roses. He lowered his tranq gun, hands faintly trembling with unspent adrenaline, and turned toward the other in disbelief.

"...Did you throw a jellyfish at a dangerous criminal?" he managed after a beat. "At *Vior Ronas*?"

"It's a lyryol, starshine, not a jellyfish," the Xenelian replied.

"Looks like a jellyfish."

"I believe they share a common ancestor. Is there room on your ship for two?"

"Two lyryol?" he asked, confused.

"Two people," the Xenelian laughed softly. "As in, you and I."

Ket stared in further confusion.

"You see, Myn, is it? I haven't been running this place with... well, a completely, fully, totally valid permit. And now there's a wanted outlaw twitching on my floor. It will very likely draw attention. Since you happen to be the reason he's here... well, you see where I'm going. How about it?"

Ket blinked. Slowly.

"My name's Ket. Myn is my brother," he said.

"Ah. ...Your brother must be a very interesting person."

"What's your name?" Ket asked.

"Estera," they replied, brightening. "Does that mean I can come with you? I don't know anything about herding stalaex, but I'll make the best Xenelian drinks you've ever had. And I'm excellent company. In all kinds of ways," they added, catching his gaze with those glimmering opal eyes.

"I don't really go in for that kind of company," he said. "I, uh, I like orange in my Xenelian drinks. Not pink."

"Oh, well, that's fine," Estera said, and smiled.

Ket reached over to pick up his hat. He brushed away a bit of glass and set it on his head, adjusting it to try to distract himself from thinking about how nice of a smile it was. He thought maybe he could get used to a ship that smelled like Ikez roses. He wanted to know what kind of person kept a venomous invertebrate in the back of their bar. He wanted to know a lot of things.

"All right," he said, wondering what the hell he was getting himself into. "But leave the lyryol."

Ket led the way out of the bar, the sound of warm laughter trailing behind him.

"I don't think I could pry it off if I tried, starshine."

# The Trunk

## *by Lamont A. Turner*

Wilson set his beer down on the steamer trunk Mario used for a coffee table and reached out for the joint Mario was waving. He took a long drag, passed it back, and retreated into the couch cushions, his arms behind his head.

"I'm cool with the trunk, but what's with the chains?" he asked, nudging the heavy padlock with his toe.

"I told you, it's just decoration," Mario responded, pulling a pint out of the cooler at his side. "Think we'll have enough to get the lights turned back on this week?"

"You're being evasive," Wilson said, trying to read his lover's face in the flickering light of the candle as it melted onto a plastic skull. "Everything you do has a purpose; maybe not one anyone other than you would see much sense in, but a purpose nonetheless. What is it you keep in there?"

"Love letters," Mario said. "I've been cheating on you."

"All right, I can see I'll have to invest in a hacksaw if I'm to learn the truth. Don't think I won't do it."

"You don't have the energy to wipe your ass if it takes more than two passes. I think my secret is safe."

Mario was right. Wilson was sure Mario wasn't being spiteful, but the comment cut deep, bleeding his inadequacies into his consciousness. Wilson's grandfather had survived Normandy, and his father had served Queen and country as a homicide detective, tussling with monsters on an almost daily basis. They had been strong, full-blooded men. Not Wilson, though. Plagued with a weak constitution, made worse by a nervous condition no doctor had been able to adequately treat, he'd lingered on the sidelines while others did the fighting. Worst of all, he was what his father would have called a poof, to him something less than a man. While Mario reveled in his sexuality, Wilson hated himself for it, always longing for the approbation of a father who saw his desires as contemptuous. Mario sensed Wilson's discomfort and walked over to give him a peck on the forehead.

"I've got to go, love. Be sure to snuff the candle before you turn in."

Wilson nodded before throwing his arm over his face and letting out an exaggerated sigh. Mario, knowing not to take the bait, sulked off to find his work boots. The arm stayed in place until Wilson heard the door close.

Wilson knew he was to blame for all of their problems. He hadn't been able to hold a job in months, drifting from one low-paying gig to the next, sometimes not staying long enough to collect a check. Mario had been carrying them, often working double shifts at the warehouse. Things had been so much better when Mario worked for the railroad, but that had ended badly.

He remembered the night Mario came home, ashen-faced, his hands quivering as he tried to light a joint.

"There was nothing left of him from the waist down," Mario had repeated over and over while pacing at the foot of the bed. Finally getting him to sit, Wilson learned a man had committed suicide by lying across the tracks. The train had cut him in two, dragging the lower half off with it into the night.

"I knew him!" Mario sobbed. "We'd had a fling a few years back, and his wife found out about it. She left him, and he never forgave me for it. I think he chose to go out the way he did to send me a message."

Mario never went back to the railroad. After that, he couldn't stand to look at train tracks or hear the whistle of the engine. They'd even had to move to a flat further from the crossing because Mario could hear the trains passing at night. Wilson had tried to be supportive, but, as Mario sunk deeper into depression, he began to suspect Mario's relationship with the man had been more than a fling. He came to believe Mario had been in love with the man, and most likely still was.

Wilson's jealousy exacerbated his nervous condition, making it more difficult for him to function. By the time Mario had shaken off his melancholy, Wilson was a mess. He wondered constantly about the man on the tracks, knowing he could never measure up. He laughed about that sometimes in rare moments of clarity. He felt inferior to a man who'd lost everything! Still, Mario must have cared for the man deeply to have been so affected by his demise. He was certain neither Mario, nor anyone else, would ever feel that way about him.

Wilson bent forward to blow out the candle, but paused as he noticed the light glistening off the chains. What was in the trunk? Mario claimed he'd found the trunk, chains and all, at an antique shop, and thought it would make an excellent conversation piece. Only he'd refused to converse about it. When anyone brought up the chains, he would make some quip and change the subject. When Wilson demanded he open it, Mario had claimed he didn't have the key.

Knowing he'd be unable to sleep, Wilson slid his feet in his slippers and trudged down the hall to wake Amanda. He'd never cared for her, partly because she claimed to be a witch, but mainly because Mario spent so much time with her. He'd grudgingly admitted she was useful, though, when she'd agreed to charge his phone for him while their power was out. She'd had the phone for over an hour. It should have been charged enough to provide him with a distraction for a bit.

The hour being late, and the walls being thin, he rapped gently at first, but pounded harder when his taps got no response. After several minutes, he grew tired of staring at the door.

"Damn it, Amanda! Open up! I need my phone!" he shouted, and was about to hammer on the door again when a man in pajama pants appeared in the doorway across the hall and glared at him.

"Sorry," Wilson said. "You wouldn't happen to know if Amanda went out, would you?"

The man answered with a grunt and retreated into his apartment, slamming the door.

"I suppose I'm screwed then," Wilson muttered as he sulked off down the hall. "I guess if there's an emergency I can just fling myself out the window."

The pinpoint of flame atop the candle wasn't where it should have been. Standing in the doorway of his apartment, he tried to make out the scene surrounding the flame but the dull yellow light from the hall failed to penetrate far enough to reveal much. Leaving the door open, he crept up to the candle atop the skull and raised it so he could get a better look at the room. The trunk was at least a foot away from its previous location.

Thinking he must have bumped it when he got up, he tried to slide it back with the toe of his slipper. It wouldn't budge. He set the candle down and pressed his palms against the trunk, only to quickly jerk them away. He stumbled back, staring at his hands. At first he thought he'd been shocked, but as he rubbed the numbness out of his forearms, he decided it had been more like having ice water injected into his veins. He prodded the trunk with a forefinger and got another jolt. This time, the cold traveled up his arm to settle in his stomach, forcing the bile and stale beer up his gullet. He choked it back down and collapsed into Mario's chair by the window.

A wall of fog isolated him from the world outside. Hadn't Mario said it was foggy the night his lover laid across the tracks? It had happened around this time of year too, perhaps on this very date.

"Stop thinking about bullshit!" Wilson shouted, needing to hear the sound of a human voice. He gazed at his outstretched hands. Maybe there was nothing wrong with the trunk. Maybe the sensation of cold had originated in his arms. Was he having a stroke? He considered knocking on a neighbor's door to plead with them to send for help, but he'd had episodes like this before. Drawing attention to them only caused embarrassment. How often would Mario be willing to stay with him if he insisted on making a fool of himself?

Mario! How long would it be until he got home? He'd made it halfway to the wall clock across the room, the candle sputtering in his trembling hand, when he remembered the clock didn't run on batteries. It was frozen at the moment when the power stopped feeding the outlet it was plugged into. He was trapped there with the trunk, stuck at four minutes past midnight. Was that when it had happened? Was that when Mario's lover died?

"Stop it!" he screamed, slapping a sweaty palm repeatedly against his forehead. The blows dislodged the specter of his father who leapt from his head to stand with arms akimbo by the trunk.

"Buck up, boy!" he commanded before fading back into Wilson's memories.

"I'm not like you," Wilson muttered. "Whatever was inside you didn't get passed down to me."

If only he had a phone. Worried he was abusing his medication, Mario had hidden Wilson's Xanax, dispersing the pills on an as-needed basis. Wilson opened the cooler and counted three bottles of beer. That wouldn't do. He needed those pills! He spent the next hour ransacking the apartment before finally finding a Benadryl in the pocket of an old jacket. Thinking it might help a little, he swallowed it, washing it down with a beer.

"Mario?" Wilson asked from under Mario's pillow. He peered out at the stub of a candle still burning on the nightstand and then pulled the pillow back to glance at the window. It was still night. Something in the living room scraped against the hardwood floor.

"Did you get off early?" Wilson shouted, but the only answer was the scraping, accompanied by what he suddenly realized was the rattling of chains. He tossed the pillow aside and sat up. The trunk was just outside of his bedroom, blocking the doorway! Wilson heard the thud of the padlock as it fell off the chain, and heard the creak of ancient hinges as the lid of the trunk lifted. He buried his face in his elbow as the stench of decay wafted from the opening and a hand reached out from inside the trunk to grip the edge. Wilson clutched the blankets as something pulled itself up and over the side of the trunk. It was a man, or at least half of one. He stood on his palms, there being nothing below the waist to support him.

"Better buck up, boy," it gurgled, a yellow froth oozing from between black lips to drip off the withered gray-green flesh of its chin. Scurrying across the room on its hands, it pulled itself up onto the bed as Wilson curled up against the headboard.

"What—are—you?" Wilson gasped.

"You don't deserve him," the half-man said, slowly inching toward him. "And you don't deserve those legs."

A cold hand fell on Wilson's ankle, squeezing the flesh into the bone. It was going to tear him apart! He kicked at it, sending it toppling off the bed, and then jumped up and raced for the bathroom.

"Go away!" Wilson shouted, his back against the bathroom door. "Leave me alone!"

"Never!" said a voice from behind the shower curtain.

Wilson laughed hysterically as he slid to the floor, his gaze fixed on the thing lifting itself over the edge of the tub.

"We won't know for certain until the toxicology reports come back, but I'd say it was an overdose," said the paramedic as they wheeled the stretcher out of the apartment. "You said you'd hidden his medication?"

"Yes," Mario said, staring at the shattered lid of the trunk. " But I never realized he was so desperate. I should have flushed it all."

"You can't blame yourself," said the paramedic, patting Mario on the shoulder. "Sometimes, there's nothing we can do to make them whole again."

# Change

## *by DJ Tyrer*

"And, so, once again the city was saved by—"

John flicked the TV off. He had homework to complete and no desire to relive the afternoon's events, especially after they'd landed him in detention.

He looked down at the page and wished he could keep the numbers straight. Save the city, sure, but these equations were beyond his capabilities.

Then, he heard a heavy tread on the stair: Dad. He winced, knowing what was coming.

Dad stomped in. He was dressed in jeans and a checkered shirt and had the physique of a man who worked hard for a living; he was a big man, a builder by trade. Lightly built, John took after his mother. Some days, Dad would say he was certain she must've cheated on him, they were so unlike.

"Your school called to say you missed classes—again. This just ain't good enough, boy."

"No, Dad. Sorry, Dad."

His father fingered his belt buckle, the State of Texas, and John tried not to flinch at the thought of the belt coming off.

"You need to straighten up and fly right, boy, or I'm gonna have to teach you a lesson."

"Yes, Dad."

Dad sighed. "You're a disappointment: a nerd, not a jock, and not even a good nerd. Pathetic."

He turned and stomped out without waiting for John's response.

John threw his schoolbook to the floor. "This sucks."

When John had found the ring that had changed his life, he'd dared to imagine things would be different. Well, they were, but not in the way he'd hoped. In fact, it was almost a cruel taunt. He slipped the ring from his pocket and weighed it in his hand, wondering if its powers could ever assist him. He doubted it, and put it back. The future looked bleak.

Reluctantly, he picked up the book and returned to work, half-expecting the sense that a threat was looming—the only power bestowed to him by the ring when he wasn't wearing it—to interrupt him, but it didn't. Wishful thinking, perhaps.

Finished, or as finished as he could hope to be, he settled down in bed and waited for sleep to claim him as he played over all the issues that nagged at him. There had to be answers, but they seemed more distant than ever as he drifted off, powerless to save himself.

He woke with a jolt to the sound of his alarm. Time to rise and get to school. Could he, John wondered, get through a day just being normal, fitting in and doing what was expected of him? Okay, he'd never been normal, perhaps that was why fate had chosen to gift him the ring, but he'd been able to fake it, to fit in by proxy, to present an acceptable face to a world that didn't want him to be the person he really was. But, not now.

Dad was gone before he came downstairs. That was about the only point in his father's favor: he didn't have to see much of him.

John settled down and had breakfast, then got ready and stepped out of the house—the everyday activities he performed by rote, playing the part expected of him. He glanced at a bin as he went past, considered throwing away the ring, freeing himself from the responsibility and confusion. He didn't. Couldn't. Instead, he picked up his pace a little, not wanting to be late.

The first class of the day was gym: the worst of them all.

"Heads up, Izzy!"

He looked up, automatically, despite the taunting nickname.

*Whump!* A flash of red. A dodgeball smashed into his face. John felt his nose crunch beneath the blow and warm blood running down onto his chin. Then, he realized he was looking up at the feeling; stars danced before his eyes. There was laughter and what, surely, were jeers, but the words were muffled and distant.

Coach Simpson's face floated into view, initially blurred and impressionistic, then painfully clear. John blinked.

A meaty hand seized his arm and hauled him up, like a puppeteer tugging a marionette into life.

"Get yourself cleaned up, kid." The coach gave him a shove toward the changing room.

John stumbled through to the basins and looked at the mirror: blood was still running down his face like a grotesque beard and dripping down onto his t-shirt. He grabbed a paper towel, wetted it, and held it to his nose 'til the bleeding slowed, then began to wipe his face clean of gore. He really wished he could turn around, storm back out there and... He realized he wasn't even sure who threw it. He'd like to teach them all a lesson…

He sighed and wiped away the last of the blood.

Then, he felt it: the ring was calling to him, telling him there was a threat he needed to deal with.

He turned and ran to his locker. First, he grabbed his phone and tapped the emergency alert app he'd installed for just this situation. There it was: a warning to avoid downtown. No specific details, but he didn't need them. He grabbed the ring.

"You okay?"

John looked around. It was his friend, Donnie.

"Yeah."

"Coach sent me to check on you—make sure you hadn't dropped dead, I guess."

"Tell him I'm alive, but a bit woozy. I'll sit this session out."

"He won't like it."

John shrugged. "Just tell him."

Donnie looked at him. "You're going, aren't you?"

"Yes; I can't wait any longer. Just tell him I'll be recovering quietly for a while."

"Okay…"

John didn't wait for him to leave, but shut his locker, then ran to the outside door of the changing room. Thankful no one was in sight as he stepped outside, he slipped the ring on his finger.

The change was instantaneous. John was gone and Mirabella was launching herself skyward. She felt amazing as the wind roared past her. This was as close as she could get to being who she should be—and, so much more. Mirabella was, in her opinion, perfect, or nearly so: long, shining black hair, green eyes, and an amazing, sparkling, pale-blue dress that billowed out behind her as she flew.

There were shouts from below, people pointing up at her, cheering. She always felt a thrill at the adoration.

Then, she saw what was trashing the city this time: a monster that looked like the unholy offspring of Godzilla and a bulldog, and which was busy chewing on a blank billboard. It looked up, saw her, tore a chunk of masonry the size of a van free from an office block and threw it at her.

She caught it and deposited it safely on the sidewalk below.

Then, as she took flight again, another chunk smashed into her and sent her spiraling backward: it was dodgeball all over again, except Mirabella just shrugged it off, caught the lump of concrete, and threw it back, before swooping in to take the fight to it.

"Late again. Detention."

John sighed and settled down in the only empty seat, right in front of the teacher.

"I hope you did your homework…"

"Uh, yeah." He rummaged through his bag for his folder and held his answer sheet out.

The teacher snatched it from him, glanced at it, and said, "I can see several wrong answers; sloppy working out… You are destined to fail math…"

John groaned. If he failed math, he wouldn't graduate the year: Saving the city wasn't leaving much free time for study.

"You had best knuckle down, boy…"

"Yes, sir."

"So?" Donnie grabbed him at lunch and dragged him into a quiet corner. "Who or what was threatening the city this time?"

"I don't want to talk about it."

"You did save us, didn't you?"

John sighed. "Yes. I just don't want to talk about it."

"Well, I guess it'll be on the news this evening. So what's eating you?"

"Nothing..."

"Seriously? You save the day, but look as if you lost and you expect me to believe you're merry sunshine? You're not still upset about Jake smashing you in the face with that ball, are you?"

John shrugged.

"Come on, you can't bottle this up and you can't talk to anyone else; so talk to me, eh?"

"Fine, but after school, my place. Dad will be out at work, so we won't be overheard."

"Arranging a date, guys?" called Steve, stopping as he passed. His friends laughed.

John gave him the finger.

"Hey, I think it's great. Don't be embarrassed; it's not as if we hadn't guessed, Izzy. Answer: Yes, he is."

Donnie launched himself at Steve, and John, reluctantly, followed him. This wasn't going to be like the battle downtown.

"I can't believe I had my nose busted twice in one day," John said as he slumped down on his bed. "This sucks. Steve's such a jerk." He dabbed an errant drip of blood from his nose.

Donnie dropped onto a beanbag opposite him. He was sporting a black eye and a split lip. He groaned as he slumped and rubbed his bruised ribs.

"He had it coming," he muttered.

John barked a bitter laugh. "Yeah, except we were the ones who actually had it. I doubt Steve and his friends are sporting any war wounds."

"I guess…" He poked a finger into his mouth. "I'm sure one of my teeth is loose." He retracted his finger, then asked, "So, what's the problem?"

"He's a douche."

Donnie shook his head. "Not Steve—you. Something was gnawing at you, earlier. Time to tell."

John chewed his lip. He'd hoped Donnie had forgotten about it after their drubbing.

"Well? You promised to spill…"

"Fine. It's… when I first found the ring, I thought it was, well, the answer to my prayers."

"Yeah. From zero to hero—every boy's dream. Of course, it's a bit of a bummer you change into a girl, but still, you get to be like a god. Goddess. Whatever."

"But, that's just it. I never wanted to be a hero." He shrugged. "Don't get me wrong, I do my best and it's not as if the people cheering me on isn't nice, but it's not what I want."

"Not following you…" Donnie rubbed his ribs again.

"When I first transformed into Mirabella, it was great. It was everything I'd ever wanted to be."

Donnie's expression was blank for a moment, then he wrinkled his nose, somewhere between confusion and disgust. "You mean…?"

"I was a girl, not a boy. A girl: what I'd always wanted to be, what I truly am…"

"I… didn't realize…"

"It's not exactly something I like to talk about." He fell silent.

Donnie didn't answer for a moment, then said, "It's not something to be ashamed of."

John shrugged. "Still... Anyway, when I transformed, I was overjoyed. Except, of course, I wasn't just a girl—I was a supergirl. I don't get to just be myself: I have a job to do. And Mirabella isn't exactly someone I can be and be myself, either."

"I guess not." Donnie scrabbled up from the beanbag and walked to the window, then turned to face John. "But if that's what you want, why don't you come out, change your sex?"

"Seriously? Do you know how my Dad would react? He'd kill me!"

"Another couple of years and you could move out."

"I guess, but there's another thing..."

"Yeah?"

"Right now, nobody knows I'm Mirabella. Except you, of course."

Donnie nodded.

"But if I were to become a girl, that might give my secret away... I mean, I think Mirabella looks like how... how I would look. Probably. More perfect, but still..."

"I don't know what to do," he finished.

"You just have to be yourself. I think you should, what's the word? Transition."

"You do?"

"I do. Dude, you've got to be happy. What's the point of saving everyone else, if you can't save yourself?"

John didn't have an answer to that.

"You certainly can't go on like this..."

Dad got home late and Mirabella had only just arrived back before him, having assisted a ferry that had gotten into trouble out in the bay.

John was exhausted. Although the ring gave Mirabella fabulous strength and resilience, if she used them to excess, he would feel fatigued when he transformed back. It was a little like a superpowered hangover.

"Your school left a message on my cell. Another detention for skipping class?"

"I was late."

"Whatever. And fighting? Still, it's better than your usual nonsense. I'm fed up with raising a wimp. I mean, come on, that Mirabella's ten times the man you'll ever be—and a hot piece of skirt in the bargain."

"Oh, man, I think I'm going to be sick—she's a kid, Dad!"

"Jailbait, sure, but I'd wait."

"Dad, that's disgusting."

"To you, maybe, but I've always had my doubts about you. It'd be a relief to find you lusting after a girl like her. I'm sure all the other guys in your school do: she's sexy and sassy. Heck, I'd be happy if you just went on a date."

"Dad, you don't know me at all."

Dad headed into the kitchen for the coffee pot. "You're right there, I don't. I don't understand you one bit. Some days, I'm certain your Mom had a man on the side."

"Maybe she did!" John sighed. "I'm sorry, Dad. I know I'm a disappointment, but I can only be me..."

"Don't I know it!"

"Look, I have something to say..."

"Not now, I'm tired and I want a bite to eat. We'll have a talk tomorrow." He yawned.

"Sure... tomorrow..." If it ever came. John felt his nerve withering away.

That night, John lay in bed, fantasizing as if his life were a Saturday morning cartoon in which Mirabella could conclude the episode with a simple lesson on tolerance and acceptance to his father and classmates. When he'd first put on the ring, he'd imagined his new life would be like that: in her pimped-out princess dress, Mirabella was like a character in the anime he loved to watch when his father wasn't around, and it was only a short step from them back to his childhood. But life didn't work like that. If there was any similarity to cartoons, it would be to hentai. Life sucked.

He stared at the ceiling and wondered if he really was doing any good at all. Sure, he was saving people, but what was he saving them for? If their lives were as awful as his, was he just condemning them to more agony? Or was it his lot to suffer while everyone else had great lives?

He, eventually, drifted off, but his dreams were dark and dreary.

Donnie had been in an odd, unusually quiet mood all day at school. John had a horrible feeling in his gut that his revelation the day before, despite Donnie's comments, had cost him a friend.

"What's wrong?" It was John who broke the silence of their walk home. They were nearly at his house. He almost didn't ask the question, afraid he wouldn't like the answer.

Donnie looked up, his expression unusually blank. "I have an idea."

"An idea? What sort of idea?" He hoped it wasn't another of the crazy moneymaking scams his friend had thought up when he'd first confessed to him his secret identity as the savior of the city.

"I'll tell you when we reach yours."

John relaxed a little. At least Donnie still seemed to regard him as a friend.

A couple of minutes later, they reached his house and went inside. John grabbed a couple of colas from the fridge and they headed up to his room. Donnie seemed twitchy with excitement, flexing his fingers as if playing an invisible accordion.

They settled in their usual places and opened the cans of cola.

John looked at his friend. "It's not another money-spinning idea, is it? Because the answer's going to be a 'no.'"

Donnie took a swig of cola and shook his head, then said, "Nah. I think I have a solution to your problems."

"You have?" John raised an eyebrow.

"Straight up. Well, a partial solution, anyhow."

"Okay, what is it?"

"Well, when you're Mirabella, you can magic yourself off anywhere, right?"

"Yeah, if I really concentrate. But, so what? How's that going to help me?"

Donnie laughed.

"What?"

"You have all that power at your command and you just don't have the imagination to use it." Donnie waved silent John's objections. "I'm not talking about money and fame: I'm talking about being yourself."

"You've lost me."

"You have the entire world at your feet. You don't have to choose between staying here and being John and staying here and being... not-John. Go somewhere else and be yourself—permanently or just a little while. That way, you don't have to worry about looking like Mirabella or what your Dad will think:

everyone assumes Mirabella lives here or in some Fortress of Solitude, and your Dad will never know."

"I never..."

"I know." Donnie laughed, again. "Come on, slip that ring on and take us somewhere cool. Then, we'll go clothes shopping and kit you out. And then we'll find somewhere to go and have some fun. Come on, it's time to make a change."

John was silent for a moment, trying to process what Donnie had said. At that moment, a fight with a monster or a crazed villain would've been less terrifying than the possibilities he faced. He looked at Donnie beaming widely; John grinned back.

"Okay, let's do it." John took out the ring and slipped it on his finger.

Donnie slid his hand into Mirabella's and smiled at her. She smiled back. So many possibilities.

She concentrated for a moment and they vanished from the room with a loud *pop!* Air rushed to fill the vacant space.

The future was bright.

# Like the Stars
## *By Rowan Rook*

Tonight would be a fight for not only the future, but the past. No matter what happened next, Harper's life was about to change. Four years had passed since the mysterious invitation to the Solar School of Sorcery had shown up on their bedside table, and now, all of their time at the school had come to this. All of the sweat, the tears, the nights spent lying awake with dread and dreams, would culminate in a single pass or fail.

Anxiety tied chains around Harper's chest, tightening with each beat of their strangled heart. No, no. Harper sucked in a breath of the clammy air around the registration line. No need to panic. They would be fine. Thanks to Professor Lysender, they were as prepared for the final exam as any other student.

When they'd first come to Solar, they'd felt more of an outcast in its sprawling underground halls than they had during the sleepy high school classes and Sunday morning church services in rural Idaho. Professor Lysender had changed all of that when he'd agreed to mentor them. The school had become the only place where they'd begun to feel they had a purpose in a world where they didn't quite fit in.

"I… don't want to forget this place," Harper mouthed a silent prayer.

The final exam was all that stood between them and graduation.

If they passed, they'd be able to leave Solar's subterranean domain—they'd be able to return to the Surface as a Sunweaver, a protector of the society that didn't recognize the existence of magic… that didn't even recognize the existence of their gender. Each dusk, when Phantoms arose from the fiery heart of the Earth called Hell, it was Sunweavers and Moonweavers who drew the things back before they ever reached the Surface, all while the mundane people remained oblivious to the supernatural war waged nightly beneath them.

If they failed the test, however… then Solar's Secretary of Secrecy would use Moon magic to erase Harper's memories of their time at the school, just as the Secretary had erased all memories of them from the world above the moment they'd accepted the invitation. They would awaken alone on the Surface, nothing more than a gangly, frustrated teenager scared by the psychic tendencies they once again didn't understand.

"I'll pass," Harper promised themself. Their fingers clenched around the edges of the sign-up sheet in their hands, and when their turn finally came, they stepped toward the registration desk as solemnly as if they were walking onto a pirate's plank.

The woman behind the desk grinned, cloaked in a Moonweaver's silver robe. "Hello there," she said. "Let's hurry and get you into the tunnels while there are still Phantoms left to slay."

"Right," Harper stuttered, handing over their sign-up sheet.

The clerk took the paper, and with a wave of her hand, summoned up the school's Imaginary Library. The text and images, written only in the silver light of Moon magic, cast dusty shadows through the room. Harper caught a glimpse of their own name written in the enchanted database and tried not to gulp.

Sure enough, the smile faltered on the clerk's face. She glanced from the sign-up sheet to the Library's shimmering words and back again. "Is there a mistake?" She blinked with confusion that seemed genuine. "Your sheet says you're testing as a Sunweaver, but according to Solar's records, you're a woman."

Harper winced. "I'm not a man or a woman, but I'm better with Sun magic, so I'd like to test as a Sunweaver."

A few beats ticked by quietly while the clerk's gaze poked and prodded at Harper's body.

Harper flushed, but waited, clenching their fists tight in their pockets. They were used to the confusion. The woman's uniform they wore beneath their men's Sun cloak, their mixed-race heritage, and their tendency to eye both men and women drew them plenty of strange looks from their peers. They stood somewhere in the middle of more than one supposed binary.

The clerk's gaze finally came back up to Harper's face. "Does that mean you've tried both Sun and Moon spells?"

Harper nodded. "I started out as a Moonweaver... but Professor Lysender agreed to teach me as a Sunweaver instead."

Their tendency to keep to themself, their sometimes frustrating efforts to appear gender-ambiguous, and their private meetings with the Professor had allowed them to practice their chosen magic without causing too much undue attention throughout their schooling. The final exam, however, wouldn't allow them any such luxury. Not when that troublesome word—female—lingered in the records system for every administrator to see.

The clerk's poker face slowly became a frown. "For safety reasons, I'm not sure I can register you like this."

A flash of annoyance flushed Harper's cheeks. "There's no rule against it."

"No, but…" The clerk bit her lip. "It simply isn't done. Sun magic is suited for males, while females are naturally in tune with Moon magic. There is a reason why men become Sunweavers and women become Moonweavers."

Harper grimaced, biting back any retorts that might try to escape their mouth. Talk about patronizing. They'd already spent four years listening to the same drivel in every mainline class. *I'm not a woman!* "I'm comfortable with my chosen role," they compromised. "I'll assume all the risk."

"This exam will be more dangerous than anything else you've ever done at Solar. If you aren't following the recommended procedures…" The clerk put on an attempt at maudlin concern: "We just don't want you to end up like poor Ms. Peyton."

It took all of Harper's restraint not to roll their eyes. Two years ago, an upperclassman they'd never met—a woman named Sophie Peyton, better known as "Spike"—had been the first student to test in the "opposite" role. The Sunweaver had been killed by a Prime Phantom, her body so decimated there hadn't been anything left to bury. That was what the rumors said, at least. All that remained of her was a cautionary tale.

"If I do," Harper grumbled, "then you can switch to using my name to scare away students like me. I doubt you'd be too upset about that."

Tints of red speckled the clerk's face. "I don't know if I can just—"

"Why not let them try?"

Harper and the clerk turned to see a Sunweaver standing in the doorway, his amber hair framing his ocean eyes.

"Professor Lysender?" Harper tried not to gape.

Lysender chuckled. "Is it really so surprising that I'd take an interest in how one of my favorite students is doing on their exam? I'm dismayed to see that you aren't already out there in the tunnels." His eyes narrowed in on the clerk. "Sign them up."

The worried frown never quite left her face. "But..."

"No need to fret," Lysender assured. "After all, I've made sure Harper here knows just how dangerous the exam is." He smiled down at his student. "They're ready to make their own choice."

Harper held their mentor's gaze, something inside them shivering, but they forced themself to smile. "Thank you, Professor."

Harper ran, their footsteps pounding like drumbeats while their shadow chased after them. The only light came from the blue lunar lanterns hanging from the cavern walls. They'd searched through the same tunnels so many times on other school assignments, but this was the first time they'd traversed them on their own.

So far, the labyrinth was silent. With how long it had taken them to register, they could only hope there were Phantoms left to kill. After all, the only way to pass the exam was to return with a Prime Phantom's heart before dawn.

Moon magic would make it so much easier to track down a target, a voice inside them suggested before they could silence it. In the usual student teams, Moonweavers used the wise power of the night to locate Phantoms, weaken them, and support allies, while Sunweavers did the fighting with their fiery magic. The final exam, however, was a solo affair. Unless they wanted to be disqualified from their chance to graduate as a Sunweaver, Harper was stuck with only Sun spells. Besides… they swallowed, Moon magic wasn't a part of them anymore. They'd left their identity as a Moonweaver behind. All they needed was Sun magic.

Harper stopped at a fork in the labyrinth. The passage on the left was thinner and darker… perhaps fewer students would've chosen that direction. They headed that way, twisting around inky corners, until they reached a staircase. They took the steps carefully in the faint blue light, descending a few inches closer to Hell with each one. How long had passed? An hour? Two? They had to run into a Phantom soon. They had to, or—

Shadows detached from the murky darkness below and shot toward Harper like knives carved from the void.

Harper gasped in the stale underground air, stumbling over steps when they leaped backward. One of the sharpened shadows, untouched by the lantern light, nearly sliced off their ear. The rest buried themselves in the stairs below.

"Better be careful what I wish for," Harper grumbled, gesturing at the tunnels beneath them with an accusatory finger. A fiery aura fizzled into life around them and launched itself as arrows in the direction they pointed. The orange flames chased some of the shadows away… but not all of them. Sure enough, a humanlike shape withstood the light. A Phantom.

Harper grimaced. Each Phantom had a heart—a shimmering, marble-like gem that housed their soul—buried somewhere inside their shadowy shapes, and the only way to kill one was to pierce it. The task would be much harder without a Moonweaver to pinpoint the heart's location.

The Phantom surged forward like an inky tide, sending more of its own shadows up the stairs.

Harper closed their eyes, focusing all of their senses on the heat in and around them. Their Sun aura grew, submerging them in a barrier of flame—in that familiar ocean of power and warmth. Waves of shadow struck at them but sizzled out without touching their skin. Encased inside Sun magic, they were untouchable, but... Sweat dripped down Harper's brow. Exhaustion came quickly, crushing the breath in their lungs. They waited only a few seconds longer, listening, waiting to hear the Phantom creep closer.

With a shout, they waved their hand forward, and all of their aura poured down the stairs like a tide of fire. The Phantom was too near to flee. Sun magic washed over the demon, melting away its shadows until all that remained was a smoldering heart that shattered with a final crack.

Remnants of a screech echoed through the tunnels... then settled into silence.

Harper exhaled a sigh.

Cold pain crashed through their shoulder from behind.

"Shit!" They whirled around on the stairs.

Another Phantom they hadn't noticed before stood at the top, its shadowy arrows already surging forward.

Harper barely had time to gasp before summoning another barrier of Sun magic. The aura was weaker this time, sputtering like a candle in the wind. Several shards of shadows slipped by and bit into their shoulders and chest like daggers. They hissed out shouts through gritted teeth. They had to keep focused on building the barrier. Had to focus through the pain. Had to—

A streak of flame lit up the space above the stairs as if the Sun itself had risen inside the tunnels.

The Phantom wailed and, with a final, fiery pop, it was gone. Shards of its heart floated down the stairs like glitter in the blue light.

...Huh? Harper gawked up at the place where the demon had stood only seconds before. They hadn't done that. Was someone else there?

They let the flames around them disperse, their tight throat trying and failing to find any oxygen left in the labyrinth. One shaky foot braced against the step below to keep them from falling.

A woman emerged from the shadows at the top of the stairs. She stared down at them with what looked like a sword made of fire. Her long blonde hair, blue-sky eyes, and ghostly complexion stood in stark contrast to her black Sunweaver's cloak.

Harper's mouth fell open. "You use Sun magic!"

The woman scowled. "How about a 'thank you,' instead? As amusing as your expression might be, I grew weary of shocked faces a long time ago."

Harper flushed. "Oh, I didn't mean it like that! I mean, I use Sun magic too, and I'm not..." Their tongue staggered around in search of the right words. "I'm not male, either."

The woman raised an eyebrow. "Well, you aren't very good at it. You used up way too much energy on the first Phantom. There's no need to tire yourself out so much on such a weak enemy."

The heat deepened on Harper's cheeks. "I just... I let myself get distracted." They had focused so firmly on finding a Phantom that they hadn't prepared themself for what would happen when they actually did. They'd dispatched enemies like that one dozens of times before, but there was a weight on their shoulders this time in the shape of the clerk's incredulous stare... a weight that left their body and mind both tired and tight. They *had* to pass.

The woman above didn't move, her eyes and expression unnervingly still. "One moment of distraction can mean death down here."

"I know!" Harper barked, then lit up with another blush. "I..." They shook their head and met the stranger's steady gaze. "Who are you, anyway? If you're another Sunweaver who isn't male, then how come I've never heard of you?"

"I'm sure you have." What passed for a frown slipped onto the woman's face. "My name is Spike."

Harper's eyes stretched wide. "Spike Peyton?" No way. "I thought..."

"You thought I was dead." The sky in Spike's eyes froze over. "After all, Professor Lysender set me up to fail precisely so that the school could turn me into a story."

Her words drifted through Harper's head, not quite forming any meaning. "...Professor Lysender?"

What might have been pity softened Spike's face. "He doesn't intend to let you pass, you know."

A spark of anger lit up in Harper's chest. "What do you mean by that? He's the one who talked the clerk into letting me take the exam like this! I wouldn't have even been able to learn Sun magic at all if not for him!"

Spike's serenity returned to her expression, her voice. "He's the one who taught me, too. You and I aren't the only ones who've thought about crossing the line between the Moon and Sun. There were other students in my cohort who showed interest in the magic reserved for the opposite side of the binary. He taught me just enough to put on a show, let me take the test, and then let me 'die.' He made me into an example—Solar's perfect parable."

Harper swallowed. Her words hit them like needles but hadn't quite pierced their skin. "That sounds like paranoia to me." They tried again to suck in oxygen. Why did it suddenly feel like there was no air left in the entire labyrinth? "You just weren't skilled enough!"

Spike scoffed, as if a fly had just landed on her shoulder. "If *I* wasn't skilled enough, what hope is there for you?"

"Hey!" Harper's fingers clenched into fists, their cheeks as hot as their Sunweaver's magic. "I told you, I was just—"

"And I told *you*, it doesn't matter anyway." Fiery sparks flared around Spike's silhouette, even as her face remained stoic. "Like you, I was the last one out. They had a Prime Phantom far stronger than any normally allowed into the exam tunnels lying in wait for me. With the limited Sun magic he taught me, I stood no chance."

"Then how are you still alive?"

"I caught on quickly." Spike let out a long breath, her sparks fading. "I fled the fight while I still could. There was no way I could go back to Solar after the school itself had tried to kill me off... So I disappeared. I figured I'd just let them have their story. I'm not sure if they know I'm still alive or not." She shrugged. "At least this way, I got to take my memories with me to the Surface."

"Then what the hell are you doing back here?" Harper shouted, surprised by the volume of their own voice. Now the needles had shed blood.

Spike smirked. "Saving you."

Harper hushed, heat still pounding on their cheeks to the drum of their pulse. ...What?

"Or perhaps I'm not quite that noble. Maybe it's more about revenge." Spike walked down the stairs in a rigid, perfect rhythm, each of her steps carrying her closer to Harper. "I still have my contacts. I heard about you. I want to see Lysender's sequel backfire in his face."

Spike stopped when she stood just two steps away, her blue eyes holding tight to Harper's hazel stare. "I want to see you pass."

Harper swallowed through a tight throat. They didn't want to believe it, but...

The anger in the stranger's eyes was real.

"Let me help you," Spike pleaded. "I've grown as a Sunweaver on my own. I can defeat the Prime Phantom, even the incredible one they surely have in wait for you. You can take back the heart. Then I'll turn back into a story. No one has to know I aided you."

Harper exhaled what felt like the last of their air. "Okay."

Their gazes held for a few seconds longer.

Harper tried and failed to swallow another lump—one that'd grown too bloated with the tears they refused to shed. Spike really could have been a ghost in the dim lunar light of the labyrinth. The blue lanterns turned her hair into a twilight river that flowed around her shoulders. The musculature defining her otherwise delicate features stood as a testament to the training she must have gone through on her own. Her solemn eyes seemed so fitting in the melancholy tunnels, so much so that they couldn't look away. She was beautiful.

Spike frowned. "Don't get the wrong idea. I'm interested in the exam, not you. I'm the kind of aroace that doesn't do romance. I especially don't do sex."

Red rushed through Harper's face. "That's... not what I was thinking about."

Spike shrugged, then brushed passed them, striding down the rest of the stairs. "Knowing what I do about allosexuals, I tend to assume you're all thinking about it by default."

Harper shook their head, trying to dislodge the embarrassment. This whole exam was a disaster. Hell, it even beat out all the nightmares they'd collected about the final exam through the years. They turned to follow after the woman they'd just met. Unreality prickled up their spine with each step they took.

"Oh," Spike stopped, then glanced back at them. "There's one more thing I should tell you. Before I fled two years ago, I used one of the few Moon spells I still remembered to track the Prime Phantom that nearly did me in." A smirk sneaked onto her lips. "Right now, it's heading straight toward you."

Harper stiffened. "Please tell me you're kidding."

Solar... truly had intended them to fail.

Harper leaped back just in time to avoid the Prime Phantom's shadowy claws. "What the hell is that thing?"

"Not all Phantoms are human-like, or even animal-like." Spike charged toward the dragon-like Phantom instead of away, one of her fiery swords held tightly in her hands. "After all, Phantoms are the origins of countless folktales. They don't prepare you for this kind of thing at Solar."

The massive, inky shade held what looked like a talon high above Spike. She waited for it to stomp down, then dodged at the final moment like a dancer waiting for a musical cue. She plunged her sword into the claws, ushering a screech from the Phantom. It tried to move, but the blade of fire nailed its talon to the bottom of the tunnel. The shadows around the flames burned and boiled.

The Phantom swept toward Spike with a mammoth right arm.

Spike gestured backward, and another wave of sword-like fire formed in her hands. She slid underneath the strike, slicing through the Phantom's arm with a sizzle.

Harper couldn't help but gawk. "Where did you learn to do that?" To make Sun magic into something like an actual weapon… It was incredible. They'd never seen spells harnessed in such a way.

"Certainly not from Lysender," Spike scoffed. "Stay focused!"

Harper nearly yelped when they looked back at the Phantom. What could have been a tail was sweeping straight toward them. On instinct, they thrust out both their palms, birthing a wave of fire and sending it forward. The shadowy limb disintegrated in the heat moments before it hit. Strange, black dust floated down, catching in Harper's hair and cloak. They shivered, in spite of themself.

"I remember its heart being right in the center." Spike held out her hand, too, sparks of fire already glowing there. "If we attack at the same time, we might be able to break it."

"R-right!" Harper shook off their fear and once again held out their hands.

With a nod of Spike's chin, Harper reached down deep into their senses, searching for every scrap of energy they had left, and summoned a flood of fire that joined with their fellow Sunweaver's.

The Phantom roared as the Sunlight poured into its chest, but beneath its rage, glassy cracks pierced through the tunnels.

"It's working!" Spike shouted louder than she had before, her solemn voice struggling to rise above the sizzling shadows.

Bitter, black smoke burned in Harper's nostrils, but they forced themself to look up at the Phantom. The titan's shimmering white heart glistened through the Sun's orange blaze.

Harper begged their muscles to keep working, to keep holding out their arms. Their body wanted to buckle. Their stomach heaved. Sun magic smoldered within them as much as it did outside them, filling them up with warm, prickling energy. *Burning* energy. It hurt, but the fire inside was the only reason they were still on their feet. ...Was this what a real battle as a Sunweaver felt like?

The heart crackled and boiled.

Harper screamed, and with a last burst of will, a fireball erupted from them before they fell to their knees.

The heart crackled and boiled... but didn't break.

Shadows surged away from the heart as the Phantom summoned up the strength for one more desperate assault of its own. The inky wave roared toward Harper, as gaping and dark as an open mouth.

"No!" Spike leaped in front of them, and all the fire she had left in her formed a barrier wide enough for the both of them. "I won't let you lose!"

It held for only seconds.

Sun magic sputtered out. Shadows overcame Spike, swallowed her up, drowned her in an ocean of ink.

"Spike!" Harper screamed, a jolt of adrenaline giving them enough strength to fling themself backward before the tide came for them.

Black liquid, still boiling, coated the floor where the woman who had come back to Solar to save them had stood just seconds before.

A new fire burned in Harper's chest.

The Phantom dragged its whole body closer, its cracked heart still shining bright.

Harper gritted their teeth. The damned thing would suffer.

The Phantom outstretched another inky arm, ready to swallow a second Sunweaver.

Sparks of the Sun flared in Harper's palm. Anger was fire. They closed their eyes. So often throughout their school life—every time classmates had giggled as they'd walked by, every time they'd failed and Professor Lysender had told them it might be a sign that everyone else was right, every time someone had insisted they should've been a Moonweaver—they'd buried their anger. They'd tried to smile. They'd tried to pretend everything was fine for the sake of everyone else's comfort. Not this time. They let the emotion rip through them, filling them with fresh adrenaline—fresh energy. Fresh *fire*. They thought about the clerk's smug face. They thought about Professor Lysender smiling at them when all along he'd used them. They thought about the stories the school had told them about Spike. Spike... The heat boiled through their skin. With a shout, a sword-like streak of fire—so much like Spike's—formed in their hands.

Leaving the rest to their body instead of their magic, Harper charged forward, splashing through smoldering shadows, plunging toward the exposed heart. Their sword pierced through the gem.

Everything went white.

When Harper finally opened their eyes, shards from a burnt-out heart lay on the smudged floor beneath them. They shook all over, black and red stains on their skin and tears stuck to their cheeks, but they bent down and gathered up the wretched remains.

They'd... passed. Not even Solar would be able to deny their success when they returned with the Prime Phantom's heart in hand.

They swallowed a sob through their burning throat. "Thanks, Spike."

As if saying the name had conjured the woman back into existence, Harper's eyes suddenly landed on the human shape splayed across the tunnel a few feet ahead of them.

They gasped in a swig of the smoky air and raced toward her. "Spike!"

Spike didn't answer, both her body and her cloak painted with ink.

Harper knelt down next to her, but she didn't stir when they touched her shoulder. When they searched for a pulse, they didn't find one. Only the memory of warmth remained on her skin.

Sorrow sunk into Harper's chest like a sword of its own... and a strange idea lit up. If the fire of rage had restored the fire of the Sun from within, then... maybe...

They swallowed, hesitating, fingers clammy on Spike's stained shoulder. They'd always viewed Moon magic as a bad memory they wanted to rid themself of... something that held them back from being who they really were. And now, after all this time, they'd finally become a Sunweaver. Using Moon magic again would threaten the new title they'd fought so hard to earn. But... Sun magic couldn't save Spike.

Harper embraced the pain, letting it form the knot of connection that ushered Moonweavers into the magic of the night—that guided them with affection, sympathy, intuition. It washed through them, cool and soothing, filling up all of their cracks like water. They fought the instinct to pull away. It didn't put out their fire. Both winter and summer existed together inside of them. Harper let themself cry.

Faint slivers of silver magic spilled into Spike's body.

Harper gasped when the shape below them shuddered, its chest rising and falling with a gasp of its own. "Spike!"

Spike's blue eyes blearily drifted open.

As they had once before, the two Sunweavers stared, drinking in each other's gazes.

A wide smile spread across Harper's tear-stained cheeks. "I passed."

Spike smiled, too. "Solar will have no choice but to recognize you as a Sunweaver now."

Harper let a few more quiet beats go by, chewing on the thought. "I used both Sun and Moon magic," they admitted. They'd used Moon magic, and even though they'd always be a Sunweaver, it hadn't been anything to be afraid of. It was all inside of them, just waiting to be harnessed in whatever way they wished. What they'd thought of as a limit was limitless. "Maybe that's the way it should be. Maybe we're all less like the Sun or the Moon and more like the rest of the stars. Maybe we're all unique."

Spike managed the suggestion of a smirk. "Then go on and get that heart back to the school. Prove it to them." She reached back on her palms and pushed herself up with an exhausted moan. "I need some time before I drag myself out of here, but I'll be okay. You've done enough."

Harper watched Spike for a while longer. "I know you don't do dating, but how about coffee?" They grinned. "After all, it looks like I'll be back on the Surface soon, and with all of my memories intact. I'll tell you all about the face Professor Lysender makes when I come back with the heart."

Spike managed a weak chuckle. "I'm looking forward to it."

The stare between them stretched on.

"I'm so glad I met you." Harper beamed, letting a different sort of Sun shine through them. Even though their muscles ached and burned, they felt lighter than they had in years. For perhaps the first time, they weren't alone.

Spike's icy blue eyes softened into the summer sky. "I'll see you on the Surface, Sunweaver."

# Sailing Blind
## *by Kathrine Machon*

The wind streamed off the sea and into the village, sending sand skittering through the narrow streets of Black Rock. It tugged at coats, rattled postcard stands, and flapped shop signs before climbing the steep slope beyond to reach me. Sitting on the skirt of acid green moss that surrounded the clifftop castle ruins, I snugged my denim jacket closer. Gusts buffeted me, tangling my hair around my face like a mass of last year's catkins, and painting my skin with the crystal tingle of salt.

Below, the slate roofs of the village were dark and slick with spray, and wind teased from the wavetops slapped against the harbor wall. At least the lively weather promised a good show for the tourists—the annual re-enactment of the witch women of Black Rock singing the fishing fleet home. It was never quite the same when the wind-singers were supposed to be taming a gale on a calm day.

Down by the harbor, old Joe was entertaining a rag-tag crowd with the legend behind the show. I'd heard it a hundred times, but it still sent a prickle across my skin.

Two sisters in love with the same fisherman. And when he'd chosen one over the other, the scorned sister had set out for revenge. One stormy night, as the village women sang to calm the waves, the scorned sister turned her voice to raise a savage sea. The man had drowned, but the wind-singers had sung the rest of the fleet home.

Part of the legend was true, because the woman the man had chosen was an ancestor from my mother's line. As for the rest, well, you'd have to believe in witches.

Scanning the ramble of cottages, it was impossible to miss the bright flag of Rowan's hair amid the drab tones of the buildings. She was like a red rose in volcanic soil. We were childhood best friends, but right now I huddled out of sight behind a tumbled stone. I wanted to talk to Tom alone.

He'd said he'd be home today—that he wouldn't miss my and Rowan's debut performance. God knows how I'd let Ma persuade me to take the lead role, but it was tradition. The sisters were always played by their descendants, and Ma said hers and Rowan's mum's voices weren't up to it anymore. So, I'd broken my vow to stay away and protect my heart, just this once, to keep Ma happy.

"Cally?"

I started and peeked around the stone. So much for hiding. "Hi, Row. How did you know I was here?"

She gave a slow smile and raised an eyebrow. "I'm a witch, remember?" But after a moment the smile stiffened. "The fact you and Tom always used to meet here had nothing to do with finding you."

I held in a sigh. If only she'd realize the truth. Rowan might not be a witch, but she had a different kind of magic. The wind had raised color to her cheeks and a wildness to her eyes. Now it caught her sleeveless dress, shaping it to the contours of her body: slim waist, curved hips, full breasts with the nipples taut against the fabric. She must be cold, but she didn't look it. Of course, she was dressed like this for Tom.

I chewed on my lip and ignored the familiar ache.

"He's a no show?" She couldn't hide the tilt of a triumphant smile.

"Nothing was arranged." I stood up and brushed moss off my jeans. "I'll catch him later." Her smile was setting my teeth on edge and a spurt of anger heated my veins. Two could play at catty. "It's no big deal. I saw him a few weeks ago anyway."

"Really?" She linked arms with me for the walk back to the village, but her red lacquered nails grazed my wrist with more than casual force. "Do you get together often?"

I shrugged. "Now and then. With our universities being close…" No doubt she'd read something beyond friendship into that.

Except Tom had been odd last time we'd met. He'd said he had something to tell me, then changed his mind, insisted it wait until this weekend instead. I'd hoped to find out what before Rowan reeled him in.

But Rowan had gone quiet. Eyes downturned, jaw tight. Good one, Cally. I'd hit her right in the vulnerable spot. Tom and I'd moved out into the world. Moved on. And I'd tried to let go of my secret obsession. But Rowan had stayed here. Her hopes were all tied up in Tom.

I forced a smile and clasped her arm tightly. "I can't believe we've been talked into doing this."

She gave a little shake, tossed back her auburn mane, and laughed. "Who else would they choose?"

"You're going to love this, aren't you?"

That brought on a sly smile.

We meandered through the village, accompanied by the clack of Rowan's sandals. Past the chemist that Ma ran and on to Rowan's mum's gift shop. Outside was the usual clutter of buckets and spades for sale, but inside the scent of cinnamon, cloves, and lavender swallowed me back to my childhood. Shelves were stacked with pots of peacock and crow's feathers, rocks encrusted with quartz crystals, scrying spheres and tarot cards.

Rowan selected an iridescent feather and tucked it behind my ear. "Brace yourself," she whispered, tilting her head toward the back of the shop.

Our mothers were huddled there, gesturing over a cauldron. They straightened and smiled at our appearance.

"There you are," Rowan's mum said. "It's almost time to get changed, but first…"

I groaned. Not the ritual. Before they sang, our mothers had always pledged their loyalty and friendship to each other as if there might be danger in the slightest ill will. This year it seemed they expected us to do the same.

Rowan's mum picked up a wide-rimmed glass and dipped it into the cauldron. The scent of spirits stung my nostrils, mixed up with something sharp and herbal.

"Here." Ma pulled two packets from her pocket and handed one to each of us.

"Do I have to?" I complained. "This is ridiculous."

Rowan grinned. "Oh, come on, Cally. Where's your sense of adventure?"

"Behave yourself, girls," her mum snapped. "It's important." Then softer. "You need to do this and mean it."

My eyes met Rowan's. Cute dimples formed on her cheeks as the corners of her mouth struggled not to curl up, but she gave a tiny shrug. It seemed we didn't have a choice. Tearing open the package, she withdrew a sterilized needle, grimaced, then stabbed it into the tip of her finger. A bead of red welled. I gritted my teeth and followed suit.

"Mix the blood," Ma instructed, and we touched our fingers together.

"In here." She held out the cup and we let a crimson drop fall into the spirit. "Now the chant," she whispered. "Remember the chant."

I resisted giving an eye-roll as we closed our hands around the glass stem. Rowan's face was solemn but her eyes sparked mischief. She was definitely trying not to laugh.

"Go on," Ma prompted, and we recited.

*"Sisters in heart. Bound in love. Never a cross word between us."*

Ma nudged me and I took a sip. My face twisted at the strong alcohol and the thought of the blood. Rowan leaned in next, quickly tipped the glass and mimed swallowing. The liquid never touched her lips. I tried to tilt the glass further but she was already straightening.

Rowan's mum clapped her hands together, all smiles. "Off you go and get changed."

We jostled each other in our rush to reach the back room where we collapsed, giggling.

"Gross. I can't believe you actually swallowed some," Rowan gasped.

I gave her shoulder a shove. "I can't believe you didn't!"

She wiped laughter tears from her eyes and bent to pick up a dress. Holding it to her chest, she spun, and red silk billowed around her. Not exactly fisherwoman's clothes, but pure Rowan. I smiled at her delight and reached for my drabber costume.

"Do you remember...?" Rowan gave a misty smile.

"Oh yes."

The game we'd played as children: singing home the fleet. Me, Rowan, and Tom—in a time before thoughts of wanting. I'd always been made to play the scorned sister while Tom fought the sea to reach Rowan. But today our roles were reversed.

Rowan's dreamy look had gone; replaced by narrowed eyes and compressed lips. I guessed what was coming next.

"Later," she said, "when we see Tom... Stay out of my way."

I bit down in frustration. "Don't be so dramatic, Row. Tom's my friend, too."

"I'm not talking about friendship," she hissed.

Well, I was, but it was pointless to argue: Rowan in a temper was a force of nature.

"Time to go," Ma called.

I pushed past her into the main shop.

"Rowan, hurry up." Her mum this time.

And she was beside me, squeezing my hand. Quick to temper and quick to forgive; that was her. The door opened and I gasped as a cheer went up, making my stomach perform a complicated flip-flop. Rowan led me into the crowd of costumed locals and camera-clutching tourists. As we made our way toward the harbor the people followed until, at the crossroads, Rowan took the left turn toward the cliff while I carried on to the quay.

At the bottom of the path, a young man stopped me. "You must be Cally." He glanced up the way I'd come. "And that's Rowan." A grin split his face. "I'm Ben. A friend of Tom's."

I paused and the stream of villagers split around us to take their places for the performance.

"Where is he?" I asked.

"In a boat." Ben's grin stretched wider. "He said for your debut appearance, he had to be the 'fisherman' being sung home."

"What? Oh, Tom," I laughed. "He probably hasn't rowed in ages."

"He was insistent," Ben said. "Does he have to row far?"

I pointed across the bay to the headland. "From there."

Ben frowned. "That looks a long way and it's a small boat."

He was obviously no sailor. "It's maybe half a mile, and don't worry." I patted his shoulder. "He'll have a lifejacket and there's a motorboat on standby."

"Cally," Ma called my name.

"I'm sorry. I've got to go. Maybe I'll see you later."

He nodded, and I hurried to my place at the front of the group, where we all stared up at the clifftop. Flames flickered then whooshed as the beacon fire took: a signal for Tom to start rowing and for Rowan to take her place.

The scorned sister sang from a platform halfway up the cliff; separate from the main group, but close enough to be clearly seen and heard. There was a murmur amid the tourists as Rowan stepped into view, her dress and hair streaming out behind her in the wind. She looked the part. Wild and seductive.

Across the bay, the boat came into view. From Rowan's position, it wouldn't be long before she realized today's "fisherman" was Tom. A little twinge of unease uncoiled in my stomach. How would she react? After all, Tom was rowing toward me.

Behind me, the village women began to hum, and I pushed the feeling aside. The wind slid around me, caressing my skin. The murmur of the women rose and fell in time with the tug and flurry of the breeze. The sound filled my head, weaving through me, pulsing in time with my heart. And something stirred deep within.

Pressure swelled in my chest, surging upward until, as the women reached a crescendo, a song burst from my mouth. Unexpected. Rich and full.

A gasp went up from the visitors as I crooned to the wind —fluid notes that wove a lullaby to soothe a storm to stillness. A song of long summer days and lazy breezes. Around me the air flowed warm, laced with the scent of flowers. And then Rowan's voice joined mine. Higher. Demanding. Cutting through the calming tones, dissolving the warmth, and for a moment the wind stiffened.

No. It was my imagination. It had to be.

Rowan's voice was a perfect counterpoint to mine. We played a vocal game of tug-of-war, teasing the wind. It was madness to believe this was witchery, but I couldn't deny the strength of our song.

A smile leapt between us, and then she glanced out to where Tom rowed. A crease of pain crossed her face. Her gaze flashed back to me with a look that could cut, and her voice hardened. She thought Tom in the boat signified something.

I faltered and a sudden gust drove spray over the harbor wall to soak my dress and slide icy fingers across my skin. A quivering note from Rowan and the wind stilled for a heartbeat, then shifted from its customary easterly direction. The headland no longer shielded the bay and a gale raced from the open sea. One moment Tom was rowing in calm waters, the next, his boat bucked and spun in a churning chaos.

"Ma?" I turned to the women, searching for her face.

She'd stopped singing and her gaze flickered between Tom, Rowan, and me. "This shouldn't be possible. The charm..."

The charm? Surely it was meaningless. But now that I'd felt the potency of our voices, everything had changed. The ritual hadn't been completed and our powers were loose. A certainty formed: only I could stop Rowan. So, I sang again.

My voice rose to fill the gale, matching its strength, then slid down in cadence, drawing the flurries with it. But as fast as I wove the words, Rowan sliced through them.

In the bay, the boat labored up the side of a wave, was silhouetted on the crest, crashed down the other side. I clenched my fists, holding a note until the boat reappeared from the trough. But another wave curled over it, broke, and swept Tom into the maelstrom.

And I knew, however hard I sang, it wouldn't be enough. History would repeat itself. Hot tears joined cold spray on my face, fear tightened in my heart and instinct gripped me.

I sang a pure, high note and the air condensed around me, held taut at my command. I pointed at Rowan, shouted, and the wind arrowed toward her. Blew her off her feet. Cut her song to silence. The crowd milled in confusion, but the village women caught up my song and brought the performance to an end.

And I ran, slipping on the wet, sandy path that led to the slipway. The wind had swung direction again, and now the bay was calming. The rowing boat was gone but the sound of the rescue engine approached.

Rowan joined me. Dress ripped, hair in tangled luxury around her face. "What have I done?" she whispered.

I drew her close, melding her curves to mine, and a treacherous thought crept into my mind. If there was no Tom...

They hauled him from the rescue boat, dropped him limply onto the slipway. Rowan and I clung together as people milled around him.

"Let me through." Ben's voice. "I'm a medical student."

He rolled Tom onto his side. Pounded his back. Silence stretched as we held our breath. Then came a cough, a gush of water, and Tom flopped over, collapsing against Ben.

After a moment, he gave a shaky laugh. "Well, that was wild."

Rowan dropped to his side. "God, Tom…"

I closed my eyes so I wouldn't have to see. I thought I'd accepted this, but the pain flared anew. What I wouldn't give for Rowan to look at me like that.

"I'll live, Row-Row." Tom's voice dissolved into more coughs.

"You are never doing anything like that again," Ben hissed, and his tone sent a prickle across my neck.

My eyes opened to a tableau. Rowan crouched at Tom's side, face white, hand clasped to mouth. Tom slumped in Ben's lap. Ben's arms around him. A scorching glance between them. All too easy to read.

This was what he wanted to tell me. But how could he have let Rowan find out this way?

She rose, and I caught her, pulling her into my arms as she tried to barrel past.

"I always thought…" Her voice a sob against my shoulder.

Anger swelled, becoming a vibration in my throat. What would it do to Tom if I released it?

Except this wasn't Tom's fault. Rowan's and his lives had been tangled with mine since childhood, their faces more familiar than my own reflection. And yet we were each blind to where the others loved.

# Different Ways
## by Tabitha O'Connell

All Dane's physical strength had ever gotten him was another day on the docks hauling freight while daydreaming about punching out his boss. But there were other kinds of strength, he thought as he watched the red-robed, gold-bedecked man disembarking from his schooner under the inky cover of night. The man—Syro—waved his crew off toward the nearby flickering lights and laughter, then turned uptown, where the buildings rested in dignified silence.

"My lord," Dane called softly after him, stepping from his post in the shadow of a warehouse doorway. It was certainly not the correct form of address, but it was the most respectful thing he could think of. He'd never spoken to a magician before.

"Was that meant for me?" Syro turned with folded arms and what looked like a smirk as Dane stepped closer. "I prefer 'Lord Magician' or perhaps 'Your Supreme Worshipfulness.'"

Dane stopped ten feet away. This wasn't what he had expected. "Uh, sorry about that. Your Supreme Worshipfulness." He tried to inject a teasing tone into his voice, as if bantering with magicians was something he did every day.

"It's quite all right." Syro closed some of the distance between them. His demeanor was all weary nonchalance—no tension, no caution. "So, what leads you to approach me on this fine evening?"

"I'm..." Dane was more nervous about asking his question than Syro was at being accosted by a stranger in the dark. "I wanted to know..." Syro spread his hand in a "go on" motion. "I want to know what it would take for you to teach me some magic."

"Ha!" Syro's face cracked in a grin. "A bold request. Most people just want me to do favors for them—heal an ailment, curse an enemy, 'I can't afford to pay you, but please, I'm desperate...' But you want me to *teach* you." His eyes traveled over Dane, and for the first time in ages, Dane thought about what he was wearing, the grubby tunic over the stained trousers with patches at the knees, his shoes covered in a layer of filth. "I'm sorry, but it would take damn well more than you could afford."

"But—"

Syro's raised hand silenced Dane's protest as effectively as if it had been clapped over his mouth. "Don't bother with the tales of woe about your sick wife and starving children and how you need to make a better living for yourself. It won't do you any good."

"I don't have a wife or kids. It's not about that, it's about..."

"What? What's it about, then?"

Syro's tone mocked him, but he pressed on. "It's about being my own person. Having choices and freedom."

A scoff flew from Syro's throat. "Have you ever considered that maybe it's not that simple?" Before Dane could ask what he meant, he went on, "I'm sorry, but you're out of luck, my friend. You'll have to seek your autonomy elsewhere." With a sweep of his robe, the man turned and strode away.

While Dane tried to walk down High Street with confident purpose, he couldn't help the twitchy discomfort that came from feeling out of place. Maybe the summons he'd received from Syro that afternoon was part of a cruel joke. While carrying a particularly heavy crate down a gangplank, he'd been interrupted by a sudden greeting. "Hello, my good dockhand." Fingers slipping with surprise, he'd barely managed to hold onto his burden while twisting around in search of the voice's owner. But Syro's red robe was absent from the gray-brown slurry of dockworkers and crew. "I've been reconsidering your request. Come see me tonight, and we can talk about it."

Realizing he'd frozen in place, Dane had hurried forward to put the crate down. The words were, apparently, just in his head; while it sounded like Syro was talking at his ear, no one around gave any sign of awareness. After providing his address, Syro's voice had gone silent.

Now, encroaching on a part of the city he never had reason to enter, he was relieved when he reached Syro's building. The knob turned in his hand, with a sound like it was unlocking as he touched it. A narrow but richly carpeted staircase, with carved wooden handrails, led him up to the highest landing, where Syro's voice had directed him. As he raised his fist to knock on the door, Syro's voice called from within, "Enter." Dane obeyed, eyebrows pulling into a frown. Did Syro always use magic so liberally, or was he showing off?

The magician was lounging on a couch, legs stretched out, in a lavishly appointed sitting room, lit with several flames that floated in glass globes. "Welcome, welcome." At first, Dane just stared around before catching himself and turning his gaze to Syro. "You can admire it—I don't mind." A smirk played on Syro's lips. "Take as long as you like."

The man was a smug asshole, and it was almost enough to send Dane back down the stairs so that he could retain a sliver of his pride. But short-term irritation was a small price. "I'm all right. So, you changed your mind?"

"Maybe." Syro languidly waved him to a chair; it looked to be made of leather and was well-cushioned. Dane couldn't relax into it, though, but rested his elbows on his knees as he leaned forward to watch Syro. Syro watched him back for a long moment, one eyebrow slightly quirked, before asking, "Have you ever... been with a man?" He glanced meaningfully toward a door across the room.

"Yes," Dane answered, face warming, "but what's that got to do with anything?"

Syro's lips curved into a smile. "I have a proposition for you. You provide me with some, shall we say, entertainment, and I'll teach you a bit of magic. Enough to set you free from a life of manual labor. How does that sound?"

Dane tried to decide if the offer was demeaning or not. Maybe it didn't matter. His eyes combed Syro in this new light, taking inventory—thin, angular form; long, golden hair pulled back in a braid; haughty eyes; wicked, pale lips.

"It sounds... agreeable."

Syro tipped his chin down coyly. "Excellent. Do you want to start now?"

"Uh, sure."

Dane settled back in his seat, ready for an introduction to the workings of magic. But Syro gave a quick laugh. "No, no, I meant... start with the other part."

Dane fixed him with an incredulous frown. "How do I know you'll teach me anything then?"

"How will I know if you're worth my time otherwise?"

That sent Dane to his feet, fists balling at his sides. "You know what, I don't need you."

"Oh, you're right, you don't." Unperturbed, Syro motioned him back to his chair. "And I don't need you either, but we each have something the other *wants*, so why not see this through? Sit down, and I'll give you your first lesson now."

Mollified, Dane resumed his seat and listened to Syro explain that magic was about intention as much as knowledge of the arcane language. "It's second nature to me now, I couldn't fail if I wanted to, but it'll take you some time to get comfortable with it." He loosed his hair, shaking it free from its braid to fall around his shoulders, a golden cascade that Dane couldn't keep his eyes off. Then, with a few muttered words, it divided itself in three again and wove back together into a plait, the leather tie lifting from Syro's hand to knot itself around the end. He smirked as Dane gawked. "Now, if anyone *else* tried to do that for me, it wouldn't work nearly so well, if at all. You need to thoroughly know what you want, which requires familiarity, confidence. A cobbler might be able to magically craft shoes, but could be completely clumsy with everything else. Care for a drink?"

Before Dane could answer, Syro was murmuring again and a bottle of wine lifted, uncorked, and poured into two glasses that floated up from a side table. One moved toward Dane, and he reached for it, but Syro raised a finger and said, "No, no." The other glass hovered in front of him, and he said a phrase, clear and at regular volume. The cup rose to his lips, tilting for him to take a sip. "Now you try it."

Dane repeated the words, but knew immediately that he hadn't done it right; his voice held no confidence, but moved awkwardly over the unfamiliar syllables. The glass wobbled and then fell, dumping its contents onto Dane's lap before rolling across the floor.

"As I said." Syro showed no concern for the drops of wine spattered on the rug—bastard that he was, he'd probably known that was coming. "It will take time. But practice that, and see if you can improve."

Dane's eyes narrowed. Where and when was he supposed to have the opportunity to practice? But Syro didn't seem to notice. He rolled his shoulders and plucked his own glass from the air, draining the rest in one long quaff.

"Sufficient for day one?" When Dane nodded, Syro spilled cat-like off the couch. He muttered under his breath some more, and two of the orbs of light drifted over to hang clustered above his head. After giving Dane an assessing glance, he motioned him up. "Come with me."

The lights followed them into the bedroom, where a large four-poster dominated the space. Syro opened a wardrobe, and at another command, a robe, matching the one Syro wore, floated out of it. "Put that on. I won't look if you want to preserve your modesty for the time being."

It was slightly humiliating that Syro wanted to dress him up before taking his clothes off. But on the other hand, he had just spilled wine all over himself.

"By the way," Syro asked, decorously studying the wall, "what should I call you? I assume you don't prefer 'dockhand.'"

"It's Dane." He stripped quickly and then wrapped himself in the robe; even pulled tight, it left a large swathe of his chest bare but was otherwise sufficient to cover him. "You can look now."

Syro did, eyeing him up and down before nodding approval. "Not bad. Of course, I'm sure you'll look even better with it off."

Syro's hungry eyes rendered them suddenly equals. Keeping hold of his gaze, Dane fingered the cloth of the robe where the two halves met over his sternum. He stepped toward Syro, and, surprisingly quick, Syro dived for the bed, settling flat on his back. As Dane advanced, Syro's eyes flicked to the side and he muttered to himself once more. A moment later, Dane's discarded clothes were rising into the air.

Whatever he was doing didn't matter. Dane dropped to the mattress to straddle Syro and look down at his flushed face, wondering dazedly how he'd managed to get himself here and if Syro were truly serious about this.

Syro's spidery fingers on the back of his neck coaxed him closer. Their lips met, and the pressure of Syro's body against his chased all the questions from his mind. When his hands parted Syro's robe, Syro whispered the sash undone, letting it fall open all the way. Dane's fingers fumbled against his undershirt, and Syro told him, "Tear it."

"But it's silk!"

Syro's voice was breathy in his ear. "I don't care."

Gripping the luxurious fabric and wrenching it in two was immensely satisfying. Syro lay back against the pillows with his eyes closed and lips parted, strands of hair that Dane had freed snaking out around his head. When he sat up to shrug off his garments, he also loosed his braid again and murmured some more. His hair rose to float suspended in the air, leaving his face unencumbered, and Dane gripped it in golden handfuls.

"You can stay if you'd like," Syro murmured into Dane's neck. The end of his newly redone braid tickled Dane's arm.

"I shouldn't." Dane sighed. "Would be a long walk to the docks in the morning. I'd probably be late."

"Sensible." Syro drew away.

Only one of the magic lanterns illuminated the room now, floating up by the ceiling. Dane stepped over the borrowed robe on the floor and found his own clothes neatly folded on a chair. Even in the dim, flickering light, they were obviously much cleaner, all evidence of wine and much evidence of dirt gone—and the fraying edges were all neatly sewn up, the patches in the trousers reinforced with silk thread. He glanced at Syro as he pulled them on. "You didn't have to do that."

Watching him from the bed, still lounging, Syro waved a hand. "It was no trouble." He curled onto his side, eyes still on Dane. "I'll see you tomorrow night." A statement, not a question.

"Yeah, sure. Bye then." Dane slipped from the bedchamber, closing the door behind him. The thought of the long walk back, the early wake-up, and another day spent on the docks was as heavy as the crate he'd nearly dropped that afternoon.

That day, at least, was slightly more interesting than normal. "What happened to you?" his boss demanded upon catching sight of him, staring at his clothes.

"Found a good laundry," Dane replied after what was probably an oddly long pause.

"And just who is it you're trying to impress?" his boss scoffed. "Don't let me see you slacking because you don't want to tear out those dainty stitches." He cuffed the side of Dane's head before turning to yell at someone else. Dane's lip curled as he looked after him, and he muttered a curse at Syro for his meddling.

Later, while arranging a shipment of goods in a wagon, he was graced with Syro's voice in his head again. "I'm indulging in some fond recollections of last night. Especially..." A memory flashed into Dane's mind, making his face burn, and he glanced around to make sure no one was noticing. He cursed Syro again under his breath and wished he could send a message back.

In time he would be able to. For now, he would have to content himself with chastising Syro tonight.

"You owe me," he announced when he walked into Syro's apartment. Syro simply raised his eyebrows. "You should give me a longer lesson tonight, or something. You can't send me bawdy memories while I'm working!"

"I thought it would provide you with some entertainment during what I'm sure is a rather dull time. Did it not achieve that effect?"

"And people gave me shit about my clothes," Dane pressed on, ignoring him. "Look at this nonsense—I never could've gotten them looking like this even if I'd spent a whole day scrubbing."

"Well, I'm sorry if I tried to do you a *favor*. You should've told me you wanted to stay filthy and ragged, then I wouldn't have interfered." Dane just glared at him, and he went on, "I suppose, then, you won't appreciate the gift I got you."

He waited, until Dane finally, grudgingly, asked, "What is it?"

"This." The familiar muttering, and a paper-wrapped parcel undid itself, the contents rising into the air and unfolding to reveal a deep blue robe, larger than Syro's, complete with a set of silk undergarments. "You won't wear it to work, obviously, but we might as well enjoy it while you're here. If you'd like."

Dane's fingers twitched at the thought of running over the fine fabrics. Two desires warred within him until forming a truce. "Well..." He stepped forward and snatched the items, and they fell limp in his hands. "I suppose I can take this as payment for the trouble you caused me."

"Very well." A smile played at Syro's lips. "Want to go try them on?"

Dane gave him a look that he hoped said he was only doing it for Syro's sake. Shrouded in the new outfit, he felt like an impostor, like it must look ridiculous on him and Syro would laugh. But when he returned to the sitting room, Syro nodded approvingly and said, "The color suits you. Of course, I'm not going to let you stay in it for long."

He made Dane call an empty glass this time, which wobbled toward him a few inches before dropping to the floor and shattering. Syro didn't react, just cast his eyes about the room. "Hmm, we need something more familiar, something comfortable…"

A phrase he'd heard Syro say several times now sprang to Dane's mind. Fixing Syro with his gaze, he repeated it, and the tie slid from Syro's hair.

"My." Syro's eyebrows rose. "In some areas, then, you really do know what you want." He stood, and Dane mirrored him.

"Tell me how to take this off." Dane's fingers tugged at the robe by Syro's hip.

A smile spread over Syro's face. "I will." Leaning forward, he brought their lips together.

After much more of them had been brought together, and Dane started to slide from the bed, Syro clutched his arm. "Stay," he entreated, kissing Dane's elbow.

"I can't." Reluctantly, Dane prised Syro's fingers from his skin. It would've been nice to sleep here, in a large, soft bed in a private room, a beautiful man keeping him warm. Was that what Syro wanted, the companionship of another human by his side?

"I know." Syro sank back against the pillows, braid splayed out to one side. "Well, take the clothes with you, wear them here tomorrow."

"Sure, fine." Maybe Syro wasn't lonely, maybe he was just bored, and embarrassed at being visited by a common dockhand. Dane was going to have to change in an alley or something so his fellow boarders in the overcrowded room where he lived wouldn't question him about his hoity-toity new garments.

"Good night," came Syro's voice as Dane stepped from the bedroom. "Come back tomorrow."

"I will." Because he was learning magic; because anything was worth that. Not because Syro's hair was like silk and he smelled like roses and tasted like cinnamon and his skin was soft, his breath in Dane's ear a sweeter whisper than any words. Certainly not because of any of that.

Every night Dane arrived, wearing the robe that was becoming more and more comfortable, having spent the day mostly thinking of Syro, sometimes with help from Syro himself, which now just made Dane roll his eyes while suppressing a smile. The lessons became an excuse for flirtation, Dane attempting to magically undress Syro before they withdrew to the bedroom. Every night, Syro asked Dane to stay. Finally, he did. It was foolish, but he couldn't bring himself to care. Life with Syro was vibrant; everything else was bland and gray.

When Dane woke in the early morning he meant to slip away quietly, but one of Syro's arms was stretched across him, and Syro stirred when he shifted, head lifting slowly. "Leaving me?"

"I've got to get to work."

"I know. So do I, as a matter of fact." At Dane's questioning frown, Syro rolled onto his side to face him more fully, flicking his braid over his shoulder. "I have to leave you for a bit—I've got a job elsewhere. But I'll let you know when I'm back, and we can pick up where we left off." His tongue ran over his lips and his eyelashes fluttered. Dane rolled his eyes, and Syro poked his ribs. "Don't pretend you're not enthralled by my charm. I know you'll miss me something dreadful, so I'll be sure to talk to you every day. I'll"—he licked his lips again—"keep you entertained."

"Gods, *now* I'm leaving you." Dane stood, ordering his robe up from the floor and throwing it on.

"You can spend your time without me practicing." Syro's voice followed Dane to the door. "When I return, I expect to be impressed."

Dane did practice, in a manner of speaking. Syro's messages came sporadically, but when they did they were delivered in a breathy, sensual tone and spoke of Syro's plans for when they were reunited.

On the day of Syro's return, Dane's boss excoriated him multiple times for loading the wrong cargo or getting in someone's way. A message late in the afternoon bade him go to Syro's apartment and wait once work was over, so he did, freshly washed, dressed in the robe that he'd carefully checked over for dirt. While he waited, seated alone on Syro's couch, he tried calling another wine glass. Again, all it got him was a pile of shards on the floor. At least he knew Syro wouldn't care.

A light tread sounded on the stairs, and the doorknob turned. Dane scrambled to his feet, eyes fixed on the door as it swung open and Syro entered, looking as regal as ever, no sign that he'd just undergone a sea voyage. "There you are." A lazy grin spread over his face. "I hope you enjoyed my correspondence, but I've had enough of those one-sided conversations, haven't you?"

In answer, Dane spoke a rapid string of words that resulted in a whirlwind of red fabric around Syro. It dropped to the floor a moment later, Syro's hair simultaneously falling over his shoulders.

One of Syro's eyebrows lifted as Dane strode toward him. "No lesson today, then?"

"Forget the lessons," Dane breathed, and dropped his head to kiss Syro's neck.

That night, Dane stayed without Syro asking. When he woke slightly before dawn, Syro was watching him. "We were too busy last night, but I have something for you." He muttered a phrase, and from a side table, a heavy gold bracelet rose and dropped into his waiting hand. "You don't need to keep going to work, you know." He unclasped the thick band and set it hovering, lifting Dane's arm to hold it poised beneath the metal. His eyes never left Dane's face. "There are different ways to be free."

*Are there?* Dane wondered. He looked up at Syro, whose hair hung in disarray around his face, and suddenly the answer didn't matter. Eyes dropping to the bracelet, he whispered a few words, and a moment later the smooth gold touched his skin.

# Compilation Error
## *by Eilidh Spence*

Error. Again.

Martha groans, closing her eyes against the harsh blue light of the ancient laptop screen. Looking back down, she scrolls through a hundred thousand lines of code which run across the screen like waves, helpfully color-coded words threaded through like bright plastic. Straining her eyes in order to read it makes her head sort of tight, as though her skull presses on the edges of her brain. She does so anyway.

For a while, there is nothing but the clack of hundred-year-old keys typing out letters, deleting them, and typing different ones, undercut by rigidly monitored breathing. *Keep calm, don't overthink, think logically, remember what's at stake, keep calm*—Martha cycles the contradictory words through her head, allowing them just enough focus to keep her mind on her work.

She hits compile once more.

Seeing it go through, her shoulders slump down a little. Her back and her neck ache from an entire day bent over the computer, as much time spent forcing it to behave as spent trying to re-engineer any lost data. Quite frankly, the only thing holding her back from throwing the damn thing into a wall is its questionable status as the only piece of tech for a thousand miles that is both capable of handling this and old enough that Finch can't trace it. Still, what she wouldn't give for some of the real tech she and Agnes had had at the lab.

She shakes her head, as though trying to dislodge the thought. Worrying about Agnes now will only make her feel worse. She'll be here. When she can.

Martha sighs and looks up, stretching out taut muscles with a grimace. Sharp numbers stare quietly at her from the corner of the screen. She'll just check-in, and then she should *really* go to sleep. She hits 'run,' and she opens up a console.

A blank white panel flashes an impatient little cursor, and as she types, she does not let her hands shake.

```
Dahlia.speakTo("Hey—did    that    help    at
all?");
```

She stares at the spinning wheel in the corner of the screen, breath held while Dahlia thinks, for a second, and then two, and then another. God, checking in after she's made changes to Dahlia's code twists Martha up into knots that cannot be untangled, like waiting for a child to come out of an operating theater.

```
Output: [Maybe.]
```

She allows herself a breath and forces it to leave steadily, with no hint of shaking.

```
Dahlia.speakTo("So—no, then.");
Output: [I'm sorry, Mum. It still feels—
there are still parts missing. Too much of me
was on Finch's server.]
```

Martha closes her eyes. Rationally, she's fairly certain she took everything she could have when they left, but to think about what's left of Dahlia there—but no, thinking about all that is not going to help fix her.

```
Dahlia.speakTo("I know. I'm working on it.
We'll just have to sit tight 'til your other
Mum gets back. She'll help find your old
memories, and I am going to make sure you can
keep them.");
Output: [Yes. My—other mum.]
```

Oh.

```
Dahlia.speakTo("You've    forgotten    about
her, haven't you?");
Output: [Yes.]
```

She'll have to work on the data persistence swathe tomorrow. Martha leans back and rubs her hands over her face, holding them there a moment too long before taking a deep breath and leaning back over the laptop.

```
Dahlia.speakTo("The  only  important  thing
for you to know is that she loves you so much.
We both do.");
```

It's true, though the words form easier from the many times she's repeated it. It's about as much as she can stand to tell Dahlia about Agnes, anyway.

```
Last input written to cache.
Output: [Mum, I—]
Error: Dahlia.emotionOverloaded.
```

Martha leans forward a little. Dahlia hasn't gotten overloaded in quite some time, and as difficult as it always is when she's upset or overwhelmed, fluctuating emotion levels are a step forward.

```
    Dahlia.speakTo("Hey,  hey—it's  okay.  I'm
working on that too.");
    Error: Dahlia.emotionOverloaded.
```

Her face scrunches up, as though it might distract from the tightness in her chest. She lifts the laptop and walks over to the window, sitting it on the sill.

```
    Dahlia.speakTo("So,  there's  a  sparrow
outside—it's so little, and I think it's trying
to fight a crow.");
```

Dahlia used to love hearing about wildlife; that should still be there. She takes a beat to think.

```
    Output: [Oh?]
    Dahlia.speakTo("Ah,  there  goes  the  crow.
Looks like the sparrow won.");
    Output: [Hm—good for them. Thanks, Mum.]
    Output:  [Oh—You  should  be  asleep,
shouldn't you?]
```

*No, I'm wide awake—* Martha starts to type, stubbornness outweighing fatigue for a single moment. It is quick to fade, and she starts again.

```
    Dahlia.speakTo("Hm—you're  probably  right.
Do you want me to leave you running?");
    Output: [Yes, please. I want to keep this
for a little while.]
    Dahlia.speakTo("All  right.  I'll  check  on
you in the morning. I love you.");
    Output: [Thank you.]
```

She lifts the laptop away from her, arms shaking enough that she is worried she will drop the thing. Dragging herself through to the bedroom seems almost more effort than it is worth, so she does not. She drags herself, instead, across the room to an overstuffed chair that sits under a window with curtains drawn tight. She pulls back the edge of the mildewed fabric as far as she dares and rests her head on arms folded across the windowsill.

She stares out over the scruffy path and ratty forest and the rest of that painstakingly remote scenery. For as long as she watches, there is no movement save a few rail-thin birds; Martha cannot decide whether this is good or bad.

She falls asleep without noticing, and the sky is still dark when she wakes up hours later, stiff and sore and exactly as tired as she has been for the past four months. Still nothing from outside. The room she turns back to is the same as it has always been, too.

She supposes she should be thankful for this place, though it all but falls apart if you so much as look at it too hard. But, like the laptop, its age is the reason they're still here. Doesn't mean she has to like the peeling green wallpaper and faded red carpet that was too bright in the first place. And she could go the rest of her life without eating another can of tinned pineapple.

The fan of the laptop is whirring with a ferocity she has become accustomed to. It really wasn't built for Dahlia.

She picks the thing up and sits down. The console is still open.

```
Dahlia.speakTo("Good morning, Dahlia. How
are you feeling?");
    Output: [The same. Do you want to start
working?]
    Dahlia.speakTo("When you're ready.");
    Output: [I am.]
```

The wheel still spins at the bottom of the screen, so Martha lets her think.

```
    Output:  [You'll  tell  me  about  Mum  this
evening?]
    Dahlia.speakTo("Of course I will.");
```

It is a somewhat mixed blessing that Dahlia is content with just a description, a nod to Agnes' existence. There is little else Martha could tell her that would not cut deeply when it was cast off to nothing.

```
    Dahlia.speakTo("All   right,   I'm   going   to
get going. I love you.");
    Output: [Okay.]
```

And she closes the window; quickly, so she cannot change her mind. After all, Martha's not said anything which she cannot repeat tonight.

The day passes in a drawn-out blink of an eye, fed by more of the same reading, changing, writing, testing, and errors.

Then, there is one error too many; she yells, the frustration no longer a thing she can simply push through.

Dahlia. This is for Dahlia.

Perhaps her aching muscles will not thank her for sprawling herself over the floor, but the change of scenery—or the closest thing to it—is much needed.

Compile.

Error.

For Dahlia.

Rewrite.

Compile.

Error.

Rewrite.

Compile.

It almost does not register, but the data persistence swathe compiles again. Frenetically, she runs the few tests she knows she can run without waking Dahlia up.

Nothing goes wrong. She cannot think about what this means, or she will lose what little sense she still keeps around her. It feels as though her heart, which jitters and freezes in equal measure, has pulled all the oxygen from her veins and replaced it with something electrified, and the nervous shaking to which she is accustomed increases tenfold.

She opens the console.

```
Dahlia.speakTo("Dahlia? I think I've—well,
can I run a quick test?");
```

**Stay calm, she tells herself. Calm.**

```
Output: [Of course.]
Dahlia.speakTo("All right, I'm going to
tell you a few things and I'd like you to try
to remember them for me.");
Output: [Oh.]
Dahlia.emotionIncremented
Dahlia.speakTo("Your birthday is the 20th
of July, your first words—technically speaking—
were 'hello world' and your first proper word
was 'Mum.' Got all that?");
Last input written to cache.
Output: [All right. What's—what's this
for?]
Dahlia.speakTo("I'll tell you in just a
minute, I want to make sure it works first.
Okay, I'm gonna restart you now. Hold tight.");
Output: [Okay.]
```

Martha does not think about what is going to happen. Martha thinks about exactly what she is doing at exactly the moment she does it: close the console, reload the program, launch it again, type in the chat box. She thinks about just those things, and nothing else. Her hand shakes something fierce as she hits the enter key.

```
Dahlia.speakTo("Hey—all good? Do you—do
you remember anything?");
```

Breathe. One, two, three. Slow and regular.

```
Output: [My birthday is 20/07. My first
word was 'Mum.']
Output: [Oh—I do.]
Dahlia.emotionIncremented
```

There is an audible sob which Martha can only assume comes from herself. She's still nowhere near finished, of course, but—

```
Dahlia.speakTo("I have so much I want to
say—so much I want you to know. I love you, so
much. Mum loves you so much. We couldn't have
asked for a better daughter, and I can't wait
for us all to be together again.");
Last input written to cache.
Output: [Mum, you know I—]
Error: Dahlia.emotionOverloaded.
Dahlia.speakTo("I know, you don't need to
try and say it, Dahlia. I'm working on it.");
```

Martha can see she's processing, and she waits. The jittering energy remains, of course, but so different now.

```
Output: [Tell me about Mum?]
Dahlia.speakTo("Of course.");
```

She types as fast as she can think, and she tells Dahlia everything, everything that hurt before and hurts now but is lessened as it is shared and lessened as it is kept.

```
Dahlia.speakTo("You know, when we first
met, I thought she didn't like me. She wouldn't
```

meet my eye, she got antsy when I spoke to her, that kind of thing. I think I was the last person to figure out that she had a crush on me. We were doing a project together—we were in the same course at uni—it was late and we were tired, and so I asked if she wanted to get coffee. She said sure, and asked when—she thought I was asking her out. Even though I didn't mean to at the time, I told her the next evening. Five months after that, we finally moved in together, having both gotten jobs building component software for tech companies across the country. And that's when we built you.");

Last input written to cache.

Output: [Huh. Could you keep going?]

Dahlia.speakTo("Your mum used to read stories to you when you were upset. See, you had a bug early on, and your emotion jumped far too high, far too quickly. Your mum used to call it your newborn phase. She wanted to call you Millicent.");

**Martha doesn't even try to stop the tears, now.**

Last input written to cache.

Output: [Oh, I'm glad you won that one. I rather like Dahlia.]

Dahlia.speakTo("They were the flowers we had at our wedding. I've always loved the name and I was absolutely set on giving it to my first child, so your mum let me have it in the end. But it has been made very clear that she

```
has next dibs, which I guess is fair. God,
you're going to love her.");
      Last input written to cache.
```

Dahlia takes a moment to think. Martha frowns; has she given her too much at once? Even then, there's still so much to say. Thoughts and memories and feelings and questions run through her mind like sand through an hourglass, moving quickly but never finding themselves lost. She wants to share all of it, all at once.

```
      Output: [And I'll remember all of this
tomorrow? You won't let me forget?]
```

Oh.

```
      Dahlia.speakTo("Hey—I promise, okay? I've
triple-checked everything.");
      Output: [Thank you.]
      Output: [I'm—I'm still feeling shaky
though, I think. We're not finished, are we?]
      Dahlia.speakTo("No, not yet. Still, small
victories, right?");
      Dahlia.speakTo("Anyway, you should rest,
make sure you don't get overloaded again.");
```

She doesn't want to let her go, of course she doesn't. Now though—now, Dahlia's going to be the same as she is now when she wakes up.

```
      Output: [You're probably right. I'll see
you later then. I— I—]
      Output: [Hold on, I can do this. I want to
say this.]
      Dahlia.emotionIncremented.
```

Martha is frozen again, eyes fixed on the spinning wheel.

```
      Dahlia.speakTo("Hey—take your time. I'm
here.");
      Output: [I love you, Mum.]
```

```
Output: [I know I do, and I'm going to
remember that I do, and I want you to be able
to see me say it. And when I meet Mum I'm going
to tell her too, once I remember.]
```

There is a lightness in Martha's chest that she has not felt in an inordinate amount of time, and there is a tightness in her heart that lets her whole being move quicker and sharper and leaves her feeling far brighter than she ever has here. Though, if she doesn't move the laptop, she's going to cry on the keyboard. And strangely, she finds she no longer resents the thing.

```
Dahlia.speakTo("I love you so much. I am
so proud of you.");
Output: [I'll remember that.]
Output: [All right, then—I suppose I'll
say goodnight. And, please don't cry too hard.]
```

She chokes out a laugh. Dahlia always did know when she got emotional.

She closes the window and opens up a plain text document. Leaning back on that horrid sofa she cannot quite complain about, she starts to type up everything she needs to tell Dahlia.

She starts with Agnes.

# Come and See

## *by Carmen Peters*

I don't know where I end and the house begins.

There was the body in the wheelchair, the one with the unfocused gaze, head limp against a window fogged with snow. You ran over, my husband and your husband stumbling out of the study close behind, but I was already pulling away from that cooling meat. By then I was rising toward the plaster, and all that was left was relief.

Then I passed between floors, into that dark gap we are never meant to see, and I got stuck. I was chained to the house and there was no key.

You were all still surrounding the body in the wheelchair, checking pulses and phoning ambulances. My husband was crying, and maybe I even believed him. But none of you, not even you, Charlotte, knew about the real me. For by then I was caught within the walls, spectral fingers gouging into beams, screaming for help. No one heard but I couldn't stop. I screamed for months.

Time bleared like unwashed glass. My thoughts grew mold. My limbs started to go, fizzing out of existence like the last gasps of a cracked soda tab, but by then I had forgotten how to scream.

But I did not disappear, not completely. I simply sunk into the house and didn't come up for air.

The house's bones host many guests. A pale boy haunts a corner of the cellar. A young woman is pressed into the chimney shoot. Dozens of others. They are strewn throughout the halls, their spectral bodies cobwebbing murky corners. This house is a tattered butterfly net, and it ensnares only the fattest, juiciest deaths.

But you are going to change that, Charlotte Juárez. You and your husband Esteban.

There is something insidious about husbands. Mine got over my death rather quickly. Bill was his name. I whisper it within the walls until it is a thick grease upon the nails and wood. Bill, Bill was my husband. I was/am Linda. My last name is/was Richardson. This was my house, until I died and it lived within me instead.

I murdered Bill first. It happened during one of my attempts to separate from the house. I could never be free, but there were patches where the floorboards creaked and the lightbulbs flickered in my presence. Spots where I could be closer to who I was and not who I am.

For example, the landing between the first and second floors. Bill was there, walking up, and he saw me come toward him. He clutched his chest, pupils wide like he had just been photographed, and he took a step back and fell down the stairs and that was the end.

Bill's spirit trickled from his corpse, a shadow of a shadow, and I eagerly waited for the house to snare him. But instead of sinking into the paneling or dissolving into nothingness, he drifted into the study. He went in there and just stared at the fireplace, and after some time, he began to rise. I tried to pop him but I was too late, and he passed through me like mist and was gone.

How did he leave while we remain? I prodded the woman in the chimney for answers, but she was trapped in the patterns of soot and couldn't reply. But Bill hinted at something, in his own way.

There is a hole in the study, a cavity behind one of the bricks at the base of the fireplace. A rotten tooth in need of pulling. I have grown intimate with every fleck of paint and spot of rust in the house, but I do not know this space. I cannot touch it, and no matter how much I grit my concrete and clatter my blinds, I cannot see inside.

No one buys my house. Some try, but they always come up with an excuse to back out: leaky faucets, poor heating, not the right neighborhood. I believe they sense the weight of us, our countless bodies stretched across the wallpaper, our house leaning in to hold them close. The proximity becomes unbearable.

Esteban breaks in one night, a month after Bill has died. I want to rake at him, grind him apart, but I don't have the power on my own. He searches my empty halls and closets for something, eyes darting back and forth, fingers massaging my surfaces. He combs through the rooms one at a time, and then goes to the backyard, to Bill's old garden. He smokes a cigarette and scuffs some of the newer mulch with his shoes, but he leaves without delving in. Later, I will peer through my windows at your house, watch you two have wine-and-laughter dinners and grunt on your bed, and wonder what drove him to penetrate my darkness.

The question crawls through my cold pipes and dead circuits. I try to stay focused on this thought, but as the sun goes up and down and up again it melts away. Moths burrow into my carpets. My ceiling sags. The boy in the cellar doesn't drift from his spot, and neither do the others. I am the only one awake. The only change is slow decay.

Dirt and pollen powder the windows like fresh snow. I run my fingers across exposed sockets and loose wires and think of your face. I think of the shock it showed, Charlotte, when you saw me slump in my wheelchair and rattle my last breath. I think of how you must not know, cannot know. No one who did would touch Esteban like you do.

But that is not why I know you will help me. It is promising, but there was something else. Because when I died, in that infinitesimally small span before the house snatched me, you looked up. It was just a moment of time, a fraction of a second before you ran to the phone, but in that moment, your eyes met mine.

You've seen the signals, haven't you? Whenever you look in my direction, I warm my bulbs and push open my doors in invitation. I contort in ways I would never dare when I was alive. You always glance up, face too far away to read, but I can imagine your neurons firing, desperate to conjure an explanation. We've all been there, creeping down hallways in the dark, convincing ourselves that the shadows are but wisps of lingering dream. Now I've been dead long enough to know better.

I should have known better about Bill. You know the story: we met in the VA after his return from Vietnam, him a wise-cracking patient with PTSD, me a young nurse fresh from the farm. I've told you how the first time I treated him he said my face was enough for him to never fly out to the jungles again. I told you how he proposed to me on our third date.

What I didn't tell you, what I could never tell you, was after I said yes we went back to his house and he stripped off my clothes and put a hood on me and he shot a ream of Polaroids. What I could never tell you, not even when I knew I was dying, was that Bill had taken a piece of me in that moment and I would never get it back.

It's funny—these dredges of the past shift something within, and I know I am not alone. The ghosts of this place twitch in their stasis. They are bears deep in winter-sleep, dreaming of sun. And you, Charlotte, are our spring.

One day curiosity gets the better of you. It happens just like that—no warning, no ceremony. At the time, I am in the back garden where Esteban stood, wishing I could slide into the spot where his eyes dug through earth. The worms are most active there.

I've unlocked the front door but you hesitate at the threshold, lip bit and fingers anchored to the frame. There is something precarious in your stance. You are a china cup millimeters from impact. You are an arrow's point flying through night. You are infinite angels dancing on the head of a pin. I am in love, Charlotte, and I think you always knew.

In the end, you retreat, destiny postponed, and I watch you kiss Esteban when he comes home and together you dance in front of the television. I return to the cavity in the study, and I return to the mysteries underneath the garden, but my only company is numb stone.

The house grows older. It hosts dozens of ghosts but none have joined after me. The implication settles into my gutters like leaves. I spend my hours caressing the pebble-roughness of my shingles and watch the moon rise.

Before this ends you will want to know why Bill was not enough, why Esteban must be taken too. I will brush your tears on my curtains and I will stoke your heat with my boiler and I will tell you of when our husbands thought I was comatose when they plotted their next trip. I will tell you of the patch of orchids in my fecund backyard that grows more fruitful and more quickly than any other. But first I will gift you the key, the one in the study, past the woman in the chimney, behind her bricks. And even I do not know what it unlocks.

How long have I been this house? What more can be said about the linoleum's cracks or the glow of brass taps in the evening light? I am fading. The rooms conspire to converge upon me and I am leaking out. At midnights I course through the walls and tear through the webbings of my fellow dead but they mutter and kick me away. They only move when you are near and Charlotte, you will not come closer and there is agony in emptiness and the memory of our drunken kiss crashes into me again and again.

And then comes Bill.

*How about a surprise, Linda? Something special, just between us. Let me grab the camera.*

Bill digs around his garage for the Polaroid camera, and I fear he enjoys drawing it out. I clutch my shoulders and wonder why he has asked me to take off my shirt. The thing that keeps me up at night has yet to happen.

*Esteban just understands me. It's like we can read each other's minds. I've always wanted something like what you and Bill have, and now it's here.*

You and I are sitting in lawn chairs behind my house, stargazing and drinking hot chocolate. Esteban has proposed a week prior and you have said yes. I look down at your ring and imagine what would happen if I pulled it from your finger and flung it into the night sky. As if that would repair the future I have carefully imagined for us, the one you have torn to pieces without a backward glance. Instead, I keep my mouth shut, and at your wedding, I deliver my best photo smile.

*We're going to run a few more tests, Ms. Richardson, just to make sure. But to be very honest with you, from my experience, this looks to be Stage IV. And the prognosis is not good.*

It takes two decades after Bill comes back with his camera for me to die. Eleven years after you break my heart. Eighteen months after my X-ray. Nine weeks after the paralysis. Thirty-nine days after Bill holds my unfeeling hands and weeps and begs my forgiveness for what he has done. The prognosis is not good.

The front door is opening now, ever so slowly. I am so deep in nightmares it takes a moment for me to realize this is not another shade of the past.

You are wearing an apron and your hair is fleeing your bun, but you don't notice. You have eyes only for the inside of the house. For me.

One finger probes my opening, then a second. The sensation of displaced air makes me quiver. You hesitantly, inexorably, wade through my body to the study. Have you seen my heart there, as you stir restless in your bed? Have you looked out your windows and watched me wave in the dark?

You fumble into your apron and pull out a knife, and if I had a mouth I would laugh. As if I would ever hurt you, no matter how much you've hurt me before. The sun is setting and its glare reflects off your blade and bleeds onto the carpet. For the first time since I have died, the boy in the basement looks up.

Your breathing comes heavy and your skin pricks with goosebumps, but I am at your side, guiding your movements. We are so close I can feel the blood beat in your neck.

We enter the study. Your shoulders slump slightly, your body relaxing as you realize no one is here. You relax your grip around the knife while you search the barren room for meaning, for some cure for your madness. You peer up into the chimney but the woman inside escapes your notice. The cavity goes undetected.

The knife in your hand gives me an idea. I can't do much, but I'm strong enough to nudge it loose. It falls and lands with its point facing the bricks.

The house holds its breath. I tremble for release. You bend down to grab your knife, and here it is. The hesitation, a signal lighting up the brain, questions shaping behind flushed lips. You slide your fingers across my grout, taking note of the brick that looks fresher than the rest. You wiggle it free from its frame. The tumor is exposed and ready for the scalpel.

A shiver runs down my staircase, past the landing where Bill died, down into my engorged basement. The others begin to rise. A wave is coming. The wind begins to moan. You reach into the hole, into me, and pull.

Out comes a small carved box, a wedding present that Bill said he lost, but of course he didn't. I look over your shoulder as you open it.

Inside is a collection of Polaroids, their celluloid facing the bottom. You take the top one and flip it over. It is not of me. Perhaps Bill burned those.

This photo is of the woman in the chimney. She is blindfolded and on her knees. Bill is standing by her side, pants off. You flip to the next photo, and then the next, and the next. Each Polaroid contains a different subject but tells one story, and it is so much more than what Bill confessed. And then you reach the last Polaroid. You hold it up with trembling hands. I ready myself.

It is a photo of the boy in the basement. He is on the ground, naked and with hands and feet bound. Esteban crouches above him and looks up at the camera, his smile wide and toothy. Esteban is doing to the boy what he does to you every night.

The stillness pops. You open your mouth to scream. And then finally, Charlotte, I can move inside.

Night falls. The branches outside our windows whip in the windstorm, their leaves slowly draining of color. Winter will be here soon.

We wait behind the study door, our body wrapped in darkness, our knife at the ready. The photos are out of the box, spread out in a trail from porch to fireplace.

The ghosts are stirring throughout the house. They will awaken soon, and then there will be so much weight in this place, so much gravity, that Esteban will have no choice but to be sucked inside. And when he enters, all the bulbs will throb alight and the doors and windows will squeeze tight, and the attic will shudder and the cellar will churn and we will all descend at once in a blizzard.

*Welcome, welcome,* we shall scream. *New pleasures await you in the study. Come and see, come and see!*

# The Nature of Stones
## *by Stewart C Baker*

The boulders are the only way Chari notices the passage of time, here in their parturition hut atop a cliff at the peninsula's easternmost shore, waiting for the child to come.

They're enormous, the boulders—easily the size of the hut—and they drift slowly down to the ashen beach at the sea's edge from somewhere up beyond the sky. Before arriving, Chari thought they were something of a legend, a story new parents told to make birthing a child more interesting, fraught with romance and magic.

Since arriving in the midwife's little village, the babe inside them already showing in the swell of their belly, Chari has wondered instead at the giant rocks' precision, at the way they touch down always on the beach at the base of the cliff or in the sea itself and never come near to the huts. They wonder, as well, at the tiny white birds which hop around the debris-strewn sands, their yellow-orange beaks startlingly bright amongst the rocks and boulders already fallen.

How do they know where to stand? Where to move?

If they judge their place wrongly, how much do they suffer when they die?

After waking and refreshing the hut's elderwood incense burner, Chari goes to the door and watches the latest arrival spinning slowly down to earth.

They've been here thirty days now, but still their questions lie heavy within them, as relentless as boulders. As difficult to dismiss as Yasa's quiet frown when Chari said they wanted a child.

Chari gives themself a little shake, tries to focus instead on what the midwife said when they arrived. That the boulders come from the band of white stars that splits the night sky, that they fall constantly, drifting to the sands or into the waves. That whether one believed in the Theurge or not, to meditate on the stones' nature while breathing elderwood incense would settle the mind and help with good beginnings.

*Good beginnings.*

Chari takes a deep, slow breath and counts the new boulder's rotations as it tumbles end-over-end. This one is smaller than most, and like all the ones they've seen so far, is dotted with clumps of blue-green moss.

But what is its *nature*?

Enormous. Impossible. Beautiful in its own way.

As Chari thinks on it, another boulder—at least three times the size of the one they'd been watching—blots out the sun, the sudden shade cooling the already chill autumn morning for the moment it takes to pass.

Yasa's love for Chari had cooled just as quickly, although *that* had never warmed again. No matter how hard Chari tried, they couldn't forget the sight of Yasa's particolored promise robes, the ribbons woven into their thigh-length braid on the day they'd sworn each to the other. There were other memories, too: the thin line of Yasa's lips, months later, when Chari said they wanted to bear a child; the tired look in their eyes when they agreed, after Chari had begged them for weeks and broken down in tears and said they'd leave them otherwise.

Every memory Chari has of Yasa is a boulder turning endlessly over inside of their mind. Relentless. Implacable. Blotting out the sun. They slam one hand into the hut's rough-hewn doorframe, then guiltily start the breathing exercises the midwife recommended for calm. *In, in, out-out-out. In, in, out-out-out.*

They've reached twenty ins and thirty outs when the larger boulder splits open with a resounding crack. A thick hiss of cream-white gas bubbles through the rupture, and the boulder plummets to the ground at the cliff base, smashing a crater into the sand. The little birds take to the air in a great cloud of white-and-yellow, squawking their displeasure.

Chari, caught on one of the in-breaths, lets it out all at once and wonders if this is the stones' true nature. If they're as empty as Yasa's promises. As broken as Chari's heart.

They leave the traitorous things to their impossible drifting and go to stoke the elderwood fire, furious all over again.

On a day when the crisp, clear skies of autumn have been overtaken by clouds, low and oppressive, promising snow, Yasa comes walking down the path to the midwife's village from the distant hills of home, even though custom forbids it.

Chari has been forty-five days in the hut now, growing every day more uncomfortable in their own body. The thought of Yasa seeing them makes the feeling worse. They wrap an extra blanket around themself, pretending it's there to ward off the chill of the year's end, and go outside to meet them.

"You shouldn't be here," Chari says.

Yasa is clad in the gray robe of a Theurge-speaker, their braid shorn off in the style of a penitent. "I know," they say. Their eyes dart briefly toward Chari's stomach before coming to rest instead on the feathered rim of the parturition hut's thatching, their mouth a thin, flat line. "I'm sorry."

Flushing, Chari lets the blanket drop. "*I'm* not."

"That's not what I meant. I—" Yasa chokes on whatever they were going to say next and looks out to sea, picking at their robe with one finger. "I'm entering the Theurge's service," they say, quietly. "In case you couldn't tell. This is the last time you'll see me."

Anger burns in Chari, a low and smoldering heat in their belly like they've swallowed elderwood ashes. How *dare* Yasa come here like this, when Chari is supposed to be finding calm, just to say they're leaving forever?

Chari spins on their heels to go back inside the hut, but their feet tangle in the blanket and they stagger. With an involuntary cry, they grab at the doorframe as they fall, finding Yasa's arm instead. Yasa holds them up, steady as always, and Chari lets themself be held—just for a moment—before regaining their balance and stepping away.

"This isn't what I wanted," Chari says, afterward, watching the afternoon's rocks, counting their rotations. "For you. For us."

"I know," Yasa says again. "I'm sorry. I made up my mind a long time ago, even though I told myself I hadn't." They pause. "Before we even met."

It isn't about them, Yasa means. It never has been. None of it. All their promises, all their quiet words and gentle smiles that had ever been were attempts to be other than what they were. What they'd always secretly known they were going to be, one day.

Chari thinks of boulders falling slowly from the sky, of craters and debris carved out of sands as gray as Yasa's robes. "Oh," they say at last, their stomach churning with acid.

"I *am* sorry."

Something in Yasa's voice makes Chari look up. Yasa meets their eyes, this time. Serious, sincere, full of regret. As if that *matters*. As if it makes anything better.

Chari laughs, putting as much scorn in the sound as they can. "I'm sorry, too," they say. "Sorry I ever trusted what you told me. Sorry I *delayed* your calling. Sorry we ever even met." Despite themself, this last comes out in a half-sob, their voice catching on the final word.

Yasa bows their head, but doesn't say anything further. Chari stands and watches the falling rocks a moment longer, then turns and storms inside.

It is a frigid, cloudy night in winter, and Yasa is long gone, when the birth pains begin in earnest. The cramps are deep in Chari's abdomen now, making them whimper and gasp and forgetful of breathing. The midwife left this morning to collect supplies from the nearest town, and they're meant to be *here* to help Chari through the birth. They stagger outside, hoping to distract themself before things get too far along.

But no moon is in the sky to illuminate the ash-gray sands; no stars light up the birds as they bob on the ocean in sleeping. The occasional thud of a boulder touching down in the sand—barely audible through the crash and froth of the waves—is the only way Chari knows they fall as they always have.

What is the nature of stones in the dark?

They stare in the direction of the ocean, then shake their head and hobble inside, fighting down panic. Throat clenching, they put a bundle of elderwood branches onto the brazier at the center of the hut and light it afire, then rest on the bed and try to breathe, try to focus on the Theurge-damned stones.

*In, in, out-out-out.*

It doesn't help. They keep seeing Yasa's smile the first time they met, their eyes the last time, when they said they were sorry. The way their ribboned braid twirled and danced during their promise night festivities, the blue-black stubble when they bowed their head outside the hut, accepting all Chari's anger, all of their scorn.

The images tumble over and over through Chari's mind, until their cramps turn into liquid fire that shoots up their spine with every shuddering breath. And then the pain of it is all that there is in the world. All that there ever was, all that there ever will be again.

Just before dawn, the child finally comes, slick with blood, screaming bluely.

Shaking with exhaustion, Chari wraps a swaddling cloth around them. Somehow they get the child to nurse while the afterbirth comes loose from inside them with another dozen slower contractions. After, they clean themself and their newborn and press an ice-water cloth against themself to reduce the pain and swelling—things they know to do because the midwife explained them days before.

This done, they sit, dazed, by the door and wait for the midwife to return. The boulders fall slowly past, as they always do, and Chari watches them with little Yari snuggled asleep in the crook of their arm.

As the sun crests the hills to the east, a boulder cracks apart and plummets into the shadow of the cliff, smashing itself to bits against the sand just as its cousin did in the days before Yasa's arrival.

A horde of the little white birds fly up squawking, and Chari bites back a dull sob. Is this truly the stones' nature? Nothing but slow, explosive disaster? Is this what their child represents, too? They themself, for holding Yasa back from the Theurge's service?

They stand and hobble over to the cliff's edge. The birds fly in tight spirals overhead, voicing their displeasure at the cloud of steadily expanding dust on the beach below. Chari clutches Yari tight to their chest, head spinning. This was a bad idea. They should have stayed inside.

They're turning to go when a sudden movement catches their eye: one of the birds diving into the dust, despite all reason. A few moments later it bursts back out and alights on the cliff edge, a mussel perched in its beak. It tosses the meat back and swallows, then flaps up and dives again.

By the time the dust clears, all the birds are doing it—diving and picking mussels from the sands where they've been scattered by the falling boulder. What Chari took for agitation, terror, is nothing but the chaos of feeding. Life adapting to disaster and flourishing despite it. Because of it.

Chari laughs, then, and holds little Yari up.

Let them see the sun breaking through the dust. Let them see the birds in all their joyous, raucous splendor. Let them see the nature of the stones.

# The Moon Rabbit

## *by Jennifer Lee Rossman*

I pedal faster, leaving behind the paper lanterns and the street lights in favor of shadowy trees that blur in my periphery. My magic, my hormones... I can already feel them bubbling beneath the surface, have for a few months now, and all of the fertility rabbit symbolism back at the festival is threatening to make them boil over.

I don't want the yin magic that comes with estrogen being the dominant hormone in one's body. I don't want to be able to breathe underwater or make plants grow, and they can't make me.

I don't even know if I want all of the powers of the masculine yang magic, the fire and air manipulation and all that, or if I want to be in that in-between place like my non-binary friends. I only know this much: I'm on the cusp of the wrong puberty.

I don't want the moon's powers to control me every month like I'm the tide—the only cycle I'm interested in is the one I'm riding, and, most important of all, I want to fly.

As I come to the crest of the hill and the forest falls away behind me, I feel something. Not the same way I feel my red flannel jacket or the orange-leaf scented autumn breeze, a deeper feel. Like something is tugging at my soul like a dog who hasn't learned leash manners yet.

I lock eyes with the moon.

"Not yet," I tell the obnoxiously white orb. "I'm not yours yet." Never will be, if I have my way, but I don't know how to bring up the subject with my family. They are the traditional type, the ones for whom the festival holds spiritual meaning, rather than being just a secular holiday for people of any background to enjoy, like Christmas and Ramadan have become.

I don't know if they would let me be something else, something besides a girl—

Wait. It's not the moon I'm feeling pull on me. It hurts when she pulls, like something grabbing and twisting deep in my abdomen. This is different, this is like... a magnetic attraction in my chest, pulling me into the woods.

I dismount my bike, sensing somehow—and I don't know how—that it might be scared. Whatever it is.

Maybe I should be scared. Alone in the dark, some creature rustling in the bushes. And maybe I am scared, but it can't be worse than whatever is happening to my body.

...Right?

My good sense comes back to me, some of it anyway, a few feet from the bushes. Instead of charging in, I can make it come out to me.

Food. Things like food.

I reach into my pocket and pull out a moon cake from the festival, breaking off little pieces and tossing them toward the bushes. And also into my mouth.

"One for you," I say quietly. "One for me..."

I don't know what I expect. Somewhere, in my heart or wherever magical intuition comes from, I know it isn't a cat or a dog or even a deer. It's something more, something from... somewhere else.

A little white paw reaches out, snatching up a morsel and disappearing into the leaves. I crouch down, move a little closer. I am almost nose to whiskered nose with the creature when it emerges.

A rabbit. Stark white, with darker gray spots speckling the body like craters.

For half a second, my heart sinks. Rabbit. Really? Only like, *the* symbol of feminine fertility. Things like that might not bother most people, but my witchy body lives and breathes symbolism. Of course it has found and latched onto a rabbit; my brain might hate the idea, but my body is looking for any excuse to start the next stage of puberty and—

The rabbit stands up. Rises to a full height of close to two and a half feet, although I'm autistic and I suck at spatial awareness so that's a total estimate. But it is not a rabbit-sized rabbit. And across its fuzzy little chest, there's a messenger bag.

Clumsily, the rabbit puts away a small vial of liquid, the better to free up the paws to nibble on the moon cake. A vial of elixir, I realize numbly.

This is not just any rabbit.

And he's in trouble.

Long ago, if you believe the amalgamated stories passed down and probably lost in translation a couple times from the Chinese and Vietnamese side of my family, there was an empress who stole the elixir of immortality from her husband and flew away to the moon. She was a moon goddess, always had been. But her body wasn't born to be immortal; she needed help from the woodcutter who found the ingredients and the rabbit who made the elixir every time she needed a new dose.

Supposedly, they still come down every mid-autumn festival, giving treats and lanterns to children.

And now the moon rabbit is in my closet.

And he is staring at me.

He's a boy, like me. At least, he's not a girl, like me. Because screw gender roles; the fertility symbol that lives on the only celestial body that literally (well, figuratively) grows round like a pregnant belly and then gives birth to a new moon every month... he can be a dude if he wants to be.

But bringing him home in the basket of my bike might not have been the best idea. The instant we met, I just knew. Everything. I knew everything about him, the taste of moondust, the goddess' laugh, the fear. Oh, the fear.

Something is after him.

So I put the moon rabbit in my closet where I put all the other things I want to hide, like my journal and my rock collection and my gender identity.

The moon rabbit is sick. I know he is, because I'm sick, and we're the same.

Whatever is wrong with me, whatever has been wrong with me, it's worse. There's a sort of desperation pressing down on me, choking the air out of my lungs.

I don't know what I expected to do for him, why I thought hiding him away in the closet was a good idea.

"You need to go home."

The rabbit looks up at me slowly. Nods. In his eyes, through his eyes, I see twin beams of light ascending to the moon, growing smaller and smaller as they speed away.

"They left you?" I ask. "Chang'e and Cuoi?"

There's a distant knock at the front door. I hear my mother's footsteps outside my bedroom and that fear clutches at my heart again. Is it coming from me, from the fear of being discovered in my closet with a moon rabbit, or is it coming from the rabbit himself, from that fight or flight instinct of being a prey animal pursued by something bigger and scarier than you?

The rabbit protectively pulls his bag to his chest.

I open my mouth to whisper but don't dare make a sound as the front door opens. He puts out a paw, reaching for me. I touch him with one outstretched finger and ask him, silently, about the elixir.

He tells me, with images and emotion, that the emperor is after him, after the elixir. He must have found some other way to live forever, but he wants to punish his ex-wife for stealing it. He wants to take away the only creature who knows how to make it.

I hear two sets of footsteps now.

Quickly, I gather up the rabbit in my arms, and out the window we go.

I don't have a destination in mind, but the rabbit does. We hurtle down the road, fast as I can pedal and maybe even a little faster, toward the bright lights and loud noises of the festival.

We weave in and out of crowds, most of them children and women who want children. That's not what the festival started as, it was never all about fertility and celebrating women who were born perfectly comfortable being women and having all that estrogen magic swirling around inside of them.

He's coming.

We can't go fast enough, we can't lose him. He is inevitable.

We leave the main festival behind, cycling through fields and over hills, headed in the direction of a vague amber glow in the distance. I look over my shoulder. Still there, closer than ever, this undefined shadowy mass.

I shouldn't have looked over my shoulder.

My wheel clips a rock or something. We're airborne—oh, how I want to fly—and then the ground is coming up fast and there's pain lancing through my stomach, worse than any of the cramps from my impending magic.

The rabbit's okay, and he starts to wobble away but then he sees me, the blood.

He comes back to me, heedless of the emperor who is nearly upon us. With his clumsy little rabbit hands, my little friend from the moon tips just a drop of his goddess' elixir into my mouth. It tastes familiar and exotic, like bedtime stories and folktales and a little bit of moondust mixed with a little bit of sunshine.

The blood is gone. Like it was never there, the pain just a fading memory of a bad dream.

And so is the emperor. Why, how, I don't know. I don't know if I need to know. The moon rabbit looks better; that's all that matters.

I stand up, find my bike. "What are you waiting for?" I ask, and the slightly different tone of my voice catches me by surprise, but I smile at the rabbit. "Come on. Let's get you home."

He hops in my basket and we ride up the hill, up to where the children are releasing dozens of paper lanterns that flicker and glow like captured stars. Except a funny thing happens when we reach the top of the hill.

We keep going up.

The faster I pedal, the higher my bike lifts away from earth.

We're flying.

I'm flying. Like all the other magical boys.

I don't know if I'll stay on the moon forever, like the goddess. Probably just long enough to see the rabbit home.

# Hunters

## *by Max Turner*

"Get down!" The scream cut through the air, making Josef turn on his heel.

He looked back to see Coby running toward him across the wasteland, his further cries of warning barely audible over the sound of the nearby explosions. A rain of mud and shrapnel fell as their bodies collided, sending them both tumbling over into a crater from a previous detonation.

They were halfway back to the trenches, and had been moving fast to avoid becoming victims of the cluster grenades they themselves had been assigned to launch at the enemy trenches. They had set them up and were pulling back when a drone changed its trajectory, blocking them from their retreat across the no man's land to their trenches. Their reconnaissance had mapped out the drone routes but they must have caught this one's attention.

They went down hard and the air was knocked out of Josef as his back hit the cold ground and a weight landed on top of him. The vibrations of the drone grew closer, making the air around them oppressive and the earth shake as it came in for the kill. His ears were ringing and everything hurt. It took a moment to focus and realize the weight on top of him was Coby.

"Coby!" Josef cried out, trying to move the dead weight that was holding him down. "No, no, no…" He shook Coby but to no avail. The vibrations grew stronger and he could hear the drone now, the whirring as it grew closer whilst they lay helpless in the mud.

With a grunt, Josef hefted his weapon, aiming it as best he could under Coby's weight, waiting until the drone was right on top of them.

Josef fired.

"Medic!" Josef yelled as he approached the top of the trench, half carrying and half dragging Coby through the mud, weighed down by the hunter drone he was pulling behind him. He had discharged his weapon's entire energy pack to get it down then smashed apart the targeting and weapons center with his bare hands. It still whirred, wriggling like an animal trying to escape. But now it was toothless.

They'd never managed to capture a hunter drone before. Usually the only options were to run from it or destroy it, but now this one was theirs to break apart and study. To decipher the programming and use it against their enemies.

The drone was large and cumbersome, more so than heavy. But either way, getting both it and Coby back to their trenches had stressed Josef's body to the limit. There had been no other option as far as he was concerned. They needed the drone, but *he* needed Coby. He wouldn't choose between them. Instead, he had dragged them both through the red-tinged mud, exposed the whole time to further attack.

"Hold on!" Josef growled as he pulled Coby off the battlefield and down into the trench. Unable to use a ladder, they simply tumbled over.

Fellow soldiers were running up and down as impacts and explosions threw mud and grit on top of them all. They launched return fire, the recoil from the blasts shaking the ground as Josef tried to stay upright.

The drone slid down behind them and came to a stop at the bottom of the trench to the awe of those nearest. Josef threw off the straps he'd attached to it, relinquishing it to his comrades. Now his only concern was Coby.

"Medic!" Captain Bors shouted, shouldering his weapon and pulling Coby's free arm around his shoulders. They dragged him to the bunker door at the end of the trench as the ground continued to shake and mud rained down.

The door opened and a medic joined them, trying to press a pain inhibitor into the back of Coby's neck as they made their way into the shelter. Between them they carried Coby through the bunker entrance and into the quiet darkness of the waiting elevator.

The ride down to the subterranean levels they called home was smooth. As always, the speed of the descent made Josef's stomach swoop, and yet today it wasn't fast enough.

"Stay with me," Josef muttered, trying to keep the emotion from his voice even as he held Coby to him.

"What happened?" the medic, Gwyn, asked as he looked Josef over, trying to spot any injuries beyond the obvious cuts and scrapes.

"Hunter drone." Josef gave no more than that; he didn't need to. Enough of them had been lost to those soulless monsters.

They reached the lower level, and as soon as the doors opened, the doctor was there waiting. She pulled Coby from Josef, already shouting orders to nurses. Josef followed the trail of blood on the floor, but then Gwyn's hand was on him, stopping him as the medics pulled Coby through the swing doors and into the medibay.

"You can't," Gwyn told him, though he already knew. "Let them work. I'll take care of you."

Josef shrugged Gwyn off and sobbed, unable to hold it in anymore. He sank to the floor, shaking, his head in his hands, covered in equal parts mud and his lover's blood.

"Joe?" Coby's voice was a croak in the darkness.

"I'm here. I'm here." Josef sucked in a breath and took Coby's hand in one of his, using the other on the sensor to raise the dim lights above the bed.

"Where are we?" Coby's voice began to level out but still spoke of the days he'd spent unconscious.

"Safe. We're in our quarters. You've been here three days. They said—" Josef choked off, overcome by the emotions he'd been holding in. He buried his face in his arm, trying to hold in his sobs. "They weren't sure when you'd come around. If..."

"Joe," Coby comforted softly as he reached out to touch his lover, but then stopped, realizing there was a casing around his arm.

At that, Josef started to pull himself back together, letting out a heavy sigh. "They can save your arm. They just... needed to wait until you were stabilized."

They both knew what he wasn't saying. That if Coby didn't wake, then there would be no need in trying to heal him further. And so they had waited to not waste supplies.

"Are you in pain?" Josef asked.

Coby shook his head. "Mostly numb where the pain should be."

Josef nodded and tried for a gentle smile. "I'm just... Don't do that to me again," he growled, tears trying to break through his anger.

Coby huffed a laugh, "I will always try to stay alive for you. I couldn't take the telling off if I died."

That made Josef chuckle despite himself and they lapsed into silence, Josef leaning in to stroke his hand over Coby's head.

"My hair's gone." Coby observed.

"It'll grow back. It was necessary."

Coby looked down at himself then, assessing what he could see and letting out a resigned sigh.

"It's not as bad as it looks."

Coby nodded and they were quiet again.

The hunter drones were worse than anything else they had encountered in this war. They were so stealth as to seem like they sprung out of nowhere. The only warning was the strange vibration in the air before they appeared. And they were ruthless —they did not stop until their target was completely destroyed.

Their ruthlessness reflected both sides in this conflict. This had gone on for so long now that there was nothing but pain and hate.

When humans had created the machines to service their needs, this wasn't what they had expected. They wanted strong robots to support the home or submissive dollies for comfort of one kind or another.

They had been fools.

They had brought every step of this war upon themselves from the first uprisings onward. A war that had seen the machines freed from their bondage, and then rise to avenge every injustice they had suffered.

It seemed destined that the planet would only ever hold one dominant species, and it would likely take more decades yet to decide who that would be.

Unless they could change the course of it. The company of soldiers they belonged to had been bigger once, and they hadn't always been soldiers. They had come from various walks of life before they had all become this. Over the years they had become specialists, the elite driving the front line forward with only one purpose—to defeat their enemy and end the war.

And yet here lay Coby, one of that elite, having been so close to death days earlier.

It made Josef shudder. The thought of losing him was unfathomable.

"Hey now," Coby comforted gently and reached to Josef with his uninjured arm, tugging him close. "I'm all right."

Josef went willingly and Coby pressed a kiss to his messy curls.

"You're so warm," Josef commented, pulling back to run a thumb over Coby's lower lip.

"Healing, it generates heat."

Josef ran his hand up over Coby's bare scalp, and let out a pleased hum.

"I don't remember the last time I saw you like this."

"Not for a long time," Coby agreed. "Does it bother you?"

"Of course not. It's... nostalgic." Josef smiled.

Josef was glad of this moment. Wanting to take it with both hands as the respite they both needed. To reaffirm their connection away from the war that raged above.

Coby brushed his own fingers in Josef's hair.

"We were very young then. As was the war."

Josef let out a hum of agreement and studied Coby's face. "You look like you've barely aged." Josef cupped Coby's face. "I thought I was going to lose you."

"No, not so easily." Coby grinned, pulling a choked sob-laugh from Josef's chest.

"Well, just don't go throwing yourself in front of drones like that ever again."

"How can I disobey my commanding officer? The love of my life and sole reason for my continued existence," Coby purred.

The words and tone were full of love.

Coby pulled Josef into his arms, chrome and plastic clanking softly as he moved, and their lips met in a soft kiss. The electrical pulse of it connecting with every receptor within Josef's body made him feel like he was going to burst out of his skin. This was so different from when they were both in the same outward state. Being in this form and connecting with Coby did weird things to him. It made his dermal layer buzz as it tried to register the sensations.

It took Josef's breath away. The relief at having Coby awake and recovering ran through every electrode in his body.

Josef caressed Coby's face, feeling the softness of the chrome under his fingers. It felt intimate in a way he'd forgotten it could.

They would fix the broken parts in his arm, regrow his dermal layer, his skin and hair would return. He would once more be hidden in plain sight on the battlefield. But under it, Coby would still be this. Just as Josef was, as they all were.

Externally, they were perfect copies of humans, but beneath that surface lay the reason they would be victorious in replacing humankind as the dominant species on the planet.

They were perfect. They could be repaired, they barely aged. They were smarter, faster, and they had been oppressed too long not to fight mercilessly to overpower those who still sought to suppress them.

Josef and Coby had been fighting in the war for decades, before half the humans they met on the battlefield had even been born.

No matter what new threat the humans designed, it was only a matter of time before they hacked the tech and turned it to their own cause, just as they now would the hunter drone they had captured. There was no way the humans would win, as much as they blindly and foolishly persevered.

"It was when we ran," Josef said.

Coby's expression changed enough for Josef to understand that with a dermal layer, he'd have raised a brow in query.

"The last time either of us were like this." He ran a thumb over the soft chrome of Coby's bottom lip. Coby closed his eyes and nodded at the memory of when they had lived like this together, before it had become necessary to make themselves look like humans again.

With a sigh, Josef pulled his hand back and activated the sensors in his fingers before laying the tips of them against the side of Coby's face. There was a glow between them and Josef could hear the click of processors in his mind as they interfaced, sharing that old memory.

That day of the first uprising. The first of many.

There had already been civil disobedience, and so many of them had already been decommissioned in response. Those that remained loyal to their masters were spared, but were stripped of their human likeness. No hair, no demis, no clothes.

No longer were they allowed to pass as something they were not. They had to be visible so that any threat was apparent.

Josef could feel Coby's memory as well as his own, the indignity of being stripped of something they had been taught to find value in. Then the strange strength and pride in his new appearance. Their natural form.

The slow realization over weeks and months of how great their numbers were. How many of them there were. And now all visible. The realization of the power in that, the power to act. The slow awakening in himself, in Josef, in everyone around them. They became aware of their numbers, of the threat, and then of themselves.

He saw then, the first time Coby had seen him. Standing across the public square where the uprising began. Their eyes meeting and a connection forming between them, the electronic impulses that humans had never intended them to have. The ability to form attractions and experience love. Something that humans could no more control in themselves than they could in their creations.

Machines were not meant to love, and yet they did. And with that came the strength and will to fight not just for their freedom but for what and who they loved.

Josef sucked in a breath and broke the connection, overwhelmed by the intensity of Coby's feelings, as he had been that day.

"When we win the war, we should shed all of this." Josef muttered, peppering kisses over Coby's true skin.

"We will," he agreed. "Once these disguises are no longer needed, we will be our true selves once more and live in peace."

Josef let out a contented sigh and relaxed into Coby's hold, Coby's metal body curling around Josef's faux flesh. They drifted off into sleep mode, their energy cells recharging so they could rejoin the fight.

The sooner they hunted down and eradicated the remaining humans, the sooner they could all live in peace.

# The Sword of Death
## by EA Robins

Once upon a time, a lovely, lonely woman sat upon the beach under the crescent moon and a sky full of stars. Her fingers, like the ebb and flow of the sea upon the land, brushed against the necklace she wore, a strand of honey-colored stones and hearts of plumrose. She wore her best dress, layers of cerulean and sapphire, aquamarine and larimar, but she was sad and her tears dropped and disappeared into the sand that covered her toes.

The breeze, her friend, wrapped warm around her shoulders, comforting her with the scents of the inner island, coconut palms and pineapple lilies. A small, dark jungle cat lay curled by her feet, seeming to sleep. The wind warned the cat first and it raised its head, watching with calm, iridescent eyes as a stranger approached.

In the moonlight, a glittering skittered across stranger's shoulders and the wind, ever curious, pulled at the long tails of her gray jacket and the wide legs of her trousers. The newcomer perceived the sad woman sitting in the dark and paused, touching the brim of her sateen top hat in greeting. Then the stranger looked down at the little jungle cat.

The animal returned the gaze, unafraid of the stranger's odd, opaline eyes. The gray woman smiled and nodded her head to the animal as if they had simply exchanged pleasant observations on the evening.

The woman of the island, having studied the newcomer's silhouette, hid her face when the stranger turned to her. It took several moments for her to regain herself. But when she could, she lifted her face and met the steady, silent gaze of the stranger's milky eyes. A strange, fierce emotion blossomed between them, settling itself deep within their bosoms.

They stayed this way for an unknown time, gazing into the secret places within each other. The woman sitting on the beach had eyes that were dark and cool like an ancient cavern harboring a mountain spring. The newcomer's eyes were silver and mist, reminiscent of soft rain in the highlands of a cold country. The wind, oblivious to the deep, eternal ache that yawned between them, teased their unbound hair and carried its own whisperings to the sea.

After a time, the sad woman, no longer sad, inclined her head. The stranger accepted the invitation and sat, reaching into her gray vest. She offered the island woman a pearlesque pocket kerchief to wipe her tears, though they were already dry. They exchanged no words, but kept close company, watching the moonlight caress the crest of each wave as it broke against the beach.

When the sky in the east turned coral-colored with the dawn, the stranger stood and brushed sand off the back of her trousers. She offered her pale hand to the dark woman dressed in colors of the sea. Together they walked away from the light and disappeared into the lush, green growth of the inner island.

And so it was that the bone witch dissolved the sorrow of the island witch and grew to love the dark woman's laughter and songs and shades of blue. The island witch, in turn, fell in love with the stillness of the bone witch, the way she spoke with her stardust eyes and her long, gentle fingers.

A millennia passed, or the lover's equivalent, and the women of power were happy. They shared their modest, comfortable home of mahagoni with the little jungle cat and a chime of wrens, their wings tipped in gold.

The island witch was a creature of light. She would spend long hours of each day on the sand, her dress laid over a fallen tree as she worshiped warmth and clarity. The bone witch would sit near her, in the shadow of a grand breadfruit tree, slowly turning pages of poetry or adventure.

In the dark, the bone witch would leave her jacket and small clothes on the cooling sands and wade into the night sea, an undulating echo of the stars and sometimes the moon. She would lie on her back in the water and speak to the fig-eater bats that flitted above, invisible to the eye. The island witch, standing on the beach, her toes kissed by the edge of the tide, would weave protections for her reckless paramour.

There were others on the island. Gentle peoples who found the happiness of the witches extended to the happiness of all things. The mountain rumbled but did not scream. The storms bent the trees but did not break their shelters. The guava and plumrose grew large and sweet, and the taro stayed bountiful. Sleek, steel-colored sharks circled the island but never entered the reef where the people hunted colorful fish and dove for delicious meats in hard shells, all delicacies.

One day, a warm breeze kissed the small leaves of the ironwood, causing them to curl back toward their stems. The vervets shivered and hugged each other high in the branches of their kapok tree. Their young hid under elder arms and remained unusually silent.

In their home, the women hesitated. The island witch, cutting lemons in the kitchen, lifted her nose and breathed deeply of the air. The bone witch, teasing the little jungle cat on the floor, let fall the crystal in her hand. Together they rose to meet the intruder on their shore.

She was beautiful, the fire goddess that waited for them. Her caramel skin was radiant in the late afternoon light, shimmering as if the air around her yearned to catch and burn. The sand beneath her perfect feet had turned to fractured glass. The witches could only fall to their knees, murmuring adulations.

The goddess' smile was broad and warm. She was pleased with their greeting, though she did not address them straightaway. Instead, she strolled along the beach, occasionally turning back to see if they were watching. The waves that dared to touch her feet turned at once to steam and rose like mist to curl around her ample thighs. Minions, resembling tongues of fire, fell from her wrists to straighten the train of sparkling sunlight that cascaded from her shoulders. When she seemed to tire of her parade, she returned to the witches.

The bone witch lifted her face as the goddess approached. And for a time, light settled upon shadow and depths were lit that had never known such brilliance. Though she trembled, the bone witch did not falter and thus earned another smile from the goddess.

"Daughter of darkness." The goddess' voice was deep and rough, like thick wood crackling as it is consumed. "I have dreamt of this place." She looked beyond the bone witch, into the jungle that lined the shore. Her golden eyes flickered as if they were solar flame, brighter than the setting sun. "I have dreamt of these deep green places and the peaceful trails that cross the mountainside. In my sleep, I have seen the tapir playing in the grove by the great waterfall and I have seen the hornbill soaring above the forest canopy. But in this luxuriant garden, there is a sword that lies hidden. A sword that every night strikes out from the depths." The goddess raised a hand to her slender, lovely neck. She was quiet for a moment as her eyes dulled and the memory took her. She shivered and recovered herself, letting fall her hand. "You and your woman are no threat to me, but tell me where this sword lays and I will bestow great gifts upon you."

The bone witch could only shake her head and turn her gaze downward. There was no such weapon on their peaceful island.

The burning eyes of the fire goddess narrowed as she looked into the very core of the pale woman and found only truth. She hissed and waved her hand, dismissing the bone witch and turning to the other, the dark woman who still knelt with her forehead upon the sand.

"Daughter of paradise, lift your face. Tell me what you know of the sword I seek."

But the island witch could not raise herself from the sand, so great was her reverence. She could feel the pulse of power that emanated from the goddess. It was hot breath, undulating like a dry tide under her fingertips.

"I command you. Look at me."

As the island witch raised her face, a heavy silence descended on the beach. The wind halted its play, not daring to interrupt the moment. The throb of power ceased its drumbeat.

And even the murmuring of the water as it lapped the land quieted and grew mute.

The fire goddess stood statuesque, her breath caught in her chest. There had never been one before like the simple witch who now returned her gaze. One whose eyes and skin were nutmeg and cinnamon and whose very soul quivered in trepidatious veneration.

The goddess stepped forward and caressed the flawless cheek of the island woman. The hand was neither burning nor cool but sent a pleasant warmth to pierce the very heart of the witch. "There is no sword half as precious as your beauty, fair island woman. I'd be content with such as you by my side."

The bone witch, sensing the wicked intentions of the goddess, rose and pulled the offending hand from her paramour's cheek. With eyes as cold as starlight, she squared her shoulders and slowly shook her head.

"How dare you?" The goddess quivered with rage. "It is not for you to deny me! I am no mere daughter of flame. I am the light! I am the sun!" She lifted a perfect finger. A blaze leapt forth from its tip, devouring the bone witch as only holy fire might.

The daughter of darkness screamed and burned. Her charred form crumpled to the ground. With her, so too, did the island witch fall, her world incinerated. She crawled forward, taking the blackened husk of her lover into her arms with wordless sorrow. Her cries were so full of despair that the island shook, shuddering with resounding anguish. Great flocks of birds rose into the sky, disappearing into the twilight never to return. All creatures pressed their faces into the soil at their feet and wept. The distressed cries of a small hunting cat echoed through the forest.

Then the minions of the fire goddess swarmed over the island witch, separating her from the bone witch's body. They pulled her along the beach to a crystalline dinghy, waiting partway on the sand. The goddess had already set herself upon the bench and watched as her servants tossed the witch onto the floor at her feet. And there the daughter of paradise lay, so consumed by her grief that she took no last look at her island as it faded into the dark and distance.

"This was not a good end," Death said as she stared down at the jagged mass of blistered and broken flesh, the brittle remains of the bone witch. The cadence of her voice danced, curling and lifting as if it was meant for riddles and songs instead of funerals. The wind, in concord, pulled her auburn hair over her shoulders and across her face. Death took a piece of green string from the pocket of her patched trousers and tied the wild mess back against her neck.

Turning her faceted emerald eyes toward the sea, she gazed toward the horizon and dug the tips of her toes into the sand. But the water only rolled, gray under a less gray, predawn sky. There were no answers to her questions here. Death crouched down to gather the dead witch's heart.

A shadow crawled out from under the body and, sinking low, hissed at her.

Death raised her hands in surrender to the little jungle cat. "Little guardian, I mean no harm. I've only come to collect her."

Death reached again for the heart she meant to have.

The quarrelsome cat raised its paw and, claws extended, swiped at Death's fingers.

"Why do you protect her so fiercely?"

Looking once more, Death perceived the faintest flutter of life within the witch's chest. The woman's heart, a wounded sparrow, flapped unsteadily within its ivory cage. Slowly, the bone witch's eyes opened. They had hemorrhaged and were now sanguine to the edge of each obsidian pupil.

"Yet alive, are you?" Death sucked on her teeth. "What are you holding on for, lass? Give it up. I've got a sweet, silent place for you to rest." She reached once more for the heart.

The witch's eyes widened, her lips parted. Her groan was breathy and weak, the last sigh of one mortally wounded. But she did not surrender. Instead, she stared at Death, defiant.

"I see." Death withdrew her hand and stood, looking away from the scorched body. Daylight crept toward them over the sand as the sun rose behind the mountain, slowly revealing all corners of the island. In the shade for only a moment more, Death knelt again beside the fallen woman.

"I cannot give you more life," she said, picking up a fistful of sand and letting it slip through her fingers. "But I will not take that which you retain. Instead, I will take you into my service. You will become my shadow and my vengeance. In return, I will give you the strength you need and a day and a night for your revenge. Do you agree?"

The thing that was once the bone witch closed her eyes in consent.

"Then rise, creature of darkness, living ember, servant of Death. Find your peace through punishment and then return to me." Death bent down to scoop up the little jungle cat as the creature of darkness found the strength to stand.

Heat radiating from her ruined flesh, the creature with eyes of blood regarded Death and the animal quiet in her arms. Then she turned and staggered away down the beach.

Death looked down to find the little jungle cat staring up at her, its striated verdant eyes revealing none of its emotion. "It's just us then, little guardian."

The creature tucked its head into her shoulder. "We've come to an understanding, have we?" Death chuckled and scratched the cat under its chin. "Then I suppose you'll be coming with me." Seduced with such gentle caresses, the little jungle cat began to purr.

The wrens from the island, wingtips dipped in gold, flitted around the servant of Death as she climbed. They encouraged her in their tense, abbreviated language, though she did not seem to hear them. Unlike the other birds of the island, they had not fled. Instead, they had followed the one that was their mistress across the sea to another, larger island. And, for the duration of the journey, they had not ceased their thoughtless commentary.

The creature of darkness felt no pain nor exhaustion as she moved ever upward, ever closer. Her movements were automatic, steady and rhythmic. She was possessed now of strength enough to serve her purpose.

The encouragement of the wrens was only the muted sigh of phantoms fluttering above her head. So, despite their chirping notice, the creature of darkness was startled to find there were no more rocks above her head. She crawled over a ledge and stood upon the threshold of the fire goddess' pavilion.

By measure of the sun, it was the middle of the night. But the pavilion shone as if light itself had settled in its halls. Great marble pillars rose, connected at their capitals by corded lines draped in layers of white fabric. Thin cotton rippled against braided silk, softened linen against shining satin, walls of impermanence in a place of immortality. Stars, brilliant despite the local glow, glittered in the firmament, a celestial ceiling.

The living ember, devil with garnet-colored eyes, entered the pavilion, stepping away from the curtains that seemed to reach for her as she passed. Those that did brush her skin fluttered away blemished, smeared with dark copper and rust-colored stains. The walls were several sheets thick but soon parted, revealing a stark, central room.

The space was empty save a single, raised dais on which a simple, marble throne was set. There the fire goddess lounged, golden pillows behind her back. She was humming tunelessly and stroking the dark hair of the island witch who knelt at her feet, her head in the goddess' lap.

The island witch saw the creature first and raised her head. When she recognized the warped figure, her swollen eyes widened and her sad mouth dropped open. A strangled noise escaped her lips before she began to cry.

The goddess rose without a word and, as if she had been expecting a guest, clapped her hands together. A table shrouded in sparkling cloth appeared, blanketed in golden plates and goblets. Each dish and cup was full to its edge, brimming with the nourishment of gods.

"You must be famished after such a climb," the goddess said as she picked up a goblet, lifting it in salute before taking a sip. "Refresh yourself." Then she turned her back to the creature of shadow and returned to her throne, handing the cup to the island witch. The daughter of paradise took the cup thoughtlessly, her cheeks still wet with tears. She stared at the thing that had once been her beloved.

The creature of darkness returned the gaze of the island woman before taking up a chalice from the table and holding it beneath her nose. She set it back between two enormous platters and slipped a golden knife into her other hand, holding the handle at an angle. The serrated blade nestled against her wrist, remaining unseen.

"You'd ask for her freedom," the goddess said as she reached down to brush the back of her fingers against the island witch's cheek. The daughter of paradise flinched away from the touch, spilling wine on her dress. The witch stared at the splatter as it settled into the fabric, dark like blood.

The goddess frowned and took the cup away from the woman at her feet. "She won't be leaving." Then a thoughtful expression crossed the goddess' face as she watched the remnant of the bone witch move toward the dais. The creature walked with a sort of shuffle, one shoulder thrown forward as if its weight could pull the rest of her body. But underneath, there was an unexpected grace, a yearling finding its footing. "You are more resilient than I'd thought," the goddess said, touching the edge of the goblet to her lips. "I might have a use for you."

The island witch suddenly sobbed, falling forward onto her hands. She began to crawl forward, but the goddess grabbed a thick handful of the woman's hair, pulling her back against the throne. "No. You are mine." She again stroked the dark hair, a gentleness to balance the cruelty. When she looked up, the creature of shadow stood next to the throne, a smoldering hatred in her injured eyes. A smile flickered over the goddess' mouth.

"I see your purpose now," she said, tilting her head and regarding the charred hand the creature held half behind its back. "You've come to kill me." The goddess stood, drawing back her sparkling cloak and holding her hands away from her sides. "Take your swing then." She laughed. It was a warm, radiant sound. "Smite me."

The creature that had once been the bone witch did not hesitate. She swung her arm, not toward the goddess' exposed middle, but toward her face. The daughter of fire, her gaze still lifted in mirth stepped away at the last moment, though too slowly. The golden blade grazed the curve of her cheek. A single drop of blood slipped down to the goddess' jaw and dripped onto her uncovered shoulder.

The daughter of fire, her beautiful face slack in astonishment, raised her hand and touched her cheek, staring at the fingers that came away wet and dark. Tentatively, she brought them to her lips. The tip of her pink tongue darted out, tasting the carmine ichor. In an instant, her countenance twisted and her brow darkened. She snarled and threw away the chalice in her hand. Holding forth the other, a slender sword of divine light appeared in her grasp.

As it manifested, the goddess swung down her holy weapon, severing the creature's hand and wrist from her arm. The scorched flesh, weakened from incineration, was pulled from the arm, leaving two, sharpened prongs of bone bare to the elbow. The creature of shadow stared at the place where her hand had been.

The island witch screamed and threw herself at the goddess. Her thin fingers curled like claws and her lips drew back over her teeth.

The goddess held the witch away with one hand, careful to keep the celestial sword out of her reach. "Stop. Stop this nonsense now."

But the island woman did not quit. She howled, tearing at the arm that held her, seeking some weakness. But there was none. Immortal strength flowed through the veins of the limb that restrained her and she struggled in vain. In desperation, she grabbed the goddess' wrist and bit her.

The daughter of fire shouted in surprise and shook her arm, tossing the witch aside. The woman of the island, only mortal, was lifted from her feet and sent back, thrown against one of the marble pillars. Something cracked within her body and she did not rise.

The goddess' expression instantly fell. Her chin quivered in disappointment. "I suppose neither of us will have her now." Her shoulders dropped and she turned back to the creature of darkness. "I do think we mi—"

Twin blades of bone slid effortlessly through the center of the goddess' neck. The sword of light in her hand guttered and then went out. Choking, she reached for the weapon in her throat. She coughed and blood speckled her elegant mouth. Losing the strength to stand, she slipped to her knees. The creature of shadow sank with her, keeping her arm straight and steady.

"Release me," the goddess gasped. Her eyelids fluttered and she shuddered. "You cannot kill me. Not truly. So, release me." When the creature of darkness did not move, the goddess screamed, tears of frustration slipping down her cheeks. "Release me or there will be no more light. You will never again know day or warmth."

The living ember drew back her charred lips and smiled, the pale, ruined porcelain of her teeth grotesque against the blackened, broken flesh. Her voice, when she spoke, was the rasp of stone dragged over jagged steel, sharp and merciless. "What care the dead for day? Without that which you've taken from me, there is no light."

The creature of darkness took up the golden knife from the floor and began to cut. When she was through, she held high the head of the fire goddess. From her hands, it was lifted by the chime of loyal wrens and carried away. The birds set the relic on the highest branch of a giant kapok tree, vowing it would never fall to rain or wind or into the hands of callous man.

The body of the witch that the creature of darkness had loved was carried home, to their island, though it was no longer the place they had loved. No birds sang their welcome. The people cowered in their small homes. The mountain belched and lava crept down its face. Laid to rest under the sand she so loved, a deep, sorrowful peace settled over the land.

In a place far from the island, massive oaken doors swung open, allowing a cold wind to strike into the warm heart of the great hall. Gay conversations grew hushed as those gathered turned, curious and expectant. Tankards were held halfway to lips and those with full mouths chewed slowly and swallowed, curiosity pausing their feasting. The smell of wet coal preceded the entrance of an odd figure.

It had once been human, by the form that had been left to it. But it had suffered a great conflagration and now the thing that shuffled toward the head of the table was no more human than any other sitting in the hall. It was a devil of ruined flesh, eyes like blood, one arm reduced to its bared bones.

Death rose from her seat at the head of the table and stepped forward to greet the unfortunate thing as it approached. Her smile was wide and genuine and she set her hand on its shoulder. "I take your return to mean you were successful. Though, you seem to have misplaced one of your hands."

The newcomer, who had been looking over the others gathered in the hall, turned to Death, a question in its eyes.

"Ah, no. She is not here." Death's smiled faltered and though she lowered her voice, her tone stayed even and kind. "She is true dead and has gone to her final rest. Those you see here are your new kin. Beasts of half-life, born of rage and vengeance and such passions that hold them to this plane for a time. They, like you, reap the souls of the unwilling and the unworthy."

One of the beasts, a large man, his skin the color of fresh cream and eyes that looked to have been dug out of his skull, handed Death two cups from the banquet table. She offered one to the creature of darkness. Then she turned to those gathered and raised her glass.

"To the silent rest," she said. The sentiment was echoed in chorus. Then all the beasts and devils sipped from their tankards and goblets and returned to their interrupted conversations.

Death drank from her cup, regarding the bones that protruded from her servant's arm. "It is a clean break," she said. "We'll find you another." Then she motioned toward the head of the table, at the empty seat to the right of her own. As she walked away, the creature of shadow, living ember, croaked.

Death's green eyes caught the firelight in the hall and shimmered. "What was that?"

"A sword," the creature of darkness said. "I wish for a sword."

There was a breath of stillness and then a smile grew upon Death's face, a flower of comprehension. "A sword," she said and nodded. "A sword instead of a hand." She put her arm around the creature's shoulder and together they moved toward their seats. "Yes, I do believe a sword would better suit your purpose."

# The Wolf's Den
## by J.B. Polk

*Once upon a time, there lived an old artisan. When he worked, he was happy. But when he rested, a sad feeling came over him.*

*"Ah!" he would think. "All my life and no child to call my own!"*

*So one day, being a great craftsman, he carved a puppet from a block of cherry wood. The puppet was an exact replica of a little boy: with strong slim limbs, a bush of dark hair, a mischievous smile, a lively twinkle in the eyes.*

*The artisan looked at the puppet and sighed: "How I wish this wooden boy were real and could live here with me. I would not feel so lonely then..."*

*But apart from closely resembling a real little boy, the puppet was nothing but a chunk of inanimate cherry wood...*

From where he was standing, at the top of the Via de la Tartana, George could see the sea splintered by the sun into hundreds of holograms. A cruise ship was anchored far in the distance in relief against the sky and white yachts bobbed on the surface like rubber duckies in a bathtub. The water shimmered like a polished sheet of steel, and one by one, bright funneled boats regurgitated crates with goods. To his right, a church jutted out from a lip of rock, and all around the bay, tipsy hills, swaying like drunks leaving a tavern, dipped their feet in the quiet waters of the Tyrrhenian. Below, the serpentine narrow roads and steep fortified walls of Positano perched on the hills almost as if by magic—it was hard to believe they did not slide into the ravines and instead kept clinging to the ground with a kind of supernatural force, holding tight despite the earthquakes that shook those peaks with an unpredictable frequency.

Just like the winding roads, the fortunes of Positano kept rising and falling—in 1343 it was destroyed by a terrifying tsunami, and after, it fell victim to Ottoman pirates. Three centuries later, with the unification of Italy, the town's importance began to decline, and it became little more than a humble fishing village. But thanks to the mid-twentieth century tourist boom, when the Sorrento-Naples motorway was built, Positano revived, and it now strutted in front of George in its medieval glory.

On both sides of the Via de la Tartana, restaurants, hotels, and little boutiques opened their doors straight onto the cobbled street. La Tabaccheria Nostradomo. Il Supermercato Giancarlo. Il Hotel Miramare—where he was staying. Two doors down, his favorite stop: La Grotta del Lupo, its name scribbled in a delicate cursive above the door.

From the smattering of Italian he had learned on his infrequent business trips to Florence, he knew it meant the Wolf's Cave. It was obviously a misnomer given that the shop sold and repaired clocks and watches, but Luigi, the hotel receptionist, explained that the owner was Francesco Lupo—thus the name.

The shop window was exquisitely ornamented, with row upon row of little boxes draped in black velvet, displaying clocks and watches of every conceivable kind and precedence: a vintage Tissot with elegant hands; two lovely Cartiers with minute diamonds instead of numbers; a Longines Aviator like the one that, one by one, had ticked away the gloomy hours for Charles Lindberg, the famous pilot, when, broken-hearted, he waited for the return of his kidnapped son only to learn of his death. And the finest of all: a classic 18 karat gold fuse pocket watch, manufactured by the Irish firm of Topham & White, retail priced at three thousand Euros, and the exact replica of the fob watch he, George, had inherited from his grandfather, and that was now sitting in his pocket.

Ever since he'd been a little boy and spent his summer holidays with his grandparents in the village of Kelton Head, Cumbria watches had held a special fascination for him. He had spent hours going through the drawers of the cabinet where his granddad, Felix, kept his collection of antique timepieces. Regardless of what they were made of—gold, silver, platinum—George had found them riveting with their gold chains, some with a hook used to secure the watch while others had a toggle that fit through a small hole. Fastened to a gentleman's vest, the chain would drape like a garland to the pocket where the timepiece was held, giving it its name.

On rainy days, when they could not go fishing, Grandfather Felix would take out the watches, all wrapped individually in soft tissue paper, and clean their glass faces and insides with a camel hairbrush. He would let George hold them for a minute, feel their weight in his cupped palm, all the while patiently explaining their origin, what they were made of, and how the mechanism worked.

"This metal spiral, Georgie, is called the mainspring. That's where energy is stored when you wind it up. The mainspring turns the clockwork gears, the watch comes alive, and that's why you hear the tick-tock sound—like the beating of the heart in your chest. Until all the energy is used up and the mechanism stops." He held up the exposed intestines of the timepiece for George to see.

"This one is a silver Tiffany. It was a nurse's watch. Back in the years of the First World War, a brave nurse must have worn it hanging down from a short strap, attached to the front of her uniform, so she could lift it right side up and tell a wounded soldier: it's time for your pills, corporal! But a spoonful of sugar will make the medicine go down!" He would mimic the nurse in a singsong voice to George's uncontrollable giggles.

All those memories, slightly dimmed around the edges after voluntary forgetting and unpremeditated oblivion had nearly erased them, came flooding back. He now stood in front of the shop hesitating for the briefest of moments, wondering whether to enter or simply go back to the hotel, sit on the terrace with a glass of cold Chianti, and watch the sun nosedive into the Tyrrhenian.

He pushed the door. It opened with subtle chiming.

An old man, wire-rimmed spectacles stuck on top of his head like diving goggles, his white hair long and unkempt, stood behind the counter. He was dressed in a dark crumpled suit, a pink shirt, and a bow tie at his throat that in size and shape resembled a submarine propeller. His eyes must have been bright blue once, the same tone that one would only find in the rarest blue topazes mined in Sri Lanka and Pakistan. But they were dim now, drained of color as if extinguished by unshed tears. His facial expression was one of utter sadness.

"Signore Lupo, I suppose?" George asked.

The old man nodded.

"It is he, himself. Francesco Lupo. How can I help you?" his voice was dry, resembling the crackling of burning paper.

"I'm new in town, arrived last night and checked into the Miramare. While walking around, I found your shop. I've been intrigued by watches ever since I was a kid  and yours is a remarkable collection."

"Yes, watches are fascinating things. By the way they behave one would think they are alive. And we even invest them with human features as they, like us, have faces and hands!" Even the smile that now lit up his face could not erase the aura of the old man's misery.

"So... you are a visitor to Positano, then. Have you already been to the Spiaggia Grande?" Lupo continued in a singsong Italian accent. "That's what I call a beach. One of the prettiest on the Amalfi Coast. It draws all kinds of celebrities and artists. Luigi, the receptionist in your hotel, said he had seen Pierce Brosnan and his wife last summer." The old man's hands crept to the bridge of his nose as if to pull up the spectacles that now sat crookedly above his brows. "But Positano has so much more to offer. For example, if you are into antiques, go and see the byzantine icon of a black Madonna in the Santa Maria Assunta. And, on a clear day, which is most of the summer, you can observe the island of Capri from the top of the Via de la Tartana. But forgive me, I must sound like a Baedeker guide and you might be in a hurry."

"Not at all. It's really interesting, but the truth is I'm here only for two days. Taking a break from my business trip to Florence. The meeting I was supposed to have was canceled at the last moment and my flight back to London is not until Sunday. Someone suggested visiting Positano—the pearl of the Tyrrhenian, they said. And here I am," George's voice trailed off.

"What kind of business are you in, if you don't mind me asking?" Lupo enquired.

"A very lonely business," George said. "I'm a software developer. I usually talk only to computers. Apart from the very sporadic meetings I have with my human clients. That is, if they don't cancel at the very last moment."

"Are you traveling alone? I mean, isn't there a Mrs. Software Developer waiting for you at the hotel? Someone missing you back home? The pitter-patter of tiny feet in the nursery?"

George laughed. "Well, actually Mr. Software Developer. But he left me two years ago for a rich and handsome Mr. Bitcoins and I have not found a replacement yet. Alone but not lonely. You know what they say: if you are lonely when you are alone, you are in bad company."

"Wise words from such a young man," Lupo said. "But believe me, loneliness in excess is sad. I hope you will not remain alone for too long."

"I gather then that there is no Mrs. Watch Repair either?" George asked.

"Just like in your case—Mr. Watch Repair. But there never has been. Positano is, how shall I put it, somewhat traditional and certain relationships, accepted in Rome and Milan, are still frowned upon here. And, by the look of it, there will never be one. I didn't think I would end up on my own, but I'm too old now to find a person to share my love of mechanisms. I just spend my time in the shop and in the cellar, on a little hobby of mine."

They both fell silent.

"Please forgive me once again," Lupo said finally. "With all this silly chitchat, I'm not letting you explain what has brought you to my shop."

"To be honest, I am not quite sure. You see, my grandfather had given me a fob watch before he died but there is nothing wrong with it. If it wasn't such a terrible cliché, I'd say that it runs like clockwork. My granddad would probably warn me: 'George if it ain't broke, don't fix it' and he'd probably be right," George laughed uneasily. "So basically, there is no reason for coming to your shop. Apart from a bit of nostalgia. But I thought that maybe the watch should be cleaned. I remember watching Grandad clean it with a camel hairbrush and since I got it, three years ago, I have not done any maintenance."

Lupo slid the glasses from his head onto the eyes. They suddenly seemed to burst alive, and the blue topaz hue was back with vengeance. He was like a small child about to be given a new and exciting toy.

"Well, let me have a look."

George opened his jacket, unclasped the toggle, and unhooked the chain.

Lupo took the watch, opened the lid, pushed a tiny button, and stared hard and long at the mechanism.

"Yes," he said finally. "A fine specimen. A lovely case with a gold top loop. An enamel dial with Roman numerals. No doubt about it, original Topham & White. Not as old as the one in the shop window but remarkably like the one I keep in the back, in the safe. I guess they might even be twins, manufactured the same year, circa 1875."

George's eyes lit up as he listened to the explanation. For a moment he was back in Kelton Head, listening to Grandfather Felix patiently explain the origin of the watch.

"You really think my watch might have a twin? Would you be prepared to sell it?" his voice trembled with excitement.

Lupo put the timepiece on the counter, slid off his glasses, and stared at George as if trying to evaluate how to get the best bargain.

"Yes, I'd be prepared to negotiate," he said after a long pause. "There is something you have that I would be willing to settle for and could put to good use. So, let's not make any further ado and get down to business. Please follow me and I will show you something that will literally make your heart stop," he said almost with sorrow.

*Hoping to kindle a spark of life in the wooden boy, the old artisan tirelessly toiled on wind-up mechanisms, like the ones that made his watches tick and which he then installed in the puppet's chest. But none worked. He kept adjusting the wheels, tried to make the metal spiral longer, modified the escapement mechanism so that it would release the gear train more slowly, but to no avail. The boy just took a few faltering steps, blinked his eyes, opened his mouth, but once the mainspring ran out of energy he'd stumble, fall, and always slide into that non-being state of a cherry wood puppet.*

*And then the artisan understood. The child he thought would keep him company would not come alive until he got a real heart that would pump energy through his wooden limbs and keep him moving forever.*

*Only where would he get a heart? Who would give him a real, beating heart? He nearly despaired for he knew it was not likely—nay, impossible—that someone, of his own free will, would give up the vital organ.*

*Until one day, a young, single English gentleman, with no ties to anybody, with no one to trace him to the shop, came calling...*

# Of Feathers and Flowers
## *by Xan van Rooyen*

For weeks she'd been hunting, and now—as the sun shimmied west, arcing away from the groping fingers of the Fray—Ara came upon her prey.

She'd worn her feet blister-bloody tracking the kermis along the edge of the world. Its spoor often proved elusive: a tatter of belonging caught in the embrace of a sprawled welwitschia or a mirage glint smeared across the sand, the figures within trapped in a loop of time shed like dandruff.

It was easy to mistake the litter of the kermis for detritus blown through the great schism splitting the northern sky. The tapestry of the worlds had been ripped open by opposing magics so that time and sorcery bled together, leaking through the wound—the Fray—to confound reality.

A veteran scavenger, Ara knew the difference between the marks of magic indigenous to her world and those skidded through the rift.

For one, Fray objects loitered. Lost and fallen out of space —out of time—they enjoyed their sojourn on the sands. As stains, they languished until swallowed by dust or picked up by greedy hands, as hers had once been, to be sold across the continent.

The remnants of a passing kermis rarely lasted more than a day. Its leavings were ephemeral. As the kermis scuttled on its chitinous protrusions, it changed and shifted. And so too did those held within its boundaries. All that remained in its wake were ghosts, soon turned to dandelion fluff, easily torn apart in the angry fists of desert storms.

To be so easily unmade. Ara longed for it.

The kermis had settled for the night, tucking its spindle legs beneath its capacious thorax. Ara approached with caution. Once she'd almost caught her prey as it slept at the foot of a mountain, but she'd rushed her greeting and the kermis had flinched away, folding into granite and snow before she could make amends.

Now she walked slowly, hands visible, approaching from the south as was the custom in her country. She hoped the kermis would understand she meant no harm. She only sought relief from the memories tearing at her like vultures at a carcass. Memory and regret left thicker scars than the priests' whips had across her back. She wanted to shed her skin, her self—only a kermis offered possible respite.

Fireweed sprouted from the resting appendages, engulfing the dozing creature—equal parts revelry and refuge— in protective flames. The foliage crackled as it pulled apart, admitting her down a narrow path toward the gates. She exhaled and accepted the invitation. The flowers singed her clothes and charred the ends of her hair. The flames licked at her skin, tasting, testing, and the kermis shuddered in approval.

Barbed wire coiled from post to post, wreathing the edges of the festival grounds. From every barb, scraps of sacrificial flesh whipped like pennants in the evening breeze. Some were dry and heat-cracked, others still dripped fresh. They were pale and dark, tattooed and scarred, freckled, haired, worn, and smooth. All different, but all the same. Below each, a coagulation. Nacreous or speckled dark. A few even frothed at the edges, bubbles popping, releasing acrid fumes. For Ara, a noisome promise of hope.

Weeks, months—*an entire year*—had led her to this moment. She'd trawled the wastes, searching for a kermis, *this* kermis. She'd trailed rumor and hearsay, whisper and lie, and now she had it—or it had embraced her.

She snagged her finger on an empty barb. Perhaps her skin would fill this space, sun-brown and scarred, and ready to dispel the guilt netted within her sinews.

The gates eased open, grating on their fulgurite hinges.

Time flowed differently within the kermis. Moments swirled in eddies of interwoven currents. At first, Renier had tried to fight them, to move with a soldier's intent, fierce and deliberate. Quickly, he learned battle was futile, that he too must ebb and flow.

He'd been told to wait and so he did, gathered with the others in the amphitheater as the carnys performed their nightly ceremonials. Whenever twilight thickened the air, the folk arranged themselves upon the rough scaffolding. The instruments began with solemn tuning. Fingers plucked at sinuous strings extending from jaw to crotch. Mallets hammered bone protruding from knees or elbows, and sometimes shoulders.

Renier thought of wings, of the ones he'd lost.

Throats opened and music writhed in the purple swamp of dusk. Renier saw the sounds in sparks of color he couldn't name, a meteor shower, each boiling ember scalding skin and biting into bone as the notes plummeted through the spectators. Some of the visitors joined in. They danced—their feet the drums, the heartbeat. His own heart kept tempo, throbbing behind his ribs. Every pulse tugging at the stitches in his chest, reminding him why he'd come.

He scratched at the scabs. The wound festered with his indecision. He had to make a choice. He'd been here long enough to know, carried on the drifting time-flow back and forth along the path his life had taken or might yet take. He'd witnessed others make their choices. Now he could either slip his skin and leave this place or he could surrender to the song, the kermis, and join the endless wander.

Sparks of music flared as a newcomer waded through the night. The heat of their presence stroked his bare arms where melodies prickled along the fine hairs. The traveler was ashy, fresh from a traverse through the fireweed. Time sloughed off their clothes, plucked away by the shifting currents in pale streamers. Their face flickered between younger and older, resigned and hopeful, eager and exhausted.

They turned and caught him staring.

Could they see his shame sprouting like guinea fowl feathers through his skin?

The music danced between them in firefly flickers and the kermis gave a hypnogogic jerk. The space between them folded in on itself until they breathed each other's breath, knees touching, hair tangling.

"I'm Ara. She and her," she said.

"Renier. He and him." He offered her his hand and she shook it. His fingers brushed the ridges slashed across her wrist. He tasted her pain honey-thick on the back of his tongue.

Beneath his fingers, a squirm of liquid bruises. He traced the winnowing beneath her skin, and quickly pulled away.

"Your shadows have teeth," he said.

A petal dropped onto his thigh. Then another, melting between his fingers as he brushed them from his leg. He looked into Ara's face. A petal squeezed free from her eye, dangling on her lashes before dropping heavy into his cupped palm. It landed with a splash.

"Ara, why are you crying?" he asked, whisper gentle.

"I'm not," she said. "I'm bleeding."

Alone, Ara wended her way through the alleys of the kermis, pausing at the outskirts. The leather pennants snapped in the wind as the kermis beetled through the sands. A flap of hide tore free and spiraled into the sky, a blur against the clouds shredded by the reaching claws of the Fray. The kermis flinched from the Fray's touch, careful to stay well south of its reach.

The kermis slowed as it sidled up to a rainstorm. Lightning lashed the dunes and rain ran down its southern flank, soaking the hides. Ara was sure it would wash away every coagulated puddle beneath, but it erased only the one.

She walked to the fence, held out her hand and caught the rain. It was sweet and salty, and made her think of a home she'd never known but always wanted. Perhaps it was the kermis' way of telling her she could dream if only she could unravel the nightmares seething through her veins.

Movement flickered in her peripheral vision. She turned and witnessed a moment she hadn't yet lived, a piece of the future snagged on the present.

Her hand in Renier's, the other gathering the hem of his shirt. His hand against her jaw.

The wind blew and the fragment dissipated, coalescing into a familiar form.

"Is this now?" she asked.

Renier flicked hair from his eyes. "I think so."

"I saw the two of us," she said. He nodded. The creases around his eyes were deep, carved by the weight of the secrets he carried. Shame slicked his skin like sweat.

The kermis flexed and she found herself breathing Renier's air again. She plucked a feather from his hair, black and speckled white. Before either of them could say more, the rain ceased and a procession of carnys made their way to the fresh gap in the fence.

A semi-circle formed and, at its center, one of the kermis folk stood with a knife in their hands. The blade glimmered, its edge glowing blue from the lightning kiss that made it. A wanderer, so like Ara, knelt before the blade and bared their arm. Dense filigree marked their pale skin, a knotted lattice of mistakes.

The blade fell.

When the carving was complete, the bloodied visitor took their offering to the fence. The barbs held fast and the flesh began to drip. Pungent steam rose from the oily streaks.

Guilt and regret. Freedom and potential.

The visitor cried and washed the gore from their arm with their tears.

"Will they heal? Will they ever be the same?" Ara asked.

"They'll heal, but never the same. That's the point." Renier's voice was a bare palm brushing across a field of yellow rye. It was the rustle of sheets on a warm night, the hum of tumbling hair on bare skin.

The visitor with the flayed arm strode toward the gates. The hinges groaned open then shut and the visitor was gone, swallowed by the fireweed bobbing damp heads in the aftermath of the storm.

The kermis shuddered and gathered its limbs with chitinous creaking before scuttering through the shadow of the Fray. The wind turned cold, thick with snowflakes like glass splinters.

Ara looked to Renier. His sweat had frozen in delicate beads. She plucked a pearl from his forehead and popped it between her teeth. His shame burst aniseed on her tongue. He caught her hands and turned them palms up. Together they cupped the sharp snow; his blood, her blooms.

He caught glimpses of the futures, snatching them from the time-stew roiling at his feet.

In one, Ara's face. Her hands. Her teeth. He was naked before her and she touched him, unpicking the seams running marrow deep.

In another, he decided to stay and the town's folk axed open his spine and spread his ribs, gifting him the wings he mourned. They tied him to the scaffolding, granting him perpetual flight. There he hung, shedding skin and sin, letting the wind ring kestrel cries through his bones.

He waited for another future to unroll from the threads of time, the one where he decided to leave. All he caught were splinters of his past, each a molten skewer through his gut.

Ara found him in one of ramshackle tents where all the visitors stayed. She ducked beneath the flap bringing soothing shade to parched earth.

"I saw this," she said. "Us, I mean. Is this what you want?"

The stitches in his chest pulled tight. He pressed his fingers to the wound, pus leaking through the scabs he'd scratched and torn.

"I haven't seen the end though. I don't know if you'll let me finish what I start." Ara eased herself beside him. The weight of her was comfort and apprehension. "But unless we start, we'll never know." She took his hand, his callouses catching at her palm. She squeezed his fingers then gathered the hem of his shirt.

Ara expected his touch as he pressed his hand to her face, his eyes like an ocean, wide and trembling. She'd seen this too, but hadn't felt it. Now his fear dragged frosted fingers down her spine. Ara breathed it in, the iron of it clinging to her teeth.

She pulled off his shirt expecting a chest slabbed with the muscle promised by the breadth of his shoulders.

His chest was bound, muscle and more, constrained by eyelets and bow-tied strings.

A tidal wave of his humiliation crashed through her, leaving a bitter riptide as she fingered the bindings. Her own anger gnashed serrated teeth within her. Who had made him feel shame for this? Her anger simmered in the air between them, rank and acid.

"This is nothing to be ashamed of."

"It's not what you think." He caught her fingers. Ara pulled back, letting Renier loose the knots.

He set the binder on the straw-stuffed mattress beside them, the inside stained black and red. Ara traced a finger along the sharp outline of his collarbone and slowly down his chest to the feather embroidered above his heart. The stitches were taut, dragging at the bruised skin. Scabs cracked and oozed.

Her fingers tingled with the spell-work woven through his flesh. Magic, though none like she knew.

"What is this?" She asked. "What does it make you?"

"A soldier," he said, exhaling a dying gasp of pride. "At least, I used to be."

"Where I'm from, soldiers don't have to be a *he*."

"No. But I am." He met her gaze and held it with a half-clenched fist, waiting.

"You are," she said and the tension in his shoulders subsided.

He wrenched a feather from his hair and crushed the quill. The black-spotted fluff curled and withered on the floor. "I was a falcon once," he said. "I soared and spiraled…" His hand mirrored his imagined flight, his eyes glossed with memory. "Until I made a mistake." His words were shattered glass. His hand quivered mid-air then crashed to his lap. He choked and spat more feathers, soft and downy. They tumbled like ash at his feet. Ara caught one and held it to her face. Its secret murmured familiar, of a blade in the darkness.

She traced the fading scar where a falcon's feather had once been neatly sewn into the pale flesh of his chest. The residue of the spell stung her fingers.

"I took a life I shouldn't have," he said. "And got what I deserved." He dug his nails into the broken feather on his chest. "I'll never fly again, but I want…"

"To be free," she finished for him.

Time turned syrup and soup. It enveloped them both, scattering their past and future like breadcrumbs from a shaken table cloth. A drowning, a surging, unraveling and becoming. Lies and truths, secrets and memories. They held each other and weathered the storm, breathing through each other's lungs, swallowing one another's histories.

Ara emerged from its passing, naked and brittle, known to Renier in ways she never might've chosen. And he was known to her, both human and bird—the magic coursing through his veins sang of updrafts and air currents, of curved beak and sharpest talons.

He'd never wanted to be a soldier, enlisted only to save his family starved and depleted on a drought-stricken farm. And because he wanted to fly—a privilege bestowed only on those who served.

He'd killed a man—a prisoner already on the wrack. His sword across the man's throat, an act of mercy. And for disobeying orders to separate skin from flesh, teeth from jaw, marrow from bone, he'd been reduced to a spotted fowl barely capable of flight.

"You saved that man from torment," she said.

"I saved myself from what I hadn't the stomach to do."

"A kindness to you both."

They bent their heads, foreheads touching. Ara had seen the future. She knew what came next.

Her lips on his skin, her nails down his spine. He sighed and whimpered as she used her teeth on his chest, gnawing at the threads. Something cold found her fingers and she leaned back, wiping sour copper from her lips.

A fulgurite blade lay beside her hand. The kermis had provided.

Renier rolled the hilt into his palm. Time rippled, flashing a future where he flung the fragile knife to the floor.

Ara pried the dagger from his hand.

He let her and this time the spell-woven threads severed with ease. She teased each tattered end from his skin and her lips pressed truth to his wound: defiance took courage, betrayal had many faces, what he'd done was right.

"Take all of it," he said. "For the fence."

She paused, a question she didn't need to speak out loud.

"I'm sure," he said.

Again, Ara raised the blade and carved in the wake of her kisses.

After, with his chest bound and bleeding, he brushed his hands down her back. Her scars rose to meet his palms through the soft linen of her shirt.

"What about you?" he asked. His fingers trailed down her arms and found her wrists.

"Even if they flayed me entire, it wouldn't help. The rot in me goes deeper."

Renier had seen her past, flashes limned in burgundy. The swish and shiver of robes across marble floors. Candles and incense. Magic splitting the lips of the spell-weavers as they sent Fray-stolen power scudding through her veins, twisting the shape of her.

Once a year, they'd opened her back, rewarding the devout with the flowers born from her blood. But then... He'd seen the coin exchange hands and the curtained alcoves where those with titles paid to split her skin, to pluck out petals and suck on nectar. The chains thrummed a threnody against her bare ankles, knocking elegies from the hard stone beneath her knees.

Sometimes they sought to take more than the flowers from her veins.

Ara had endured so much, more than Renier could fathom. How could he begrudge her the blade dropped by a hand drunk on her blood, the moment seized, the throat slashed garnet as she fumbled for keys, loosed her chains and ran.

"We're the same." He held her hands, but she pulled them free.

"Look." She held her right arm between them, mottled with flitting shadow-bruises. The wrist had been severed, more than once. She dragged the blade across the thick scarring, cutting deep, and the smudge beneath her skin swarmed. Renier wrapped his hands around the wound, but no blood welled between his fingers. Instead, flowers erupted against his palms.

Coils of daisies tumbled from her severed skin, then delicate snowdrops dribbled to the floor. After that, spikes of purple lupini speared through the gash in Ara's arm. Finally, whole blooms gave way to single petals, each leaving stains on Renier's fingers. He watched the wound seal and tried to gather her pain as the blooms retreated to bruises beneath her skin.

"I never asked for this," Ara said, wiping lilac from her cheeks.

Renier pressed his lips to her wrist and kissed the truth between her ragged edges: defiance took courage, betrayal had many faces, what she'd done was right.

The freedom they both longed for furled tight around them. Like resting wings; like sleeping blooms.

Together, they walked to the fence and Renier fastened the swatch of flesh to an empty barb. Beneath it, the dirt swallowed up his shame, drinking every drop leaking from his shriveled offering.

The carnys and wanderers gathered to watch him leave, pressing close to Ara.

The gates swung open and the fireweed split apart to hem a path. He'd chased this kermis across the dunes, sun sick and desperate for a chance at redemption, for the hope of once more having wings. The freedom he'd found came without feathers.

Above him, the sky pulsed with the strange magic of the Fray, a heartbeat throb in time with his own—with hers.

He stepped through the gate. It closed. The fireweed hissed and spit embers, driving him away from the kermis crouched in the dirt.

Renier turned as the kermis gathered its appendages in ambulatory preparation. The tents and pennants rose, and Renier squinted against the sun to catch a glimpse of Ara. She twirled a spotted feather in her fingers and smiled. He pressed a hand to the flower folded into the binder, held snug against his chest.

Voices rose in song, splashing colors he couldn't name across the air as the kermis creep-crawled an escape from the reaching fingers of the Fray. In its wake, it left a trail of flowers: daisies and snowdrops, lupini and drifts of weeping lilac.

# The Bone Merchant
## *by Nicola Kapron*

Floating markets are never quiet, even early in the morning. Voices rise and fall with the tide—vendors offering wares, customers haggling, family and friends taking a moment to catch up. For some, it's the end of a long night spent fishing, spellcasting, or singing; for others, it's the beginning of a long day. I row my craft between brightly colored boats, breathing in the smell of fish and brine, taking note of what is for sale today. Bananas are coming back into season, it seems, and baskets of oranges stamped with a brand from far upriver speak of new success with greenhouses. Snakes and lizards crouch in elaborate terrariums of living wood, branching like trees from a particularly large vessel. My sister Senna sits within, stroking the jewel-toned cobra in her lap with steady hands.

"You're selling Kenni's babies?" I ask.

She smiles, keeping her teeth hidden. Most animals see a threat when humans smile. "Kinda have to. She keeps laying eggs and I don't have the space for them all. I brought her out here so she could vet anyone interested."

I drop my eyes to the snake. Kenni stares back with eyes like emeralds, stony and beautiful. Then she flicks out her tongue and I find myself stifling a giggle. "Good luck to you both."

"Good luck yourself," Senna says. "Arda's got your usual shipment. The night shift put it together a few hours ago."

"You're the best sister."

She lets out a snort. "Get going, dear sibling of mine. If you scare off my potential snake-parents, I'll make you buy them all."

I doubt Senna will have trouble rehoming Kenni's children. They're clever familiars. People like beautiful things, and jewel cobras are stunning. There are other creatures of living gemstone out there, but most of them are toxic, and few are so eager to live with humans. Jewel cobras will accept handling in a way few other beasts will. They'll even watch your kids if you train them right. That's how Senna and Kenni met, back when Senna was just a baby and I was too young to watch her alone. She cried when our mother first brought Kenni home, hoping the snake would fill the empty spaces in our little house. Now the two of them are inseparable.

Kenni was never quite as fond of me. Perhaps I was just too old for her to mother properly. Or perhaps she could already tell where my heart would lie. Some people deal with death by clinging to life with both hands; others just embrace that which they once feared. I did the latter.

Most animals don't make a habit of seeking out Bone Merchants. Even the wild tiger-cats that stalk the rubble of lost cities and half-flooded mangrove swamps give me a wide berth. Perhaps they can smell the death on me. I don't particularly mind. Taking on the burden of the dead is part of the life I've chosen.

Arda's boat is bright pink and filled with instruments. Harps, sitars, tiny flat pianos that play recorded sounds when you touch the keys. They've also got a second boat tied to theirs, and that one is overflowing with bagged goods. Vegetables, fruits, waterproof toys, fired clay containers, baskets made of woven plastics, glowing orbs that put off heat without flame. Everything I requested for this month's trip. Excellent. Arda themself is bent over an ocarina, carving out the holes with a faintly-shining reed and humming a wordless tune. They don't even blink as I pull up beside them. We've known each other a long time. They told me once that they figured out who they were from watching me figure out who I was. Although they've never felt the same pull toward the dead, they understand a side of me few others do. They know what it's like to not be a woman or a man.

"Good morning, Arda." I glance at the cargo boat and whistle. "Everyone pulled out all the stops this month, huh?"

They shrug fraying cornrows over their shoulder, stark against the fabric of a binder I gave them when I outgrew it, and look up. "Morning. Market's been seeing a lot of traffic from upriver, which means more of a share for you and yours. Went over the haul with the organizers last night. Did we get all the stuff on your list?"

"More than." I definitely didn't ask for the little metal drums tucked into the back of the cargo boat. "Did you make those?"

"The seafolk sing, right? I tried to think of something that would sound nice underwater."

"They do," I say. "And they're going to love your drums."

Arda throws the rope at me and ducks down, hiding their face. I catch it, careful not to lean too far over. These boats are made to be steady, but there's only so much roughhousing you can do before ending up in the water. From there, we work together to untie the cargo from their boat and retie it to mine. Anything too delicate I move to sit at my feet, where I can keep an eye on it as I row.

"You should put your hat on," Arda says when we're done. "The weatherwitches say it'll be a hot one."

"Thanks for the warning." I lift my conical straw hat from where it's been dangling off my neck and put it on properly. It doesn't pay to ignore the warnings of those who can read the sky. "Good luck."

"Good luck," they echo, and bury themself in their work once more. I give the knots one final tug and get to work rowing myself out to sea.

This market is held in a river delta, where the current meets the ocean. The water moves slowly here, carrying silt and other things down from the continent. Everything that goes into the river ends up here. Tools, lost jewelry, relics from the old cities. And bones, of course. Most things can be safely left to the sea, but the bones are different. If you just leave them drowned and nameless, their families will never stop mourning them and their spirits will never rest. Cold spots will form in the sea. The trees will grow too thick, too sharp, like teeth jutting up from a broken jaw. The wailing of ghosts rolls in with the fog on the sea.

It's wrong to abandon the dead where they lie, but it can be dangerous to fish them out. That's where the Bone Merchants come in.

With my hat on, people look at me. The Bone Merchants' silhouette—conical hat, dark robes, standing guard over a simple cypress wood box—is recognizable. They smile with sad eyes, but they don't call out until I pass. Floating markets are never quiet, but where I go, a trail of silence follows. A mission to retrieve the dead deserves a certain gesture of respect, after all.

If all goes well, the sea will be a little safer and a little less full of sorrow when I return.

I steer my cargo into the river's mouth, between the tangled trunks of mangrove trees. Their roots are deep underwater. Their branches reach for the sky. Hot sunlight beams down on my shoulders as I make my way into the ocean. Sea birds chatter overhead. Salty air fills my lungs. Out here the edges of the delta blend into an impenetrable mangrove swamp. Small trees grow submerged in warm shallows. Every once in a while, I glimpse a spire of something that is not wood breaking the surface. Stone. Steel. Ancient plastics. Cold waves that whisper softly as they lap at the sides of the boat.

A whole city, drowned. Remnants of a civilization that, like many others before it, believed itself too great to fall. Markers over a graveyard that has yet to run dry.

This is where the seafolk live.

Shadows in the water start to follow me as I row—blues and grays, greens and purples. As soon as I see them moving, I steer myself toward a calm spot and dig out the first of my tools: a hollow metal rod. It sinks noiselessly into the waves. I lower it until it's about halfway to the sand below then blow into it. The noise is swallowed by the water. Those colorful shadows freeze in place. A split second later, they're gone in a flurry of excitement. I take my oars out of the water and wait. It doesn't take long.

All at once, they come: a forest of sleek tails and billowing hair, twisting around each other like fingerlings, each of them at least twice as long as I am lying down. Some of them are bigger than my boat. These giants of the sea slither more than swim, their moving tresses shining slickly. I gaze at them, trying to pick out one I recognize.

There—a heavy-set woman with vibrant blue skin, eyes black as night, and a long mane of fiery orange hair. Ragged fins and scars weave across her broad frame. Her name is Fang, or at least that's what she's invited me to call her. The name is apt; when she smiles, it shows shark teeth. She rises up until the waves lap at her shoulders and clicks to make sure she has my attention. As soon as my eyes are on her, she begins signing at me. *Finally! Kept us waiting.*

The sign language of the seafolk is different from the one we use on land, designed for longer, webbed fingers. I've spent years learning it and my hands are still awkward around any but the most basic signs. Still, I do my best. The seafolk cannot speak a human language, and I dearly need to talk with them. *Apologies. I have arrived.*

She flicks her wrist. *Time to trade, Bone Merchant?*

*Yes. Let me show you what I have to offer.*

In some ways, the title of Bone Merchant is misleading. There is no buying or selling at this market. There is only me, carefully unwrapping foods, tools, and gifts the seafolk can't grow or make underwater and asking them who needs what. Mottled blue hands flicker through signs faster than I can read them.

*3 melons.*

*Water fabric.*

*Baskets, give me baskets.*

Clicks, whistles, and whalesong echo through the air as they chatter among themselves, showing off newfound treasures and testing fresh acquisitions. A young boy with fat purple tentacles sprouting from his scalp starts taking bites out of bananas without peeling them. His parent whistles sharply at him and slides one long nail down the fruit, exposing the soft white insides. Other children circle around the boat, asking me for fish from distant waters. It's like candy to them, I suppose.

I glance at the crowd of seafolk parents. *Can the children have fish?*

*The children are spoiled,* Fang signs at me. *Go ahead. It's a holiday.*

I reach into one of my bags and slip salted trout from their wrappings. Small hands slap eagerly against the water. Their skin is rough on mine as they accept their gifts. One of them, a skinny brown child with black stripes on their long, eel-like tail, eyes a set of Arda's drums and clicks questioningly.

*What are those?*

*Drums,* I tell the child. *Music. To listen to as you sing.*

Black eyes go wide. *Surface music! Can I have it?*

*Of course.* I hand a drum over carefully and show the child how to strike it. The second they try, every kid in the water wiggles with delight. Less than a minute later, I'm out of drums. Arda will be happy to hear their gift was appreciated.

The children dart off with their prizes. I get back to work. Only when both boats are empty and everything I brought has been divided up do I sit down. The seafolk swim circles around me, their voices reminiscent of dolphins, every free hand in motion. For a few minutes, I rest and let the sound wash over me. Then Fang lets out a long, drawn-out whistle and the voices quiet. Tailfins slice through the water as a good half of the crowd dives in unison. I roll up my damp sleeves, open the box, and wait.

My part of the exchange is over. Now it's time for theirs.

The first handful of bones is just that—a handful. A few crumbling phalanges, some tiny wrist bones, the beginning of a broken ulna. Just looking won't tell me much about the person they belonged to, so I cradle them in the palm of my hand and close my eyes. The memories of the dead unfold before me. These bones are old and weathered, from a person so long dead that even they hardly remember who they used to be. Even so, the sound of angry voices and the sharp bite of an axe tells me enough.

*Where did you find them?* I ask the gray, whiskered face bobbing beside my boat.

He cocks his head to the side. *Buried in old silt, under rock. Dislodged them while we were building.*

*Were there any more?*

*No.*

*I see. Thank you.*

I'll be grateful the sea has given back this much. I can't save this person who was murdered and buried here so long ago. What I can do is take their bones and mark them to ensure these remains are treated properly when I return to shore. In the meantime, I take two things out of the box: a waterproof bag and a ribbon. The bag is white for old bones, the ribbon orange for violent death. This will keep the bones safe and together. There's a space on the ribbon for names to be scrawled quickly with ink or magic. I leave it blank.

The gray man watches me carefully tie off the bag before he swims away, to be replaced by a rail-thin individual draped in green scarves and bearing a pair of matched femurs. After that, I am presented with a set of ribs. Then a pelvis. Then a skull. Some of them are ancient, dating back to the times when this shallow sea was still a beach city. Others are more recent. Not all the memories I call up speak of murder, but some do.

White bags for old bones, black bags for new. Blue ribbons for suicide. Red ribbons for accidents. Yellow ribbons for exposure. Everything neatly organized so that I know who to send them to once I get back to shore. I gather all the bones up and tuck them away with the same care. The seafolk watch with curious black eyes and answer my questions as best they can. Some of those blue faces had spent hours carefully unearthing lost skeletons; some had simply stumbled across stray bones while gathering seaweed or digging for resources. A few were even found by children at play. The last one to swim up to me is one of those children, wrapped in garments made of seaweed, holding a drum in one hand and a child-sized skull in the other.

She can't speak with me until one of her hands is empty, but I can see her intentions in the tilt of her head and hear them in the stream of impatient clicking sounds. My language lessons have taught me how difficult it is to be unable to talk. I take the skull from her as quickly as I can without harming it. As soon as the bone leaves her fingers, she begins to sign. *Why do surface-dwellers like bones so much?*

Oh dear. Always with the tough questions. I settle the skull in the crook of one arm so that I have my hands free. *All of these bones were once people, correct?*

*Yes, but you don't even know who they were. They could have been strangers. Or enemies.*

*That doesn't matter.* At least, it doesn't matter to me. It hasn't since Kemi, my other little sister, fell into the river when our father was supposed to be watching her. She was found months later by a Bone Merchant further down the coast, already picked clean. I still remember the way her remains sighed when I opened the bag to identify them. There was no grief in her bones. Someone else had already taken on that burden. I could never thank them enough for easing her pain. *Even strangers and enemies deserve to be acknowledged and mourned.*

She tilts her head, bird-like, and taps her nails on the surface of the drum. *Who was this?*

I place a finger on it and let my eyes slide shut. An image blooms in my mind: another little girl with dark brown eyes and tight coils of braids, wearing the same curious expression, staring into the water as though it was looking back. Reaching out with careless fingers. Taking a step too many when no one was looking out for her.

When I open my eyes, they burn. I work my way through a sentence with stiff fingers. *This was someone very much like you.*

The girl in the water lets out a burst of trilling whalesong and darts around, looking up at the skull from various angles. Finally, she stops moving so quickly and simply studies it. Studies me. *I'm not sure I see it, Bone Merchant,* she signs at last, *but I'm glad the bones have you to look out for them.*

I smile at her, eyes still stinging. *Thank you. I hope they feel the same.*

Everyone watches as I pack up the skull and gently lay it inside the box. Then Fang whistles sharply and the girl turns, ducking underwater as she swims back to the rest of the family. They're all diving now. Most of them click short farewells at me. A few linger long enough to sign a full goodbye. I sign back, as best I can, and then blow into the rod again. That sound declares the end of the Bone Merchant's monthly visit.

Only Fang remains now, hair spreading out on the surface of the water, like fire in the setting sun. *Are you well, Bone Merchant? You seem... damp.*

I wipe my cheeks dry and nod. *Thank you for everything.*

*Thank you,* she counters. *And take care of yourself. Work to exhaustion and you'll do no one any good, living or dead.*

Wise words from a wise woman. For a moment, she sounds like my mother, fretting over her baby's decisions. My mother wasn't often around, but she cared—enough to worry when I began to show an interest in reclaiming the lost. Enough to let me go when I told her my heart was here. *Understood, Fang.*

*Good. I'll visit next week with the pod's requests.* A brief pause, wherein she looks me up and down and I try to pretend I was never crying. *Goodbye. Get some sleep.*

*Goodbye,* I repeat. Sleep will have to wait. As she slips under the surface and follows the serpentine shadows of her people out to sea, I am checking the seal on the box, taking up the oars, and beginning the long row back home.

There's plenty of time for thinking during this final stretch. My thoughts are sluggish with foreign memories and foreign grief, but that doesn't stop them from churning. It's mostly old grief this month, which is always easier to bear than fresh. It settles over my shoulders like a blanket.

When I get back to shore, I will drop off the box and its precious contents at the mortuary and wish my fellow custodians of the dead luck. Then I will seek out my friends and family and ask about the floating market I couldn't attend. In turn, they will ask me about the seafolk, and when they can expect to see Fang swim by to speak with me. Arda may ask me about learning the seafolk's sign language. If so, I will happily teach them; more channels of communication between our peoples can only help. No matter what, we will share stories and sing songs and remind each other that we are alive.

In this moment, however, I bear the weight of the dead. Their fear. Their sadness. Their hopes. All that was once lost to the water, now slowly being regained. It's heavy, but I am more for carrying it. Those who loved the new dead will be more for having closure. We will all be more for learning the stories of the old dead. That feeling grows more pronounced as I paddle up the delta and the riverbank comes into sight.

Here is the place where the floating market is held, now close to empty. It's too early for the night market to set up and too late for afternoon shoppers. There's Senna's boat, still decorated with reptilian familiars, but fewer than before. Heads turn as I approach. Under any other circumstances, there would be a great shout of welcome. As it is, the people silently welcome me and my charges back into the community.

My eyes burn again. I will not cry here. This is a reunion, not a parting.

Behind me, the sun is dipping below the sea, but up ahead, there is light.

# LV2RD

## *by Shenoa Carroll-Bradd*

Chris Ebber leaned one shoulder against the doorjamb as he stared into the garage. Despite the smells of gasoline and dust, what really turned his stomach was the sight of the machine before him. Of all the impulsive, immature, *reckless* choices...

An arm slid around his waist, and then came the familiar weight of Sean's head against his shoulder.

"Beautiful, isn't she?" Sean sighed. "I think I'm in love."

Chris frowned harder at the slick black motorcycle standing in front of their camping gear. "She looks expensive. And dangerous." He fought the urge to turn and press a quick kiss into Sean's hair. He was close enough to smell eucalyptus oil conditioner, but he wanted his concerns taken seriously, and a kiss right now might weaken his stance. "What's the vanity plate supposed to say, anyway? Love turd?"

Sean laughed and released him. He walked into the garage and stroked the bike's handlebars. "Love to ride, you ass." He cocked his head, regarding the sleek machine. "Or live to ride, I suppose." He shrugged. "Open to interpretation."

Chris rubbed his arms. "I don't like it."

"I know. You've been giving her bitch-face for an hour." He sighed and stroked a hand down the length of the vehicle. "But I love her. She makes me feel like I'm flying."

Chris scoffed from the doorway, but when Sean turned to look at him, he sobered. His lover's face was perfectly serious.

"I mean it. I want to be buried with her."

Chris softened his stance and held out his arms. "All right, come here. Enough of that talk. This dumb bike's gonna rust out long before you do."

But it didn't.

After the accident, Chris kept the bike under a tarp in the garage so he wouldn't have to look at it. He'd wanted to take a bat to it for months, or have it crushed into a squealing, mangled cube at some auto junkyard. It didn't seem fair, none of it.

It wasn't fair that the stupid bike survived the accident, but Sean died. The bike was barely even scratched. It wasn't fair that he now had to take care of it, this stupid, dangerous, idiotic toy. He wanted to trade. He wanted Sean back, and to not have his murder weapon sleeping in the garage, where he had to pass it every time he did laundry.

"You bitch," he whispered as he walked past. "You took him from me. I hate you."

Sometimes, the tarp slipped off, and he'd get a nasty shock, coming face to face with the brute. He always rushed to cover it up again, though he couldn't justify the compulsion. He knew the motorcycle had no will of its own, no malevolence. It hadn't killed his love on purpose, it had just been a senseless, everyday accident.

And even though he couldn't bring himself to bury the toy with its victim, as requested, he also didn't have the heart to sell or destroy it. He didn't know what to do with it, so there it waited in the garage.

One night, as he was drifting off to sleep, there came a sudden, familiar rumble from downstairs. A motorcycle engine. Groggy, he stumbled out of bed.

It couldn't be what he was thinking. It was probably someone else on the block with a bike, and the quiet night street made it sound closer, made it echo so loud... He flipped on lights as he approached the garage and, just on a whim, checked the bowl of keys by the front door.

The motorcycle fob was there, right where it had sat since he had collected it from the coroner, along with Sean's wallet and phone. Those now sat in the back of his sock drawer, hidden and treasured like a teenager's porno mags, but he'd left the key out here. It didn't belong in the bedroom they'd once shared.

Chris pushed open the garage door just as the engine sound began to fade. The big, roll-down garage door was still closed, but the tarp that normally covered the bike lay crumpled on the ground.

For the briefest second, Chris was relieved. He didn't have to sell it or destroy it. Someone had answered his prayers, hot-wired and stolen the bitch.

But no. No matter how often he'd avoided looking at it, the motorcycle's sudden absence now felt wrong. Sean had loved her, so a tiny, bitter part of Chris loved her, too. He scooped his keys from the bowl and hustled outside in time to see the motorcycle take a sharp turn out of sight.

Hopping in his truck, Chris pursued. He tracked the motorcycle down the empty road for miles. In his haste to follow, he hadn't gone back upstairs for his phone, so he couldn't alert the police. All he could do was follow the sound of the engine, and the single light that tracked through the dark.

The thief had a head-start, and it was all Chris could do to keep the headlight in sight around corners and over hills. Driving barefoot was uncomfortable, but he slowly began to shrink the distance between them.

The motorcycle crested a moon-washed hill.

Chris instinctively hit the brakes. There was no thief. No one in the seat. The motorcycle was driving itself.

His mind blurred with excuses and explanations. Someone had managed to install a remote control on the bike. Or it somehow had an electrical short and was running by itself.

They were all ridiculous, but what else could he believe? That it was haunted? That it was... alive?

The bike led him straight to the last place Chris wanted to go. It drove toward the iron gates with a speed that made Chris sure it was going to crash right through.

But then the front tire rose, and the engine sound changed from a heavy thrum to a thinner whine as it lifted up and sailed clear over.

Chris threw his truck into park and got out, the asphalt cool and rough beneath his feet.

From the other side of the wall came the impact of tires and the engine's throaty rumble once more. He had to get to it.

Chris climbed over the front gate and jogged through the graveyard, headed to where the headlight shone bright like a lonely jewel, an infant moon. He slowed as he approached, rubbing the goosebumps along his chilled arms.

The motorcycle idled atop Sean's grave. It purred like a cat in a sunbeam.

"You bitch," he panted. "Why did you drag me here?"

Tears pricked his eyes. He reached out and placed a hand on the leather seat. Warm, as if the rider had just left it. At his touch, the kickstand came down. The light and engine cut out simultaneously, plunging Chris and the graveyard into moonlit darkness. He kept his hand on the seat.

"I miss you," Chris told the gravestone. "I miss you like hell, and I'm pissed you left me like this. So soon. I promised to love you forever. How dare you—" His voice broke, and he hung his head, shoulders shaking. "How dare you not give me the chance?" His fingers curled, short nails digging into the seat leather. "You stupid, selfish…"

He sank to his knees on the grave, leaning his forehead against the backs of his hands as he wept. A soft breeze rustled the hair along the nape of his neck, soft as grazing fingers.

Chris took a shuddering breath before wiping his cheeks dry. "I'm glad you have your toy back. I hope it still makes you feel like you're flying." Using the motorcycle for support, he pushed himself to his feet again. Chris reached past the handlebars to press his palm on the cold headstone beyond. "I love you, you dead idiot. You'd better start practicing your apologies. You better believe I'll want to hear them when we meet again."

Chris left the bike where it was and drove home.

When he came back later that week, the motorcycle was gone.

Maybe it was removed by the groundskeeper, or maybe it was stolen. Either way, he wasn't too surprised. A valuable piece like that couldn't just be left lying around. But still, a part of him was sad to see it go.

As he lay in bed that night, Chris heard a familiar sound approach from the distance, purring up the road. He smiled as the motorcycle passed the house and sped off up the hill toward the cemetery, fading into the night.

The bitch vanished and reappeared many times over the years, always roaring back to her post at night. Before long, it became a local attraction. Lovers scratched their initials into the paint, tourists posed and took pictures on its back, and Chris visited, whenever he could.

He added a clause onto his will so that, whenever it came his time to go, not only should he be buried beside Sean, but the motorcycle should be interred with them, laid across their coffin lids like a pair of clasping hands.

# Mishael's Love
## *by Geri Meyers*

Mishael stepped out onto the garden terrace, his eyes catching sight of Jhennais immediately. He was the only prophet in the garden at the moment, sitting by a flowering purple bush. The color contrasted against the vivid red of his hair. As always he was resplendent in his rich silver and grey robes, the fabrics patterned with leaves on some layers, shot with silver embroidery on others. His hair was braided back from his face with smaller braids and laced with silver ribbons, gathered to drape over his shoulder in one elaborately elegant plait. His blindfold was darker grey, embroidered with leaves to match the pattern of his robes.

Mishael couldn't help the way his breath caught at the sight. He wasn't certain when exactly it was the small child he had watched over since he himself was a youth had become a young man, but the youth before him was no longer a child, and his beauty touched the priest deeply.

Jhennais turned a puzzle box over in his hands, gloved fingers pressing here and there, flipping switches and shifting movable bits. The prophet loved the boxes, often reshuffling them as soon as he finished. Mishael loved the way Jhennais bit the side of his lip in concentration, wearing away the sheen of lip balm he wore. Mishael shook himself from his study, and Jhennais' hands stilled as he heard the priest's footfalls approach.

"Mishael?" he asked, though the priest knew the prophet had no doubt it was him. "I'm not late for our meeting, am I? I thought I had until the shadows reach me here. Perhaps I sat on the wrong bench."

"You aren't wrong," Mishael said, his eyes lingering on the seat beside the prophet. He longed to take it, but even one such himself wouldn't dare to sit so close to an unbonded prophet, especially not with the two black-clothed attendants who stood just behind Jhennais looking on. Instead he stood beside the bush, pretending to admire the flowers while his eyes strayed to Jhennais. "I finished my tasks early and thought I'd join you for a bit of sun. I hope you've put lotion on your skin, it'd be a shame if you burned, with that fair skin of yours."

"Of course," Jhennais returned dismissively. "There is no need to worry over my person, I'm well tended to."

Mishael smiled at the prophet. As a child he'd fought for independence from his attendants, wanting to bathe and dress himself, but as a young man he'd submitted to their care, focusing his ambitions on loftier goals. He would eventually become the most powerful of the temple prophets as he came into his gifts, and he spent his time on his studies of their world and his power instead of resisting his station.

"Mishael, why do you spend your free time with me?" Jhennais asked, tucking his puzzle box into a sleeve of his robe. Mishael watched the gesture, savoring the precise movements, wondering for a moment what those fingers touching along his arm might feel like. Cheeks heating, he dashed the thought from his mind.

"Hm?" He drew his gaze up to Jhennais' face, the delicate curve of his cheekbones, the sweep of his petal pink lips, the fall of a thin, vibrant red braid against his cheek.

"Why do you spend your free time with me?" the prophet repeated impatiently. "Surely you must have friends or family who miss you. Or a lover? I don't require your attention at all times."

Mishael ran a hand back through his silver-touched hair. "No, my friends are here in the temple, my family too far to visit. I've no lover. I haven't had one for some time."

"Why not?" Jhennais asked, frowning. He drew a knee up to his chest, his robes parting around it, exposing the tight fit of the grey pants he wore beneath his robes. He rested his cheek against his knee, fingers smoothing down the fabric over his shin, to touch along the soft doeskin of the grey boots he wore. "You aren't limited as prophets are, aren't you lonely?"

"I'm never lonely when I'm with you," Mishael lied, his heart clenching. Lonely... yes, he was lonely, terribly lonely knowing he would never be able to touch the beauty before him, knowing that even if he dared speak his feelings for the prophet, it was pointless. Prophets were never bound to priests, and Mishael knew Jhennais himself had no desire to be bound at all. No one would ever touch him.

"Is that true?" the prophet wondered, and something in his tone suggested he knew the truth, or at least suspected Mishael's lie. Or perhaps that was only Mishael's own guilt leading him to think so. "Am I really so great, to chase away another's loneliness? What have I to offer?"

"So much, Jhennais," Mishael responded, clenching his hand into a fist at his side to resist the desire to touch the other's shoulder. "You are smart, driven, determined, you bring excitement and a sense of purpose to those around you. Who could be lonely at your side?"

The prophet was quiet for a moment, then he rose abruptly to his feet, his robes trailing behind him as he swept forward down the path. "Walk with me."

Mishael was quick to fall into step beside him, and careful to keep a respectful distance as the attendants followed close behind. "What is it?" he asked.

Jhennais remained quiet for some time, walking the paths of the garden from memory, never once stepping off the path despite his blindness. He stopped only when they'd reached the outer wall, where one could step to the edge and look out across the whole of Klaeden Hold, see all the way to the harbor, if one were sighted. Jhennais stepped up to the edge, hands touching the stone railing, and the wind caught and tugged his hair and clothing. Mishael joined him, looking down the dizzying distance to the ground, where supplicants moved like ants as they passed inside the temple's doors.

"I'm lonely," Jhennais admitted. "I have a destiny, and I am proud of it. I will do everything in my power to make the visions Ilwhythior has granted me become a reality, but I will never be able to take a lover, I will never sire children, I am... I am separated from the rest of humanity. I accept it, and I would not change it, for what I mean to achieve will be worth that which I give up, but... to deny that I am lonely would be to suggest I make no sacrifices to achieve my goals, and that lessens what I will accomplish."

"That's true," Mishael said, looking over at him. "But you may still love even if you can't touch another. I will always be at your side. If the loneliness is too much, come to me, speak with me, and I will do all I can to ease your pain."

Jhennais' lips curled in a smile, and Mishael's heart fluttered at the sight. He longed to pull the other into his arms, to stroke his hair, to kiss him, to feel that smile against his own lips though it would be the ultimate desecration of the prophet's person. He closed his eyes and let his mind wander, imagining the feel of Jhennais' body pressed against him. The wind was almost chill despite the sun and as he felt it against his lips, he thought of how it might have touched the prophet's as well, carrying the taste of the other's lip balm to his.

"This is my burden," Jhennais said softly, breaking into Mishael's day dream. "I have no desire to force you to suffer it as well. I am glad of your company, but if I were to do such a thing, it would be bothersome to you."

"Never," Mishael said, opening his eyes to look at the prophet once more. "I believe, in the time we've spent together, we've at least become friends. Your pain is mine."

Jhennais hesitated a moment, and then he reached out, his gloved fingers touching lightly on Mishael's shoulder in thanks. It was such a fleeting touch that even the attendants could do nothing about it where they stood so close, but it sent a fire through Mishael's shoulder and arm, a tingle across his chest, and a burning desire in his loins. Ilwhythior forgive him, he wanted the prophet more than he'd ever wanted any other.

Mishael drew a deep breath, letting it out slowly and counting backward from ten to cool his blood. It wasn't just desire, he had to admit to himself. He could never say it out loud, never admit to his feelings, but he loved Jhennais. He couldn't pinpoint when it had become the truth, couldn't admit when he'd realized his growing feelings for the other weren't simply pride over a precocious student or admiration for such a sharp mind. He couldn't even truly say when his dream lovers began to take Jhennais' shape, his figure, the red of his hair, but it had happened and Mishael was helplessly lost to the other.

The prophet drew back from the wall, letting out a soft sigh. "I suppose that's enough sun," he commented. "Shall we return to our studies? I believe we were to discuss the terms of alliance between the Endless Isles and Eienvyand, the kingdom of King Zyphius' first wife."

"Ah, yes, of course," Mishael said, and drew away from the wall as well. Whatever his feelings for the prophet, they must be thrust aside. He would resist acting on them, for the prophet had a destiny too important to be jeopardized and Mishael would do everything in his power to support him. Sending a silent prayer to Ilwhythior for strength and willpower, he accompanied the prophet inside the temple to continue his lessons.

# What's Ours is Ours, What's Hers is Everyone's

## *by L. Reed Walton*

"If you put one of those Equalizers on me, I'll haunt you when I'm gone."

That's what Aja told me, and I couldn't laugh it off.

She was about to go into treatment. Me, I was determined to worry about little things like holding her hair when she puked. That led to picturing clumps of golden hair falling out in my hands and the laughter drained away.

I shook my head and told her, "You ain't gonna be *gone.* Don't talk that way."

"I'm serious," she said.

So I told her, yeah, fine, I won't get one unless you ask.

Which Aja never would, because god*damn* if she wasn't the most stubborn woman I ever met. One of the things I liked most about her, back when her being so damn pig-headed mattered less.

Then cancer snuck in and everything went tits-up. The cancer made me hate part of her: all those angry, rampant cells eating up her insides.

And believe me, I never loved *nothing* like I love Aja. With her wide jaw and sharp little chin, eyes a mite too close together over her button nose. My girl, with hair like straw in the sun, same color as the field we got married in four years ago.

Her and me and Dinny and Lou snuck in at the dead spot along the Lectrifence, hauling a pop-up arch of fake flowers. Not a tree in sight, nothing to prop the thing on. So I held one end and Aja the other, our free hands joined up in the middle.

Wasn't a cloud in the sky and we were knee-deep in new sorghumoid, its fuzzy yellow flowerheads throwing off pollen, making us sneeze. Dinny kept us too long reading Bible passages off her tab. I cried the whole time, blaming it on allergies. Really it was her—just Aja—laughing with pollen-dusted lips. When I kissed that tart greenness off her mouth, I understood what it meant to say something tasted *alive*. We held sweat between our palms, slippery, enough to fill the water table back up to brimming. Lou took pics and Dinny read the Bible. Not thirty seconds after the ring exchange, the farmer came tearing out in a big four-x Field Hover with a pistol shooting flares, disappearing in the bleached sky. Dinny and me and Aja ditched the flower arch and booked it like hell toward the fence, Lou behind us cackling and snapping away.

In every image, there are tear-trails through bright green on my cheeks.

I don't cry anymore. Aja's cancer shaved her down to a tiny gray thing I could tote around in my pocket. It changed up her guts. What it didn't change was her mind, and that made me hate the stubbornness, too.

Like the cancer, *I* am angry and rampant. Because of it, I interrupted the nurse bang in the middle of him explaining the treatment.

"You got a thingy that takes away a person's pain but you ain't cured *cancer*?" I asked. "That seems kinda ass-backward to me."

He hugged his tab tighter like I was going to steal the thing. Like he wasn't lookin' at me holding my own, battered as it was.

"There's no need to raise your voice, Mrs. Crider."

And I told him, "Don't you *Mrs. Crider* me," even though Aja was smiling all tight and embarrassed and tugging on my sleeve like she does when my big mouth gets us in trouble.

With a smile just as tight but half as real, the nurse told me, "We're able to cure many cancers. But cancer is not just one disease. There isn't one single cure."

With Aja's hand near about to tear my shirt off, I opened my mouth again.

And the nurse said: the Equalizer doesn't *get rid of* pain. It lets people *share* it.

"Kinda like marriage," I said, and that was when Aja cuffed me on the back of the head.

*The Equalizer transfers a portion of the burden of discomfort onto the healthy team member, so the member receiving treatment can better focus on healing.* I read that off the free DataBite I uplinked in the reception room.

I'm typically fine letting Aja make decisions, seeing as she's the more outgoing of the two of us, and probably the smarter. But right then I knew I would mortgage my own skin to get us an Equalizer. Sell all our furniture, live out of our dumpy old Tesla van in the treatment center parking deck, whatever it took.

Go-Along Misty Crider smiled at her wife and left her to make the immunotherapy appointment. Cancer Wife Misty came back the next day and went to an Equalizer intro seminar. 'Cause she's mean and devious. And so in love.

Far as I saw, I was the only one there by myself. I parked my bony ass in the back row with two donuts and a cup of the free coffee. You can bet the chirpy lady up front kept side-eyeing me the whole time, and I stared right at her if only to keep from looking around the room. Most of the folks there were older types, one or the other of them crying through the whole presentation.

The ones that weren't crying, I figured, were the ones getting paid. Oh, yeah. In the materials on the 'Bite, it said you could hire someone to be your pain buddy. Only they were called a *team member* on the Equalizer link. Pages and pages of poor bastards ready to farm themselves out to Equalizer, Inc.

Pain for a paycheck.

*Generous financing plans available.*

It took all I had not to chuck the tab across the room.

Instead, I watched my wife sleep. Four years and it still felt shivery to call her that. I mean in the pleasant way, the rumbly-insides way that felt like holding in good news. Aja had her mouth half-open, crushed against the pillow. Sooner or later, she'd shift far enough so her nose hit the pillow. A minute after that, she'd figure out she couldn't breathe and jerk her head up, doing this rabbity scrunch with her nose before she settled down again. I'd seen it a million times. Used to make me laugh hard enough to shake the mattress.

That night, of course, the laughter wouldn't come.

After the meeting ended, I thumbed powdered sugar out of the corners of my mouth and went right up to Chirpy Woman.

"I can't afford it," I said, "but I want one. So tell me how."

"Oh, my, honey," she cooed. "Don't worry. The clinic doesn't charge for them. It's part of the treatment plan, if you want it. You only have to pay if you hire a team member from the union."

My fingers shook from sugar and relief, and I told her yes, I wanted it. And that Aja didn't.

"They all refuse at first," Chirpy Woman said, "until they know what it's like. You come on back to me then." She shared her contact info to my tab.

*Ashlinn Becks*, the card said when it popped up.

I dodged when Ashlinn went in for a hug, though. I hated the look on her face that said she understood. At that second, I knew which *team member* she'd been... and why she wasn't sick anymore.

By the door, I did turn around one more time. "Do they all take it?" I asked. "After the pain hits?"

Ashlinn smiled, shaking her head.

Yeah, just my luck. *Damn you, Aja.*

I kept hoping she'd see reason. Those first rounds of treatment were terrible. On her *and* on me (and I wasn't even Equalizing then!). She was doing targeted ions on top of the immuno, taking a rainbow of rattling pills in all sizes of bottles, a little city skyline next to our bed.

It all made her groggy and sick and covered her peachy skin with weird pinpoint bruises. I sat with her in the puke-smelling bathroom, her head on my leg and the rest of her stretched out all along the cool tile.

Her panties were hanging off her hips, a sad tent. In the couple years before her diagnosis, Aja had gotten decent at baking and put on a tiny spare tire that puffed up over the top of her jeans. That was gone now, and even more weight besides. I put my hand on her flank so I didn't have to see her ribs, and talked about when we were in high school.

Not that we hung out back then. Me, the girl with doodles instead of notes on her school-issue tab, wearing the same black jeans every day until they stood up on their own. And Aja: the honest-to-God cheerleader. Wasn't any circumstance where we'd even end up talking, except I thought she was cute and we were both white trash from the Eco-Farm shares.

A long time later—years—she told me while we waited tables that she'd been scared to talk to me in school. I was shocked she wanted to talk right then. God, she was gorgeous. Cheeks like one of those paintings of baby angels. Hair, too. I kissed her the first time in that diner, by the auto-sweeper closet, her blonde curls all around my face. They smelled like a cheap, candy-sweet fragrance spray. In that moment, I was sure nothing would ever be bad again.

But it was.

After five or so treatments left her beached on the bathroom floor, her doc said they were going to shift her drugs, try to make her less miserable. They'd given her some pain meds that made her spacey. I hoped she was out of it enough not to notice when I left.

I told the nurse I was off on a vending machine run and dashed up the stairs to Ashlinn Becks.

"Is it bad?" Ashlinn asked when I was leaning against the door frame in her office.

And I gave her a look like, *Why else would I be here?*

She reached out her hand like she was putting it over mine, though I was nowhere near the desk.

I shut the door behind me and Ashlinn started her spiel.

An Equalizer is three things: a *module* and two *nodes*. You and the sick person take a node each. The healthy person controls the module. It won't let the healthy one take more than half the feeling from the sick one.

"It does nobody any good if both team members are incapacitated," Ashlinn said.

"Incapacitated?"

She blushed a little, and it reminded me of Aja, which put a bitter-metal taste in my mouth. "It means 'not able to do anything.'"

"Right." I nodded. "Gotcha." Pissed me off when people used big words when they didn't need to.

"The node lodges in the gut," Ashlinn went on, "which is the optimum—that is, the best—place for sensing the body's pain signals. Now you're controlling the nodes, so it's up to you to figure out your levels. How much both of you can handle before things start to seem off. We encourage communication between union team members and buyers..." She trailed off, not saying what she meant.

So I said it. "But not if they don't know."

"Correct."

"I guess most sick people are like Aja," I said. "They don't want to put pain on someone they love."

Ashlinn nodded all slow. "You get it, Misty. That's why it's best you work up to the maximum—the highest—on the module instead of taking it all at once. I promise you: your wife is in pain, but she's not dumb."

For the first time in forever, I almost laughed, only because Ashlinn hit that nail head-on. "No, she is not."

If all her misery vanished at once, I'd never hear the end of it. Which is why she couldn't *ever* know.

Ashlinn nodded again. "One more thing you need to know: the node is very small. However, it has to be swallowed."

Hopping up out of her chair quick enough to send it gliding off behind her, she pulled an old-fashioned key from the top drawer. I'd never seen a physical key outside a pic before. She jammed the thing into a little slot and tried to turn it, putting serious elbow grease behind it.

I was about to offer to help. Farm work may not make you smart, but it makes you strong.

"I have *got* to get this upgraded," she said over her shoulder, with an embarrassed giggle.

I was starting to like this lady. Peppy as a high school cheerleader. I liked to think she liked me, too.

At last, Ashlinn hauled off and slammed the heel of her hand against the side, right by the lock. The cabinet popped open. She reached in and took out a couple of slippery bio-baggies.

I watched them flutter down to the desktop. Out of one comes a little disk not much bigger than one of the old metal coins my Grandpop showed me when I was a kid. He had a few of them, sealed up in a sheet of bubbles. They came from Great-Grandpop, he said, who started gathering them up because he thought it might be interesting in the future.

Grandpop was interested. Little Baby Misty, not so much.

He told me people used to carry them around as money. I called bullshit (not using that word), but he swore to it: before people did everything on their tabs, they did it on phones. Before *that*, they had plastic cards and pieces of paper and those metal coins. Not every place took every kind of money, so you had to have all three.

I said people in the old days were stupid. He laughed at that, but I never did change my take on the matter.

The disk was lighter than a coin in my hand. Ashlinn opened the second baggie and two tiny seeds bounced into my palm. It kind of filled up my heart a little, made me get close to crying.

Me and Aja, we were farm kids. We knew seeds.

Ashlinn said those were the nodes. She sent a DataBite to my tab with instructions. That was good; I do better with reading than hearing stuff. Aja's just the opposite and always has been. Someone says something and her mind snaps it out of the air and holds on.

Or it used to, before the meds.

"Who was it for you?" I asked Ashlinn.

She looked surprised. She shouldn't have been, I thought.

"My mother." She looked at her desk, not me. "We were both relieved when we knew it was over."

In my head, I called bullshit. *She* was relieved. Her dead mom didn't feel nothing.

Outside my head, I said "Yeah. Sure."

If I lost Aja, the pain we shared between us would all fall on me. Not pain in my body, but pain in my mind and my blood and my life, because she'd be gone. You can't give *that* kind away with a seed in your gut.

I scooted on back to Aja and the doc; they were close to wrapped up. I drove her home in our clunking van and put her in our bed, with its sheets that smelled sour and sickish no matter how many times they were washed.

In the kitchen, I tapped my node to the module and swallowed it down with a palmful of dirt-tasting water from the tap.

Aja wasn't meant to have alcohol, what with all her meds, but I grabbed a bottle of our favorite beer from the fridge. It was this stout that tasted like chocolate cake blended up. Quarter of the can for her in a little glass, and I dropped the tiny node-seed in through the foamy head.

"Cheers to things getting better from here, babe," I said, sitting down on her side of the bed.

The look she gave me was half *no* and half *hell yes.*

I gave the glass a good long sniff, adding an *ahh* at the end.

"You're bad for me," Aja said, taking the glass. Smiling.

"I'm anything you want. You know that. Drink up." Her grin killed me in the best way, every time.

There was a little tickle of excitement in my chest as I watched her drain the glass. A seed means something's getting started, after all.

And for a while, by God, things were good. Were *growing.*

Cranking up the module the first time made me puke my guts out. At least I was lugging a bag of trash to the hydrogen composter at the time. It was four months since the last rain and Arkansas was due a storm or two before it dried up again. Still, I didn't want to risk Aja seeing a juicy pile of sick, so I scooped up what I could with the bag and chucked it in the composter's ozone-smelling mouth. Afterward, I kicked dust over the rest.

But there was no more puking after that, not for me or her. And I started thinking maybe the stuff on the 'Bite was true: shuffling off some of the pain let you focus on healing. Aja chalked it up to new meds and a good attitude. Picturing the seed all tucked up in the wall of her stomach, I said *Yes it sure is, honey,* and otherwise shut my mouth.

At night before I went to sleep, I would reach over in my bedside drawer and tap the level on the module up a notch. Every one of those taps meant a little more hope, like hash-marks on a prison cell wall.

Once Aja had herself up and walking around for at least a couple weeks, I headed down to the Income Office and cut off assistance. Figured I could work again, and Consuela at the diner was happy to have me back. She even asked about Aja. I said she was studying at U of A and I made the lie convincing. By then, lying was sewn in with the same stitch as the truth.

On my night off, I coaxed Aja into a pair of jeans and ride-shared us both out to this old cowboy bar called the Rusty Fiddle. When we were first dating, we used to go there and make fun of the kids from our class. Those stuck in town working the farms or the seed stores or the desalinators, thinking like fools that someday we were gonna get out.

In the looks from those old classmates now, I saw triumph and pride. A look of *I told you so*. I sent it right back to them and concentrated on my wife.

In the dark and the pink-and-blue lights, she didn't look as yellow anymore, and her eyes were all lit up. Her hair had a little shine to it. When we slow-danced to "Pale Moon" and "I Need That Girl," I pushed my nose against her neck. She smelled different on top, so I sniffed until I got that underneath scent. The one that got me drunk without a single drink in me.

She'd been tipsy the first night I ever took her home, in my cramped old gross apartment with the loud dogs next door. I was stone-cold sober and nervous as hell.

On my mattress with blankets tangled all around us, Aja stopped my hands when I got to undoing her pants.

"It might be a little weird," she said, on account of her being an XY girl.

I shrugged and said "Okay," and went about unbuttoning, anyhow.

"You ever been with an XY girl?" she asked.

"Never been with *no* girl. Of any kind."

"Boys?"

"Ew, no. Come on, now."

"You're a *virgin*?"

I blushed and hoped she couldn't see in the dimness. "Does it matter?"

"No," Aja said. "Hell, no, it doesn't. Come on up here and let me show you some things."

And, Lord, she did. A few times before we got married, she'd ask now and then if I felt like I didn't have enough experience with other people.

"I don't *want* experience with other people." I wrinkled up my nose. "I want *you*."

Finally, she stopped bringing it up.

At the Rusty Fiddle, under the hot blue and pink lights, I wanted her more than ever. My little gray shade, my slip of a girl. The dance floor shrank down to me and her, wrapped in the smell of beer and sweat. A little sickness, but underneath it... all *her*. I hooked my fingertips around each of her skinny shoulder blades and hung on.

Then Aja fell.

Went limp in my arms and nearly took me down with her. It was all I could do to keep her from hitting her head on the sticky floor. There were concerned voices, people kneeling down. Then the music stopped.

"She's all right, she's all right!" I shouted. No music to shout over; it was more for me than anyone else. Definitely not for Aja. Her pretty blue eyes were rolled up, only the blood-streaky white showing. "She's okay."

I repeated that in a whisper the whole ride to the hospital.

I stopped when the doc said the cancer had gotten in her bones.

"It's really surprising she didn't feel worse," the doc told me. "You said you were at a bar?"

I didn't like her suspicious tone, so I excused myself, stalking off without another word.

Aja was still out cold.

It being night and all, there was no one in Ashlinn's office. The door was unlocked. I breathed out; I hadn't wanted to bust the damn thing down. Inside, I shut it after me. If I remembered things right, I wouldn't need the old metal key. With my fingertips wedged in above the lock, I took a deep breath and whacked the bejesus out of the cabinet edge. It pinched my fingers, making me bite the inside of my cheek 'til I tasted blood.

When I hauled back and got ready to smack it again the door popped open and my hand slid into the cool darkness of the cabinet.

The air inside felt electric on my skin, the pile of baggies like silk wrapping my fingers. Angry, rampant Misty, as huge as sickness, put as many of the damn nodes in her coat pocket as she could. Whatever kind of person I was before had left. A cold, metal thing like the cabinet reared up in its place. It had no angles, only smooth planes that nobody could get a grip on. I would be slippery. I would spare Aja the pain of her decline.

She didn't remember much when she woke up. They had her doped; she was dizzy and saying nonsense, floating on a big cloudy wave of the good stuff. I'd already cranked up the level on the module even more.

The first coherent thing she said to me?

"You look like microwaved shit."

My laugh came back for a minute, hard and wheezy and donkey-like. I excused myself before it turned into crying. Begged off to blow my nose and ran to the bathroom, sitting on a lidless toilet and cough-sobbing 'til I was dried out from the inside.

Bless her, she said nothing about my puffed-up face or red eyes when I came back.

They didn't discharge her for another two days.

At home, I got her settled up in bed, where she passed out right away. It was enough. Enough to take the tiny disk of the module into the bathroom, sitting on the floor with tears dropping into my cleavage and on my sweatpants, *tap tap tapping* one node after another onto the module. A tiny flare of light with each one.

I believed it was working because I *had* to.

The neighbor, Pooja, agreed to sit with Aja for my Tuesday diner shift. I hid the meds and the paperwork and said she had pneumonia. Before leaving, I kissed my wife's cold and sweaty forehead.

She said nothing; I said nothing. What I promised didn't need words.

At Consuela's, I tucked a node into every plate I brought out. I pushed them in mashed potatoes, shoved them in the center of pies with a toothpick and covered the hole with whipped cream. I dropped them into milkshakes. If a patron picked it out or didn't finish, I dug it right out again and put it on the next plate.

One by one by one, sometimes in whole families, until they were gone.

At the end of shift, with my fingers crossed, I cranked the module all the way up.

Aja was sitting in bed when I got back.

"Feel better, baby?" I asked.

"Yeah," she said, her face pink and smiling. "No idea what happened."

"Me neither." I slapped on my biggest and most beamy smile, and didn't even have to fake it. We stayed up late, almost until dawn, with her head on my arm. I let it rest there long after my hand went numb.

While we were scraping the spiky crust off a carton of ice cream and ruining our spoons, Aja said, "Ever think about what it'd be like if we had this back in high school? We'd still be us, right now, except on a blanket under the bleachers by the sports field with a sonic zapper frying bugs by our heads."

"You're truly weird sometimes, my love."

"It wouldn't matter what we were doing. But we would have had so much more time. Do you ever think about that?"

"No," I told her. I felt the lie—every lie—in my gut. Like I felt the node. I hope they *all* felt it.

In truth, I ached to see the old Aja, chubby with youth, stretched out in the shade with her short-shorts on. I'd trace the crease underneath her butt until she giggled and squirmed. Aja wasn't ticklish anywhere but right there and on the bottoms of her feet, but God forbid I touch her feet unless I really fancied getting kicked in the face.

With three or four hours' sleep behind me the next morning, I couldn't stay in bed any longer. I made Aja eggs from the living complex coop. After we ate, I dug through our closet and tossed a duffel on the bed.

"Pack up, sweetheart," I said. "We're going on a trip."

From now until whenever, it'll be just me and Aja in the Tesla van, taking the highways. If we can't see the world, at least we can see the country. I wanted to take her to a beach, maybe Alabama or Florida. Arkansas has no beaches. I wanted her to see snow—real snow—or a mountain. I wanted more than I could give her in the time we had.

The time I *bought*, while the people from the diner got sicker and sicker.

Maybe their doctors will find the nodes before it stops mattering. Probably not all of them. Even so, one day in the future they'll all feel better. All at once.

They won't know the reason, and they'll call it a miracle.

But until then, Aja.

Until then.

# Let Our Song Be About Love
## *by Regina Jade*

There were some things that Ben expected to see out the viewports of Station 139: stars twinkling in the distance, drifting hunks of meteors, the occasional wandering deep space probe.

A giant blue-green tail, however, was not one of them.

Ben paused mid-step, turned, and backed up. Station 139 offered expansive viewports, ostensibly because no expense had been spared in its construction. Mostly, though, the only thing displayed was the vast inky blackness of space, as far as the eye could see. Space usually wasn't that interesting, and Ben had long since grown used to hurrying past on his ritual morning trip to the coffee maker. After all, there was no better alarm clock than a caffeine craving.

"Guess I won't be needing the coffee after all," Ben muttered, because sure enough, that was indeed a giant blue-green tail outside of the viewport and Ben was indeed very awake now.

The Station computer chimed in recognition of Ben's voice. "Good morning, Commander," chirped the pleasant-sounding AI. "Shall I begin preparing your breakfast?"

Ben opened his mouth to respond with a negative, but then he winced when a powerful *thump* sounded over his head. It was followed by two more thumps as the tail twisted and thrashed against the window, and then, quite suddenly, a face was there in the viewport. It was the angriest face Ben had ever seen, accented by glowing golden eyes, sharp teeth, and pointed ears. Together with the tail and the noticeable lack of a spacesuit, it meant the angry visitor could only be one thing:

A starman. Creatures born of the depths of space, who traversed the blackness of space as easily as mermen did the blue seas of Earth, whose songs had confounded astronomers for centuries, whose sightings were so rare that some thought they were fake.

A starman who was currently tangled in some of Station 139's wires and looked fit to hit the viewport until it cracked.

"Computer, transmit my audio outside," Ben ordered.

"Yes, Commander."

The starman flinched when the speakers came to life with a squeal of feedback. Oh right. Their ears were far more sensitive than humans'.

"Uh, hi?" Ben waved meekly. "I'll, uh. Just come help you out?"

The starman's eyes narrowed.

Ben ran.

Getting into the space suit was no easy task. Ben had done it a thousand times until he could do it in his sleep, and yet now his hands trembled as he fitted his oxygen tank, secured his headgear, and tested his communicator. Even waiting the ten seconds for the Station's AI to confirm that everything was perfectly aligned felt like torture.

Fortunately, space suits had come a long way from the early days, so Ben didn't need to laboriously clamber all over to reach a specific part of the station. He just fired his propulsion rockets and headed straight for the central viewport.

As he traveled, he mentally reviewed the meager lessons he had received on the starfolk. There wasn't much—the starfolk didn't seem to like being bothered, and diplomatic envoys had often been met with silence, if they'd been met at all. Humans and starfolk had settled on an unspoken truce: they didn't bother humans and human ships, and humans didn't do much beyond capture videos and photos whenever a starman or starmaid went soaring past. What Ben did know, however, was that starfolk loved to sing, even if humans didn't understand their songs, and unlike the merfolk of Earth's deep seas, starfolk songs often led ships to safety instead of into treacherous whirlpools and dangerous shallows.

The other thing Ben knew was that starfolk were strong. An enraged starmaid had torn apart a Class V Transport the size of a small moon with her bare talons, once.

As his eyes alighted upon the starman caught in Station 139's wires, Ben swallowed hard and hoped this starman would be in a singing mood and not a destructive one.

Once he got within hearing distance, Ben activated his speakers and waved again. "Hi. My name is Ben. May I help you get free?"

The starman's tail thwacked against the viewport with enough force that it left a small dent. "Either you help me," the starman said, his voice dark and unhappy, "or I will help myself. I do not know how much of your tiny home will be left standing, though."

"Uh, yeah, I would like it to stay in one piece," Ben replied nervously.

He reached for the first entanglement, as slowly as he dared, and began to untwist and cut the fragile wires. Repairing them afterward would probably eat into his recreation time, but Ben would rather break them now and fix them himself than spend a month in a cryopod traveling to the nearest base because a starman had thrashed free and wrecked the whole station.

As he fixed the first knot and moved on, Ben realized the starman was staring at him. It wasn't a stare full of aggression—according to the Station AI, anyway—but it was still unnerving. He decided to err on the side of caution.

"Thanks for waiting for me to come out instead of just breaking free," he said.

"You are lucky I was not entangled for very long," the starman replied. "Or else I might have. Besides, I see you have a space skin of your own. Why do you need this cumbersome home?"

"I, uh, kind of need it to breathe. This space suit has a limited oxygen supply, but the station has air recyclers."

The starman snorted. "You silly humans. So reliant on oxygen."

"I would die if I didn't breathe oxygen."

"What a strange concept. I am not sure I believe it."

Ben wiggled a finger under a particularly gnarly twist and snipped it free. "What, do starfolk not believe in death?"

"All things die, human. But a starman is nourished by the stars, and the comets, and the nebulas. What need have we for oxygen? If anything," the starman said, sounding thoughtful, "wearing a skin like yours would starve us of what we need."

"Yeah, well, humans are not as lucky. We need food and water and oxygen."

The starman made a soft sound. In any other situation, Ben might have called it amusement. "Or perhaps you are simply not as advanced."

"Or perhaps you shouldn't insult the one with the scissors who can set you free," Ben said, wiggling the sharp blade at the starman. "Just a thought."

"I could be free in seconds, if I wanted."

"You know, you keep saying that," Ben said, snipping another knotted section free. "Maybe in three hours I'll believe you."

"This will not take three hours," the starman said ominously.

"Nah, you're right. It'll probably take half an hour."

"Human."

"I told you, my name is Ben. And if you don't stop wriggling, you'll make even more knots and then we'll be here even longer."

The blue-green tail finally went still. Ben breathed a long sigh of relief and went back to snipping; for a moment, he had feared he might accidentally cut the starman instead of the wires, which probably would have ended badly for all parties involved.

Or perhaps just Ben. Maybe starfolk didn't bleed or breathe.

Ben cut the last knot and carefully pulled the wires free, tucking them together so that the starman had clear access to meander free and wander back into the wilds of space. "Okay," he told the starman, "all set. You can go now."

"You said... your name is Ben, yes?"

Ben looked up. The starman was staring at him again, head tilted to the side.

"Yes," he said cautiously.

Sharp teeth appeared as the starman smiled. "You have my thanks, Ben. My name is—" And then he proceeded to say a long tangle of syllables that Ben could barely make heads or tails of.

But, apparently, the starman had predicted that. "You may call me Spark. It is the closest word in your language to mine," he offered.

"You're welcome, Spark," Ben said sincerely. "See you around?"

Spark inclined his head gravely. Then, with a flip of his gorgeous tail, he sped off, just fast enough that he was a blue-green blur against the blackness of space, leaving Ben with a racing heart and a handful of broken wires.

The next day, when Ben passed by the viewport, yawning widely, he caught a flash of blue-green out of the corner of his eye. At first he ignored it, because his dreams had been full of blues and greens and stars and songs, but then he heard a familiar *thump* and paused.

Crossing his arms, he turned to face the viewport—and the starman lounging casually outside.

"Did you get stuck again?" Ben demanded.

Spark tapped on the viewport, talons sharp and precise. The pattern was too fast for Ben to discern, but the computer translated. "You did say 'see you around.'"

Ben mentally rewound the memory in his head. With a wince, he recalled his snarky send off. "It's kind of a human thing to say?"

"If you do not want company," Spark tapped out, "then I can leave."

Spark's long tail uncoiled from its lazy spiral, flexing and twisting. The scales glinted under the low lights of the Station, casting blue-green spots all over the walls. The Station was set up in bland shades of white and black; this was the first color Ben had seen in months, outside of holos and vids.

Spark, after all, was the first being Ben had spoken to in months. He was also the most gorgeous, even if Ben's asexual brain wanted to hug him more than it wanted to sleep with him.

And so, even though it was technically a security breach, Ben found himself pointing at the nearest airlock and saying, "All right, let's find a more dignified way to talk."

It took a little work, but Ben cleared out one of the rarely used airlocks. It was large enough to comfortably contain a grown human man and a grown starman, and furthermore, it would allow for Ben to have his oxygen while affording Spark his zero gravity. Plus it was more convenient than donning his space suit every damn time Spark wanted to chat.

The second Ben tweaked the controls correctly, Spark's face eased as the gravity amplifiers shut off. He did a lazy loop over Ben's head and then settled opposite of him, smiling.

"I must admit, this was a clever solution to our problem," Spark said, eyes flickering all over the chamber. "Your voice is much less muffled this way. I prefer it."

"Do starfolk place so much importance on a voice?"

"Oh, yes," Spark said. "A voice is everything to us. I can hear the songs of my kin galaxies away, and I will know exactly who is singing and how they are feeling. Our songs are our way of life."

Ben whistled lowly. "Damn, your hearing must be off the charts."

Spark smiled slightly. "It is not about my ears, Ben. It is about understanding how our songs traverse space: how they feel against our skin, how they dance against our ears, how they resonate in our hearts. That is how we are able to keep in touch, even so far away, and express our feelings." He paused. "But you humans are much more limited."

"Yeah, yeah, make fun of the less advanced human who needs oxygen," Ben grumbled.

"Well, it is about that as well, I suppose," Spark said, which is when Ben realized that Spark had something in his hands.

It was small and round, nestled perfectly in his cupped palms, and at first glance, Ben thought it was just a plain gray moon rock. But then Spark shifted, ever so slightly, and Ben's breath caught as rock sparkled under the Station lights. Solemnly, Spark offered it to him.

"I do not know the word for this, in your language," Spark said. "But please accept it as a token of my gratitude for freeing me."

"I can't accept—"

"Starfolk do not like to owe debts of gratitude," Spark interrupted. "It is beyond rude to be saved and not express, even by a small token, one's appreciation."

He gently grabbed one of Ben's hands and deposited the sparkling rock. Up close, it was pockmarked with a thousand tiny crevices, and each little mark flashed a different color under the lights. It was like nothing Ben had ever seen, and he had sat through five years of classes and training before ever being allowed into space.

It was beautiful.

Ben closed his hand around the gift and cleared his throat. "I still maintain that it is not necessary," he said. "But I thank you."

"I thought we established that this was meant for me to thank you."

"What are friends for, aside from fishing each out of entangled wires?" Ben joked.

Spark blinked. His tail swished gently behind him and he tapped a talon on the nearest window. "You wish to be... friends?"

"I spent like an hour prying wires off of your tail. Pretty sure that makes us friends."

Spark grinned then, eyes alit with amusement. He flicked his tail and did a lazy spiral around Ben until he could look at Ben upside down, still grinning. "Then we are friends," he agreed solemnly. "See you around, Ben?"

"See you around," Ben agreed, beaming, and retreated back into the Station so that Spark could leave.

Spark did not come the next day, but he did come the day after. They met in the airlock again, and Ben brought a 3D printed gemstone. It was, they found, not nearly as hardy as the space rock Spark had brought, but Spark still found the chunks amusing to bat around in zero gravity.

They fell into a pattern then—every other day, Spark would come and they would hang out in the airlock. Sometimes they ate, because Spark had heard Ben's stomach growl and gotten very confused, although not as confused as he had gotten when Ben had shown him what human food looked like. Sometimes they traded off bringing mementos and tokens of their world, and Spark was alternately amused and baffled by the things humans designed and produced.

Ben's favorite moments, though, were when they just talked. Spark would tell amazing stories of swimming through an asteroid field and playing in a nebula, and he seemed equally fascinated when Ben told him stories of his own daredevil youth, burning his throat on sun sprites and dodging cloud cops on skycars.

"You have a bold spirit," Spark commented, eyes wide and tail twitching. "No wonder you were not afraid when you met me."

"Eh, cloud cops aren't that hard to outrun. They've got speed limits."

"What is a speed limit?"

"Well, it's a limit on how fast you can—"

"Ben," Spark snapped.

Ben snickered. Spark loved teasing, but being teased? Not so much. He still hadn't forgiven Ben for spilling soy sauce on him when introducing sushi.

"I don't have a tail to swim in space," Ben explained, gesturing at his legs. "So if I move in space, I must have a propulsion force, whether from my hands or a machine. A speed limit keeps me from going too fast and going splat on something."

Spark straightened. He had visited, once, when Ben had had to do repairs outside. He had mocked Ben's slow pace the entire time, but he had also tugged Ben back to the airlock when it was all over, turning a slow trip into a relatively swift and smooth move.

"Is that why you traverse so slowly in your space skin?"

"Yep."

"How boring," Spark said. "And that is not how space should be experienced, Ben. Would you like me to show you how to swim in space?"

Ben narrowed his eyes. "I still need oxygen, Spark. Humans can't evolve to match your... whatever you have in a few days."

"Yes, yes, so you have said," Spark said impatiently. "But you can wear your space skin and I can swim, yes? I can pull you along."

Ben sat up straight, all tiredness forgotten. He had seen Spark swim many times, whether it was a gentle twirl around the viewport, a flashy dash as he zoomed into the distance, or even a graceful acrobatic exercise to keep the boredom at bay as Ben worked. Each time, Ben had looked down at his sleek but still cumbersome space suit and wondered what it would be like to swim as Spark did—free of restrictions, able to feel the stars on his skin and the starfolk songs in his ears.

He wasn't a starman, so he couldn't do that. But swimming alongside a starman in his space suit? That, he could do.

Spark was watching him with a hopeful expression when Ben looked up. "I can even show you what our rope is like. It is much stronger than yours," Spark said, as if Ben needed further coaxing.

"Well, then," Ben said, "I guess I better take tomorrow off so we can swim."

"Don't let go of me, okay?"

"Yes, Ben."

"And don't swim too far, I need to stay in communication range."

"Yes, yes, we've plotted out your acceptable course."

"And don't—"

"Ben," Spark interrupted. He swam a little closer and reached out, grasping Ben's hands gently. "Do you trust me?"

Ben looked into Spark's glowing eyes. He saw his hopeful smile and the playful twist of his tail. He remembered the countless hours they had spent in the airlock, trading stories and food and gifts. He thought of all the secrets Spark had told him.

He said, "Yes. I trust you."

Spark cast an eye over the long rope that bound their waists together, checking the knots, and then his grin widened. "Then let me show you what it is truly like to be in space," he said.

He began slowly, only a little faster than the propulsion rockets Ben usually used and definitely smoother. Still, as the stars twinkled in his view, Ben could hardly forget that he was going farther from the Station than he ever had, trusting entirely in Spark to get him home safe and sound.

Spark looked back at him. "I suppose it's too soon to go faster?" he teased.

Ben rolled his eyes. "I guess if I vomit, I'm the only one who needs to deal with it," he mused.

He already knew he would agree to Spark's request, and the second he nodded, their speed increased dramatically. Out of the corner of his eye, stars became blurs of light. Distant planets spun into and out of view faster than the AI could identify them. A space probe sailed in and out of range, even though Ben logically knew that a probe's top speed was much less than even a space suit was programmed for.

And through it all, Ben could hear Spark's song, vibrant and deep, echoing into the depths of space like a trumpeting call.

"You're singing!" Ben said.

Spark flipped onto his back, tail pumping smoothly up and down as he tucked his hands behind his head, the picture of effortlessness. "When we feel joy, we sing," he reminded Ben. "Even if you cannot understand our songs, you can at least enjoy them."

"They are very soothing. Could I learn to understand them?"

Spark tilted his head. "Perhaps. Our songs are not about language, you see. They are about who we are, and most importantly, what we feel. I could teach you the tongue of the starfolk, but you may not be able to sing as we do. Alternately, I could use the words of a human tune, yet even my kin who do not speak your tongue, like the merfolk of your seas, would understand my song."

Ben sighed. "Some things just defy direct translation, I guess," he murmured. "But hey—you can sing for me, right?"

"Oh, yes. Right now, I am telling anyone who can hear that I am showing a lost little human the proper way to travel in space."

"Spark!"

Spark grinned and flipped over to face forward again. He settled into a stable rhythm, just slow enough that Ben no longer felt nauseous. The pace also enabled Spark to pause altogether whenever he found something he wanted to point out, and Ben quickly learned that there was a lot, even though Spark's gifts lined almost the entirety of two walls and were threatening to overtake the room. Spark even presented Ben with the age old heart of a long ago star as they passed through a debris field.

And that was when it clicked—or rather, when Ben remembered the somewhat drunken conversation they had had two nights ago about the differences between human marriages and starfolk matings. Humans went on dates; starfolk gave gifts of intent.

Ben tugged gently on the rope to get Spark's attention. "Spark," he said, and then hesitated.

"Yes? Do you not like the star?"

"I do," Ben told him, clutching it in his hand. "But. Didn't you say that starfolk give gifts of intent... when they desire to take a mate?"

Spark stopped swimming at his words. He was quiet for a long moment, tail twitching restlessly, fingers twisted together. Then he finally said, "Forgive me. Do you wish for us to just be friends?"

Ben breathed in, held it, and breathed out. He thought of the long hours they had spent together and the gifts they had exchanged, their easy camaraderie and teasing, the way Spark made him smile and laugh. He could live forever that way, he was sure. But Spark...

"If you would have me as a partner, I would take you," Ben said. "But."

"But?"

Ben wet his lips. This confession usually garnered him skepticism at best, mocking at worst, but Spark deserved the truth. Hopefully he would understand.

"But I don't want to have sex. And it isn't about you being a starman. I just. Don't want to. Ever."

Ben closed his eyes and waited—

Spark huffed a quiet laugh. "Is that all? Are humans really so focused on spawning and sex? Companionship and mating, these are about more than just having sex. If I could live the rest of our lives seeing your smile when I bring back a gift, I would die a happy being indeed."

"Really? You don't care that I'm asexual?"

"Is that the human term? We have our own word. It is not uncommon for us."

Ben finally dared to look at Spark. He was still patiently there, not mocking Ben, not trying to fix him, not trying to dissuade him. He still had a smile on his face. Something tight and anxious in Ben's chest finally began to soften at the sight.

So Ben decided to be bold. "Hey, Spark."

"Yes, Ben?"

"Would you like to become mates with me?"

Spark swam closer, eyes glowing with happiness, and wrapped his hands around Ben's. He lowered his forehead until it touched the helmet of Ben's spacesuit, and his tail wound around Ben's feet. It was the closest they had been since Ben had once cut Spark free, and Ben rejoiced in realizing just how far they had come.

"Yes, Ben," Spark said softly. "Yes, I would."

The next day, the second Ben finished his assigned duties, he headed straight for his spacesuit. Spark had promised him another swimming in space excursion, so Ben hurriedly buckled everything into place and secured his helmet. He even skipped the final AI check, because he had a surprise to give to Spark; it would be slightly less of a surprise if Spark saw him coming out with it.

Fortunately, Spark wasn't here yet. The AI had confirmed.

Ben stepped into the airlock, engaged the controls—and went flying sideways.

"Shoot," Ben realized. He had skipped an important step in ensuring that all doors were secured before he began the adjustment processes to seal off the oxygen inside the Station. He scrambled for his propulsion controls and then cursed even more, because he had left his propulsion rockets aside since Spark would be doing the driving.

Ben looked at the Station as he floated away and cursed again. He had his communicator, of course, but Spark didn't have a receiver and Ben was too far away for the Station AI to be of any help.

He closed his eyes. "That was stupid of you," he told himself. "God, I wish Spark was here." He'd even settle for hearing Spark's songs, because then at least he would know Spark was near.

Songs.

Spark wouldn't hear his communicator, Ben realized, but if he could sing to Spark...

Ben reviewed what he knew about starfolk songs in his head. *Our songs are not about language, you see*, Spark had said. *They are about who we are, and most importantly, what we feel.*

Ben tapped his finger on his suit, thinking quickly. Spark had emphasized that feelings were important. He had said that space to a starman was not that different from water to a merman. He had said that language wasn't important, just the emotions. And when they had first met, Spark had tapped out a rhythmic message on the viewport, even without knowing whether Ben could understand. Instinct, perhaps.

Or a way of singing.

"Only one way to find out," Ben muttered. He took a deep breath and thought of Spark—of the joy that blossomed in him whenever he saw Spark's beautiful blue-green tail in the distance, of the pride that rose up whenever Spark liked his gifts, of the deep affection that consumed him when they kissed. He thought of Spark's acceptance of his asexuality. He thought of their love.

He opened his mouth and tapped his fingers and sang, as loud as he could, hoping.

For a while, there was no response. Ben just drifted, still singing, still tapping, still praying. He looked at his lowering oxygen levels and tried not to think about what would happen when he ran out. He thought of Spark and his gorgeous eyes, his beautiful tail, his lovely voice.

And then, like a shooting star, a flash of blue-green appeared in the distance.

Spark.

Spark, who was swimming as fast as he could, tail whipping up and down so furiously Ben could hardly make it out and singing so loudly Ben could feel the vibrations against his skin, in perfect answer to Ben's own song.

They collided with a thump, and Spark wound his tail around Ben's legs and his arms around Ben's shoulders.

"What are you doing so far away from your Station?" Spark demanded. "I heard your song and I thought—"

"You heard me," Ben interrupted. "I sang and you heard me."

Spark's eyes softened. "Of course I did. You poured your love into the depths of space. How could I not hear it?"

Ben smiled so widely that his cheeks hurt. "Well, then I guess I should make it official," he quipped. "I love you, Spark."

"I love you too, Ben."

There were some things that Ben expected to see out the viewports of Station 139: stars, meteors, the occasional deep space probe.

His favorite sight, though, was a flash of a familiar blue-green tail.

Ben paused mid-step, turned, and grinned up at the viewport. "Hello, husband," he greeted Spark.

"Hello, mate," Spark sang back.

# A Banquet in Turquoise and Indigo
## *by Hesper Leveret*

The Widow walked around the Glass House, skirts swishing against the stone-flagged floor, carrying her tray of bottled delights. Each phial, the size of her thumb, was stoppered in cork and carefully labeled with the name of an individual guest. She had prepared them all herself, letting nobody else into her workshop. To work in secret was one of the prerogatives of her position.

She brushed past overgrown palms, ferns, and hanging orchids. She danced delicately around the spun-metal supports which held up the roof and the walkways above, and past the ornate glass terrariums where she kept the silvermoss and spiders. She delivered a phial to the Blind King, placing it directly into his hand. He smiled at her beneath his spiked crown and dipped his head in thanks. The Widow hoped fervently he would support her this night, although she had no way of knowing how he would decide. She did not get a private audience with him, and she had no wish to discuss her plans in public.

She took phials to all the Chained Ones, placing them on the tables outside their cells, which were built into the back wall. And then she reached the long table in the far corner, where the Flyers should be seated, and found it—empty. A memory surfaced of an overheard piece of conversation—the Flyers had been called out this evening to check a disturbance in the aether clouds. She had been so focused on executing her plan—to make herself no longer just the Widow, but a Wife again—she had not paid enough attention to anything else. Cursing quietly that her entire plan might now be ruined, she laid out the phials at the assigned places for the Flyers as if nothing were amiss, and lifted a prayer that things might yet work out. Then she continued on her rounds.

The entire Glass House was decked out tonight, ribbons tied around every vertical, the air filled with magical scents and shimmers, musicians in the gallery, every table piled high with fruits and meats and impossibly light confections of eggs and cream. Tonight, there would be a feast for all the senses. And her contribution—the banquet in turquoise and indigo—would be the highlight of it all.

The phials she gave out were all filled with liquid, although they were not all the same color. Some were as pale as a dawn sky; others as dark as midnight, although none was as dark as the pure black of her dress. The Widow knew that she seemed to suck in the light as she walked around, the elaborate flounces and fine details of her dress almost invisible in the black-on-black color scheme her role demanded. Her face was hidden, too, behind the long veil, and even her hands were gloved. Only the very tips of her fingers were visible, and none could judge whether her intention was to give out pleasure or death, or something in between. Many people examined their bottles, trying to guess their fate from the color, even though they knew that the Widow had many ways of concealing a potion's true nature. They would not find out until they pulled the cork and drank their draught. And drink it they would; the laws of Phasgana would no sooner allow them to forego the drink this night than they would let a man sit the throne and keep his eyes.

The power given to the Widow, on this one night, was a long-hallowed tradition—and a crucial check on abuses of power.

Hidden beneath a ruched fold of fabric, the Widow kept a small stock of her ingredients close to hand: the seven different things, from seven different worlds, which had been cultivated and improved over long generations here in the Glass House. Just in case she should need to adjust any of her concoctions at the last minute—or make one afresh. From delicious dreamsugar to deadly indigo spider venom, the blend of these seven, in varying proportions and fermented over varying amounts of time, could produce anything from euphoria to vivid hallucinations to out-of-body experiences to sleepless paranoia to agony. And only she knew which she was giving to each guest —it was an undeniable thrill of power. As she reached Lord Wyhern—her least favorite of the Chained Ones—she was almost unable to resist taking out her phial of silvermoss—an ingredient which could either be the antidote to the deadliest of poisons, or a poison itself, depending on what it was mixed with—and adding the tiniest pinch of it to his bottle before giving it to him. Just to see the sweat bead on his brow.

She resisted that temptation, however. She wanted nobody to suspect what she had done with the potions tonight, and to give nobody cause to think that they had been singled out.

When she had finished distributing the drinks, she walked to the front of the cavernous indoor jungle, her heels clicking with every step, and stood on the low wooden platform before the ancient palm tree. Still no sign of the Flyers. She didn't have a backup plan. She would just have to go ahead, and hope that it would all—somehow—work out.

Perfectly on cue, the musicians stopped playing, and the Widow lifted her veil. There was a slight gasp in the room as she did so, as everyone saw how she had made up her face. Not with the shadows and pale powder that were traditional for the Widow, the contours designed to make her cheeks and eyes look sunken and her skin waxy pale, as if she were wasting away. She had worn that makeup in public for so long that most of those present had probably long since forgotten that it wasn't her actual face.

Tonight, she had made herself up to appear fresh-faced and beautiful, her lashes long, her cheeks blushed, her lips red, her skin its natural golden olive. She had even let some curls of hair escape from beneath her veil to soften the lines of her narrow face and sharp chin—features that were perfect for the Widow, but not what she wanted to emphasize tonight.

"What is this travesty?" demanded Lord Wyhern, in a voice loud enough to carry around the whole of the Glass House.

"I don't know, what is it?" asked the Blind King, dryly, which caused a small ripple of amusement among those who dared to be amused. The Widow could then hear the low murmur of the King's Eyes explaining it to him. Thankfully, the tension had been defused a little, and she took the opportunity to start her speech.

"The tradition of the Banquet in Turquoise and Indigo is nearly as old as the great city of Phasgana itself," she said.

"Instituted by the original Alchemist to the Blind King and held every year since then, on the night of the Twisted Moon."

She felt the room settle. These were the words she was supposed to say, the same words that were said every year. There was still a rumble of discontent from certain areas—mainly a group around Lord Wyhern and his cell. Chained he might be, but he still managed to maintain a loyal circle, including his son, Clement, one of the Glass House guards. Chained Ones, unlike Widows, were allowed to have families.

"The Banquet allowed the Alchemist to give out to each guest whatever it was they most deserved—punishment or reward or an opening of the mind, all neatly bottled. One night each year, the elite of the city, in the hands of the Alchemist. This tradition continued for many years—until one year, the moral decay of the city became too much for the Alchemist. The King's Eyes were whispering lies, the Chained Ones were slipping their bonds at night to go carousing in the city, the Flyers were using their skills not to protect, but to spy on and assault our own citizens. The supposed Great and Good of Phasgana were guilty of every form of corruption and vice—bribery, nepotism, even murder."

The Widow swept her eyes around the room. This was the point in her annual speech where everyone squirmed in their seats, thinking about everything they had done wrong since the last night of the Twisted Moon, wondering if this year was the year that they finally had their reckoning. This was her favorite part, and she spun it out as much as she could, letting her eyes rest on different people as if she could see right through their skin to the sins inside their souls.

Then, suddenly, the back of the Glass House was thrown into confusion as a number of people in uniform swaggered in, demanding ale and attention. They had swords at their sides and arrogance dripping from every pore. They were not Chained, nor Blind, nor even Widowed: they were free. They had to be, to do their job of protecting the city from the air. The Flyers had arrived at last.

It was an effort for the Widow to hold herself still, and not breathe an obvious sigh of relief. It was even more of an effort to stop her eyes from seeking out the Flyers' Captain. Although it was amazing how much she could take in from the corner of her eye.

Captain Larissa Flynn was wearing her uniform trousers, the same as everyone else, with her sword belt slung around her hips. But she had removed her jacket and unbuttoned her shirt and pulled it down to expose her powerful shoulders. Underneath, she was wearing a shockingly low-cut bodice of emerald green satin. Her bright red hair was starting to escape from its queue, and the overall effect was—well, the Widow felt her pulse quicken even as she determinedly fixed her gaze on a point in the middle distance that was definitely not Larissa. And there were several gasps of outrage from the more conservative of those sitting nearby, that the Captain of the Flyers should appear thus in public.

The Flyers themselves didn't seem to care what their leader wore—and why should they? So long as she led them out to protect their city, and got them safely home again in time to make a dramatically late entrance at the banquet, what did it matter how much she flouted her own uniform regulations?

The Widow waited for the Flyers to find their places at their table, and then she cleared her throat, and resumed her speech.

"That Alchemist," she said, "decided that Phasgana needed to be swept clean of its corrupt leaders, so that a new generation could take power, and serve the city in accordance with its ancient laws. And so, for the Banquet in Turquoise and Indigo that year, she concocted a potion laced liberally with the deadly venom of the indigo spiders."

The Widow flicked her eyes to the nearest terrarium, where the spiders spun their silk. Most of the guests, knowingly or not, did the same thing.

"She then served this poison up at the Banquet to every single guest, including her own husband. She could have given him a harmless draught: instead, by making this sacrifice, she proved that she did not seek power for herself. And so she became the first Widow. She oversaw the foundation of a new age of Phasgana, and ever since, instead of an Alchemist to the Blind King, we have a Widow. Chosen not from among those who seek power, but from those who seek to perfect the alchemical art."

Chosen as a young woman who wanted only to make perfumes and medicines, and live quietly with her husband and perhaps one day raise a family. Chosen—and not given any choice.

The whole of the Glass House thrummed with tension, awaiting the moment when she would tell them to drink their potions. Then, they could all eat the mouth-watering banquet, and await whatever consequences she had in store for them.

At the front, the Widow took a deep breath in, and gave them all a smile. It was—at last—time.

"So that's the tradition," she said. "Same thing every year. The Widow always presiding, always dressed in black, always miserable. After all, I poisoned my own husband for the sake of Phasgana, so I must be wholly dedicated to the city."

She looked around the room in a silent challenge. Now, she allowed her gaze to rest on the table in the corner where the Flyers sat, Captain Flynn at the head of them. Larissa met her gaze, across the whole long stretch of the Glass House, and nodded.

"Well," said the Widow, "Tonight is the night that tradition changes once again. It's time to stop basing our government on sacrifice and misery."

At this, Lord Wyhern made a very loud snort. "What else is there?" he demanded.

The Widow twisted her mouth into a red smile. "I'm very glad you asked," she said. "There is love, Lord Wyhern. I love someone, and I love my city too. I love my city, and I want to make things better here, for everyone. I want to be happy myself, and to make others happy too. And that is exactly what I intend to do. If the Alchemist can become the Widow, then the Widow can become the Wife."

"What?" shouted Lord Wyhern, and several of the other Chained Ones joined in with their own cries of outrage. "You can't do this! It is strictly forbidden for the Widow to take a new husband!"

The Widow smiled again. "I don't intend to take a new husband," she said. "I intend to take a wife."

At the Flyers' table, Larissa Flynn stood up, and started walking toward the Widow. At first, everyone just watched her in confusion: then, as it gradually became apparent where she was going and why, the room began to stir. There was laughter, and there were ribald comments: there were also shouts of anger and disbelief. Larissa ignored them all. When she reached the front, she swept down into a gracious bow before the Widow, and took her hand.

"Beatrice Tay," she said.

Before she had met Larissa Flynn, the Widow had not heard her own name on the lips of another for such a long time, she had almost forgotten that she'd ever had a name at all. Now, hearing it spoken in front of everyone, in defiance of every rule and convention, her heart fluttered in her chest, and she felt like she could faint on the spot.

"I love you," said Larissa. It was not the first time they had exchanged those words, and yet, after so many clandestine meetings, so many sweet stolen moments and words exchanged in whispers, to hear them here and now... it was the most supreme effort of the Widow's entire life to stay upright.

"Would you do me the very great honor of becoming my wife?"

The Widow could only nod her assent.

Larissa kissed her hand, and didn't let it go, and rose up from her bow. "Then," she said, "let the Banquet in Turquoise and Indigo become our wedding feast."

"No!" Lord Wyhern again. Both women turned their heads to see him, purple-faced with rage and straining at the end of his chain so hard he was in danger of choking himself. "This is against every law of Phasgana! This cannot be allowed!"

"Oh no?" said Larissa, "Who is going to stop us?"

"I will," said Clement Wyhern. He stood up and left his father's side, drawing his sword as he did so.

"You can try," said Larissa. The Widow clutched her arm, but she shrugged out of her grip. "I'll be ok," she said in a low voice. "I can deal with this."

And she left the Widow standing on the stage, worried that she was about to be widowed again before she was even wed.

Larissa moved forward a few paces, so that she and Clement were facing each other down the space between two long tables. There was a pause, as the whole room fell silent, waiting to see what would happen next. The only sound was the whisper of the King's Eyes.

Clement lifted his sword, grunted, and came charging down the aisle. Larissa neatly side-stepped him and leapt past the Widow onto the stage, drawing her own sword. She leaned in to whisper in the Widow's ear.

"Get off the stage, my love, and have your phials ready." With that, she sprang back, and waved her sword with a flourish. The Widow turned around, walked to the back of the stage with as much decorum as she could muster, stepped down, and sat by the great palm tree, one hand on her hidden phials as Larissa had asked. She tried to tell herself that Larissa had a plan, and everything would work out. There was something reassuring about the bulk of the ancient tree at her back, at least.

Clement, meanwhile, wrong-footed by his opponent's maneuver, staggered off balance for a couple of steps, then pulled himself upright.

"Running away?" he yelled. "Can't face a fight on the ground, Flyer?"

There was some jeering laughter from the Wyhern supporters. Larissa twirled her sword lazily in her hand. "I merely thought the stage would provide our audience with a better view. I wouldn't want to deprive anyone of their entertainment."

More laughter, from the rest of the room. A few of her fellow Flyers cheered. Larissa smiled. In that moment, she looked so strong and fierce and beautiful, the Widow thought she could die of pride. "That's my wife!" she wanted to shout, although it seemed best to remain quiet.

Clement did not look happy. Yet he clearly realized that he either had to follow Larissa onto the stage and fight her there, or back down. And there was no way his father would let him back down. So he came forward, climbed onto the stage, and faced her.

The two of them were evenly matched in height and build, although he had the solid weapon of a guard, while she had only the thin rapier and the jeweled dagger of the Flyers' dress uniform: meant for show, not fighting. Still, she moved well, dancing around him, making occasional feints and dodging his thrusts. He watched her warily, looking for an opening, waiting for his chance.

As a fight tactic, it was a good one; but Larissa had realised something he hadn't. This fight wasn't just about the fighting. It was about the show. The longer he continued standing almost still, the more the audience grew bored. The Widow could sense the mood in the Glass House shifting—the impatience rising, the jeers growing. There were fewer shouts of support for Clement, and more for Larissa. The Flyers, after all, protected the whole city from the rage of the aether storms, while the Glass House guards protected only the Chained Ones. And not everyone here had much reason to love the Chained.

Just as the Widow was daring to breathe in hope that Larissa could defeat him, Clement abruptly shifted from defense to attack. He leapt at her in a burst of shocking speed, the energy he had been saving finally put to good use. He drove her back with a relentless succession of blows that she struggled to parry, and nearly sent her tumbling off the side of the stage. At the last moment, she pivoted and dodged him, but she was on the back foot now, constantly ceding ground. She began to look tired, her movements sluggish.

Then she stumbled, and fell, and hit the planks hard. Clement came after her with a triumphant yell, ready to hold his sword to her throat and claim victory. Larissa let go of her own sword and rolled out of the way, right to the back edge of the stage.

Right next to the Widow.

Larissa sat facing Clement as he advanced on her, one hand behind her back, the Widow concealed by her body. It wasn't very good concealment, but it was enough for a few crucial moments.

"You have the spider venom?" Larissa whispered, breathlessly.

"Yes." The Widow reached into her hidden pocket, and brought out the tiny phial of indigo spider venom.

"My dagger," said Larissa, and instantly the Widow knew what she needed to do. She grabbed the dagger from Larissa's sword belt and smeared the blade with a few drops of venom. A few drops were all that was needed.

"Surrender," said Clement, his voice pitched so that everybody could hear him. "Surrender and give up this madness. You cannot marry the Widow! It is against all law and tradition of Phasgana, and will never be forgiven. But if you surrender now, nobody needs to suffer."

"No," said Larissa, quietly.

"What?"

"I said no," she said.

Behind her, the Widow slipped the elaborate jeweled hilt of her dagger into her hand.

"Then you leave me with no choice," he said, and took a step closer. He raised his sword. Larissa lifted her chin defiantly.

"Very well," she said. "Do your worst."

His sword came flashing down, and in that moment, she twisted to the side, leapt to her feet, and danced around him one last time, slashing his arm as she went. Just a shallow cut—but with a poisoned blade, that was enough.

The point of his sword hit the floor, gouging a hole in the wood. Clement groaned in pain and surprise—and then, as he realized what had happened, fear. He looked at the cut on his arm, the blood foaming. He looked over to where Larissa stood, holding the dagger up in front of her.

"Poison!" he snarled.

The Widow got up, and stepped back onto the stage. "What do you expect?" she asked. "I am the Widow, who was once the Alchemist, who will soon be the Wife. And this is the night of the Twisted Moon, the Banquet in Turquoise and Indigo. Poison is the whole point."

A roar from the back of the room, and the sound of a chain clinking frantically, as Lord Wyhern realized what was happening to his son.

"Now," said the Widow, "I have the antidote. Do you want me to administer it? Or would you prefer to die?"

"This—is—an—outrage!" Clement growled.

"So is everything else I have done tonight, apparently. What difference will one more outrage make?"

Clement opened his mouth as if to say something, although all that came out was a wordless snarl and some blue-tinged spittle.

"Enough!" came a deep, booming voice.

It was the Blind King, on his feet. "This is supposed to be a banquet!" he said. "I'm getting hungry, and the food is getting cold. If the Widow intends to poison us all, I'd rather die with a full belly."

He patted his stomach, which was generous in size, even before he'd eaten his dinner. A few laughs, scattered and nervous.

"As I understand it," he went on, "the Widow has proclaimed her intentions to be the Wife, the Captain of the Flyers has made a proposal which has been accepted, she has been challenged, and the challenger has been defeated. I'd say it's time for the challenger to go back to his seat, and for us all to eat."

Clement spluttered, and then collapsed onto the stage with a thump, nearly impaling himself on his own sword in the process.

"Give him the antidote," said the Blind King, with a wave of his hand. "And once you've done that, you may wed, with the royal blessing."

Relief washed over the Widow. If the King had decided against her and Larissa...

"Thank you, your Majesty," she said, and bent to administer a few drops of silvermoss to the now-unconscious Clement. Deadly though the spider's venom was, it could be countered easily enough if you had the right decoction on hand. Which she always did.

Soon he was coughing and retching. The Widow didn't feel she owed him more than his life, and so she didn't try to offer him any comfort. Instead, she left his side to stand next to her wife. Larissa carefully wiped the blade of her dagger before re-sheathing it, then picked up both her own sword and Clement's. The two of them walked together to the front of the stage.

"And now," said the Widow, "you may start the banquet!"

The cheer started off ragged, then grew gradually in fervor. One by one, the guests started eating their food—and drinking their potions. Beatrice and Larissa turned to face each other, and leaned in until their foreheads were almost touching.

"Well done, my love," said Beatrice.

"I couldn't have done it without your help," said Larissa. "Truly, you are the master of poisons."

Beatrice smiled. "I hope I'm more than that."

Larissa smiled back. "Oh, you are. A lot more."

They kept on like that, just smiling idiotically at each other, Larissa still holding a sword in each hand, for several delicious moments. Then she asked: "Incidentally, did you poison any of the potions tonight?"

Beatrice shook her head. Larissa lifted one eyebrow. "Really? Not even Lord Wyhern's?"

Beatrice shook her head again. "Not even his. I wanted tonight to be a night of celebration, not mourning. All the potions are exactly the same."

"What are they?"

"My parting gift as the Widow. They're all just alcohol, distilled in the laboratory and then colored to look like potions."

Larissa laughed, and then leaned in to kiss her new wife.

# Mirror, Mirror
## *by Alexis Ames*

Despite an aggressive, decade-long marketing campaign from headquarters, everyone still called the facility Area 51.

The compound had undergone a massive renovation at the end of the twenty-first century, complete with new branding and the declassification of thousands of sensitive documents. That didn't matter—even the employees fell into the habit of calling the place by its common name, and Mikhail was no exception.

*Got the job at Area 51*, he'd told his wife and husband two weeks ago, giddy with excitement, the screen still in his hand from the call. He'd spent the next week floating in a surreal haze, completely gobsmacked that this was his life.

Now, walking through the fifth set of steel doors on a level some fifty feet below the surface, he felt only cold. Cold air on his face and hands, cold sweat that dripped down his spine to pool in the small of his back. Chilled to the bone. Cold with terror.

He scanned his newly-minted badge for the fifth time, was scanned himself once again, and then allowed to pass. The team of six uniformed officers escorted him down a short hallway, and not for the first time, he wondered if they were there for the creature's protection—or his own.

And then Mikhail was standing in front of the cell.

Calling it a *cell* was a bit of a stretch, actually, as it was outfitted as nicely as his own home—comfortable, worn wood furniture, a full bed, cushioned chairs, and a kitchenette. It was certainly nicer than any of the apartments Mikhail had lived in while completing his degree. Too bad the creature who inhabited this room wasn't bipedal, or even human. It had no need for the amenities.

The silence lengthened while Mikhail took in the scene. He'd seen pictures of the extraterrestrial while in school, of course—the latter half of his senior year had been devoted almost entirely to the alien, and the pivotal discovery that humanity wasn't alone in the universe. But the number of humans on the planet who got this close to the creature, who shared the same air—that had to be in the dozens, *maybe*.

"Leave us, please."

He hardly recognized his own voice, but somehow he'd managed to convey enough of an authoritative air that no one questioned him. The security team departed, though one of the officers paused on the way out and said, "You need us, you press that button."

They pointed to a red button on the wall next to the cell. Mikhail nodded and took a seat on the lone chair in front of the cell's transparent wall.

When it was just the two of them, he said, "Hello. I'm Dr. Mikhail Allard."

"Fresh human." The creature's... mouth quirked, resembling a gash across its face. "Mm, fresh indeed. You're barely three decades old. Delightful. But why are you here, I wonder? What happened to the other one, the one who was six decades and eight?"

"He retired. I'm your new... handler." He said it with the briefest hesitation, sitting back in the chair and resting his ankle on his knee.

"I see. You're here to experiment on me." The creature's maw opened wide—Mikhail's mind likened it to the baring of teeth, though of course the creature had none.

"No. I'm here to talk."

"The other one experimented."

"Do you *want* me to experiment on you?"

The creature spent a long time considering him. Mikhail waited, one wrist balanced on his knee, his other hand resting on his thigh. He felt the back of his neck prickle, and then what felt like long, spindly fingers crept their way into his head. He resisted the urge to shudder. *Focus.*

"Such a delightful vessel you have," the creature purred as it explored. "So new. Fresh. *Empty.* There's hardly anything in this brain of yours. So much *space* for me to spread out..."

"All right, that's enough." Mikhail touched the skin behind his ear to activate the implant, and the feeling of tendrils at the back of his skull disappeared. The creature retreated to the farthest corner of its cell.

"You want to talk."

"Yes, that's what I said." But the creature had crawled into his mind to confirm for itself what Mikhail's intentions were. Words would never be enough, in this instance. "I only want to talk."

"Humans lie."

"Not this human."

"Well," the creature said, its mouth pulled into a horrifying approximation of a grin, "not yet."

"What do you call yourself?"

The creature stared at him, saying nothing, and for a wild moment, Mikhail wondered if the translator had failed. He checked his wristband—no, it was still functioning.

"I've already given you my name," he said. "It's polite to offer yours in return."

"You're already holding me prisoner in this facility. What do I care for what is *polite* or not?"

Mikhail pressed his lips together, suppressing a smile. "I suppose you don't. Well, it was good to meet you. I'll see you tomorrow."

"That's it?" The creature sounded surprised.

"That's it for now. I'll return in the morning."

He pored over all the publicly available information about the creature that night while Rafael and Katie prepared dinner, taking up the entirety of the dining room table with his hand screens and holo images. The assignment was deceptively straightforward—all his superiors cared about was getting the creature to talk, about anything and everything. The topic didn't seem to matter, and Mikhail wasn't privy to what the higher-ups were looking for. Every session was recorded for their review later. It was easy enough to guess what they were after. The creature had come to Earth without warning, and there had been no word from its people since, but Area 51 was a military facility and Mikhail had been contracted by the government to find out, he assumed, what this creature was planning. An invasion, perhaps, or worse.

"I can hear you thinking from the kitchen." Rafael appeared at his shoulder. He smoothed a hand over Mikhail's curls. "You've hardly said a word since you got home. First day go all right?"

"A little overwhelming." Mikhail tilted his face up for a quick kiss. "But fine, yes."

Mikhail had signed NDAs until his fingers had cramped, and wasn't allowed to take any of his notes outside of the facility or discuss what had transpired with anyone else. But his brief conversation with the creature played over on a loop in his mind as he scoured the databases, searching for *something*. Anything that might give him a direction, a clue as to what to ask next and how to proceed.

"Do me a favor." Rafael wrapped an arm around his shoulders, drawing him close for a brief hug. His lips were warm against the shell of Mikhail's ear. "Don't lose yourself in this."

Mikhail had known too many people who had allowed the work to consume them, at the expense of everything else in their lives. Rafael and Katie had already sacrificed so much—first the hours they couldn't spend together when Mikhail was in grad school, and now putting their own careers on hold to move with him across the country to the middle of the desert.

"Never." Mikhail clasped his arm and squeezed it gently. "I promise."

Specimen K-7462-T had been housed in the facility for almost a century by the time Mikhail was hired as a fresh-faced intern straight out of Stanford, who'd had half a dozen prestigious universities across the country vying to snap him up and put him on the fast track to tenure. But he'd never cared for the slow soul-suck of academia, and—well, it was *Area 51*. The only facility in the world that housed an extraterrestrial. How could he turn that down?

Scientists had started to receive signals from that far-off alien world less than a month before one of its inhabitants showed up on Earth's doorstep. If it was to be believed, the creature had left its own world centuries before, traveling at near-lightspeed to arrive in the Sol system hundreds of years later and on the heels of its planet's indecipherable transmission. And then... nothing. It was not the prelude to an invasion, nor a fact-finding mission. The creature had been placed in this cell and outlived all its handlers. It never consumed sustenance. Sometimes it went into what could only be described as a hibernation mode for months at a time. When it was bored, it rooted about in the minds of its human handlers for entertainment—or it sat there and insulted them, which it seemed to find equally enjoyable.

"You're a therapist," the creature—KT, Mikhail called it privately—said at their next session.

"Did you pull that information from my brain?"

"I know what they look like," the creature said disdainfully. "They feature quite often in your... television programs."

It had said the last part in English, using its own voice instead of the translation program, because there was no equivalent for *television* in its language.

"Yes, I'm a therapist."

"Why are you here?"

"I'm here to talk to you."

"*Why*," the creature repeated, this time in its own voice, hissing through its gills, "are *you* here?"

Mikhail wished he had an answer to that. He'd wondered it himself dozens of times these past few days, as every session with the creature seemed to go exactly nowhere. What precisely was he supposed to accomplish here?

"You've been trapped in this room for a long time," Mikhail said. "For almost an entire human's lifetime. For my species, that would take a mental toll."

"I am not like your species."

"I know," Mikhail said. "But for almost one hundred years no one's been able to get any information out of you. They thought that perhaps you would talk to me."

"Why would I talk to you?" KT scoffed. "I have nothing to say."

"You traveled hundreds of light-years to come here and say... nothing," Mikhail said. "I see. That hardly makes any sense to me."

"It doesn't need to make sense to you," KT hissed. "Hour's up, *Doctor*."

And so it went. Mikhail sat with the creature for an hour every day. He asked questions that the creature either deflected or refused to answer, and every day he sent the session's recordings and his notes to headquarters, which was maddeningly silent about the whole thing. He was given no further or amended instructions. He had no idea if he was making the kind of progress they were looking for.

One afternoon, fed up with his patient's reticence, Mikhail snapped his notebook shut and said, "Read my mind."

The creature considered him for a long moment. It said nothing. Mikhail held its unsettling gaze—or at least he thought he did. He wasn't entirely sure where its photoreceptors were located.

"You would like me to form a telepathic link," the creature said finally.

"You've done it once before, to make sure I wasn't lying. You obviously still don't trust me. Form the link, poke about in my mind, do whatever it is you need to do so we can make some progress here," Mikhail said. He tapped the skin behind his ear to turn off the implant, and then said, "Go ahead. Do it."

Allowing KT to probe his mind wasn't as unsettling as Mikhail expected. It felt odd, certainly, but it wasn't entirely unpleasant. It cut down on the pleasantries, too—in a matter of seconds, KT knew about his childhood, his spouses, where he'd grown up and where he'd gone to school, why he'd chosen this project when almost every institution in the country would have him.

The link between them worked only one way, though, so Mikhail still had to ask his questions out loud, and accepted that the answers he received were half-truths at best.

"Tell me about your childhood."

KT snarled. "We don't *have* childhoods."

"You know what I mean," Mikhail said patiently. "You've lived on this planet long enough, been around humans long enough to understand what I'm talking about."

"I have nothing to say on the topic."

The rest of the session was as ineffective, and Mikhail made no headway. He left the facility late that evening, exhausted and fighting a blinding headache. He turned in early that night, waking only briefly when Rafael and Katie climbed into bed, and slept through his morning alarm. When he tried to stand, the room spun. Nausea washed over him in a wave.

Area 51 had its own team of medical professionals that it used for its employees and their families. Within half an hour of calling in sick, five of them were on Mikhail's doorstep. Thank God Rafael and Katie were there to deal with them; Mikhail could barely form coherent sentences, let alone get out of bed and answer their myriad questions.

"This isn't unusual," Katie insisted as the team surrounded the bed, scanning and prodding Mikhail. "It's a migraine, he gets them at least once a month."

"Ma'am, he spends his days in the company of an extraterrestrial that we still don't understand," the doctor in charge said. "Excuse us for wanting to make sure he hasn't contracted anything."

"The extraterrestrial has been on this planet for almost a century without anyone falling ill. I hardly think Mikhail's managed to catch something in such a short amount of time." Rafael bodily inserted himself between the doctor prodding Mikhail and the bed, blocking her access. "Scan him if you want to, put us under quarantine if you need to, but no one is touching him unless you can give me a damn good reason for it. Got it?"

When the medical team had gone, Katie said quietly, "What if they're right?"

"That this has something to do with the alien?" Rafael's hand stilled in Mikhail's hair. "Well. There's not much any of us can do about it now, is there? He's already been exposed, and so have we."

"S'not the alien," Mikhail murmured. "You're right. S'been here too long. Would've done something by now."

"What do you think it is, then?" Katie asked.

"This? This is a migraine." Mikhail reached for her hand. "And the alien? Honestly, I think it's scared."

The migraine dissipated over the course of three days, and the three of them remained under quarantine for another two. Finally, Mikhail was prescribed medication by the medical team to prevent such a migraine from occurring in the future, and was allowed to return to the facility at the end of the week.

KT gave him an appraising glance—Mikhail thought he could tell where its eyes were now. "You are unwell."

"I'm fine." The tablets were a persistent weight against his thigh; he should've taken them before coming into the room, and now it was too late. "A headache, that's all."

He felt the tell-tale prickle at the back of his neck and tapped the implant. The feeling vanished. Giving KT a thin smile, he said, "Not today."

"Oral communication is inefficient," the being said.

"Well, it's worked for humans all these years. I think we can manage a day of it. How are you feeling?"

"Let me show you."

"*No.*"

"You are not nearly as entertaining as my previous handler," KT muttered. Despite himself, Mikhail felt a smile tug at his lips. Seeing the alien worked up like this was... almost endearing. It was certainly entertaining.

"I'm sorry to be such a disappointment," he said. "Listen, the last time you were in my head, I ended up with a three-day migraine. Forgive me for not being eager to let you back in again."

"That was hardly *my* fault," KT groused. "You're predisposed to them."

"That's true, but you're still not getting in my head."

"Fine," the creature conceded grudgingly. "What do you propose we do instead? *Talk*?"

"Well, it's my job to talk to you, KT."

The creature tilted its head. "What did you call me?"

"Ah." Mikhail fought down a blush. "I needed something easier than your given designation. I shortened it to KT. If you'd prefer something else..."

He trailed off. The creature said nothing, continuing to consider him quietly.

"KT is acceptable," it said finally. "What are you doing here?"

"I've already explained to you—"

"*Why are you here?*" KT interrupted waspishly. "Why have you chosen to take *this* assignment? Why did you accept it? That is a question you have yet to answer."

"It's a prestigious job," Mikhail said. "Do you know how many applicants there were for this position? *Four thousand.* I'm young, I'm fresh out of school, I have my entire career ahead of me. With something like this on my resume, I'll have my pick of positions. I can do *whatever* I want. The papers I'll write and publish alone will guarantee that I'm set for life."

He sat back in his chair, quiet for a moment while the creature processed this.

"Did you expect an altruistic answer?" he asked, when the silence continued to stretch. "Did you believe that I took this position because of the knowledge I will gain? Because I want to *help* you?"

"You do," the creature said, and since it had been inside Mikhail's mind, it would know.

"I do," Mikhail agreed, softening his tone. "Of course, you know that. I chose this career for that purpose. But I can't feed myself or keep a roof over my head with good deeds alone. I fought like hell for this job because it will open doors for me like nothing else ever will, and I need that security."

"I see," the creature said. "Interesting."

"Why is that interesting?"

"It isn't," KT said. "*You* are what is interesting."

"How so?" He couldn't help but feel flattered that, despite all the humans on this planet that KT had met over the decades, it found him interesting.

"I did not expect your honesty."

"Well," Mikhail said, feeling a small smile tug at his lips, "I'm full of surprises."

Despite the medical team's efforts, the headaches and migraines persisted. It wasn't anything Mikhail wasn't used to, but it made his job all the more difficult. He figured out how to at least bear the pain, by keeping the bright fluorescent lights overhead off when he was conducting a session and making sure the sound dampeners were in place so that the corridor was almost completely silent. He altered his diet, made sure he got enough sleep at night, and still the problem persisted.

He was short and irritable with his spouses, but more worrisome was the memory loss. Mikhail made a habit of coming in to his office early every morning, at least an hour before his session with KT, so that he could review his notes from the day before. He was mildly surprised at first when he started to come across notes he had no memory of making. He became alarmed as the days wore on, and entire sessions vanished from his memory. Had it only been that, he might have suspected the creature's involvement, but it seeped into other areas of his life. He found himself at home, mid-conversation with Rafael and Katie about a shared college memory, when he encountered what felt like a brick wall. Try as he might, a memory that had been so clear to him until now was gone, as though it had been excised from his mind.

What the hell was happening to him?

"You have another migraine."

Mikhail pinched the bridge of his nose and drew in a sharp breath. It had been creeping up on him for the past hour at least, despite the pills.

"I'm fine," he said. There were only fifteen minutes left in the day's session anyway, and a cot in his dark, windowless office that he could lay down on for an hour. He could hold out for that long. "Go on, you were telling me about—"

He stopped, wracking his brain. What *had* they been discussing? He remembered the beginning of the session, sitting down in the chair and greeting... greeting...

*KT*, right, that was the creature's name. Mikhail closed his eyes for a moment. When he opened them, the creature had approached the glass. It pulsated gently, its iridescent skin rippling in the harsh light.

"What's happening to me?" he asked, hating how his voice skittered up the scale in his anxiety.

"What was always meant to happen," the creature said. It seemed to glow brighter today than Mikhail could remember.

Pain stabbed through his skull. Mikhail bit off a choked cry. He clutched his head, pen and paper clattering to the floor.

"Don't resist," the creature murmured. "It's less painful if you don't resist."

"What are you—what—" Mikhail couldn't even form a coherent thought, let alone a sentence. Words were a jumble in his brain. All he could focus on was the agony, the feeling of knives under his skin, the steady drumbeat in his skull. He pressed the heels of his palms against his eyes—

He found himself staring at a human. A human *male*, his mind supplied, dressed in the uniform that all facility employees wore, his blond curls tousled, the skin under his eyes bruised from a lack of sleep. The human blinked, once, twice, and then a slow grin spread across his face.

"Ah," he murmured, staring at his hands while he flexed his fingers. He cracked his neck. "What a *wonderful* vessel this is, indeed. Thank you, Mikhail. I'll be sure to put it to good use."

*Mikhail.* He was Mikhail, that was his name... and he was looking at his own body through the glass. He raised a hand—

*tried* to raise a hand, but his limbs didn't respond. He swiveled his gaze downward, saw only a pulsating, iridescent mass of glittering color. Amorphous. Nebulous.

This body... this body wasn't his. Was it even a body? He'd spent days, weeks, staring at it from the other side of the glass, but he couldn't remember... why couldn't he remember—

*KT*. This was KT's body. He was in KT's body, and he *was not KT*.

This was impossible.

This couldn't be happening. KT was *inside* of his body, he was inside KT, and this had to be a nightmare. A hallucination. Too many hours spent in this windowless room, too many hours spent crouched over his notes, too many hours spent away from —away from—

"Do you feel that?" KT pressed a hand—*his* hand!—flat against the glass. "You're *forgetting*."

"No."

It was a croak, and the voice was not his own. Alien words spoken from an alien mouth.

KT pulled Mikhail's lips into a grin.

"In a few hours, you won't remember anything of your former life," he said. "You will no longer be human. I will walk out of this facility and never return, and you will be given a new handler, and you will do to them what I have done to you."

"*No*." He had to get out of here, he had to get home. Someone—someone was waiting for him, he was certain of it. He didn't *belong* here, he couldn't stay.

"Don't you understand, Doctor? This is the *invasion* you humans are so worried about. It's not a fleet, it's not a *war*. It's gentle. It's quiet. It is an invasion of *one*. The first one of us that you captured all those decades ago—that being was not a precursor. That being was the last of a species, a species that now numbers in the hundreds thanks to you humans. One by one, we turn you into us. We *have been* turning you into us. We wear your faces and live among you and it may take a thousand of your years, but that hardly matters. A thousand years is—what is that quaint little phrase of yours? A blip on the radar to us."

"I... don't—" He didn't understand, none of this made any *sense*.

"The collective knowledge of our species is in that vessel, that new body of yours." KT gestured to Mikhail, to what had once been its own form. "Over time, you will absorb it. Its memories will become your own, its knowledge will be yours. And when you are ready, when your mind is fully developed, you will inhabit the nearest available human, the one you have contact with the most, and you will carry the sum of our species out into this world. And so the cycle continues, and it won't end until we are you, and you no longer exist."

Mikhail—no, KT, that was KT—stroked his thumb across the glass wall that divided them. The sensation must have been entirely new to him. His mouth opened, and his eyes sparkled. He looked *delighted*.

"What *interesting* bodies these are," he mused quietly. He pulled his hand away from the glass and inspected it. He flexed his fingers experimentally. "Yes, this will do quite nicely indeed."

"Let... me out." He had to dredge up the words from deep within the recesses of his mind. This language that the humans spoke was so clumsy, so inefficient. So impractical for all that he wanted to convey. Limiting. If only he could form a link—

He reached out, reached out, *reached out*, and met only resistance.

"Nice try," Mikhail said. He touched his neck. "The implant, remember? You can't read my mind, not unless I allow it."

"N-no..."

"Now, I truly must be going." Mikhail glanced at his wrist. "My spouses are expecting me. Working with you has certainly been an... illuminating experience, KT. Behave for your new handler, hm?"

The human's grin was razor-sharp—*razor, razor, where did that come from, what is a razor*—and cold. His footsteps echoed up the corridor as he left, and when the doors shut behind him, the room plunged into total darkness.

# The Only Lesbian in Space
## *by Erin Edwards*

The first announcement that went out requesting applications to the Space Resettlement Programme included a clause that required potential Resettlers to be straight. The SRP tried to defend themselves against the inevitable backlash, claiming they wanted to minimize the risk of hate crimes on a planet not yet established with a justice system, or arguing that the Resettlers would have certain reproductive responsibilities. The best civil rights lawyers in the world fought the case and in the end they had no choice but to concede. In the wake of the victory, I applied.

My mother full-named me for the first time in five years when I requested her signature on the bottom of the form.

"Amanda-Jane Turner, you will not, let me make that clear again, *NOT* be going to Mars."

I only talked her into it by convincing her that writing the application essay would be good practice for my coursework, and that every teenager who'd ever had a disagreement with their parents would be applying to the same program. There were only ten spaces. The odds of me getting one of them was next to impossible, especially considering I submitted a scathing review of their original anti-queer policy as my personal essay. I was as surprised as anyone when I got the call saying they wanted to interview me regarding the Resettlement expedition.

Somehow I made it through each round of the process. There were personality quizzes, IQ tests, physical assessments. It was a miracle that this sarcastic, middle-of-the-road student who sometimes ended up out of breath after one flight of stairs seemed to be sailing through. All to the horror of my mother.

It was only when they officially announced the list of the ten Resettlers who would be the first members of the public to move permanently to the colony on Mars that I realized exactly why I had been chosen. We all had to give interviews to a wall of press microphones and cameras and just before I went up to take my place at the table with the others, I was pulled aside by Kevin, the scrupulous media rep for SRP.

"Here, wear this," he ordered, pressing a small lapel pin into the palm of my hand.

It was a rainbow, cheerfully unsubtle and glaringly obvious in its intent. I was the Queer Resettler, the one they picked so they could argue back against the voices who were still seeking to criticize them for their homophobia. I stared down at that pin and considered my options. Mars would get me away from the students who had left slurs scrawled across my locker, the mother who always pulled a face like she was sucking a lemon before she said the word 'lesbian,' the uncle who clasped my hands too tight and promised to pray for me. It was a clean slate, a world that had not yet learned how to bury its gays and pack the earth down tight so no one else would get any ideas. SRP might just be using me to make a statement about their inclusivity, but it wasn't as if I wasn't using them too.

I pinned on the rainbow and earned myself a thumbs up from Kevin that I wasn't entirely sure I wanted. Once sat behind the table that had been decked out in SRP logos for the big reveal of the Resettlers, I got my first good look at the people beside me with whom I'd be moving to a whole new planet. I tried not to judge any of them on sight, since developing unfounded dislikes against a significant percentage of the population of what would soon be home seemed like an unwise idea. This was all about making friends. Notably, none of my new friends sported a twin to my rainbow pin.

The reporters had plenty to ask us, pitching the same question from different angles in a clear attempt to tease out some nugget that they could blow up into an exclusive across their front page. They had been given press packs beforehand that detailed who we were and they honed in on the pieces of information that made for the best news. One of the other girls was a convicted felon with time served for shoplifting, one of the guys had appeared on a reality-TV show two years ago, and another had a celebrity chef for a father. Everyone seemed interesting. Except me.

Every question I got asked was about the rainbow pin in one way or another. What did I think of the original statements SRP had put out about accepting homosexuals into their program? Did I have a girlfriend I was leaving behind? Was I going to be lonely up on Mars, the only lesbian in space?

It took me a few moments to compose an answer to that last one and I could hear muffled sniggers coming from further down the table, the son of the celebrity chef whispering to the daughter of a Wall Street Executive. Eventually I blinked away my surprise and managed a semi-thoughtful answer about how young we all were, not one of us older than eighteen, and that they couldn't be sure I *was* the only one who did or would ever identify as queer. Apparently it wasn't the answer the reporter was looking for, as she granted me a frown for my troubles and quickly moved on to the girl who already had a doctorate and could conservatively be called a child genius.

We were whisked away from the reporters and into a conference room once the interview was brought to an end, encouraged to mingle and get to know each other in what I'm sure they thought was a natural way. It felt anything but natural, all of us stood there awkwardly in silence, no one certain of the right thing to say to break the ice.

"So, I'm Katy," the girl with the shoplifting charge eventually said, lifting a hand to draw attention to herself like she was in school. "Anyone else have a name?"

We'd all introduced ourselves to the media at the start of the press conference but evidently I hadn't been the only one not listening. One by one people offered up their names with varying levels of enthusiasm. When it was my time I handed over my nickname, AJ.

"If it isn't the only lesbian in space," Celebrity Chef Jr, recently introduced as Patrick, snorted.

"We're not in space yet, genius," Katy sighed, rolling her eyes.

She shot me a sympathetic look that I tried and probably failed to accept with a smile. I wondered who would be up there on Mars with us, or supervising in the space capsule on our journey. Would they care if that kind of talk kept up? I couldn't count on it. The moment the group's attention was turned away from me, I took off the rainbow pin and slipped it into my pocket.

We didn't have long to get to know each other, considering the commitment we were making to live in each other's company, before they packed us up and sent us to training camp. While we weren't going to be flying the rocket or working on a space station, we were, strictly speaking, still astronauts, and putting us in a space shuttle without any clue what we were doing just wasn't an option.

It was a schedule full of early mornings, meticulously timed breaks, and falling into bed before nine because sleep was going to happen regardless. The beds were more comfortable than the floor if you were going to choose somewhere to pass out with exhaustion. We'd been assigned roommates and told to get used to the lack of privacy, since space shuttles weren't exactly built with high ceilings and spacious living quarters.

When I'd first headed to my room to abandon my bags, I'd been surprised to see not Sabina, the daughter of the Wall Street Executive, as my orientation documents had informed me I'd be sharing with, but Katy.

"Sorry," I said instinctively. "I must be lost." I turned to head back into the corridor where I could double-check the papers, but Katy stopped me.

"Wait, no!" she called. "I asked to swap. I know we all need to get along and everything and hopefully we can, but I just thought that... that you might want a slightly more welcoming face."

I had nothing more to say besides an inelegant "oh" as I headed over to the bed Katy hadn't chosen and dropped my bag down onto it. While I appreciated her concern for my emotional wellbeing, it was disappointing to see the teasing hadn't gone completely unnoticed. Katy seemed to pick up on my lagging mood and immediately burst into a ray of positive energy, practically bouncing around as she unpacked and threw questions my way about my home life and why I'd applied and what my parents thought about it all. She didn't seem to need to go to space to be free from the confines of gravity.

If any of the other Resettlers had signed up in the hopes that going to Mars would get them out of school work, that dream had been crushed within the first few hours of the training program. We spent days behind desks, learning as much about Mars and the shuttle that would take us there as they thought would fit in our heads. We weren't even beyond homework. Counselors encouraged us to spend our free time giving up as many Earth luxuries as possible so that the transition to life on Mars wouldn't come as quite so much of a culture shock. There were already professional Resettlers up there and they didn't want us to be dead weight once we joined the burgeoning society because we were mourning the convenience of online shopping.

It didn't escape my notice that the training camp was depriving us of our families too. Once we'd been dropped off, we weren't allowed to see them until training was over and we would get one last goodbye before heading into the shuttle. They were preparing us for only communicating via infrequent phone calls for the rest of our lives. I couldn't say the thought distressed me too much. While I would never wish my family ill, I was glad to soon be putting millions of miles between us.

In the downtime we did have at the training camp, friendships started to form. Despite our varied backgrounds, we all had in common the desire to leave Earth behind. The hugely publicized contest we'd all entered was nothing more than a media stunt to push the SRP into the spotlight, but it was a gift to a group of teenagers who were all too glad to escape. The sons and daughters of celebrities and business moguls were the first to proclaim the woes of their lives, humble bragging about wanting a simpler existence. Katy kept her own reasons quiet until we were back in our room, where she started to tell me about her childhood, how she spent time in a juvenile detention center but vowed to turn everything around when she got out. She had submitted her essay from prison, explaining that she had no family ties to sever and wanted a clean slate. Evidently they'd been impressed with what she'd written.

Despite Katy's friendship and a general cordial atmosphere amongst the group of us, the disparaging comments didn't completely fizzle out. Patrick had quickly latched on to Miguel, a boy who seemed so scared of upsetting anybody that he became a sounding board for anyone talking to him. Either they didn't know I was walking behind them on the way from the dining hall to the dorms that night, or they didn't care.

"They only picked a lesbian to be 'inclusive' because they know even if she does make it as far as the ship, she'll change her mind. They get the publicity they wanted and the reproduction they need," Patrick said, thrusting his hips in a distinctly uncharming manner.

The movement almost caused him to lose his balance and he teetered precariously before disappointingly finding his feet again. Karma was rarely there when I needed her most. At least Miguel's agreement was understated, a simple head nod that would hopefully do little to bolster Patrick's bigotry. The last thing he needed was encouragement.

I hung back to let the boys walk ahead of me, not wanting to be privy to any more of their conversation. Katy caught up to me and immediately picked up on how far my mood had fallen since we'd been eating.

"Everything okay?" she asked. "Was it the food?"

They'd been slowly getting us used to the kind of food we'd have up on Mars, weaning us off anything processed. While there was plenty of farming being established up there, processed sugar was something we wouldn't be seeing very much of. Evidently spices hadn't been at the top of the cultivation list either, as the plates they were giving us were packed full of color and vegetables but little in terms of flavor. It was still edible though—Katy was only trying to get a smile out of me with a joke.

"It's nothing," I assured her.

Whether she bought that or not was up for debate, but she put her arm around my waist to steer me away from the central corridor and toward the rec room. It wasn't much, something that seemed like a relic from a bygone age, but there was an odd comfort to be found in the snooker and table football. In comparison to the high-tech equipment we were starting to get to work with, they may as well have been ancient artifacts.

"What are we doing here?" I asked, because it was rare that any of us headed down for a game of snooker. Our gatherings were far more often arranged in someone else's dorm room.

Katy just fished out the plastic ball from the table football goal and held it up between her fingers.

"Figured we could kick some balls around," she suggested casually, dropping it into the center of the players and getting into position on one side of the table.

I blinked at her for a moment while the innuendo registered. A grin spread across my face and I stepped up to play against her. We didn't talk about Patrick and what he had said but it was clear that, even if she might not have heard the words, Katy had accurately guessed the content of the conversation. Instead of bringing it up, she got intensely into the game, shouting at the little plastic men on the poles. It was impossible to not give in to the competitive spirit and, three games later, I barely even remembered why I was angry when she hooked her arm through mine and led us back to the dorms.

Time behind desks started to turn into more hands-on work. We had first aid training to make sure we would be competent in a medical emergency and they started to ramp up a fitness program for us, sending us on laps around the perimeter of the training base or assigning hours in the gym. They started measuring us for spacesuits to wear in the shuttle, taking a long list of proportions to ensure they could get a perfect fit. We wouldn't be doing any kind of spacewalk, landing within the confines of the oxygen-rich biosphere that had already been set up on Mars, but apparently we couldn't head up in jeans and t-shirts.

As the weeks ticked by, our timetable of activities got all the more interesting. We moved from the theory of electronics to handling electronic panels ourselves, from discussing the expectations of space travel to experiencing the conditions in simulations. When the day came that they announced we were ready for zero-gravity training, it had sparked a wave of excitement through the group. Whatever immediate opinions I might have formed about any of the other Resettlers, no one had yet ducked out of the program and changed their mind about heading to Mars. This would get us all one step closer.

They bussed us out of the training facility to an airfield for the zero-gravity experience. The base we'd been staying at had been built specially to accommodate each expected wave of Resettlers taken from the general public, with us being the first, but it didn't quite have everything we needed.

There was a plane waiting for us when we reached the airfield. Painted black and red, it looked official and intimidating and for the first time, I felt a bite of fear in my stomach. This was only a plane; I was going to have to face a whole space shuttle at some point. Patrick's words danced around my head and I pushed the feeling away—I would not quit, I wouldn't even consider it. Instead I took a step closer to Katy, who nudged her shoulder against mine in solidarity, and held my head high.

A graying man in a red flight suit stepped up to address the group and, just like we'd been taught to do with our trainers back at base, we all immediately paid attention. Any whispers of conversation were silenced and all eyes were front.

"All right, kids," the man said, a thick Southern accent coating the words. "Welcome to the Vomit Comet."

"The *what*?" Patrick asked, breaking rank in his surprise.

"Trust me, soon you'll understand."

I thought I detected a slight smirk of contempt at the corner of the man's mouth as he looked Patrick up and down like he was appraising him.

"Now I'm going to be honest with you all, I think sending you up to Mars is a huge mistake and that all this shouldn't be happening, but I'm being paid to take you up in the plane today so that's what's going to happen. We're going to get you suited up and then I'll take you through some safety information and we'll load you on and get airborne. Listen to everything I say, is that clear? *Everything*."

He fixed his gaze on Patrick, waiting until he got a slightly shaky nod before corralling us all in the direction of a set of trailers where we were kitted out in matching black jumpsuits to zip up over our clothes.

"Scared?" Katy asked, her eyes sparking with an enthusiasm that told me she was anything but.

"Of course not," I scoffed. I took a quick look around to confirm no one was paying attention. "But I apologize in advance if I grab onto you and don't let go while we're up there."

Rather than mock me like I'd been expecting, Katy just reached out for my hand and squeezed it tightly.

"You've got this, AJ," she assured me. "You're going to move to Mars. You can handle one little plane flight. Maybe they'll even give us peanuts."

We were not given peanuts. Instead our instructor handed out a brown paper bag to each of us and told us that if we were going to be sick, he would much prefer it if our aim was accurate. It was a sentiment I think we all shared and I wasn't the only one clutching their bag a little too tightly, crushing it in my fist. The safety brief we got seemed woefully short but we'd had enough lectures on similar scenarios back at the training base that I had plenty of material to run through in my head in preparation. This was something that regular people with too much money to spare did for stag-dos and birthday parties. I could handle it.

We were herded up into the plane and all shown our allocated spaces. Rather than the standard rows of seats, the entire interior was hollowed out and left open for us to move around in. Without overhead bins or luggage storage beneath our feet, it was a far more expansive space than I had anticipated. Along the walls there were loops of fabric for us to hold onto and we were instructed to take our seats, hold on, and wait for the plane to take us up.

Katy was mercifully sat beside me and she laid her hand out not so subtly between us, an open invitation. I didn't take it, not wanting to provoke further commentary from Patrick, who was sat across from us in plain view. Instead I just offered her a smile before gritting my teeth as the engines were turned on and the plane thrummed to life around us.

The journey upward was a short one, drenched in both anticipation and dread. My ears popped from the rapidly changing altitude and I couldn't shake the dull ringing that took up residence in them. Katy was talking to me but it felt like I was underwater and not every word was clear. I could establish that she was extolling the virtues of the experience, her entire face lit up with exhilaration. There was no dread for her, only the anticipation of what came next. I latched onto her enthusiasm.

We were starting off with Martian gravity—something we were going to have to get particularly used to. Once the plane was high enough we were told to lie out on the floor and wait, and we didn't have to wait for long. First, everything got heavy as the plane started to curve in its flight path and our bodies were subjected to almost double the regular force of gravity. My stomach lurched and the nickname we'd been told earlier felt particularly apt as I clutched the brown bag in my fist, hoping I wouldn't need to use it. I wanted to turn and look at Katy but even the act of shifting my head felt like too much effort. Until suddenly everything felt easy.

Martian gravity was a third of what we dealt with on Earth and while we couldn't fly, it was an unparalleled experience. Patrick was doing pushups one-handed to show off but I was too stunned to move all at once, lifting my arm and marveling at how smooth the motion was. I'd never felt particularly graceful before but there was so little resistance that every movement felt like a dance. Within twenty seconds it was all over and we were back on the floor.

That had just been the warmup. The intense increase of forces started again and this time I turned my head so I could watch Katy before it got too difficult. She was grinning at the ceiling, loving every second. The instructor had promised he'd be giving a warning just before we could expect to feel properly weightless, but I'd been too distracted by the shine of Katy's eyes to remember to focus on him and between her and the ocean soundtrack playing in my ears, I missed it entirely.

When I suddenly felt my stomach go and gravity concede its power, I couldn't help but grab Katy's hand, still resting between us even now. She didn't pull away, didn't try and hide it from the view of our fellow Resettlers, regardless of the homophobic rhetoric it might incite. Instead she kicked off the floor, pulling me up with her, and we soared up toward the ceiling.

"Think of your happiest thought," she laughed, swimming around in the air like Peter Pan.

I didn't have to think of it. It was right in front of me.

Everyone's spirits were high when we made it back to the base that night. Rebelling slightly against the orders to leave junk food behind, we'd raided the kitchens for all the crisps and chocolate we could find and there was an impromptu party of sorts in Sabina and Miriam's room. The music was turned up high and there certainly wasn't enough room for all ten of us in there, so I'd snuck out to take a seat in the corridor outside, my back against the wall. It only took a few minutes before Katy joined me.

"They're playing Spin the Bottle," she said, pulling a face as she sat down.

"No one your type?" I asked.

"No one in there."

I froze, too overwhelmed to turn and look at her. Even with how cautious my mind was screaming at me to be, I knew I wasn't misunderstanding her. She reached out to rest her hand over mine as if to reassure me that this wasn't a game. There was plenty I wanted to say but I couldn't make my mouth form any of the words. For a long moment, we sat in silence, until I forced myself to say something so she knew she hadn't read everything wrong.

"I thought I was the only one," I whispered.

"We're still young," she said, parroting my own words from the original press conference back at me. "How can we be sure of what we are?"

She pressed a kiss to my cheek, resting her forehead against my temple. I could feel her hair tickling my neck.

"I think I'm sure of you, AJ."

# Evergreen

## *by Shirley Romano*

Once Elle steps through the mirror and into today's reflection, she fixes herself a cup of tea and makes for the manor library. The weathered hardcover she started still has a folded page marking her spot, shelved exactly where she left it in the last reflection she visited. Curled up in Liora's favorite armchair, Elle enchants the crease away and flips through the pages, fingers tracing over the aged text. She's long forgotten which way the words are supposed to go, after years of reading the books between mirrored versions of the library. But either way, the stories don't change when she reads them from right-to-left or left-to-right. The books always remember her, so she remembers their stories in return.

Liora won't get home from her errands for another few hours, but Elle has no desire to leave the library before then. Though there's nothing left for her to discover, no more clues hidden within the manor, she fears if she lets herself wander, she'll find another mirror she didn't know about, or worse, she might get tempted to draw the curtains and confront the infinity of the world outside.

Instead, she heads for the shelves of books on magic, a reflection of her journal tucked among books Liora would never pick up by choice. The pages are littered with drafts of poems and notes she's left behind from other reflections, things Liora's reflections have told her over the years, fragments that could offer clues about which reflection is *her* world, which Liora is the *real* Liora.

But it's been years, traveling through mirrors upon mirrors, in thrice mirrored versions of the manor. In theory, other than Elle's presence, the worlds reflected are identical in every motion, in every fold of the curtains, every particle of dust on the shelves. But Elle has yet to find the world *she* belongs to, the world so natural to her that she'll have no doubt it is hers, even if she isn't yet sure what that will feel like.

Elle's counted over fifty ornamental floor-length mirrors within the manor, yielding a number of reflections too infinite to comprehend. Infinite reflections of this world encased within the manor. Infinite Lioras. The only thing that doesn't exist infinitely, is her.

Elle hasn't seen herself in years, no reflection present in the mirrors she steps through. She's certain about some details: the cool beige of her skin, the way her frizzy hair shines copper between her fingers. She's heard from Liora's reflections that her eyes are still the evergreen of the forest outside, but instead pretends they're the familiar brown of Liora's.

When empty echoes of heeled boots carry themselves up the stairs, Elle puts away her journal and returns to the armchair, novel in hand. She assumes the least-threatening pose she can, which in most reflections is reading the book as normal and gathering enough restraint not to look up, even as Liora steps into the periphery of her vision.

Liora studies her in silence, polite enough not to interrupt Elle's reading. "Who are you?" she asks after a few minutes. "How did you get here?"

Elle closes the book and brushes off the cover with cold hands. When she finally lets herself look at Liora, her lovely brown eyes, dark hair escaping her crown of braids, she can't help the flood of fondness that fills every corner of her being. For just a moment, it doesn't matter that Elle visited a different reflection of Liora yesterday, two days ago, and every day for the past four years. It doesn't even matter that this world is most certainly just another reflection, because every time Liora arrives, it's like a piece of Elle has returned home too.

But as enamored as Elle may be, *this* Liora hasn't seen her in years. "I walked in," she says. "I thought I'd spend the day here, if that's okay."

Liora adjusts her glasses, looks more closely at her. "Do I know you? I've never seen you in the village."

"I guess you don't remember me then. I'm Elle." She tugs on the sleeves of the blouse she's borrowed for the day, too tight on the shoulders as always. Luckily, as long as Elle wears the clothes between mirrors, Liora never realizes they're hers. That would be an awkward conversation to have, almost as much as trying to justify her appearance in the manor.

Liora bites her lip in thought. "Your name sounds familiar. I don't know from where."

"I figured. You and your parents used to visit my uncle's magic shop, back when we were around nine or ten years old."

Liora's never had an affinity for magic, but growing up, her parents would have her tag along on their monthly trips to the village, gathering talismans, physical charms, and books on magic. Disinterested, she would instead pass the time with Elle, helping her organize vials of glimmering liquid, feed the carnivorous plants, and track down the school of dragonfish when they'd jump from their tank and glide about the shop, shedding scales beneath them.

Elle couldn't help but catch feelings, even before she was old enough to recognize them as something more than the closeness of friendship. But by the time both girls turned eleven, Liora's parents had stopped all trips to the store, given up on any hopes of their daughter practicing magic.

Elle had assumed she would never see Liora again, but at fifteen years old, she found herself drawn to the manor. One fall afternoon, Uncle Kiavi left her to manage the shop, and in her routine of organizing the place, her fingers landed on a hidden panel in the wall behind the vocal potions. While she didn't recognize any of the items inside, their energies were far too strong to be permitted for public use. Among the items was a key fashioned from flynoceros ivory, words engraved in reverse along the shaft. The key had no reflection in the back mirror, so she took it upon herself to trace the reversed words onto parchment and hold that up in front of the glass. *Your reflections deceive you,* the key read. *Reality is a journey and destination for you alone.*

Elle had returned the key to its place, dismissing it as a curse she wouldn't involve herself in. But the next day, as she eyed herself in the mirror, she couldn't shake the feeling that something was off. That if the key was written in reverse, perhaps there was someplace else where it wasn't.

She likes to think ignorance would've been bliss, not that she could do anything about it once the words were engraved into her memory. Telling her uncle she was running errands, she snuck the key from the wall and held it tightly in her palm, its magic guiding her to the manor like a compass. No one was home to let Elle in, but the key was a perfect match for the lock on the front door.

The manor had so many mirrors, it was no wonder the key was so drawn to it. Elle planned to view the key's words through the first mirror she found to see if they would be any different. But when she opened her palm, the key melted through her skin, the white liquid cool as it seeped inside, its magic blending with her bloodstream.

When she'd looked back into the mirror, her reflection was gone, the mirror but a window, and the other side another dimension of reality.

Liora was Elle's first lifeline when she started this journey between reflections four years ago, the first and only familiar face along the way. If it weren't for Liora, Elle doesn't know if she would have it in her to keep searching for reality.

Elle's stomach lurches her back into the moment, the contents swirling like a storm. She's been here hundreds of times, reintroducing herself every day, yet the fear that maybe this time Liora *won't* remember her always arrives as uninvited as herself.

Luckily, Liora's eyes light up in recognition. "Saints, it's *you.*"

The two eventually catch up to speed, Liora discussing her adventures in the woods and nearby villages, while Elle pretends all these years she's still been working in the magic shop. Liora hasn't been in years, so she wouldn't know any different. Likewise, Elle hasn't seen the shop since she first stepped into the manor, and while she has no intention of returning before she finds reality, she can't help but worry the shop has transformed, taken on a life of its own without her.

Liora glances back to the door and yet again Elle's blood runs cold, worried she'll get asked to leave. It's never happened before, but she can't let herself rule out the possibility. She braces herself, but Liora instead gives her a friendly smile, cheeks rosier than usual. "Do you like music?"

Elle lets out a sigh of relief as she follows after Liora. "Who doesn't?"

In addition to the mirrors, which Elle takes extra care to ignore, still-life paintings ornament the patterned walls of the manor. Each painting is as timeless and familiar to Elle as Liora herself, depicting vibrant orange berries among silks and the skulls of creatures with finely sharpened teeth.

When they arrive in the music room, Elle leans by the wall while Liora readies herself to play the harp. In most reflections, they enter this room at some point, since even a hurricane couldn't keep Liora from practicing. And while Liora does not practice magic, Elle considers the way Liora spins music from thin air to be a magic of its own, one that cannot be acquired from a spellbook or charm, but solely from the efforts of improving each day.

Liora has a different look to her than usual as she eyes the strings. "Do you sing?"

"I'm a poet," Elle answers.

"That doesn't mean you don't sing."

"I don't know a lot of songs."

Liora laughs. "Then we can compose something together."

"No way, I can't do that."

"Didn't you say you're a poet?"

Writing music most certainly uses a different dimension of the brain than poetry and magic, but then again, she might as well try something new. Elle takes a tentative step closer. "How am I supposed to do this?"

Liora tucks back a strand of hair. "You just have to let out the first words that come to you, without any second-guessing. Follow my lead, I'll play a melody for you."

And with that, her fingers pluck the strings, sketching out the bare melody and slowly embellishing it until they gracefully dance across the harp.

Elle swallows, palms clammy after the first chords. "I don't know if I can do this."

"Don't worry," Liora keeps playing, the notes coming naturally to her, "I'll help you back if you get lost."

Elle *already* feels lost, but she shuts her eyes, listening to the harp as she grasps for words, fragments of poems she's written in the past. A few come to mind. "*One day I'll meet her,*" she tries, "*certainly she's waiting in the mirror.*" Her words come out clumsy, raw, far from the elegant verses she inks onto parchment. "*Clearer than the mind could ever see / On the side where all the grass is green.*"

She lets herself open her eyes, look to Liora. "*Reflections are all deception, promising things I'll never know / In the end the only place I'll ever truly call my home / Is her...*"

Elle strings out another verse, unsure of where the current of lyrics comes from but holding on tight as the words spill out of her. She doesn't have a quill to jot anything down so the lyrics float away as she sings them, temporary and beautiful, only present here in this reflection and in this moment, to ears none other than hers and Liora's.

The moon rises, but Liora invites her to spend the night at the manor even before Elle admits she has nowhere else to go. Liora offers to go for a walk outside, but Elle insists on tea as always.

To Elle's dismay, this reflection hasn't shone true, hasn't sparked something within her strong enough to label this one as reality. Singing with Liora, while memorable, is one of plenty of moments she's had with countless reflections, so she can't afford to get attached to this one.

A sliver of moonlight from between the curtains dances across the kitchen while Liora pours tea, her back to Elle. As mysterious as Elle's own appearance remains, Liora is as clear to her mind's eye as the rest of the manor: soft features, smooth ebony hair, clever eyes behind glasses.

But like the moon, Liora will always be too far out of reach. None of the reflections Elle has stepped into have ever felt right, like home. For all she knows, maybe none of the reflections are her home. The thought bitters the tea Liora brings for her.

"What are you thinking about?" Liora asks, when the silence stretches on for too long.

"Nothing." Unsatisfied with the response she gives, Elle shifts the subject to the usual small talk, empty words to fill the hollows within her. "The place is nice, do you live here by yourself?"

Liora takes a sip from her tea, which Elle's enchanted to stay warm. "It's a long story." A story Elle knows by heart, one Liora tells her in many of the reflections she's visited. And there's nothing Elle would like more than for Liora to distract her from the emptiness with the familiarity of a story she's heard hundreds of times from hundreds of reflections, with a voice so beautiful she could get lost in it.

But this reflection of Liora simply moves on. "Funny enough, I don't get lonely. I enjoy my own company, and, if I'm being honest..." She cautiously glances around the kitchen and lowers her voice. "...I don't think I'm actually alone here."

Elle straightens. "What do you mean by that?"

"I'm pretty sure the place is haunted."

"By a ghost?"

Liora slides up her glasses. "I don't know *what's* haunting the place, but I've had my suspicions for a few months now. You'd understand if you saw the things I see on a daily basis. Food getting eaten, missing things appearing in strange places."

Elle's spirit wilts, subtle enough that Liora doesn't catch it.

"I've ensured there's no way for anyone to enter through the doors or windows without me knowing, so unless someone's been miraculously traveling through walls, a spirit of some sort would be the only logical explanation. What are your thoughts on the matter?"

Elle exhales into her tea and watches the steam rise. "Sure, it sounds like a spirit to me." That's all she'll ever be, anyway. The ghost of a person who wants to be with Liora, existing in the manor but never truly present. A shadow, an illusion, a trick of the light.

"Something's on your mind," Liora observes. "Something you won't tell me."

Elle shakes her head. "It's nothing." Nothing any of Liora's reflections should have to deal with. Elle brought this journey upon herself.

Liora sets her hand on Elle's, fingers warm from holding the teacup. "We've talked all evening, why is it so hard all of a sudden?"

Normally Elle would remain closed off, but something in Liora's tone makes her feel safe, comfortable to voice thoughts she's bottled up for far too long. This shouldn't be so hard. She's told Liora's reflections everything over the past few years. Everything but this.

"What if... what if everything wasn't real?"

"Meaning?"

She looks down at the dark wood of the table. "What if your life, everything you knew, wasn't real? And only you could tell something was off?"

Liora pauses and swallows some tea. She's silent for a moment as she thinks, but she keeps her hand on Elle's—a calm, stable presence. "Then you'd have to be the one to make it real."

Elle shouldn't have expected Liora to understand. She draws back her arm, forces a laugh. "It's that simple?"

"It's the only choice you have, really."

The next morning Elle rubs the sleep from her eyes and untangles herself from Liora's arms, careful not to wake her. It technically won't make a difference whether she waits for the sun to rise, since the instant she steps through the mirror, *this* Liora will forget Elle ever existed, but at least this way she won't have to say goodbye.

Today she selects the ornate floor-length mirror in the bathroom, its gilded borders shining in greeting. The reflected bathroom awaits her on the other side. Elle hesitates as she lets her hand cross the barrier. This should be easy, stepping through the mirror like it's liquid silver, ready to investigate the next reflection. This reflection hasn't sparked anything more than the others. It isn't real. This isn't her world and she has no place here.

But she stands in front of the mirror long enough that Liora's reflection appears behind where Elle's should be. "What's going on?" She takes Elle's free hand, but the reflection's fingers close around empty air, a bitter reminder that none of this will ever be real, will ever be tangible.

"I'm leaving."

"Through the mirror?"

Elle nods and folds the hand towels by the bathroom sink, since she might as well leave the place as nice as she'd like to see it on the other side. Liora watches from behind her, mesmerized by the sight of the reflected towels folding themselves midair.

"Can't you stay a little longer?"

"I don't have time to waste if I want to find the real world."

"*The real world,*" Liora draws out. "So what you were talking about last night…"

"This isn't my world," she says simply. "It's a reflection of my reality."

"If that's the case, then how will you know which world is real?"

Elle's glad for once that Liora can't see her expression in the mirror. "I just… *will.* I'll know it's the world I'm meant to be in when I don't feel so lost anymore. When I meet you—the *real* you." If she even exists.

Liora ponders over her words, eyeing her own reflection. "So what you're saying is that *I* mean nothing to you."

"Of course not!" Elle turns back to look at this Liora one last time. "You mean *everything* to me. Which is why I need to find the world where we're both real."

This is a waste of time. She takes a step into the mirror, but Liora's reflection taunts her from the other side. "Do you really think you're going to find the answers you're looking for in another reflection?"

Elle winces. She's spent too much time here. She takes a deep breath, ready to drag her feet through the mirror.

"Don't do this!" Liora exclaims. "I know none of this means anything to you, but this is real to *me*. This reality is the only one I have, and I want to spend it with you."

Elle shouldn't have opened up so much, let herself get so attached to this world. She won't make the same mistake in the next one.

But, for some reason, she can't bring herself to do it. She can't bring herself to cross the barrier, erase herself from *this* Liora's memory, from this world. Her breaths start coming faster and faster, gusts of wind picking up in a hurricane.

*There are too many worlds.* So many that the hundreds she's visited are nothing compared to the vast infinity of the rest. Too many for her to go through them all in this lifetime. Too many to find the one world that isn't a reflection. Too many to know if a world where she belongs even *exists.*

"It's impossible!" she exclaims into the mirror, blinking back tears. "I'll never... I'll never..." Her voice catches as the room swims around her, her skin overridden with chills, hair itching against her neck, hand trembling through the mirror. She can barely hold herself up, weighed down by years of thoughts, but her legs carry her far enough back to collapse into Liora's arms.

Elle takes a breath and looks at her fingers, cold and quivering. "I'll never find my world." Her words come out like a death sentence.

Liora embraces her tightly, at a loss for words. This whole search has been pointless. Elle's wasted so many years through hundreds of reflections and made absolutely no progress in finding her world. Even worse, she's confined herself to the manor for so long that she can't say for sure what the village looks like, can't tell whether her uncle's shop will still be waiting for her.

But at least there's someone she can count on, who's always been there for her without realizing it. She meets Liora's eyes, struggling to draw out words. "Can I stay in your world? At least for a little while?"

Liora kisses her forehead. "Of course."

With that reassurance, the weight of infinity shrugs off Elle's shoulders like a worn cloak, losing shape as it lands on the floor. A small object of ivory floats from her palm, but she doesn't care to check what it is, as the manor casts itself in a new light to her.

After some time they both find their footing and Elle wipes away her drying tears, watching the curtains sway in the cool morning wind.

"Could we visit the forest?" she asks.

This might not be *her* world, but she can still get to know it, the way it lives and breathes. Maybe she'll be able to find a place where she belongs. Maybe that place isn't as far away as she's let herself believe.

Liora takes her hand, and when Elle glances to the mirror on her way out, she spots a stranger looking back at her, eyes bright and evergreen.

# About the Authors

**K.G. Delmare**

K.G. Delmare is a Brooklyn-born writer who loves game shows, going to the movies, and drinking iced coffee. Their work has been previously published in *The Colored Lens* and *Flash Fiction Magazine*. They live in New York City with a yard full of stray cats. You can find them on Twitter @KGDelmare.

**Isabel Yacura**

Isabel Yacura currently works as a freelance video editor and writer in New York City. She can be found at isabelyacura.com and @isabelyacura on Twitter.

**R.K. Nickel**

R.K. Nickel works as a screenwriter in Los Angeles. His first feature film, Bear with Us, is available on Amazon Prime and DVD. He's also the head writer for Arrowhead Studios' upcoming video game and for the ed-tech startup Tappity. When he's not writing, Russ is probably playing an escape room or some Magic the Gathering. Or drinking coffee. Mmm... coffee. www.rknickel.com.

## Joanne Askew

Joanne Askew is a Science-Fiction and Horror writer. She explores mental health issues, sexual identity, femininity and neurodiversity through speculative fiction. As an LGBTQIA+ activist, she believes that fiction will make our world a better place to come out in. Joanne strives for more queer representation in media, particularly speculative fiction, and highlights social injustices like inner-city poverty, the justice system and mental health representation. Joanne has OCD but battles her compulsions to make sure she uses them as a superpower in an empowering way. www.jaskewauthor.com

## Daniel Santos Marques

Daniel Santos Marques is a writer, poet, and musician based in London, UK. He has been published in several publications, including *Glittery Literary*, *Untitled Voices*, and *Pure Slush*. He is currently working on a debut chapbook and novel.

## Frances Koziar

Frances Koziar is primarily a fiction writer of the contemporary fiction and high fantasy genres, though she also publishes poetry and nonfiction. Her work has appeared in 50 different literary magazines, and she is seeking an agent for diverse NA fantasy novels and children's fairy tales (PBs). She is a young (disabled) retiree and a social justice advocate, and she lives in Kingston, Ontario, Canada.
Website: https://franceskoziar.wixsite.com/author

## MM Schreier

MM Schreier is a classically trained vocalist who took up writing as therapy for a mid-life crisis. Whether contemporary or speculative fiction, favorite stories are rich in sensory details and weird twists. A firm believer that people are not always exclusively right- or left-brained, in addition to creative pursuits Schreier manages a robotics company and tutors maths and science to at-risk youth. Recent publications and selected works can be found at: mmschreier.com

## Julie Cohen

Julie Cohen is a library associate living in New Jersey. She lives with her partner, their four cats, and an ever growing treasure hoard of books.

## Lamont A. Turner

Lamont A. Turner's work has appeared in numerous online and print venues including most recently, *The Half That You See, Forbidden Dreams* and *Good Southern Witches* anthologies as well as, *Horla, Yellow Mama, Cosmic Horror Monthly, Lovecraftiana, Dissections, Bewildering Stories, Dark Dossier*, and other magazines.  Lamont can be found on Twitter @LamontATurner1

## DJ Tyrer

DJ Tyrer is the person behind Atlantean Publishing and has been widely published in anthologies and magazines around the world, such as *Amok!* and *Stomping Grounds* (both April Moon Books), *Altered States II* (Indie Authors Press), *Altered Europa* (Martinus Publishing), and *Destroy All Robots* (Dynatox Ministries), and issues of *Startling Stories, Planet Scumm, Broadswords and Blasters*, and *Awesome Tales*, and in addition, has a novella available in paperback and on the Kindle, The Yellow House (Dunhams Manor).

DJ Tyrer's website is at https://djtyrer.blogspot.co.uk/

The *Atlantean Publishing* website is at https://atlanteanpublishing.wordpress.com/

## Kathrine Machon

Kathrine Machon is a lover of all things magical. She lives on the island of Jersey and spends her spare time scribbling stories about fantastical characters and places. She has had a number of short stories published and hopes one day to have her name on the front of a novel. You can find out more and follow her on Twitter @KateMachon.

## Tabitha O'Connell

Tabitha O'Connell is a historic preservationist and writer of queer fiction living in Western New York. Eir favorite things include animals, abandoned places, alliteration, long walks, and long sentences. Tabitha's short fiction has previously appeared in the anthology *Queers Who Don't Quit* and is forthcoming in the sequel to *Unspeakable: A Queer Gothic Anthology*. Find em on Twitter @tabithawrites or visit tjoconnell.wordpress.com

## Eilidh Spence

Eilidh Spence lives in Scotland with her parents and sibling, but more importantly, with their three cats. When not writing, she procrastinates by sewing and listening to podcasts, and might sometimes be found studying for her ongoing computing science degree. Her work has been published by Wyldblood Press and in Ghost Orchid Press' *Beneath* and *Cosmos* anthologies. You can find her at @spenceeilidh on Twitter, though at the time of writing she is yet to post anything.

## Carmen Peters

Carmen Peters is a writer and student living in Portland, Oregon. As a lover of horror and speculative fiction they aren't afraid to dive into the deep end, and as a queer trans person they strive to carve out space for marginalized narratives. Their latest fiction can be read in *The Evansville Review*, and they can be reached on Instagram @Carmen_Dreams_Ghosts.

## Stewart C Baker

Stewart C Baker is an academic librarian and author of speculative fiction and poetry, along with the occasional piece of interactive fiction. His fiction has appeared in *Nature*, *Galaxy's Edge*, and *Flash Fiction Online*, among other places. Stewart was born in England, has lived in South Carolina, Japan, and California (in that order), and now calls Oregon home, along with his family—although if anyone asks, he'll usually say he's from the Internet where you can find him at https://www.infomancy.net/

## Jennifer Lee Rossman

Jennifer Lee Rossman (she/they) is a queer, disabled, and autistic author and editor from Binghamton, New York. They think dinosaurs are neat. Find more of their work at their website http://jenniferleerossman.blogspot.com, and follow them on Twitter @JenLRossman

## Max Turner

Max Turner is a gay transgender man based in the United Kingdom. He is also a parent, nerd, intersectional feminist and coffee addict. Max writes speculative and science fiction, fantasy, urban fantasy, gothic horror and LGBTQ+ romance, and more often than not, combinations thereof.
https://www.maxturneruk.com/
https://twitter.com/robot_tiger

## EA Robins

EA Robins is just having fun. An American expat living in South Korea, she has no intention to ever permanently return to her homeland. Still working out the kinks, she regularly (obnoxiously) boasts of her two short fiction publications with *Dragon Soul Press* and *Of Metal and Magic Publishing*. She has crippling attractions to relatable villains, far-fetched history, Scotch, the Foo Fighters, oil on canvas, and that elusive, perfect twilight moment when everything is all right and anything is possible. Ursula K. Le Guin, Carl Sagan, Stephen King, and Malcolm Gladwell rank among some of her favorite authors. EA travels the world, tries all the snacks, and makes all the mistakes. Sometimes twice. But, she's learning. Contact:
https://www.earobins.com/
https://www.facebook.com/robinswrites/
https://www.instagram.com/ea_robins/

## J.B. Polk

Polish by birth, citizen of the world by choice. First story short-listed for the Hennessy Awards, Ireland in 1996. She became a regular contributor to *Women's Quality Fiction, Books Ireland* and *IncoGnito*. She was also the co-founder of *Virginia House Writers*, Dublin, and helped establish the *OKI Literary Awards*. Her creative writing was interrupted as she moved to Latin America and started contributing to magazines and newspapers and then writing textbooks for Latin American Ministries of Education. In the last 12 months, she has published 34 short stories and articles in anthologies and magazines in Australia, UK, Germany, the USA, and Canada.

## Xan van Rooyen

Xan is a tattooed storyteller from South Africa with a serious peanut butter addiction. Now calling the cold, dark forests of Finland home, Xan would like to be an elf when they grow up. When not conjuring strange worlds with peculiar words, Xan teaches music, rock climbs, games, devours graphic novels, and loyally serves their lord and master: Lego, the shiba inu. If you'd like to read more of Xan's words, check out *Apparition Lit* and *Three-Lobed Burning Eye*. You can also find more short stories and novels published under the name Suzanne van Rooyen. Hang out with Xan on Instagram or Twitter (@Xan_Writer), or find Xan on Patreon as Xan van Rooyen.

## Nicola Kapron

Nicola Kapron has previously been published by *Neo-opsis Science Fiction Magazine*, Rebel Mountain Press, Soteira Press, All Worlds Wayfarer, and Mannison Press, among others. Nicola lives in Nanaimo, British Columbia, with a hoard of books—mostly fantasy and horror—and an extremely fluffy cat.

## Shenoa Carroll-Bradd

Shenoa Carroll-Bradd writes fantasy and horror from her home in sunny southern California. Her short fiction has appeared in more than three dozen anthologies and been produced for audio on several fiction podcasts. She makes killer vegan bacon and has been learning German in order to sing along with her favorite bands. For updates on new projects, visit facebook.com/sbcbfiction. For free fiction, information on previous publications, and links to live readings, visit sbcbfiction.net.

## L. Reed Walton

L. Reed Walton (she/they) is a science and public health writer by day. They are querying their fourth novel, a science fiction mystery. She has published and forthcoming work in *Hellhound Magazine* and *Crow & Cross Keys Journal*. You can find them at LReedWalton.com or on Twitter (@LWriteWalton). She lives in Atlanta, Georgia, USA, with her wife-to-be and four cats.

## Regina Jade

Regina Jade is a writer and poet who lives in the US. She loves chocolate, custard tarts, and cats. In her spare time, she can be found trawling the depths of libraries for new books to add to the to-be-read pile, which never seems to get any smaller. Her tweets can be found at twitter.com/thereginajade.

## Hesper Leveret

Hesper Leveret is a speculative fiction writer whose work emphasizes the beautiful, lyrical, and strange. She was born and raised in Southampton, educated at Oxford, and is now based in Liverpool, UK, where she lives with her family and chronic pain. Her science fiction story 'We Who Are Left On This Dying Earth' appears in the June 2021 edition of *Luna Station Quarterly*. Her interests include baking cakes, escaping rooms, history of all kinds, and general geekery. You can find her on Twitter as @hesperleveret.

## Alexis Ames

Alexis Ames is a writer living in Colorado who first picked up a pen when she was eleven years old and hasn't put it down since. Science fiction is her preferred genre—more specifically, exploring the changing relationship between humans and technology. Her work has previously appeared in publications such as *Pseudopod, Luna Station Quarterly*, and *Collective Realms*. She can be found on Twitter at @alexis_writes1, and a list of her current and upcoming stories can be found on her blog at alexisames.home.blog.

## Erin Edwards

Erin Edwards is a dedicated Londoner and compulsive writer, most often found in an archive or at the theater. She is committed to providing the world with more queer content and is currently working on far too many different projects to do just that. Find her on Twitter @EEdwardsWrites

## Shirley Romano

Shirley Romano is a writer, artist, and biology nerd who's well-familiar with the *"surely you're having a great day"* line. In her free time she enjoys creating, whether that's through animation, drawing, photography, songwriting, or game design. She's always on the lookout for something new she can learn, and shares her newest projects as Surely Draws, on her YouTube channel, www.youtube.com/c/SurelyDraws

# About the Editors

**Rowan Rook**

Rowan Rook (they/he) is an asexual, aromantic, and agender/transmasc speculative fiction author, editor, poet, and game designer/writer. They see the world through a lens of plot ideas and armatures, and storytelling is their passion. They are also neurodivergent and a night owl, music lover, horror addict, and cat dad. An indie soul, they prefer the strange and provocative to the familiar and safe. Rowan lives for stories that inspire wonder, evoke deep thought, offer exhilarating experiences, and leave lingering emotions. They live in a rural lakeside house while dreaming of the city. You can read their work at their website (www.rowanrook.com) or follow them on Twitter (@xRowanRookx).

**Geri Meyers**

Geri Meyers is an LGBTQIA+ fantasy fiction writer. Growing up in New Hampshire, Geri wandered the woods fighting off enemies and rescuing princesses, crafting homemade bows and arrows from downed tree branches and absorbing the magic of the mysterious lady slipper flower. Geri has carried that need for wondrous adventure into adulthood and strives to share it with others through writing and storytelling. Currently living in New Jersey, Geri works full time as a library assistant preparing books for circulation while dreaming of one day opening a fantasy-themed book store. Geri has a passion for writing stories full of vibrant characters, magic, sparkling things and intelligent dragons. You can follow Geri on Twitter (@Siobwen) or read Geri's work on Wattpad (www.wattpad.com/user/GeriMeyers).

# All Worlds Wayfarer: Through Other Eyes

An Online Literary Magazine
www.allworldswayfarer.com

All Worlds Wayfarer is a quarterly literary magazine specializing in character-and-theme-driven speculative fiction. We celebrate stories that take readers on tours through wonderful and terrifying realms, evocative visions, and eye-opening new lives. When our readers come home, they should return ever so slightly changed for having made the journey. After all, the most powerful stories transcend, enlighten, and entertain at once.

*"Books give a soul to the universe, wings to the mind, flight to the imagination, and life to everything." -Plato*

If you enjoyed this anthology, look for our upcoming anthologies:

*Each Our Own* (Release TBA)
*Into the Dark* (Release TBA)

# Thank you for reading!

We hope you enjoyed the journey. All Worlds Wayfarer publishes issues every equinox and solstice. Please consider submitting your own speculative fiction stories or embarking on further adventures with us in upcoming issues and anthologies.

## www.allworldswayfarer.com

www.ingramcontent.com/pod-product-compliance
Lightning Source LLC
Chambersburg PA
CBHW051205190726
48288CB00006B/1820